PUCKSHAW

Island Interrupted

JULIE M. DRYJA

Dedication

For Jack and Franny

BOOK ONE: LIFE ON THE ISLAND

BOOK TWO: DEATH ON THE ISLAND

BOOK ONE

Life on the Island

P*ROLOGUE*

The antique clock announced the end of the day with twelve ominous chimes as Henry Macguire—silent and numb—pondered his newest confusion. Perhaps it was fatigue. Or was it just his deep loneliness—gnawing at him yet again with the sharp teeth of a rat? How to escape this self-induced chaos? What to do? Ah, yes! The aging reporter blocked his ears like a spoiled child and fled into the arms of the only comfort he knew these days—his beloved journal.

September 1, 1993.
Good evening Kind Friend!
I hope you are ready for me tonight! Yes, I am filled with confusion and on the brink of another descent into hell. Of course, you are probably thinking, "Again?" Yes, again! But honestly, I am bewildered by the reaction I've had to a very sad but not uncommon occurrence. For no reason, I have been surprisingly upended and disarmed and—as always—I turn to you to unravel my deepest and most vulnerable feelings. Let me tell you what happened.

This morning, around eight-thirty a.m., one of *Puckshaw's* **beloved summer residents returned to the island's warm, welcoming shores by way of the mighty Atlantic. Propelled by a stiff wind, her tiny, naked body arrived on a crashing wave of foam and was left to rest against the shimmering seascape of a deserted cove. Aside from bruises and scratches—presumably inflicted by the buffeting which her defenseless body must have sustained on the journey home—she appeared unbroken and convincingly at peace as the lone witness, wandering aimlessly in the deserted cove, sped to her side. Having spotted the body as it washed to shore, the old doctor carefully inspected her for any sign of life before hastening to alert the authorities.**

A few hours later, as I looked down on the scene from atop a twenty-foot cliff, the young woman was being

carefully lifted from a rocky area of triangular shaped boulders rising out of the sand like miniature pyramids. What an incredible sight to behold! Momentarily suspended in mid-air, the victim was raised gently as muscular legs and experienced feet jockeyed for a solid position from which they might safely transport her through the rocky path!

Finding myself sandwiched between two hacking octogenarians and a profusely sweating stranger—whose obese presence dominated--I held my breath *and* my ground as I stretched and twisted my neck to get a better view.

As a reporter should be, I was early to the scene though quickly dwarfed by breathless islanders arriving to witness the unfolding drama below. (No surprise here; word of the tragedy had spread across the sun-drenched isle like a brush fire!) As the crowd grew, my position became jeopardized by the arrival of taller, wider, and more aggressive thrill-seekers. I wanted to move—but hesitated; I could end up further back in the crowd and that wouldn't work well for me since I was already at a disadvantage—short in stature and carrying extra equipment.

I opted to stay put for the time being.

Anxious to satisfy my growing curiosity—which *is* part of my job—I raised my high powered binoculars and trained them carefully on the drowning victim. I observed with astonishment how wide open and oily her blue eyes had remained in spite of her rough sea voyage home. I shiver when I think of this, but for a fleeting moment I thought I spotted a glint of light flashing in one of her eyes—really! I jerked my binoculars away and shook my head in an attempt to refocus; in that moment there was a flurry of activity and without further ado four of the island's finest sets of rescuing hands firmly repositioned her unclothed body and prepared to carry her to the waiting stretcher.

The area was rugged and slippery and I was told that in the interest of safety the experienced team of volunteers had opted to use their gloved hands instead of the stretcher that waited some twenty-five feet away. They were gentle to a fault—reason enough for me to wonder, bizarrely, if she was still alive. (What is that all about?)

In the blink of an eye, a human throne was formed by eight strong arms that raised the blue-eyed victim up in mock repose—her head having fallen to one side. Red hair and slimy sea weed covered part of her face and I concluded with a twinge of sadness that the distorted position could be the result of a broken neck—perhaps even the cause of death.

Elbowing my way forward, I stared shamelessly at the pale, sculpted body so gently wrapped in layers of transparent, water-saturated skin. Oh, what uneasy beauty!

With every detail magnified by the telescopic lens of my new camera; it was hard not to notice the limp wrists, bloated hands, and fuchsia-glazed finger-nails—nails so recently groomed! Spotting the tiny gold band on the third finger of her *right* hand, I automatically assumed that she was unmarried and somewhere in her mid-twenties. Such a lovely thing who probably would have been deeply embarrassed at the way her young breasts had parted and carelessly fallen to the sides of her boney chest. And yes, how her (probably) once-flat stomach and pointy hips sank deeply into parted thighs, forming a kangaroo-like pouch. Pardon my graphic detail, but in spite of the grotesqueness of it all, I must continue.

From perfectly squared kneecaps, her shapely calves and swollen ankles flowed gracefully into puffy, pale blue feet—so modestly suspended in mid-air! She sat regally— seeming to cooperate with the four young men who moved with caution toward the waiting gurney.

Believe me, Kind Friend, I have seen many funeral processions and those young rescuers appeared to be grieving pall-bearers who may (or may not) have had a personal connection to the victim. They walked with such pronounced solemnity—taking short, military steps toward the gurney. Such precious cargo!   Beautiful! Delicate! Tragic!

I was standing there mesmerized when suddenly—out of the blue—I was overcome by a wave of rage. Why the hell hadn't they covered her up? That stupid, flimsy piece of plastic wrap kept slipping away as they moved her about! What the hell was wrong with them? They must have known there would be a gathering crowd; there always is! And why were they carrying her that way? Was this some kind of a joke or was I dreaming? I trembled with anger and insane elation; what was going on with me? (Cramer explained, later that they had expected to use a stretcher with proper covering, but as it turned out...because of the rocky terrain...and blah, blah, blah.)

In an erratic move, I broke away from the group and headed toward the *off-limits* concrete stairs that led through a tunnel and down to the beach below. Confidently flashing my reporter's credentials for the young deputy's approval, I nonchalantly attempted to pass him and guess what? The damn fool darted in front of me with childish authority and thrust his halting palm in my face. I tried to sound official and patiently explained my presence at the scene; after all, I *was* the island's ranking reporter. No! Not good enough for him! My clever little ploy was met with icy resistance. Lucky for me, Sheriff Cramer miraculously appeared and silently nudged me toward the rusted railing of the off-limits stairs.

Descending, I caught the harsh flashes of the coroner's relentless camera as it exploded again and again in an assault on the unfolding tableau. Half-way down, I stumbled—hesitating to go any further. There were only ten or twelve stairs left, but I was feeling dizzy and nauseous—seriously considering whether or not I would make it to the bottom without passing out.

I blamed my condition on the fumes that had emanated from the overweight chap who had been standing so close to me, earlier; perhaps his toxic fumes had finally reached my coffee drenched stomach! I took a deep breath and moved forward slowly, clutching the dangling railing and swallowing sticky balls of saliva—surely to cause an attack of retching if I didn't get some air soon. This had never happened to me before!

I saw it as a bad omen—perhaps the first warning shot had been fired across my bow!

"Come on, Henry; keep moving! Jesus, haven't you ever seen a naked woman before? Move! We've got work to do and it'll be your by-line on the front page tomorrow morning. Why not get it right the first time around, huh? Ha-ha!"

That goddamn Cramer picks the worst times to be a joker! I didn't think there was anything to laugh about at the moment. A young woman was dead!

Reaching the bottom of the stairs, I let out a long sigh and stepped out onto the tiny cove where I secured my footing in the sand and took up a favorable position among the dozen or so VIP's who were standing around, casually whispering. I barely had time to give them much thought; I was too struck by the unexpected emergence of the victim's body. She was so close I could almost touch her!

Her crystal clear features, glowing in the rays of the near-perfect New England sunlight, stunned me. My eyes and feet were riveted as I marveled at the haphazard way the red ringlets framed her face as it rested on her right shoulder. The unsightly tangle of seaweed had fallen away and she looked so beautiful that I could hardly breathe. A Madonna!

I certainly wasn't prepared for the lightening-quick movement with which strong arms lay the victim upon the black rubber body-bag that had been duly prepared to receive her. Directly, the ever-present latex-gloved hands began their cruel, zippering journey from her toes to her parted thighs. With increased speed they covered her sagging stomach and bony chest, hesitating for just a moment before covering the expressionless face with those haunting, wide–open eyes of blue liquid—still staring blankly. I let out a long sigh as the Velcroed flap was pulled over the top of her head and fastened tightly.

Raising the gurney to shoulder height, the four young men with seemingly choreographed sharpness disappeared into the tunnel of concrete stairs.

Turning in unison, we watched in silence for their emergence at the top of the bluff. In moments they appeared and quickly moved toward the waiting ambulance with its motor purring and its rear doors flung wide open, waiting somberly in the driveway of the small cottage. Some said it was a summer home to the victim. I pause here momentarily...words...fail me...

Quickly recovering from his unexpected sadness, Henry resumed his entry a few moments later:

What confusion reigns over me! What can I say? Why would this beautiful creature—or anyone else, for that matter—*elect* a death which is certain to involve resistance to such frightening suffocation? I use the word *elect* because for some reason it seemed to be patently assumed by *you-know-who* that this was no accidental drowning. I could tell by the way Cramer and those phony *Puckshaw* officials were staring straight ahead—tight-lipped and arrogant. I knew that those bastards were trying to hide something; they had that *official business* look that shuts one out.

It could have been an accident, but I don't think so. She could have been murdered, you know; but...it's more likely to be ruled a suicide—for some unknown reason. That's exactly what I mean; I wonder if I'll *ever* know the truth—probably not! I'm trying very hard *not* to imagine the horror of her final moments; yet...I bet she fought back at the last minute—panic-stricken. Was there pain or regret? Did the end justify the means? Hopefully, she just surrendered to blessed relief; after all, it seems to have been her decision—or maybe not! Oh God! Listen to me. I am being irrational again—am I not?

Now I ask you, Kind Friend; why do I feel such a curious sadness? Is this not just another Labor-Day Weekend accident which I am obligated to report on? And what is this gnawing pain in my chest that so resembles indigestion? Could it be the sign of an ensuing heart attack?

Something is definitely not right with me; whatever it is that I saw this morning has thrown me into utter turmoil. So I fret and I whine and then flee to you—as usual.

It's already passed midnight and I doubt I will sleep much tonight. I should be tired! After all, I spent an hour in the library very early this morning. I looked at archived articles and photographs before leaving for the scene of the tragedy. I spent at least three hours at the cove—gut wrenching!

There was no one there to sob for her—just curious onlookers and notorious gossip mongers—champing at the bit to wag their tongues in eyewitness glory! Isn't that despicable? That's *Puckshaw* for you!

Later in the evening I went to the newsroom for two more hours. I was almost overcome with emotion as I readied my story for tomorrow's front page. It was sad and deeply depressing to revisit the past life of this reclusive victim, but I've done my best and written only what I know to be true—at this point in time. Now I have to trust that the boys in the production room will wave a magic wand over the presses and roll out an exciting morning issue of the *Sunny Islander*. Front page! *Macguire's* by-line! Big news! Big deal! Yuk!

But oh, how I worry that no one will care about this dead woman. Do you think that's just another excuse for me to push the envelope? I do.

Now if you'll please allow me just one more observation, I promise to say good-night!

We both know that *Puckshaw* is an over-rated summer haven for high-bred locals and low-budget tourists. The economically-challenged arrive in hoards, gawking at celebrities, drinking too much, and driving too fast; while the elite—tanned from a day at sea on resplendent yachts—hobnob in their oceanfront mansions, sipping too many cocktails served up by white-gloved attendants. To add to the insanity of it all; both groups turn a blind eye as their underage offspring roam the island at will—seeking alcohol, drugs, and the opportunity for sex.

Don't you agree that *Puckshaw* plays host to a summer-long festival of risky behavior—for adults and youngsters alike?

The scene is set! All the componements for drownings, overdoses, and a variety of other tragic accidents are guaranteed—every season—right here on *Puckshaw.* STEP RIGHT UP FOLKS!

Why am I carrying on so? Why can't this drowning just be a simple accident…or suicide…or….whatever the hell you want to call it? Why do I have this morbid desire to make such a big deal out of it? Sounds crazy—I know—but isn't that just like the old fool that I have so recently become—*that singular, eccentric, goddamned Henry Macguire?*

Okay, now I've said it and I'm glad!

I'm very tired and I must reveal that I'm ashamed of my behavior at times like these. Listen how I babble on; perhaps true madness is at hand—who knows? All I ask is that you be patient with me, for at this very moment thousands of demons are scrambling my thoughts and converging on my soul. Soon they will break down the door and I fear I will be defenseless. I must fight back, I must fight back.

I think that I am at the beginning of a long journey—a journey that I must take—one that will challenge my integrity, drive me to dangerous distraction, and even…threaten my very being. Am I losing control? Yes and no. We'll have to see.

I must sleep now, Kind Friend—conserve my strength for the morning. Who knows what awaits me? Good night, for now.

HM

1 *The Cove*

On December 15th, 1993, Henry once again shares his distress over the increasingly morbid interest he has taken in the Labor Day drowning victim.

December 15, 1993
Hello, Kind Friend!
Much has been happening to me in the last few months. I am overcome with very troubling thoughts and wish to babble on to you for a moment or two. God, I hate nights like this when darkness falls too suddenly—leaving me alone and unarmed against my relentless demons.

I'm foolishly angry with myself for missing the sunset tonight; I rarely miss the orange ball plunging into the ocean, even in winter when it is only visible to fools like me. My devotion to the ritual makes me feel like I'm maintaining some sort of control over my life; rather like allowing the day to end and the night to move in with my express permission. Hmm! Interesting!

Well anyway, I interpret missing a sunset as some sort of an omen. I'm like that, you know; always reading a stupid message into a normal occurrence—it's asinine!

Tonight I'm feeling darkly out of place—as if I should be somewhere else—separated from myself. To complicate matters, a chronic backache is now threatening to spiral out of control and sideline me for at least two or three days. I'll have to keep myself occupied with writing to you, dear friend, and yes, editing my mind-boggling manuscript. Imagine me, the author-in-waiting! How about that? Ha!

More pain! God, I really wish I hadn't moved that heavy desk yesterday, but my eyes aren't what they used to be and I could no longer work by the light of that small north window. I had to do something or totally lose my patience *and* my mind! I love my old desk even though I should have thrown the ancient albatross out last year; I just never got around to it. But isn't that just like me? I'm sure good old Ed Sims would have helped me to get rid of the cursed thing, but now the damage is done and that's that. The desk is in its new place and I have a new back-ache and I'll probably keep it for another ten years; the desk that is—not the backache. Well, I'm certain I'll muddle through the spasms; after all, it's not the first back ache I've ever had.

I'm worried; I'm not at all convinced that I can successfully cope with this troubling mood that I've been sliding into at such breakneck speed. You know what I'm talking about, right? Yes, the drownings. There were three, you know, and I can't seem to stop obsessing over them. I am spending far too much time thinking about the girl and her mother. I must take some action soon or else...who knows?

From where I'm standing, there seems to be a deep black hole at my feet—beckoning me to jump! Not at all promising! Yet, I feel sort of drawn to it and we both know that's nothing new for me. Hell I've had those dark leanings for as far back as I can remember....only this one does feel somewhat different. The fact is, it's been creeping up on me for the last month or so, causing a persistent and penetrating sadness which is quietly eating its way into my spirit like the proverbial worm in the apple. Is it any wonder that its eerie presence gives me pause?

But anyway, I have chosen this night—a cold, moonless one—to indulge my curiosity over this off-putting state of mind. You *do* know what they say about curiosity and the cat; but I think I'll take my chances. I hope I'm not making a mistake, but this inner restlessness is pushing me further and faster into uncharted territory. It reminds me of the same feeling that prevails when one gets a second-hand invitation to a birthday party. Remember those? You never knew what to expect if you went and you worried like a damned fool about what you might miss if you didn't go.

So, kind friend, I wonder if I should just go to bed and think things through a bit. What do you think? No wisdom in trying to make a decision about anything tonight. I'll probably feel a lot better in the morning; so for now,

while I'm safely tucked away under my quilt of comforting darkness, I'll just ponder until uneasy sleep comes.
Good night, kind friend.
HM

A few nights later, in the premature darkness of a late December afternoon, Henry Macguire wandered along the secluded, crescent-shaped beach in a tortured state of mind. Lately, he was more often than not plagued by cluttered thoughts and conflicting moods—his emotions see-sawing at will. Fully aware that in the last few months he had spent more time walking in the cove than any other place on the island, he could no longer stop himself. Only the cove, with its familiar sounds and salty spray, showered him with welcoming peace. There was much to think about, but something was preventing him from deciding where to start.

Weeks of pondering the unexpected predicament in which he had recently found himself had already resulted in one undisputable conclusion: he was a troubled man who needed help in sorting himself out. If he wasn't prepared to take the necessary steps; he might well be doomed to wander the naked beach alone—trapped in his presumed madness.

To protect himself from the stinging night air he thrust his aching knuckles deep into his pockets and exhaled clouds of steamy air he could feel but not see. Cocking his head to one side, he listened intently to the steady throbbing of his temples as it competed with the roar of the icy Atlantic.

Henry loved the ocean with all his heart and soul and if he recalled correctly, it was the main reason he had decided to settle down on the tiny island called *Puckshaw*—almost twenty-three years ago, when he was just a young, wandering reporter. Now, since he had been thinking about death with increasing frequency, he made a mental note to leave instructions for his ashes to be scattered over the Atlantic for all eternity—if there was one.

With deliberate disregard for the changing seasons, Henry was still unfashionably clad in tennis shoes as he playfully teased the foaming surf into snapping at the hems of his pant-legs. When he finally became bored and cold he danced away gingerly, escaping the last wave before heading in the direction of the crumbling, concrete stairs that were dangerously slippery with decaying leaves at this time of year. Tonight, his water-soaked tennis shoes would make the climb even more treacherous to negotiate, but Henry nonchalantly shrugged off the soggy inconvenience and proceeded absentmindedly.

These days, the *off-limits* area was rarely visited by the islanders—it having been deemed *too unsettling* by most residents. Even though a few local teens could occasionally be spotted sneaking down for a quick smoke or a forbidden beer; the freezing waves were high and dangerous—a solid deterrent to loitering in the cove—even for fearless, thrill-seeking youngsters.

Henry Macguire was blissfully unfazed by the danger.

In the last twelve weeks, the increasingly perturbed reporter had come to know the area on a very intimate basis and he felt perfectly safe—even on a moonless night—without the slightest trace of visibility. The few individuals who had become aware of Henry's reclusive wanderings and strange behavior could never have imagined just *how* familiar he was with every inch of the cove—including the dangerous stairs and the newly-neglected path that led to the abandoned clapboard cottage; yes, the very cottage once called *home* by three drowning victims.

It was December 17, 1993, and barely three months had passed since the most recent drowning over which Henry had become obsessed. As of late, he depended solely on his lengthy visits to the cottage for peace of mind and inner strength as he tried desperately to sort out his feelings and assess his strange behavior. Having had little success, he continued to spend hour upon hour perched atop the lonely cliff—hovering over the empty cottage like a scarecrow guarding a newly-planted field. His daily presence had become questionable—*at best*.

Fully committed to this curious routine, the brooding reporter had recently experienced a few particularly crazed episodes during which he had circled the cottage non-stop—unaware of time or space—changing direction every now and then to break the monotony.

4

He complained to his close friend—Ed Barton—that lately he often felt gripped by an indescribable *force*; "Could this possibly be a form of *madness*?" he had asked—in all seriousness.

Ed had good-naturedly used the universal sign to indicate that one was crazy and tip-toed away chuckling.

Though Henry had regularly indulged in trance-like periods of contemplation accompanied by soft humming or whistling, things were subtly changing. On this dark night, he quite shockingly found himself fully engaged in conversation—an unprecedented display of eccentricity which alarmed him and rightly so. Frightened, he kicked a shower of sand and leaves into the darkness and wailed, "What is going on? What have I done to deserve this?"

He remained silent for a moment—as if expecting an answer—before anxiously continuing his ramblings. "Is it possible that I have sold my soul to an invisible enemy—one that has robbed me of my use of reason? If this is true, (Henry raised his eyes to the darkened sky) identify yourself, you coward! Tell me who you are and why you burden me with such overpowering emotion and bizarre behavior!"

He was shouting now and it frightened him, anew.

"Leave me alone; just leave me alone!"

In this volatile state of confusion he paced aimlessly, struggling to sort out the indescribable feelings that had been holding him hostage for the last few months. He had begun to experience other strange episodes: certain razor-sharp images and sounds had been presenting themselves to him on a regular basis—even when he was among friends or working at his desk in the newsroom. During an episode he would either explode in a burst of anger or recoil in cowardly fear and flee to his bed for the rest of the day. This behavior was shocking and unacceptable to the once unflappable, fiercely-in-control journalist known as *Henry Macguire*.

His friends and colleagues had always seen Henry as a bit of a loner—likable but quirky. Most days he was guarded and quiet but could be devilishly prankish on his good days. He was respected as an intelligent individual who, as an experienced reporter, had trained himself to remain detached and professional—avoiding over-emotional behavior—until just recently.

Aside from his visits to the local coffee shop to collect harmless tidbits while breakfasting; he concentrated on his thorough and painfully truthful reporting that appeared in the *Sunny Islander* almost daily. He kept to himself and encouraged others to do likewise—especially when he sensed they were getting too close to him. It was the way he chose to conduct his personal life.

Only lately something had changed—something he had patently refused to admit to himself.

So what was it?

The hard truth was that after almost three months of Henry's indiscreet visits to the deserted cove and its hauntingly sheltered beach; he was now insanely referring to the presumed area where three drownings had occurred—within feet of each other—as *sacred ground.* No one had ever attached such a blatantly religious connotation to the site of the tragedies; suddenly, Henry was heard carelessly dropping the term in casual conversation.

Some had noticed the change—others hadn't; but Henry was mentally and physically deteriorating at an alarming pace. During his endless walks in and around the drowning site, he was convinced that he heard the cries of the victims—pleading and moaning; alarmingly soulful cries that only the seriously pained or injured had the right to make.

He tried hard to play down his vivid imagination, but contrary to his efforts, he seemed to have established a personal relationship with the victims since he now sensed their pulsing presence both spiritually and physically. Something from within was propelling him into a constant replay of the last moments of the most recent victim's life. Henry questioned himself over and over; was she murdered or had she defied fate, thereby offering up her last hope for happiness by willingly bringing her life to a catastrophic end? Was it not a replication of an earlier suicide—that of her beloved mother—which had occurred just over a decade ago in the *same* cold surf, in the *same* deserted area, and in a *strikingly similar* manner?

So what was going on? Was there some kind of curse in play here?

As a seasoned and respected reporter on the island of *Puckshaw*, Henry Macguire had heard it all—many times over. Some residents held the childishly superstitious belief that a *hex* had been cast upon the cove and cottage, thereby cursing all those who dwelt within its confines.

Anyone who spent more than one season on the island was bound to have heard the wild rumors about the old *Carter widow* who had lived alone in the aforementioned cottage for many years. Henry had heard how, toward the end of her life, she had roamed around the deserted cove in her nightgown and sleeping cap, singing *Wagnerian* arias in the thick, German language of her childhood.

Many of the old-timers who frequented the coffee shops and newsstands recounted how, as children, they had skipped around the cottage cruelly chanting, "Witch, witch, jump into the ditch," just to entice the old lady outside to shout at them in her native tongue; but that was years ago—probably in the fifties. Now, once again, the absurd stories were making the rounds of the diners, beauty shops, and—ironically—the *Sunny Islander's* conservative newsroom.

Henry chuckled up his sleeve and remained true to his cynical nature of taking everything he heard on Puckshaw with a very large grain of sand.

Whatever the truth was and regardless of what anyone believed, one night the old widow seemed to disappear into thin air, leaving her flowing nightgown and lace cap to rest on a jagged-edged boulder—a mere twenty-five feet from the pounding Atlantic surf. The body had washed up several days later in a nearby cove—bloated and bruised from battering waves and the treacherously rocky shoreline.

The old widow's death was flatly ruled an accidental drowning—not exactly the stuff of which legends are made; at least not until a young woman by the name of Belle Adams bought the abandoned cottage in the early seventies. Newly repaired and remodeled, it became a private, charming, summer get-away for her and her only child.

The islanders occasionally spotted them shopping about the island, flushed with joy at their new surroundings, but by 1981, Belle Adams was dead—having perished into the Atlantic as the result of an apparent suicide. Hence, the eerie legend "found legs".

In September of 1993, barely three months ago and nearly twelve years after Belle's death, the legend was once again yanked to the forefront of the gossip mill. Another drowning…same place…same circumstances.

In August of '93—only one month before the Labor Day drowning—Henry Macguire had been feeling depressed and out of sorts. Puckshaw—the very island he had called home for the last twenty-three years—had begun to feel like a prison to him. Prematurely grumpy, he had reached his mid-fifties bored and disenchanted with his comfortable but empty lifestyle. He was tired of chasing non-stories and too-often bored to distraction with the lack of stimulation in reporting *Puckshaw's* banal news. Secretly, he wanted to wind things down and concentrate on developing his beloved journals into a *bona fide* auto-biographical manuscript. In short, he was ready to step aside and give some up-and-coming youngster a fresh opportunity at the island's only paper.

Though still young, Henry argued an excellent case for early retirement—*a retirement that was not to be.*

He was caught unaware by the news. It was over a decade since the Belle Adams case had made the front page; yet again Puckshaw was fully engulfed in a media frenzy surrounding the *third* drowning of a summer resident who had occupied the now-fabled cottage. The victim: *Sonny Adams*—Belle's daughter.

The *Sunny Islander* was gearing up—Henry was told to *turn it up a notch.* As one of the area's lead reporters on the story, he was obligated to enter the fray with his respected style of investigative, *truth-in-reporting* coverage. His colleagues were hopeful that it would help him shake off whatever was bothering him as of late.

The moody reporter was surprisingly invigorated by the challenge—as opposed to his recent malaise and jaded attitude toward his job. The deeper he dug, the more he became engrossed in the mysterious, disjointed pieces of information that were beginning to define the persona of the youngest victim. Confident in his findings, he wrote in detail—feeling no shame in delivering to the public what he thought to be true. Conversely, he felt uncontrolled rage when blatant falsehoods appeared in the mainland (Boston) papers or when innuendos were carelessly tossed about by Puckshaw's incessant gossip mongers.

Whether protecting the reputation of Sonny Adams, like a defense lawyer, or openly criticizing the shoddy behavior of long-standing islanders and their loose lips; Henry felt compelled to write of the unraveling mystery at length, adding depth to his pieces with each new scrap of information he received or uncovered.

His contacts in Boston supplied him with endless tips and leads—some good, some not; unfortunately, by the time he meticulously checked them for veracity, his competitors in the surrounding areas would often print the story—true or false—before he had a chance to lay his findings out in black and white. Henry didn't mind if they got it right, but when they didn't, he would hit the ceiling in an uncontrollable rage.

Spurred on by his editor-in-chief to *keep the pots boiling,* Henry began to see the developing drama as *his* story—perhaps the most poignant of his career. One month into the exaggerated coverage the re-energized reporter *owned it*; the continuing *novella* could be found spread across the bottom half of the front page of the *Sunny Islander* almost daily—preceded by Henry's by-line and accompanied by new photos of the scene—also Henry's handiwork. The process was exhilarating—a breath of fresh air for him. Someone had thrown him a life-preserver just as he was about to sink into a sea of unremarkable retirement. He felt *saved.*

Unbeknown to most, Henry, at the ripe, young age of fifty-four, had already completed his evolution into a lonely, withdrawn figure who never expected such a bizarre assignment to arrive on his doorstep so late in his career. Heart-wrenching and exhausting as the research would eventually prove to be, he thought the task to be well within the realm of his journalistic capabilities and life-long quest for *truth in all things*.

Though the well-known and equally well-liked reporter was unaccustomed to finding himself as embroiled as he was in the quasi-sensational Adams case; he was suddenly aching with a new sense of purpose. As he plunged headlong into unfamiliar territory, he was sadly unaware of his ill-preparedness for the toll it would take on his shrinking world and his already-diminishing existence in it.

The life-altering journey through the history of the Adams family would lead Henry Macguire through the valley of despair and darkness for some time to come.

A black sky hung over the cove like a heavy canopy muffling the silence of the cold, moonless night. Only Henry's childlike voice could be heard as he rambled on with ease, since his was a solitary presence in no danger of being seen or heard. He whispered and wailed; wondering if he was losing his mind or, at best, entering an early dementia. Thoroughly perplexed by his unorthodox behavior, he would not be intimidated; he was determined to see his obsession through to the end—whatever the outcome.

Shuffling along with his pronounced limp and aching back, Henry Macguire cut a comical figure—short, stocky, gnome-like—chuckling, crying, and waving his arms about as he mindlessly retraced the steps he could now take with his eyes closed. Up the stairs, round and round the cottage, down the stairs to once more pace the sandy shore of the lonely beach.

With raised, bloodshot eyes—too often deprived of sleep—Henry glared with misplaced anger at the hungry and arrogant sea vultures, imagining how they must have boldly mocked the desperate cries of the women who may (or may not) have died in their presence. He now saw the once-gracefully soaring birds as ugly, raw-winged predators, boldly sweeping through the dark sky to invade his thoughts with their fearless squawking. Brilliant, yet harebrained, they swirled throughout the cove, continually at risk of being sucked into the surf and condemned to stony silence.

Henry rubbed his eyes until they ached and blocked his ears like a child, shaking his head violently to bring his thoughts into sharper focus—without success. "Be gone, you wretched creatures!" he shouted, as if he could actually banish them with a wave of his hand, "Get the hell away from here!"

As rumor had it, the silent cove, was the only witness to the journeys of the three ill-fated women—from their idyllic beginnings in the cottage, to their tragic endings in the ocean—but Henry's suspicious nature and truth-seeking persistence led him to believe that such an assumption was disputably simplistic. As far as he was concerned, the first victim's demise was academic. Surely, the second time around, someone had seen or heard something when Belle Adams had ended her life early one morning while the sun shone and the birds sang and her young daughter slept peacefully in the enchanted cottage.

And the third time...?

Henry made a mental note to make another stop at the island's police station just to make sure that he hadn't missed anything—any tiny scrap of information that he could further explore. He blinked rapidly; the little voice in his head reminded him anew that there *was* something he could look into again. The hushed rumor about a lone witness, high on the cliff above the cove, had yet to be confirmed or denied and every time he inquired about the unverified report, he hit a brick wall. Even Cramer, his close friend on the island's force had grown defensive. "Leave it alone, Henry; just leave it alone."

Something was amiss and Henry hadn't been able to shake the chill it brought to his spine every time he thought of it.

The truth was that shortly after the Labor Day drowning, Puckshaw's law enforcement team had moved swiftly to squash the rumor about a lone, white male who, in good faith and to avoid the expected media frenzy, had volunteered a signed statement in return for a ninety-day immunity period to protect his privacy and that of his family members. And yes, he was presumed innocent...

When Henry finally cracked that little story, he didn't like it—didn't believe it—and questioned why the individual needed immunity if he was so innocent. Seeking answers, the irate reporter was propelled into a fact-finding rampage.

During his twenty-three years on the island, Henry Macguire had reported—with authority—on everything from *agoraphobia* to *zucchinis*. He was patient, had the memory of an elephant, and the determination of a bull dog. That being fully understood by one and all, he was not going to let this meaty bone go. *Cramer & Company* could withhold the name of the *Caucasian male* for as long as they chose, but Henry continued his inquisition—publicly badgering the island's Police Department through his weekly column—demanding full disclosure. He was prepared to wait for an answer—no matter how long it took.

Regardless of the fact that a reasonable amount of time (three months) had passed since the story broke and all the dirty laundry remotely connected to the case had been thoroughly aired out; the guys at the island's precinct continued to be evasive. They were making Henry sweat. He knew if he didn't ask the right questions at the right time and from the right person, he might just be left in the dark. On *Puckshaw*, it wasn't really about what you *asked,* but rather what they *chose to tell you.* And even though the guys at the station had always been respectfully fond of Henry, they were now being stubbornly standoffish with him.

If they knew anything about Henry Macguire; they should have known that any unwarranted behavior toward him would only serve to arouse his suspicious nature and feed his tenacious appetite for the truth.

Henry blew warm air on his aching knuckles to distract himself from his welling anger and confusion. He was in a rage for reasons he could no longer explain. In turn, he cursed his mother and father and the disastrous day he was born. He cursed his beloved sister, *Laura,* for reasons unknown or too challenging to think about. Thoroughly exhausted, he cursed the *unknown* powers (he no longer used the word, *God*) for having taken young Belle and Sonny Adams at the peak of their physical comeliness with such dark violence.

Covered with confusion these days; his spirit failed him more and more—faith and hope having been relegated to the land of tarnished virtues which he had long-ago discarded.

The truth was that Henry Macguire was filled with an immeasurable sadness and on the verge of collapse.

"What a pity!" he shouted into the cold darkness. "They had everything to live for, hidden away in their enchanted cottage with the roaring Atlantic at their feet! What was it that destroyed them—one by one? *What* was it? *Who* was it?"

Henry meant to find out.

The Carter woman's death could easily be put down to dementia and neglect as contributing factors to accidental drowning. She had probably been walking in her sleep when she made her way down the stairs, disrobed, and stumbled into the cold surf, dying within minutes. Case closed. Henry had already put that behind him; but now, with every bit of new information he became privy to, he came closer to concluding that the lives of the mysteriously private Adams women were, more often than not, darkened by periods of spiritual and physical pain as well as the heartbreak of personal abandonment. Was it really true that these two desperately isolated women—pushed to the edge of inescapable hopelessness—had sought the ultimate solution?

He couldn't answer that question—yet.

Hours passed and it was almost dawn as Henry seated himself on the frosty ground atop the steep cliff. He he pulled his stiff and aching knees up to his chest and drew in an icy breath. In anticipation of the next couple of hours, he actually became excited as his mind played out a series of cinematic frames, over and over, like a loop from a silent movie.

With a sardonic grin he recalled and deeply regretted the media attention that had so recently created a circus atmosphere on the island of Puckshaw. Several foolish residents, anxious for their moment in the spotlight, had unashamedly trampled over one another to wax philosophical over their unique connections to the two fragile figures in question.

They had babbled *ad nauseam* about the idyllic lifestyle on their *precious* island.

Henry had turned purple with fury when some of his friends and colleagues had bowed in awe before the influx of *outsiders* who, in Henry's opinion were "nothing but bloody newshounds" that had descended over Puckshaw like "a small army of housewives, begging for old photos and encouraging *bogus* friends and relatives to pay lip service to the Adams women".

At the time, still under pressure to *keep the pots boiling,* Henry, too, had been forced to beat the bushes—flush out new information just to keep up with his competitors—even though he thought it was invasive and disgusting the way salacious stories about the defenseless women were making the rounds from island to island. To him, they were blatant lies, rumors, or pure innuendo—all of which he strongly desired to prove false...*if he only knew the truth.*

He had done his job to report the facts—scant as they were; now he could barely wait for the *Sunny Islander* readers to become over-saturated and rebel against the pointless trivia and emotional drivel that they were being force-fed; then and only then could he embark on his journey to find the truth.

At last, one could hear the collective sigh of relief as a reprieve from the print invasion was granted! As expected, the story finally died down with a few obligatory updates each week; then—without missing a beat—the *Sunny Islander* went about its business of discovering or *creating* the next eye-popping event that was sure to sell newspapers and insure its *dignified* presence on the island.

After all, it *was* December and Henry hypocritically counted on some heart wrenching, holiday sob story to break soon. It only took one unexpected event with the right number of calamitous components and (presto!) a daily headline would be guaranteed for weeks—or until the public nonchalantly turned a blind eye, at which time the savvy publisher and his trusty editors would *make it* disappear. That was their job—plain and simple.

Of course, the secret of success was in knowing exactly when the public had had enough.

By mid-December the Labor Day drowning was no longer the leading topic of conversation among Puckshaw's meddling year-round residents—everyone having gratefully moved on.

Only Henry continued to indulge in a morbid interest in the lives of the Adams women and their abandoned cottage, high on the bluff above the roaring Atlantic. For some unknown reason a dark curiosity of his youth had been unexpectedly unleashed and he seemed stubbornly reluctant to abandon his quest for knowledge about the two women and their combined tenure of twenty-three years as fascinating summer residents of Puckshaw.

Having never been a sound sleeper, days and nights passed before the near-dysfunctional reporter slept for more than three or four hours a night; and those hours, once precious, were now continuously interrupted by dreams and haunting visions of Belle and Sonny Adams.

Henry poured over his notes, articles, and journals. He re-read everything that had been printed—true or false—about Puckshaw, the now infamous cottage, and the drownings. He sent inquiries and made calls—mostly unacknowledged—but he would not be daunted by the snail-paced flow of information.

Deeply puzzled, he questioned the numerous missing blocks of time so apparent in the tragically interrupted life-spans of the Adams women. The women seemed to appear out of thin air and unexpectedly disappear for years at a time. *Who* were they? *Where* were they during those missing years? His obsessive curiosity was getting the best of him and he felt compelled to search for accurate, eye-witness information. He knew of no law that prevented him—in the interest of truth—from further researching their lives.

As he pondered his new challenge, it truly amazed him that he still had any desire left to pursue a story that no longer held any particular interest for the reading public. After all, he *had* been thinking of an early retirement in order to spend his final years reading, writing, and perhaps even getting his beloved journals published.

That would have to wait.

Still seated atop the icy pinnacle overlooking the mighty Atlantic, Henry was the picture of a leaderless warrior. He needed a plan—yes, he needed a *real* plan.

Wearily dropping his head into his hands, he prepared to drift into a deep reverie which he increasingly found peace in, these days. These self-searching exercises were cathartic and centering, in regard to putting his past into proper perspective and his future into calm contemplation. When he was a young man he would have thought that indulging in this quasi-oriental practice was fool-hearted and a waste of time; only lately, he was appreciative of the way it kept him focused—even driven.

Tonight, he chose a seductive, meditative scenario in which he sat before a mirror speaking in a soft, melancholy voice, reflecting on recent events and his reaction to them. Though questionable and time-consuming, the dialogue was exactly what Henry Macguire needed. He could ask and answer his own questions, thereby retaining complete control of the meditation. He would be the first to admit, with fairness, that the method was somewhat unorthodox; maybe so—but it accommodated his, by now, extravagantly quirky needs.

Finally, in the semi-darkness that eerily precedes the sun-rise, he very deliberately pulled the woolen collar of his jacket up around his neck, forming a tight, warm cocoon to protect him from the wind. Then, dropping his shoulders, he gently closed his eyes and gratefully slipped into his chosen reverie.

~ * ~ * ~ * ~ * ~ *   * ~ * ~ *

Before the end of his self-designed meditation, Henry was at ease with the direction his decision was moving in. Bizarrely, he was about to move forward into the lives of Puckshaw's private, yet most-celebrated, women. If he didn't, madness would surely seize him and most likely destroy him. He was left with two choices: he could detach himself completely and close the book on the Adams women and perhaps Puckshaw itself; or he could stoke the fire in his belly and widen his search to include their lives as they existed before their arrival on Puckshaw as fascinating summer residents.

Without seeking advice from a friend, or perhaps consulting with his physician, who undoubtedly would have sent him packing to a mental health expert; Henry resolved to go in search of the truth—wherever it was hiding. He would satisfy his ever-increasing desire to untangle the web of secrecy and rumor that surrounded the lives and deaths of Belle and Sonny Adams.

As he saw it, the dead women, obviously at a serious disadvantage in setting the record straight, needed him to peel back the facade and expose the stark truth regarding their lives and deaths. They certainly didn't deserve a tainted legacy based on rumors or falsehoods.

On the other hand, Henry needed Belle and her daughter, Sonny, to validate his obsessive search for the truth to make the shattered puzzle whole again.

So the deal was struck; Henry would be the Yin to their Yang. He would find the truth and write about it and in the process, the women would receive their justice.

2 *Henry: The Early Years*

Early on in his life, Henry Macguire had faced the fact that he was not—and never would be—a literary genius. For a young reporter, that might be considered a very humble and realistic assessment of his talents as revealed in an introductory essay he wrote for a prospective employer:

"Sir, I am no journalistic genius; I am just an average guy with an average number of limitations that any one of my previous editors would gladly attest to. Am I Thorough? Yes, and very highly-motivated, if I must say so, myself. My god-given talents are few, but I continue, on a daily basis, to make the best possible use of them.

I am original and consistent in my approach to reporting newsworthy events and one fact about me is indisputable: I unfailingly write the truth—no matter what the cost is.

Dripping with confidence, he continued:

I guess you might say I'm a simmering pot kind of guy; I never get terribly excited about anything or overly-impressed with any person or group of persons. I search for and focus on the truth. No frills!

When I was very young, a not-too-friendly editor criticized me for being a reporter that wasted too much time searching for the truth. I took it as a compliment and he fired me! Perhaps he needed to do a little searching of his own?

I believe it is to my credit that I have spent most of my adult life ferreting out interesting and newsworthy facts with the sole intention of assembling them in the meticulous manner required to create reliable and readable copy—just what the discerning public demands and deserves. I am persistent in seeking the inner core of any story—big or small—no matter how long it may take. One more thing, sir; I'll even take a flyer and say—with respect and humility—that I have already achieved a reasonable amount of success in building my career as a worthy reporter. I would truly like an opportunity to work for your company. HM

Henry later noted in his journals that he got the job.

The youngster who went by the name of Henry Macguire—never Hank—had actually drifted into journalism quite by accident in the summer of 1959, having enrolled at a Community College in the vicinity of Portland, Oregon. It was one of the few regional colleges that had invested in three small dormitory buildings—one of them a renovated Sears & Roberts warehouse. A respectable two-hour drive from his home, Henry planned to enjoy campus life to the full.

Naïve and lacking in direction, the farmer's son arrived on campus a wide-eyed kid without a care in the world. After a mind-boggling orientation, he volunteered to help out a sophomore with reporting duties at the small, liberal *Campus Review*.

"Just collect a few campus tidbits and cover breaking news—if there is any," the kid had said, nonchalantly.

Breaking news? It was almost 1960!

To Henry—young, unsophisticated, and away from home for the first time—the newsroom seemed like a great place in which to make new friends or just "hang out" in case he became lonely; he obliged his new acquaintance with gusto!

At nineteen, along with the rest of the student body, the youngster sat poised and unsuspecting on the cutting edge of the monumental youth movement that was about to rock the free world through the sixties, seventies, and well into the eighties before finally losing its head of steam.

Although one might not imagine the rural youngster as being at the forefront of such a powerful revolution; the kid fell in love with the fervent independence of the unwashed and outspoken, blending in and trying hard to forget everything he had ever been taught by his rural-minded parents and teachers.

In time, he became accepted into the small group of *newsroom elites*—brave, bearded, young souls who sometimes recklessly wrote what they felt with the intention of curing the global malaise of every kind—all with one monumental stroke of their righteous and inexperienced pens!

Henry—summarily dispatched with pen and notebook to sniff out campus news whenever and wherever possible—was on the hunt. Elated, he roamed the campus relentlessly; literally knocking himself out with page after page of daily observations while secretly basking in his new status: a wobbly-kneed fledgling flouting his new sense of belonging and purpose.

That summer, with some regret, he never left the campus. Homesick and almost penniless—he lived on a few dollars a month that his mother and sister were sending him.

He lived in the newsroom during the day—eating free doughnuts and pizza—and spent his evenings holed up in a tiny dorm room located on the top floor of a newly-renovated building—without air-conditioning or vending machines. There he poured over his notes and assembled what he thought to be edgy and current campus news to be served up in eye-witness reports, opinion pieces, and a Q&A column. He wrote—totally committed—by the seat of his pants and later observed that "it was not pretty, but always truth-filled".

When he finally learned the identity of the few patient professors who performed obligatory advisory duties to students running the campus publications; he stuck to them like glue. It was the fine, graying academicians that taught him about being accurate and concise—the very first principles to be applied to his still-in-the-infant-stage reporting career. He worked hard at "getting it right, without rambling all over the page". Principles were one thing, but skill was another and the youngster had a long, long way to go.

Even though their time was rapidly passing, the "war horses" of the college faculty were willing to impart some obviously absent skills to the new breed of up-and-coming-journalists who would one day come to realize that they would spend more time *searching* for the truth than *writing* about it. Should the premise of that maxim ever come to be reversed; a valued professor told Henry Macguire to, "Just pull the plug, kid".

Henry stood by that advice throughout his career of journalistic endeavors. Once, when he *waffled* on a "hot button" campus issue and fled to one of his mentors for help on explaining his position; the old professor looked him straight in the eye and answered without the slightest hesitation, "Henry, when in doubt, write the *truth!*"

The earnest novice might have been guilty of a lot of mistakes in the early years, but he was always vaguely aware of his natural ability to assess a situation and write about it in a fair and cohesive manner. Being an avid reader and youthfully passionate about current events, young Henry loved to express his opinion—more often than not insignificant. Lucky for him, the campus paper gave him a legitimate position on its "soapbox".

It was during his *so-called* academic era that a fellow student in the newsroom encouraged Henry to keep a journal in order to practice and experiment with his writing skills. "Try it, *brother;* you can actually freeze events in real time. *Like,* someday you might want to write your memoirs and you'll be able to re-visit your youth in the turn of a page. Write what you're thinking and feeling, *my brother*; you never know when you might need the information again! *Dig?*"

Later on, Henry would write about his student friend. "He was one *cool cat!*"

As he stumbled along in his daily entries, the budding writer/reporter discovered another advantage to journaling; that would be venting one's emotions. He knew all about keeping the lid screwed on too tight. His father had an explosive temper though he was seen as a quiet, gentle guy by those who didn't live with him. Henry loved his father dearly, but he never wanted to be *that guy*—the one who calmly endured a devastating tornado without blinking, only to explode violently over a glass of spilled milk at the dinner table.

After a particularly stressful day, the youngster would pour his rages and disappointments onto the pages of his journal before walking out of his dorm—*de-fanged.*

Changing and growing were important steps to take if Henry planned on being an engaging and successful print journalist. Though he was maturing slowly and somewhat of a loner, he seemed to be on the right track most of the time. He was faithful to his chosen craft—writing almost daily. Sometimes he was amazed at what he wrote and at other times—aghast! He would write and then wonder; shall I keep this or flush it? Eventually he came to peaceful terms with his journal—he stopped second-guessing himself. "Don't ever be ashamed of what you have written—just let it be."

That was *Henry's Law* as it applied to keeping a legitimate journal.

The kid paid ninety-seven cents for his first hardcover journal—the first in a collection of event-filled volumes that would eventually serve as psychiatrist, friend, and father confessor to him and his highly developed alter ego.

A pretty good investment, the way he saw it.

Early on, he took a bold and mature step to impose strict reporting rules on himself: he would be as fair and accurate as was humanly possible, never apologizing for anything he wrote, as long as it was written with one significant guideline in mind: *the truth.* He knew that there was no way of controlling how *he* felt about the issues he was reporting on, but he planned to be faithful to the truth under any and all circumstances. That meant no *yellow reporting*, no cutting corners, no waffling!

It was 1961—young Henry automatically grew the mandatory pony tail and beard, drank a lot of coffee, tried a few drugs, and wrote a lot of drivel—all to his dislike. Time was not particularly of the essence, so he ended up sticking around the college newspaper department for a full two years—passing a few courses while he was at it. He was fast becoming fiercely independent and held the *brilliant* opinion—one of the follies of youth—that sitting in the classroom was a waste of time; especially when he could be in his room writing or slinking around the campus searching for a story. There was so much going on and his youthful, searching spirit literally soared with ideas. He was soon down to one course.

As Henry recalled, "One night during a lonely semester break and a prolonged coffeehouse poetry binge, I made a conscious decision to pursue the *writing* as a career—make a living from it; that important affirmation out of the way, I felt the burning itch to move off campus and try to make it on my own. I enjoyed solitude—no serious danger of getting lonely or missing student interaction."

Or so he thought.

He secured a tiny, furnished, studio apartment outside the perimeter of the campus and blindly applied for a half-dozen newspaper gofer jobs within a twenty-minute walking radius—landing one within a few weeks. It lasted for six days; they asked him to scrub the toilets when he wasn't delivering the mail or serving coffee from a filthy little cart. *Uh, uh! No thanks!*

He completed—just barely—one more course and spent the rest of his time sending opinion articles and essays to as many publications—large and small—that he could possibly afford the postage for. He entered—and did not win—dozens of contests with rocket speed; his formal submissions suffering a similar fate—rejection. The quirky kid didn't seem to mind; he was young, free, and an *American; h*e thought *that* to be a pretty damn amazing resume in those days.

That was Henry Macguire at his youthful and truthful patriotic best.

Young Henry continued to willingly take his share of odd jobs. He cleaned an apartment building until he ended up in the emergency room, having been bitten on his ankle by a rat early one morning. He even tried carrying garbage out of a fast food restaurant until he was mugged in the alley late one night. Finally, after attempting to fill the position of a *Department of Sanitation* intern, he wised up—applying only for jobs that were indoors and offered a free hot meal.

Though frequently out of work—broke and exhausted—he never once considered giving up writing. He would rather write than sleep or eat.

After eight months, he finally had one tiny success; a local *penny sheet* printed his insightful essay on the freewheeling youth culture and its long-range effect on society. (As Henry recalled, twenty years later, "I had no idea what the hell I was talking about!") A few of his friends claimed to have seen him "floating on air" after seeing his words in print—at a newsstand! That was his cue! He took his leave of the academic community with more confidence than money or college credits and began a ten-year odyssey during which he freelanced his way across the country—learning the ropes and paying his proverbial dues.

He would laugh and cry and make foolish mistakes; but most importantly, he would learn about the complex world and his place in it—all the while journaling his every discovery in touching detail.

Unreliable car, dingy motels, lousy food—he did it all. Henry gained "a little knowledge here and a little experience there" all while achieving the distinction of writing some pretty mediocre stuff that he was not proud of. He drove from town to town and paper to paper, seeking advice from *whomever* would answer his questions about *whatever.* He typed copy in Indiana and composed obituaries in Illinois. In Ohio, he worked—really worked—for a small village newspaper. He loaded the truck, drove it, and after dropping off bundled papers at designated locations, parked it, and slept in it—all for sixty-eight dollars a week, after taxes.

With a stroke of luck, the one and only reporter at the paper fell ill and Henry begged for a chance to make the fellow's usual rounds and write some sample copy. He offered to take his own pictures and continue to help with deliveries—all at his current pay.

His boss checked every word he wrote and deleted unnecessary or inappropriate comments or opinions. He always gave it back to Henry for his final perusal and approval and in time, the young reporter went from the anonymous *staff writer* to *H. Macguire.*

Whenever Bob Racey, editor-in-chief of the *Ohioan,* was asked how his young reporter was getting along, he answered, "Great! He's a natural!"

With direction and encouragement, Henry was turning out clean, colorful pieces and making a very small name at the very small paper. His boss liked him, his co-workers—consisting of a pressman, a *new Henry,* and the secretary/receptionist—also liked him; even the residents of the small village that he had come to know through covering the local scene were *very fond* of him. So it was unanimous—they all thought he was a *fine young chap*!

The young reporter often breakfasted with the Police Chief, lunched with the school bus driver, and had coffee with the guys from the garage. By all standards, young, trusting Henry Macguire—still unscathed by malice in the work place, corporate mayhem, or the vicissitudes of life in general—was considered an asset to the paper and a fine addition to the serene village. When he wasn't spending an evening with Lucy, the young library assistant, he was tucked away in his room at a cheap but clean boarding house, writing articles and opinion pieces for small magazines whose editors had come to respect his work in the last few years. He received a few dollars *here* and a few dollars *there* for his freelancing and was planning to invest in a good typewriter—pretty soon.

At twenty-five, Henry Macguire had no master plan for his life's work. What he did have was a notebook filled with contacts at regional magazines and small newspapers. At one time or another, most of them had sampled the surgical precision with which he reported on current events or his truth-filled treatments of special interest groups. He had recently begun to demonstrate his skill in shining the light on up-and-coming local politicians—their ugly warts and shameful behavior not excluded. He held the mature opinion that it was a waste of time and money to support a public figure that was known to have a *loaded closet* just waiting to explode—thereby catapulting him into political oblivion on your donations. He ended his piece with, "IT'S YOUR DIME. WHY WASTE IT?" The villagers loved it.

He was almost ready to buy that new typewriter.

Shortly after the Christmas holidays, one of Henry's contacts in Arizona called to ask him if he was interesting in contacting the editor of *The Texas Star; he* was looking for a fresh young writer—free of controversy or "grandstanding". He needed a *big favor.*

Henry made the call within minutes.

John F. Burrow, editor of the aforementioned paper, explained that he had secured permission from the Governor for a reporter of his choice to interview a convicted serial killer sitting on death row in a Texas prison. Burrow preferred an unknown journalist whose recognition factor would not overshadow the story, itself. Did Henry want it?

Henry was overjoyed and accepted the offer on the spot.
He was told nonchalantly that it might go into syndication—if it
was good enough.

After eight one-hour interviews, Henry flew back to Ohio and spent every spare minute editing his intense, factual reflection on the killer's cold-blooded murders, icy lack of remorse, and seemingly fearless journey to the death chamber. The eight-part series made it into syndication and Henry made the front page of the *Ohioan,* becoming a *big* celebrity in the *small* village.

Spring was on its way and Henry, feeling frisky—the time-honored privilege of youth—randomly applied for positions at small publications in New York, New Jersey, and Massachusetts. He dreamed of working on the east coast—as close to the beautiful Atlantic as possible.

He received a few flattering calls along with more "thank you for applying" rejections. Undaunted, he sent out a dozen more applications.

Because some people actually enjoyed reading his pieces; Henry Macguire concluded—with no little amazement—that he more often than not *felt* like a writer—however *that* was supposed to feel. In spite of his growing stability, almost a decade would pass before Henry would allow himself to declare with confidence that he made his living as a writer. It wasn't until the end of his ten-year, self-imposed apprenticeship that he had become a fine reporter—applying his journalistic skills and unique style to a wide range of topics.

Henry Macguire had almost arrived!

Eighteen months passed before he announced with very little emotion that it was time to move on. "No, there's no problem, Mr. Racey, Sir; just want to spread my wings. You know what I mean? I'd like to get to the east coast and try to settle down a little. Just not quite sure; know what I mean, *my brother?*"

Henry continued to sell whatever he wrote to whichever newspaper outlet or magazine that would pay him a fair price for his work. He was content. He was competent. He had a long list of contacts. All he had to do now was find a place to settle in with some permanency—plant some seeds. He soon found settling down to a bigger challenge than becoming a writer had been.

During his remaining seven years of zigzagging up, down, and across the country, he had miraculously matured without incident. Having left his teens behind with little regret and triumphantly marched through his twenties—so full of promise—he steadfastly remained a loner. He continued his vigilance when it came to involvement with any one person or group; if he was to remain unbiased in his reporting, he would have to avoid affiliating with controversial religious or political groups with obvious agendas. (He would become much more judgmental and opinionated later on in his life)

Young Henry kept his guard up lest that feeling of entrapment yet again hover over him as it had when he was in his late teens and coldly obsessed with escaping stifling ties— hence, his hasty departure from Bob Racey and his friendly *Ohioans*.

He liked things neat and uncluttered—no baggage for Henry Macguire. It was assumed by those who knew him—albeit casually—that he had a normal childhood; no deep, dark secrets of axe-wielding parents with cultish religious affiliations or cruel tendencies toward children. If the truth were known, his parents were level-headed and low-keyed rural citizens of Oregon—without the slightest tendency toward demonstrative affection.

They had nodded "fine" when he decided to go to Community College and "fine" when he decided to hit the road just before his twenty-first birthday. After all, it *was* the 60's and life was calling him and "sure" he should go.

His sister Laura—three years his senior—was in no hurry to join the exploding youth counter-culture extravaganza. She had a *short-haired* boyfriend with a job and a car and all they dreamed of was getting married and having a bunch of kids—just live happily ever after in their "picket-fenced home". Basically, all systems were *go* for her debut into the conventional, satisfying life of a young housewife in the Oregon *rain forest.* At least that's what Henry derisively referred to Portland as.

At that time, Viet Nam was only a strange sounding place without the remotest possibility of ever affecting Henry or any of his peers; if and when the long arm of the *Draft Board* ever reached out to him, "my flat feet will keep me out of the running—*no pun intended,"* Henry had written to Laura.

On the other hand, Russia was warming up the "cold war" with its new catalogue of big bombs, using its littlest satellite, *Cuba,* to bully the great US of A.

"*Cuba*—only ninety miles from the US—they couldn't hurt a fly, could they?" Henry wrote in several pro-peace, anti-violence and anti-invasion articles. "Hell," he stated flatly, "it just doesn't sound like any of those places needs the likes of me meddling in their lives—does it?" (Henry was a staunch pacifist and would have surely sought the very unpopular *conscientious objector status* if called to serve.)

Oregon didn't seem to need Henry either; nobody really begged him not to go. He figured they all knew they would do bloody-well without him and with that understood; his dad checked the old Chevy over and his mom gave him ten new one-hundred-dollar bills and told him to drive carefully, eat well, and stay away from alcohol and loose women—in that order.

He promised to obey the above commandments but the heralded counter-culture was calling him and he really had to run. He wasted not a minute in packing his scarce belongings—the usual clothing, his high school dictionary, (the only one in the house) and two rolls of toilet tissue (on his mothers advice)—and hitting the "highway to paradise".

During the first six months that he was on the road he dreamed about his parents constantly; his mother's knock-out cooking and his father's dry humor made him crazy with sadness. He couldn't count the mornings he woke up with every intention of going home "come Sunday". He spent hours daydreaming about the long hours he and his sister spent together as kids when she would beat him at *everything*—hide and seek, worm digging, broad jumping, and creek-swimming contests. And "oh, those long hot summers filled with mosquitoes, cook-outs, and lemonade!" Some days he couldn't remember why the hell he *ever* left home.

Now, without any warning, he was missing Oregon—"of all places!" he sobbed into his journal.

Henry answered his mother's letter and told her that he had managed to get into a few night courses at the University of Central Wyoming and yes, he was fine and would be calling soon. Actually he was taking *one* journalism course and working in the Library. The rest of the time he roamed around the UCW campus or read and wrote in the quiet of the library. Occasionally, he slept in someone's dorm room—usually someone he hardly knew. In order to save some money, he often ate cheap fast food or "mooched" his lunch from a fulltime student that he had become acquainted with.

Students and professors were kind and a few of those "loose women" his mother had warned him about had occasionally helped to distract him from his loneliness, but nothing filled the longing for home that haunted him for months on end.

He discovered early on that alcohol could never be his friend; more likely it would be his undoing if he tried it again. Put simply, it made him violently ill and almost sent him to the hospital late one night after downing a few drinks; booze scratched off his list of possible creature comforts with great speed.

Fast food—cheap and available—quickly became a big problem for Henry. He was used to hardy, wholesome foods his mother had placed on the table every day of his life. No matter what or where he ate, he felt uncomfortable for hours afterward. (Early signs of the ulcer he would be plagued with for much of his adult life.) He finally found a healthy and economic solution: he bought fresh fruits and vegetables in the supermarket along with jars of peanut butter and boxes of crackers; he "grazed" peacefully throughout the day while driving. No fuss, no mess. Pizza became his only comfort food, which he could eat hot or cold—any time, any place. He treated himself to pepperoni topping only occasionally. "It doesn't keep well when you don't have a refrigerator," Henry wrote to his sister on a lonely night.

One quiet afternoon in the library, Henry Macguire concluded with no little guilt that he had broken every one of his mother's parting commandments before the first sixty days of his extended road trip had passed, yet the first flush of autonomy far outshone the blush of shame and self-condemnation. With smug satisfaction in having survived the first two months on the road; the path to independence seemed much less formidable with every mile he drove.

The young journeyman with little education, less experience, and no money, was finally on his own; he was making decisions, earning a very meager living, and with an enormous amount of luck, he was on his way to a successful journalism career.

He felt like a man of the world writing about such lofty topics as religion, politics, and the Cultural Revolution that he was *so* a part of.

Henry wrote to Laura about "how glamorous" it all was; he never mentioned that he spent most of the time in his car, even when it wasn't running. And yes, how he had discovered that he could sleep pretty comfortably in the back seat, write an article about the roar of a freight train, and eat a pizza—all for only a few dollars. Often, in the interest of saving that few dollars, Henry bought a couple boxes of sugar-coated cereal and a quart of milk and *gulped and crunched* his way across the country's highways.

When the spirit moved him to write, he pulled over at a rest stop, jotted down his ideas, and took a quick snooze. There were tons of kids on the road, then; Henry never felt frightened or intimidated to spend an afternoon chatting with young bearded kids—mirror images—frequenting rest stops or gas stations in search of a ride to *wherever*. That's just the way it was then; the young trusting the young—or something like that. If anything, it was definitely a time of experimenting with drugs to expand one's mind, doing your own thing, and not trusting anyone over thirty. *Henry agreed with some of it—but not without coming to the conclusion that he still had a lot to learn!*

So there he was; among the richest kids in the world and living in the freest and bravest country on the planet; at least, that's what he had been taught. He soon came to understand that his country *did* have a few *dirty little secrets* that the government was working on, but by and large its citizens were definitely riding the crest, especially if one was twenty-something and on the road. Henry had no way of knowing how close he was to the national calamity that was waiting to bring him to his knees and ruthlessly rip open his guts, thereby bursting open the floodgates of public wailing.

November 22, 1963

Hello, Kind Friend:
I am barely able to speak but I ask you:
Who in their right mind could have predicted or even
imagined the unthinkable act of a single madman who calls
himself Lee Harvey Oswald?
HM

The hours blurred into days and then into weeks of numbing disbelief. Henry cried and wrote and wondered. It was mass gloom and he didn't know how he was ever going to get through it. Given the unbearable circumstances and his shaky state of mind, it was no wonder that—for the first time in his life—he found himself to be desperately in need of a friend on that snowy Sunday in December of 1963.

The holidays were nearing and most families and friends were huddling close—trying to steal whatever comfort they could in each other's warmth and Henry? He was somewhere in the Mid-West', alone, in a dingy motel, with a small black and white T.V. as his only companion. As he saw it, most of his countrymen were deeply depressed and he was no exception. That day, seemingly anesthetized, Henry sank into a deep, dark hole of loneliness that brought him to the brink of heading back to Oregon—yet again. Only the unreliability of his beat-up car and the cost of gas and food prevented him from attempting that feat; in the most profound confusion he spent the day confiding in his journal.

Dec 16, 1963
Hello, Kind Friend,
This dreary night finds me lonely, cold, and without any appetite for food, books, or companionship! I am preparing to leave Chicago and make my way to Breezing, Pennsylvania, where I'm to have an interview with the editor of a small newsmagazine called *Cool Breezes*. Maybe I'll stop in the Poconos and then it's on to *I don't know*; I hear it's pretty there. Anyway, the interview sounds interesting doesn't it? It should be right up my alley—mostly because it

is an opinion-driven publication and even the highest powers know how opinionated I am! But, Kind Friend, I confide to you on this saddest of days that I'm afraid I no longer *have* an opinion left in me to share with another living soul. It's all been said, day and night, night and day. Everybody just keeps asking, "Why? Why? Why?" But nobody has an answer and I just can't stop thinking about it: A bereft widow, two fatherless children, a riderless horse, and a leaderless country; now what? No one can make things better—we're doomed—and I'm only in my twenties!

Oh, how I wish I were home in the lush green of Oregon; there, I would never be alone in my father's house. There would be a barking dog, a scratching cat, and a screeching sister—telling me to move my big feet. Mom would be reading the paper, giving Dad bits of news that she thought he should know because he no longer read the paper—said he just didn't have the stomach for it anymore. And there *I* was, destined to be a writer someday! How do you figure *that one* out? But that's how it would be—all Ozzie and Harriet-like. "Hello, Mom. Bye mom, hello dad, bye dad." You know what I mean don't you?

But what do I do now? Maybe I should just go home and stop all my senseless dreaming. I'm so tired of it all. I wonder if it's really worth it. Look at our President; was his life worth it? Was his death worth it? I don't even know what I mean, anymore. Doesn't make sense to me at all! I'm trying hard to pull myself out of this darkness, but nothing is working. Can't listen to music, watch television, or even read a magazine or newspaper. Maybe if I move on and try to put down some roots; you know, maybe if I tried to stay in one place long enough to get a permanent job and find a real swell girl, I might feel better. I don't know.

But right now it looks pretty bleak so I won't make any hasty decisions tonight, while I'm feeling this way and the snow is falling and my soul is shaken and yes, while I feel like crying. I think I'd better just turn out the light and hope that tomorrow is a more tolerable day.

At a time like this you, alone, give me courage. So, I bid you goodnight, kind friend.

HM

By February, 1964, Henry seemed more up-beat as he wrote with some degree of optimism.

February 9, 1964
Good evening, Kind Friend.

I have just turned the television off and picked up my pen and journal quite lightheartedly for the first time since *you know when.* I think I can safely state that tonight, the national grieving that has paralyzed our beloved nation since November 22, 1963, has been put "on hold" for the better part of an hour.

Thanks to Ed Sullivan—television's square jawed, no-neck, variety show host; four young lads from Liverpool, England, stepped into the country's living rooms and brought a collective sigh of relief to America's mourning masses. While thousands of teenagers were propelled into screaming ecstasy—just short of levitation; perplexed adults were left shaking their heads in disbelief—even that reaction was a welcomed emotion after the weeks of prevailing sadness. That was some kind of wonderful reaching out from across the Atlantic to say, 'I wanna hold your hand', wasn't it? I hope the sad spell is broken and we can get on with our nations business of solving the problems at hand; there are so many issues that we young people want to lend our support to. Believe it or not, some of us *do* have informed opinions and we truly hope our nation's new leaders will listen to us and let us help.

Tomorrow I'll be leaving for New York to participate in a 'Future Journalists of America convention. The guest speaker is Pierre Salinger: the cigar-chomping press secretary to our fallen president. I am very excited! This is my first attendance at a seminar with *real* professionals on hand to give much sought-after advice. I am filled with optimism.

Sweet soul mate of mine, I confide to you with so hope tonight, that 1964 is looking good!
Good night, HM

By the end of 1964, both of Henry's parents were dead. Having been stricken with cancer—they died within months of each other. From that time on he considered himself a gutless coward of the highest degree. He had not returned to Oregon to see them during their ill health nor did he honor them with his presence at the time of their respective deaths and burials. (This pattern would repeat itself time and time again as Henry grew older.)

His sister had kept him informed of every sad step along the way and when it was all over, she informed her brother that she never wanted to speak to him again.

Why should she, Henry asked himself; I've been a lousy son and a lousy brother.

It was a grim but true; he would think of Laura every day for the rest of his life.

3 *Puckshaw*

The cove was dark and cold as Henry sat with his knees drawn to his chest. He squeezed his eyes shut and pictured his mother, father, and beloved sister in a time and place he would never again visit. With warm tears streaming down his cheeks, he said *good-bye.*

Aching with arthritic discomfort from the bitter cold, he shifted his painful position and mentally forced himself to return to his reverie and the recollection of his magical arrival on *Puckshaw*—the secluded island that had captured his heart forever.

~ * ~ * ~ * ~ * ~ * ~ * ~ * ~ * ~ *

With no purpose other than to improve his reporting skills, Henry drifted for a decade before he finally felt the urge to settle down. It was all quite by accident, as he would recall time and time again during his life.

He was spending a few days on the little island in August of 71, covering a regatta for the regional sports magazine, *Sail Away!*

Upon his arrival, he immediately realized that the big hoopla was not about the exciting competition, but rather the presence of *old-money families* and their high-profile celebrity guests. Henry was irritated; he loved both leisure and competitive water sports—especially sailing and that was *exactly* what he planned to write about this week. He was determined not to mention the snotty, high born kids of rich politicians and screen-idols, all running around clad in monogrammed summer get-ups and worn-at-the-heel loafers. Big hair, big teeth, and loud-mouthed, they roamed the competition's VIP area with sass and swagger.

Henry groaned.

Regardless of his irritation, the young visiting reporter was thrilled with the clean beauty of Puckshaw; it was a sight to behold: clear skies, blinding sun shimmering off blue-green water, and the most breathtaking beaches he had ever seen. He looked forward to his time on the island with tingling excitement.

Attending the first two competitive events, he wrote his coverage piece quickly, took a few photos, and as soon as the crowds thinned, disappeared to tramp about the island, sipping soft drinks, sunbathing, and snoozing. With three more days of events to cover, Henry relaxed, drank in the sunshine, and admired the beautiful Atlantic. It was during that sunny week of sea-food lunches on secluded beaches and hours of lazily reading his favorite authors that Henry became serenely aware of something remarkable: he wasn't anxious to leave. Not one bit!

The enticing island seemed to have drawn him into its magnetic center. The unique little spot was a welcomed relief from the bustle of Boston, where he had spent the longest period of his adult life—just over two years—busy with freelance projects and long-range commitments from Chicago to Buffalo, New York.

Not a single city, job, or person had yet been able to nail Henry down long enough to lay roots, but Puckshaw was a different story. He loved being surrounded by its sparkling water and saw it as a challenge to survive *Mother Nature's* wicked sense of playfulness. There were no bridges in sight; one could only sail, fly, or ferry to and from the island and its tiny key—though one or two high born residents claimed to have parted the waters on occasion.

Deep in his soul, Henry knew that he could make this place his home—if they would have him! Upon completion of his assignment, the diminutive stranger made a quick move to the island. Under cover of darkness, he had packed his car and ferried over at eleven p.m. on a Friday night. Upon receiving directions from the harbormaster, he registered at a local motel and went to bed.

He couldn't help it and didn't mean to offend anyone, but he found humor in the suspicious attitude that the islanders exhibited toward *everyone* and *everything*—from a sudden afternoon downpour to the *uninvited stranger* that had suddenly dropped into their midst, unannounced. He suspected that the year-round residents—so deeply embedded in this magical island and its traditions—expected a *divine sign* to explain his presence. He also held the firm belief that it might take some sort of a *divine miracle* in order to win them over.

Henry, known to be prankish at times, made up his mind with characteristic arrogance; he wasn't going to try to impress them. After all, as far as he was concerned, they were sheltered and misguided in the belief that they actually *owned* part of the Atlantic Ocean. Who the hell did they think they were, anyway?

If the truth were known, Henry Macguire fell recklessly in love with Puckshaw and everything it had to offer; many years later, he would finally admit that he had never really gotten over the thrill of a blazing dawn or the delightful suddenness with which the night fell. An entry in his journal attested to the beginning of his twenty-five-year love affair with the island.

September 20, 1971.
Hello, Kind Friend,
Good News! I think I've finally found a great piece of real estate to plant my flag on! It's about forty-minutes out of Boston. After several years of searching for a place where I could work as a journalist, tend to my manuscript, and live and write in privacy; I have stumbled upon a little gem quite by accident! The sun is delightfully bright and the water is crystalline. The sky, like a flawless baby-blue canopy, cools the hot beaches, knee deep in sparkling sand. What else can I say? Oh yes, year-round residents are high born and snooty while tourists—also known as *outsiders*—are generally raucous and ill-mannered. It's really hysterical observing the waspish behavior of the local residents; sometimes I can't believe my eyes and ears, but I love it! Hell, after spending the first twenty years of my life in the rainy outback of Oregon, I consider myself a lucky bastard to have found such a Utopia—yes, right under my nose! It's pure magic!

Did I tell you that it's an island? Yes, it's an island called *Puckshaw*. It's named after an obscure Native American Chief called Kambi Puckshaw. It's wonderful!

Within days Henry Macguire began feeling comfortable on the island; he had only *dreamed* of ever having the privacy that he so craved for most of his young life and there it was—an enchanting hide-a-way; just begging to meet all his quirky needs. In calm seclusion, he could finally work on his *manuscript*—a compilation of his journal entries, along with various humorous character sketches and essays about his *so-called life* as a reporter.

Some thought it was pretty ambitious for someone who had barely turned thirty, but for some reason Henry already felt old. The truth was that the young reporter had *always* felt old. He had sought a solitary existence that rendered him friendless at a young age. Old and alone at thirty—he figured he deserved it. He was the first to admit that he was a lousy human being—his own family couldn't count on him—he had proven that!

He was secretly convinced that he didn't deserve such a beautiful place in which to live and early signs of paranoia drove him to worry that Puckshaw might be snatched away from him prematurely. He planned to soak up as much of the island as he could.

Having been paid pretty well for his work for the last three or four years, Henry—never having been extravagant with money—or anything else, for that matter—had accumulated a healthy little nest egg and felt no pressure to *gettajob* immediately.

He planned to hold on to a couple of long term writing jobs, covering special sporting events for two regional magazines in the Northeast. He had also recently renewed a contract to read manuscripts and play "book doctor" for two fledgling publishing companies in the south. He also planned to write his monthly instructional piece on current events for a *Weekly Reader* small press. His income was steady and his savings were doing fine; he had every reason to confidently roam about the island until he found the right spot to plant his feet.

After securing an introduction to Ed Barton, Editor-in-Chief of the *Sunny Islander*—still a three-times-a-week publication in the seventies—Henry offered his reporting services; "Maybe I can contribute something to your *little* paper; what do you think?"

They *just happened* to be a little short-handed in the newsroom. "Yes, there *are* still a few late summer events to be covered but...I don't know; I've never even *heard* of you before."

A few days later Henry Macguire was hard at work covering Puckshaw's last sporting event of the season—a junior sailing contest—and its popular Jazz festival. Before long, Barton had added the day-to-day soft news to his duties and, as expected, he quickly became a regular in the newsroom and around the coffee shops.

The usual busy-bodies wondered *who* he was and what he was doing on *their* island. They would, so Henry jokingly put out the word that he wasn't any sort of pedophile or serial killer; just a hard-working reporter, who *happened* to fall in love with the island and did they mind *terribly* if he stayed.

He had already made up his mind—he was staying for a long time.

Every summer was break-neck-busy on Puckshaw; Regattas, speedboat races, and a variety of music and art events—all designed to lure *old money* families and their *delightful celebrity guests* out of their secluded sea side mansions and into the island's venues. The summer festivals drew thousands of modest-income summer vacationers, along with temporary hospitality workers, and the usual array of *paparazzi*, relentlessly pointing their cameras at anyone that even resembled a celebrity.

The islanders—from the coffee house wait staff to the *Maître D* at *La Provence Bistro*—thrilled to the annual appearance of presidents, ex-presidents, and their fleets of secret service protectors and *hangers-on*.

Henry marveled at their *naiveté*.

"Jesus, you'd think *The Almighty* had arrived the way you bow and scrape," he howled at the coffee shop staff and their raised eyebrows. "C'mon, people, those rich ones are just like anyone else—except for their endless amounts of money and offspring."

"Right, Henry," Vera piped up. "Just keep talking while we make our tips."

Henry noted with renewed disdain how *the glitterati* kept a strict routine: Upon landing in small private planes, they posed for photos and shook a few hands before boarding cool, sleek limousines waiting to transport them to *The Crown & Anchor Marina,* where fully staffed white yachts—the biggest and the best—awaited their arrival. Stocked with expensive wines, caviar, and various *goodies* indulged in by the rich and famous, the showboats cruised around the bay, honking their arrival, before departing for their private mansions to prepare for elaborate dinner parties and the next day's activities.

They were "the beautiful people"—an assortment of handsome politicians, socialites, and luminaries; all with good-looking wives, girlfriends or both, along with hoards of athletic kids, nannies, private chefs, and caterers. They descended like little military platoons while tourists and islanders alike screeched with delight. After all, every breath the summer celebs took meant precious dollars in the island's coffers.

Henry loved to annoy them by practically ignoring their arrival for the summer events. It was the seventies and he wondered who the hell they thought they were. He'd just say the *Kennys* or the *Sullivans* were seen boarding the Helicopter or arriving by ferry. He thought they were phony and useless—living on inherited wealth the way they did. But it really wasn't any of his business and nothing he wrote or didn't write was going to change their status on the island. He didn't know why he even let it bother him—it had been going on for decades and showed no sign of abating.

Once the summer was finally over there was little to report on the island. The *touristy* events came to a halt and that was the signal that Henry could do his own thing, which consisted mainly of sleeping a little later in the morning and roaming Puckshaw at will. He didn't bother anyone—just sort of observed the local scene, drank a little too much coffee, and worked on his journals; *that* he did faithfully, with an eye to getting them published someday.

Henry showed a flair for humor throughout his writings, though he didn't intend for his journals to be comedic; an occasional comedy of errors—maybe—but comedy club funny—no! For instance, he never saw anything funny about the endless reflections on his chronic and sometimes debilitating depression and paranoia; or his mysterious searches that, more often than not, ended in defeat.

Frequently, his quirky compulsions or inexplicable obsessions led him on week-long quests of driving for miles and searching for some unknown or unattainable information in connection with a story he was working on. Searching, searching, searching—that was Henry Macguire. Finding the truth? That was the ultimate "high" as far as he was concerned.

One thing was for sure—he didn't see any sense in hiding his problems from his journals. After all, he saw himself as a deep-in-a-dark-tunnel sort of guy and he couldn't change that. Actually, he never even thought about trying.

During his first fall and early winter on the island, Henry Macguire just sort of hovered around the coffee shop for the town gossip and filed a local interest story every now and then. His duties were light; cover the town meeting, interview the fire chief or the mayor, and report on the local kids who had made the dean's list or received an award for some minor achievement. The islanders really loved that *tripe*—as Henry called it. What they didn't like was when he deliberately reported some mischievous behavior or property damage perpetrated by the local youngsters. When they objected too loudly, Henry would reason very gently, "Its news. Not *good* news, but news."

He also wrote a column on boat safety—more like an admonition—pointing out the number of boating accidents they had on Puckshaw every year; they didn't like that, either.

Henry enjoyed the freedom that the winter allowed. On his own time he observed the *waspish,* yet interesting, islanders and continued his writing; a little poetry, a few short stories for the *Atlantic Quarterly,* and a monthly column for *Boston Boater World*—all in addition to his other manuscript reading commitments. There was always something for him to work on— generating a steady stream of income.

For a guy that liked to refer to himself as "a little lazy at times" he was always meeting a deadline of one sort or another. One could hardly call him lazy.

He still thought people saw him as the kind of guy that had nothing to do all day and that image suited him just fine; after all, everybody didn't have to know what he was doing every minute of the day. Relatively speaking, the *Sunny Islander* was just his speed; laid back and tight-lipped, with an occasional screaming headline—maintaining a tricky balance of fantasy and reality which kept him employed from season to season. He was more than happy to spend the next ten years riding the waves and becoming an islander. And after that, who knew?

There was plenty to write about in the early days of his first decade on Puckshaw and he willingly filled the editorial page with commentaries on national and international issues and their effect on the bland little Island—neatly tucked away off the coast of Massachusetts. He laid his own opinions squarely between the lines while still giving his readers what they wanted and deserved—the truth.

With the sixties behind him, Henry found ample material to write about during the seventies. Of course, there was Vietnam. In late 1972 Henry was still railing against the machine. "When will they stop the bloodbath? When will they stop the body bags and flag-draped caskets from coming into our living rooms every night? Who are these kids and their families that are bearing this unconscionable burden? Are we ever going to end this fiasco? Then with a splash of light-heartedness Henry added, "I don't mean to be disrespectful, folks, but is Disco-dancing for real? Please say it isn't so!"

By August, 1974, we had said good-bye to a tax-evading vice-president and hello to a hotel with a strange sounding name that was destined to become a household joke. A politically motivated, botched break-in brought down a president who narrowly escaped impeachment, along with dozens of career employees who were dangerously close to the doomed leader.

Henry focused on the shamed president's traumatized wife and daughters bravely facing the public condemnation of their loved one—while he stubbornly maintained his innocence.

Ashen and forever remembered for his five o'clock shadow and greasy beads of perspiration, a *potentially* great statesman fell from grace. Smiling and mischievously delivering the victory sign, he boarded a military helicopter waiting to fly him into disgraced retirement.

Henry Macguire continued to report the daily news while more and more bouts of depression gnawed at his guts. He needed fresh topics to write about. Frantic, he researched arms proliferation, contemporary art, inter-galactic travel, and the truth behind John Updike's *Rabbit, Run.* Finally in exasperation, he opened one of his widely read Sunday commentaries with, *"WHAT NOW?"*

He answered his own question with, *"Well, there sure are a variety of mind-numbing, illegal drugs one can turn to while legally wearing a brightly colored polyester leisure suit and a string of love beads! And yes, you could be dancing nightly in some pretty dazzling and dizzying paisley prints, all designed to distract YOU, THE AVERAGE AMERICAN, from noticing the state of social chaos that you are being sucked into. Can't you see that you are being force-fed wide-screen heartthrobs, bikini-clad pin-ups, and a shimmering crystal chandelier that swings and sways to the throbbing beat of a disco tune? Listen folks —it's all contrived to numb your senses and lull you into idiocy.* Henry ended his rant with, *"Wake up, little Susie!"*

The column sent the island into overdrive and forced Henry to hide out in his cabin for several days—blissfully writing and chuckling at his prankish deed.

Meanwhile, behind the scenes, the nation's leaders continued to apply band-aids to a hemorrhaging society that, without much ado, slid on its backside into first base and the "big eighties"—the mighty *Reganomic* era. Henry didn't like to complain *too* much because even though he saw the president as nothing more than a *B* actor, he would make a lot of money from his unique economic agenda before the end of the decade; that was his business and he, like many others, *rode the crest all the way to the bank.*

Though Henry Macguire may have found a magical place to live and secured a decent job to make a quiet living from, he did not have the same luck in making friends. The reason was obvious: whenever a mere acquaintance showed signs of becoming a true friend, he tested them by cruelly rebuffing them. If the candidate persisted, Henry then reversed his position and took his responsibilities of loyalty and confidentiality quite seriously. Unfortunately, many good and kind individuals walked away from him; they didn't have the stomach for his routine of "vetting" his prospects.

Henry figured he had made about three or four good friends on Puckshaw, his favorite being Ed Sims.

Now, a wide grin crept across Henry Macguire's drawn face as he sat hunched over in his soul-searching meditation on the freezing bluff above the Atlantic; he was thinking about his first meeting with Ed Sims—back in the late seventies, early eighties—when the larger than life attorney had just taken a small apartment on the island. Ed had been seen around Charlie's Coffee House looking for new clients with a kind of desperation that screamed, "HIRE ME!" By today's standards he might be considered an *ambulance chaser*, but this particular morning he was just another customer having breakfast.

Sitting at the long, low counter—side by side—Sims suddenly thrust his hand between the newspaper and Henry's face to introduce himself as *Ed Sims*, attorney at law. Henry was taken aback; the islanders just didn't do that sort of thing, so he had to assume that the man was a newcomer—also known as an *outsider.* He gave him the quick once over and made a mental note about his appearance: overweight, sweaty, shiny suit, and stained tie. "Ugh!" Henry quickly concluded that this poor guy could use a few bucks and a makeover.

Ed slid his business card over and said something about..."if I can ever be of any help..."

Henry squirmed a little, recoiled from shaking his sweaty hand, and nodded as he picked up his card and returned to his sports page. (He hated being bothered so early in the morning, when he had hardly opened his eyes.)

After consuming his second cup with a satisfied sigh, Henry turned to say goodbye to his new acquaintance, faintly aware of the flushed, pained look washing over the stranger's face.

"Are you alright there, Mr. uh, Sims?"

Ed Sims shook his head vigorously.

"Not sick are ya?"

Sims was panting now, almost hyperventilating. He ran his chubby hands through his thinning hair and mumbled something.

Henry had read you should ask, "Are you choking?" when someone showed unmistakable signs of distress in a restaurant. So, a bit exasperated, he asked Sims the question.

Sims looked down toward his lap. Henry followed his glance and peered, somewhat embarrassed, in the same direction. Beneath the low counter and the shiny stool there was a space, about eight inches long—just enough room for one's knees to fit under comfortably—with a short drop to the floor for ones legs and feet. But the owner of the coffee shop, Charlie, aware of the discomfort of children and adults whose feet did not reach the floor, had installed a raised wooden step that served as a footrest. It was similar to the step you might see running along the bottom of a bar—a footrest of convenience for those patrons who had been cheated, when it came to leg length.

Anyway, Ed Sims must have considered himself to be one of the short-legged customers, for he had wedged his hefty thighs into the limited space provided under the counter and raised his swollen feet— already stuffed into too-tight loafers—onto the little step; unknowingly, he had squeezed himself into a pretty tight spot. The problem was that now, after a big breakfast, a glass of juice, and two cups of coffee, Sims was unable to free his legs in order to stand up and make a necessary trip to the washroom. A very necessary trip, as he would recall, years later.

Henry took a closer look and shook his head from side to side with a low whistle. Later, he would describe Sims' thighs as "two huge ham hocks, wedged into a mailbox".

He studied the problem like a mechanic looking under the hood of a disabled car.

"Now why the hell did you go and do something like that, young man? You're in a little bit of trouble here."

Sims was breathing heavily and in some pain. "Can you help me out of here, buddy? Please. I uh, need to use the men's room—soon."

Henry bolted off his stool and knelt on the diner's greasy floor grabbing Sims by the ankles, but they, too, were wedged over the little bar with his heels and toes pasted flat against each other without room for a single hair between them. His lower body seemed to be cemented to the floor and couldn't be budged. Sims was actually putting the full weight of his heavy legs and thighs on the outer sides of his ankles. Henry was afraid he might break something if he continued to pull on them.

He had every reason to be concerned. He could see and smell how hot and swollen his legs were as his pant legs rode up to reveal several inches of bulged flesh above the elastic on his damp socks; he wondered why the hell this grown man had twisted his ankles around like a little ballerina. Henry quickly answered his own question. When Sims felt the pressure he must have turned his feet inward to rest on his ankles and buy himself more room—too late.

Henry pulled himself up and stood behind Sims to think for a minute before putting his arms around his huge waist to pull him back, thinking that might help, but Sims' thighs seemed to be ballooning by the minute under the counter, wedging him in tighter and tighter. Ed let out a gas pass and Henry felt a little quiver of laughter rising from his belly to his throat, but quickly looked away—stifling it; he reasoned that it wouldn't be polite.

A tiny group of regulars had by now, put their newspapers down and were watching in sheer amazement. Sort of a "will he or won't he" look on each of their faces. Henry knew he couldn't laugh now; after all, the man was in a predicament. He bit his lip and stifled another smile before grabbing Sims under each armpit and shaking him from side to side like a mad dog trying to free a bone from a carcass. He couldn't budge those huge thighs, try as he did. Ed's neck was bright red and Henry was getting scared. He had to think of something fast. Christ, he thought, this guy could have a stroke, right here, and his having to go the bathroom and all...it could be quite messy. He thought of asking Charlie for a crowbar to rip a piece of the wooden step out as a last resort to relieve the pressure, but he suddenly heard a voice out of the crowd shout, "Come on, Henry, you can do better than that!"

It was Jerry, the *Marlboro guy*. "Show us what you got!"

With that bit of encouragement—accepted as a challenge—Henry dropped to his knees, grabbed Sims around the waist, and literally began to twist him from side to side; it was a comical sight: Sims dancing to Chubby Checkers' *Do The Twist*. At the time that Henry was putting the slightest spin on the chrome stool, Sims began swinging his backside back and forth; soon the stool, wet with perspiration, was beginning to spin on its own. Not that you could see it, because it was covered by Ed's large backside, but you could hear it squeaking under the pressure.

The cheering, shouting crowd was now fully engaged in the hair-raising event; it was the best entertainment Charlie's had offered in a long time and would not fade into anyone's memory any time soon. Before long, both bodies were twisting and turning with increased speed and determination. One large grunt from Henry and a corresponding one from Ed Sims, and the newspaper flew in one direction while Ed's half-filled cup flew across the counter to send a stream of cold coffee toward Vera, a seasoned waitress, who had stopped snapping her chewing gum to open her mouth and stare in amazement. The tug of war continued as they rocked from side to side.

With perspiration dripping down his back, Ed wished he had been a little more generous with his *Mennen's Speed Stick,* earlier.

Henry was just about to give up, when the chrome stool spun with a fury, dislodging Ed's short, swollen legs to the right, and flinging his body after them. Henry, with his hands firmly grasping Ed's waist, was still holding on when he felt his feet leave the floor and his own small frame, sail over this stranger's back and finally land in a sweaty heap with Ed Sims rolling over the top of him. All three hundred pounds! The breakfast crowd roared and applauded and ran to pull them to their feet. Sims was red faced and weak-kneed as he thanked Henry and shook his sweaty hand, with gratitude. He excused himself and made his way to the washroom to cheers of victory and "high-fives".

Returning quickly—albeit a little red-faced—with water slicked hair and freshly-tucked-in shirt; Sims hiked up his trousers and placed his hands on his wide hips, asking, *"What?"*

Vera rescued everyone from the awkward silence with a typically sarcastic and facetious offer. "Hey, you both look like you could use a cup of coffee! Sit down and catch your breath. Right there, *IN A BOOTH!"*

Shortly after the roar of laughter subsided, Ed Sims and Henry Macguire began a close friendship that would last for the rest of Henry's life. In the remaining years, to Henry's knowledge, Ed never again sat at the counter in Charlie's.

4 *The Drowning*

Henry became visibly agitated as his reverie led him to a more recent day in September—just a few months ago—when he was informed of the early morning suicide of one of the island's young summer residents. He squirmed and breathed rapidly, practically working himself into a hyperventilating fit before slowly regaining control of his emotions. Adjusting his collar against the chilling wind, he retreated back into his exercise, wishing he had a video of himself during one of his trances; he never was absolutely sure of his behavior and assumed a video would preserve his moods and physical reactions more accurately than his memory could.

He let his mind travel to the first day of September; the day that had changed his life forever.

Then, leaning forward like a priest in the confessional, he began quietly communicating with his self-designed alter ego. He recalled the dreary September morning when he had nonchalantly sauntered into the newsroom, only to be greeted with an exasperated growl by the cranky editor of the *Sunny Islander*.

"Henry! Get the hell in here! Where have you been? Tell me—what the hell's happened on Crescent beach?" And before he could respond, Ed Barton continued, "and please don't say you haven't been down there yet! What the hell is going on with you anyway?"

Henry had already heard from the guys in the newsroom that Barton was on a tear, so he was somewhat prepared—*don't overreact.* Some young woman had drowned early that morning and now it looked like Barton was guilty of overreacting. .

"Jesus, chief," he said rather playfully, with just a hint of disrespect, "Take it easy; it was probably just another love-struck kid going in for a late-night dip to drown her sorrows. I guess she sort of *got in over her head*—if you know what I mean." (He raised his eyes to the ceiling and folded his hands in mock prayer)

"No, I don't know what you mean!" Ed bellowed, "And you don't know what the hell you're talking about; get the hell out of here and see if you can get the story on it before every other reporter within a hundred miles arrives. Sheriff Cramer said they got the tip around six o'clock this morning and they're down there now searching the area. Some of the locals have already called in and are claiming that the young woman was related to another suicide victim you *just might* remember because you covered it about ten or eleven years ago.

Listen to me Henry—I'm dead serious. If this kid is who I *think* she is, everyone in town is going to make a big fucking deal out of it; now get the hell down there and have something in by press roll tonight—or your ass will be hanging from the flagpole tomorrow morning. Beat it—now!"

Ed Barton never lifted his eyes to meet Henry's; he just reached into his drawer for his bottle of antacids. Henry's shoulders jerked at the loud crack of the drawer closing as he walked away shaking his head. As he checked his mailbox he heard Ed let fly that they would probably be reading about it in Hong Kong before he got around to filing his story. Henry thought he *could* be right—though he tended to exaggerate. Most small town editors were *like* that—highly excitable and over-reactive; the exact opposite of a guy like Henry. Yet, for some odd reason, Ed Barton and Henry Macguire were comfortable enough to call one another *friend.*

Henry sauntered, somewhat resentfully, towards his reliable *Puck Jeep;* he called it that because it resembled the souped-up dune buggies that most of the year-round *Puckies* drove in winter, while their shiny, four-door sedans were locked away in a garage. He headed down the main drag of the island, stopping only to pick up the NY Times and a steaming cup of bitter coffee from *Charlie's.* Sitting in the idling jeep he quickly perused the paper, slowing down only long enough to read the sports page and blow on his coffee; soon he was going to have to dig his heels in and sort out what the hell all the fuss was about.

There had been so many boating accidents, drownings, suicides, and disappearances over the last twenty-two years that he found it daunting to remember the facts regarding the incident that had occurred on *Puckshaw* twelve years ago. "Hell," he had snickered on his way out of the office, "I can't remember what the hell happened last month; how am I supposed to remember a story that I filed eleven or twelve years ago?"

If the truth was known it was not likely that Henry had ever really forgotten a front page story with his by-line on it—he was just playing a little game with Barton's head that they both enjoyed.

Puckshaw was a summer haven for those who loved to swim, boat, and participate in a variety of, sometimes dangerous and stupid, water-related activities; Henry wondered what the hell was so shocking or special about this drowning accident—or suicide—or *whatever*. He shook his head and swore under his breath as he considered buying a pack of cigarettes.

Bless me father for I have sinned, it's been too many years since my last cigarette.

Henry hadn't smoked a cigarette since the eighth grade.

He scanned the rest of the news, turned on the radio to ease his aggravation, and headed over to the newspaper's archives library—located at the end of the business district. He wanted to refresh his memory about the suicide that had occurred ten or eleven years ago and run a quick file photo search on the new drowning victim.

Sandy, an eighty-year-old islander with the memory of an elephant, maintained the gleaming, recently whitewashed, former church in sparkling condition. It was rumored that the aged archivist was so quick and accurate that he could *almost* match an electronic data base in speed and accuracy. *And he could also make Henry wish he hadn't gotten up that morning.*

"You're late, Henry," he said with a knowing smile. "We've already had a *million* calls. Everything you'll be wanting is piled on the table in the back; please… handle with care."

Henry stared at him with newly awakened hatred. *God, what a pain in the ass this guy could be.* He pulled a folding chair over—cringing at the scraping sound it made on the recently polished hardwood floor—and began to review the twelve-year-old file on the suicide of '81.

The pictures of the stunning red head jogged his memory. He remembered that case and felt a *twinge* because he had seen the young woman and her daughter around the island many times; usually at Charlie's on a Sunday morning. Henry was sure he would have made an entry in his journal about this suicide and made a mental note to check the date—July 14, 1981. By then the young woman and her daughter had been coming to the island for about eight or nine summers—according to his front page story.

The mother was a dazzling red head and her little girl was a typical carrot-top beauty-in-waiting. Both sported summer freckles with a trace of hidden pride that red heads seemed to possess—but would never dream of admitting to. Although they often had breakfast in Charlie's on Sundays—unlike the locals—they never indulged in idle gossip; just ordered their breakfast and chatted privately while they ate, occasionally looking up to see what the loud laughter was all about. Not that they were rude—just reserved and mannerly.

Henry was aware that Belle Adams had overseen the renovation of the old cottage and had taken deep pride in its stunning make-over—blushing bright pink at the compliments that the islanders generously doled out. Of course, there were some *locals* who insisted that the old *Carter woman,* who drowned while living in the place, still haunted it, but most of them were finally silenced by the enchanting new look of the cottage and its lovely summer occupants. No one had mentioned anything about it being haunted in years—as far as Henry knew.

His clear recollection was that the Adams mother and daughter were thought to be friendly enough; just preferred to keep a polite distance from the busybody islanders, which seemed fair enough. Henry figured that was a good decision on their part—probably what made them so likable.

He turned his attention back to the photos and began to calculate that the kid had been about fourteen at the time her mother disappeared into the surf on a hot summer morning in

1981, while she slept. He had heard that the youngster made the call for help. Henry would check those details out at the station.

Belle Adams had been terminally ill with cancer, although there were some that said she died from a *broken heart*. Henry shook his head, having learned in the last ten years just how Puckshaw's year-round residents reacted to bad news—looked for something dramatic and morbid to harp on. There was even some foolish talk of *murder*—it had been duly noted that *outsiders* had visited the tiny beach just a few days before the drowning.

On Puckshaw, just being innocent visitors qualified one for being suspect; but murderers? Sure, why not?

Henry continued reading the old newspaper articles from 1981; pressed for time now he read quickly. He jotted into his notebook that her full name was *Bellmara Peterson Adams* and her friends called her Belle. She was almost thirty-seven years young at the time of her death—survived by a fourteen-year-old daughter and a few distant relatives. It made the back pages of the Boston papers even though it was the city in which she lived and worked. Though it was no big deal there, it sure had rocked *Puckshaw*! That's all they had talked about and Henry became annoyed just thinking about it. Everyone had carried at least one newspaper under each arm so they could discuss the case with singular accuracy. He wondered why on earth *anyone* would use the *newspaper* as a sole source of accuracy!

After a few days, regional papers had dropped the "possible murder" angle and concentrated on the plight of the fourteen-year old daughter, sadly left behind with few known relatives. It was later reported that she was whisked off the island and sent to live with relatives or *possibly* her father.

Most people agreed with the opinion that a ghostly pall seemed to have settled over the doll-like cottage—yet again. Some folks said the kid visited the place occasionally over the following few summers, usually accompanied by an elderly couple—just a few "hellos" were exchanged. The youngster's visits became far and few between.

Later in the day, Henry found out from a pretty good source at Charlie's that the young daughter began to return on a regular basis after several years had passed. She was probably in her early twenties by that time and *her* full name was *Carena Peterson Adams*; she was fondly called *Sonny*—an obvious reference to her disposition. Henry was secretly glad that they hadn't called her *Carrie*; he hated that name with a passion.

And that was it in a nutshell. Sonny Adams was *probably* the victim that washed up on the beach earlier in the day and had most likely drowned. What ever happened had happened shortly after dawn—according to the police.

Henry had a story to put together before the night was out; now, he would use all his skill to construct a compassionate and fact-filled profile of this young lady whom he knew so little of. He was going to have to come up with some reasons why she *might* have wanted to end her life. He hoped it was an accident—all the facts weren't in yet—maybe it wasn't.

He had a few contacts he could start with, but first he had to get to the cove where the cottage was located. It was the tiny beach below the bluff that the kid had been found on. For some reason Henry was already feeling like a rat gnawing into her private life.

He pushed the pile of folders across the table, scraping his chair on the newly waxed hardwood for the second time, as he rose to leave. Just as he placed his hand on the heavy brass doorknob, old "peppermint Sandy" tapped him on the shoulder and conspiratorially handed him an envelope with some photos in it. Henry let out a long sigh. *What the hell was it now?* It just so happened—the way old Sandy put it—that someone had gotten hold of a few snapshots and given them to him with the stipulation that they remain anonymous. Henry opened the door and held them under the sunlight; his eyes were getting worse every day and the little troll seemed to be enjoying his struggle to focus clearly. What a bastard he was thought Henry, as he turned his attention to the photos again.

One was a tiny wrinkled photo of a little girl in a floppy hat with red hair bursting out on all sides; she was playing on the beach with a little playmate.

No big deal. Henry shrugged his shoulders questioningly at Sandy.

The second snapshot was also unremarkable—probably a reproduction of a high-school yearbook photo—turtleneck and wavy red hair to boot. Henry placed it back into the envelope and pulled out the last one. It stopped him in his tracks. It was a more recent photo of a stunning young woman looking over her shoulder and waving to someone. Her red hair was tied to one side with a black velvet ribbon and her blue eyes sparkled at the sight of someone who was luckier than hell to have deserved such an adoring look.

So this was Sonny Adams! The radiant look of this young lady was absolutely breathtaking and Henry suddenly became aware of the peppermint scent emanating from old Sandy. Though he had turned his back on him, he was acutely aware of Sandy standing a little too close.

Sandy was peering over Henry's shoulder and eyeing him as though he was reading his mind. Feigning condescension, he grinned, shook his mangy head, and gave the visibly irritated reporter a dismissive wave.

He was like that; treated Henry as if he was twelve years old.

"Jesus, some days I really hate you more than words can describe," Henry muttered as he left the library. He almost wished Sandy had heard him, yet, he was grateful he hadn't. He wouldn't have really wanted to hurt the old guy.

So this was the young victim of the unfortunate drowning accident; Henry only knew a few things about her. It was a fact that Sonny had recently reached the promising age of twenty-six and rumor had it that she had been spending a lot of time at the cottage *alone*, having split from a close companion in the last six or seven months. The source of the statement was, of course, anonymous and the assumption was just one of many rumors that were unfurling with increasing speed. Copycat suicide, murder, and other absurd plots were recklessly being hurled about Charlie's during the breakfast hour and although it was not Henry's style, he had to jump in somewhere.

She was fair game, now, and that was a lousy position for her to be in.

"Damn it."

Henry thought it was a lousy position for anyone to be in—dead or alive. It pissed him off the way the locals would buy into such idiotic plots when obviously bogus witnesses appeared right out of thin air. It was pretty cut and dried—as far as his experienced reporter's instinct was concerned—she had drowned. He was unsure as to whether it was of her own volition or not. *End of story.*

Henry Macguire walked out of the library and took a deep breath of damp, September air—a clear warning of the fall to come. It felt good; almost cleansing after the new-wax-job stuffiness of the library, combined with the stench of old "peppermint Sandy".

He climbed into his Jeep and secretly hoped the kid really hadn't committed such a desperate act, but on the outside chance that she had, he asked himself what the hell could have gone so wrong in *her* young life. First the mother and now the daughter; what the hell was *that* all about? Flipping on the radio he caught the tail end of an "oldie" and stepped on the gas.

Feeling a little unhinged after reading the articles and seeing pictures of the kid, Henry drove to the beach slowly—countermanding Barton's order to get out there, pronto. He had very little desire to intrude on this young woman's privacy and now, he had no choice but to dig up something that was true and present it in a compassionate, readable fashion. The aging reporter hated the invasive aspect of reporting—like when the person in question wasn't around to tell his/her side.

Henry never minded blowing in a lying politician or a madman who ran a hedge fund—he loved ripping them to pieces. Unfortunately, *this* sad story had to jump out of the front page of the *Sunny Islander* in the morning and he felt a little sick about being responsible for plastering the young woman and her mother all over the front page.

After examining his reporter's conscience, he felt as though he really didn't have a choice; it was a story that had to be written and no one would deny that there was plenty of fodder here; two previous probable suicides—one being the victim's mother. There was plenty to write about and if he didn't do it, someone else would. Not to mention that he was in danger of getting his "lazy ass" kicked if he didn't write something sensational for Barton.

The next five hours left Henry reeling. By the end of the day, he would question his own sanity and wonder whether or not he had dreamed the whole thing up.

He headed to the scene of the accident and got there just in time to see the pale, beautiful body of a young woman being carefully retrieved from a rocky section of the beach. He shivered with excitement and unrestrained curiosity. When the long process from the beach to the waiting ambulance was over, Henry had a few words with Sheriff Cramer before hurrying off to interview a few of the victim's neighbors, after which he contacted some coldly-distant, *almost-relatives* by phone.

By the time Henry went back to Charlie's for some local opinion, he was feeling crummier by the minute. After a quick bowl of soup caused a cesspool to form in his stomach, he stumbled out of the coffee shop and headed straight for the newsroom to write what was expected of him.

He had a job to do and today it was a *dirty* job. This girl was young and beautiful and the ugly story was shaping up to be a very tragic event in *Puckshaw's* growing history; at least, that's what Henry Macguire thought and if the earth was still spinning on its axis—that's what Henry Macguire would write.

He had stopped at his cabin for a moment to check what he had written in his journal about the young mother's suicide back in July of 1981. To his surprise it was a mildly graphic and brief entry—a description of the accidental drowning (suicide) of Bellmara Peterson Adams, long-time summer resident of Puckshaw. A short bio indicated that she had left behind a young daughter. As he read the entry, he concluded that he had been a little overzealous, having used phrases like "ravaged by a ruthless disease", "disappeared like a ghost at dawn", and yes, "motherless child". Lord, such drivel, he thought. He chalked that kind of dramatic detail up to his mid-life-crisis-forties. He also concluded that he was a much better writer now, with much more sensitivity. A little voice in his head told him he just might be getting *dangerously soft,* but he wasn't listening.

He turned a few pages to see if he had written any follow-up on the Bellmara Peterson suicide but he didn't see any other references to her. He flipped a few pages back and came upon a grand description of the *Royal Wedding of 1981*. He laughed out loud at his use of the hackneyed phrases like "etched in our collective memory" and "fairy tale come true"!

He grimaced. Here, you had the toad like Prince of Wales and the proverbial sacrificial Virgin uniting before almost a billion viewers, unexpectedly bringing an unfamiliar smile across the faces of those *dour Windsor's*.

As Henry looked back now, almost thirteen years later, (1993) one more hackneyed phrase came to his mind. *"How's that working out for you?"* he whispered.

By early December when the sensational drowning suicide story had started to die down and the gnashing of teeth was over, Henry was fatigued. He had spent most of October, November, and early December, doing the usual coverage, follow-up, and wrap-up that every major story deserves. And one had to face it; the suicide of Carena (Sonny) Peterson Adams was indeed a major story that had sold its share of newspapers on Puckshaw.

As he recalled, he had that story in his head and on his lips day and night; like a worm, it seemed to have taken up permanent residency deep in his spirit and he had no idea how to deal with this eerie set of circumstances.

Cold and confused, Henry remained still, preparing to end his reverie.

Instead of the usual peace and calm that usually accompanied his recollections, he felt exhausted and haunted. Never in his wildest dreams could he have imagined the dark mood of silence and melancholy he had descended into.

He drove home slowly, as if under a spell. Upon entering his cabin, he turned the light on, slipped out of his muddy shoes, and glanced around the cold, neat cabin. He was struck by the pain of his new loneliness. Plagued with insomnia, detecting the arrival of a new ulcer, and fearing madness, he admitted with no little shame that his life had spun out of control.

He had deliberately avoided the newsroom, letting the machine pick up his messages to avoid lengthy conversations with colleagues or friends. On Wednesdays he usually dropped off his column and current coverage of local topics of interest and said hello to Barton before hastily making his way to Charlie's for a cup coffee.

He wrote during the day and visited the cove and the cottage late at night—in search of an answer.

For the first time since the quirky reporter had arrived on *Puckshaw,* he was surprised by the swift change of seasons. Of course, he had never roamed the beach in November and December before—hence his heightened awareness. It was mid-December and the freezing winds had come early, paralyzing the partially decayed leaves into amazing patterns covering the driveway that had once served as a private playground for a carefree child, fittingly called Sonny for her bright and cheerful demeanor.

In his dazed visits, Henry had made it a habit to circle the clapboard cottage and peer through the windows into the private sanctum that he had no right to enter. At first, the window panes shone and were easy to see through, having probably been cleaned for the last time in late August. In October, all too soon, they became dusty and covered with spider webs, obscuring his view. In the end, when the sleet and snow came, the windows became frosted over with ice—at which time he was forced to scrape little circles with his gloved hand in order to peer in and assure himself that all the contents were intact and nothing in the cottage had been violated. The little man had unwittingly become the self-appointed custodian of the seemingly abandoned property—honored to stand guard over it and its deserted surroundings.

It was during one of these visits that a mere shell of Henry Macguire realized to what degree his selfish and empty life had deteriorated. He had had fallen under the spell of a haunting pair of deaths and a dangerous obsession now gripped him.

"What to do. What to do?" he sobbed as he flung himself to the ground, the ice and snow burning through his pant legs as he lay, spread eagled, silently gazing at the starless sky. Despair reigned and just as the last shred of hope left his body, the massive blanket of darkness was ripped open by a flash of awareness. In the drama of that fleeting moment, Henry Macguire's eyes were opened and he saw himself poised on the brink of redemption.

Invigorated, he rose and brushed the debris off his clothes, rushing back to his jeep. He knew what he would do. Laughably, the icy door refused to open and in his excitement Henry kicked and screamed at it to let him in. When, at last, the door flew open, surrendering to his violent efforts, he jumped in and started the motor running, tears running down his cheeks. As the heat kicked on, he rubbed his hands together before the warm-air vent. It felt good. He felt good. Without warning he was once again filled with the elation of his youth—the butterflies-in-the-belly feeling he had felt when, as a young man, he had fallen hopelessly in love for the first time.

5 *Fatherhood Lost*

The last and only time Henry Macguire had fallen in love was a faint memory now; but not so faint that he couldn't remember the thrill of it all. She was a lovely, naïve, eighteen-year-old, living in a shabby development in a run-down Boston neighborhood. Henry was just passing through—or so he thought. It was late 1969 or early 70' and the exhilaration and passion of the surprising affair resulted in the birth of his son—a son he chose not to welcome into his world. It was a deliberate and cruel act to have perpetrated on the unsuspecting young woman and Henry would someday bitterly regret it.

He had written, without emotion, of his final decision regarding the coming birth of his child and now, on a dark December day over twenty years later, feeling alone and dispirited, he re-visited his journal entries regarding that regrettable deed—and wept.

~ * ~ * ~ * ~ * ~ * ~ * ~ * ~

March 9, 1969
Bad news, kind friend,

Susan tells me I'm to become a father. It is not welcomed news; at least not to me. It's not that I don't like her; it's that I don't *love* her and I'm just not ready to be a father. Hell, I can barely take care of myself. Anyway, I always thought I would have a kid with someone whom I was *madly* in love with. You know—long term; the "I'll love and honor you forever" kind of thing. My time with Susan was never based on love; it was just youthful lust, I guess!
I'm at a crossroads—what to do? Where to go?
HM

June 10, 1969

Hello, kind friend. Susan is doing well. I am not. I really want to move on and she kindly says, "Go ahead." I know it's a lousy thing to do, but there is so much I have to accomplish in my life, yet. I can't be tied down so soon. I don't think I'd be good for her or the child, anyway. I'm thinking of taking a summer assignment on the cape somewhere. I think it's called *Puckshaw*; it is supposed to be beautiful—tiny, private, and a good place to write. What do you think?
HM

October 30, 1969
Hello, kind friend,

I guess you can congratulate or condemn me. Susan has had a little boy. They are both fine. I've made some arrangements to take care of them. I know I can and will help them financially; obviously, I can be of no help emotionally or otherwise. Now I'll have to be much more serious about earning enough money to hold up my end of the bargain—if I'm really going to keep my word. Susan is being terrific and I'm an ass. God, I'm ashamed of myself for wanting to abandon them, but I can't seem to change anything. I have not seen Susan or the boy and will soon move on. I'm so ashamed. Gloom visits me daily, now, and sleep is hard to come by. Give me courage, dear friend.
HM

~ ~*~*~*~*~*~*~*~

It was late in 1991 or early '92 when the desire struck like a bolt of lightning! Henry Macguire was filled with a burning desire to find the boy. Many years had passed since his scoundrel-like behavior and he agonized for weeks and months about whether he even had the right to walk into this young man's life; after all, he had not been a father in any meaningful way—other than to send a pittance toward his support every month. He had never held him, kissed him, changed his diaper, or rolled on the floor with him. Did he dare intrude on his life, now, he asked himself. He wasn't even sure of his age, anymore, without looking it up in his journal. Twenty-two, almost twenty-three or something like that. He'd been so detached for so many years that he felt utterly unworthy—though strangely compelled—to do something.

He had been feeling off balance and queasy for some time and hadn't quite been able to put his finger on the cause of his malaise. Barton had talked him into getting a physical, but he had put it off, once again.

Henry had never had anything more than a bad back and recurring bouts of depression, but this was totally different.

What could it be?

Henry, nearing mid-fifty, was feeling the pangs of fatherhood lost.

Flashes of desire to know his son now struck with regularity. He reasoned, with uncharacteristic pride and vanity, that his son *should* know him. After all, he *was* a successful journalist; maybe he could help the boy, now. He had plenty of money and could probably clear up any bills he might have. He could pay for his college—whatever the kid needed. There were endless possibilities to explore. Maybe the kid would even want to spend some time with him. He had so much to tell him, but deep down he was frightened; what if the boy wasn't interested after all these years? His seeking nature got the best of him and he made the decision to move forward.

It was late '91 or early '92 when Henry Macguire contacted Susan; she had graciously supplied him with his son's name and number. Oddly, the number would connect him to Scott's boss. He liked the name Scott and if it was the only way to reach him, he would gladly go through a third person. Strangely, it was also the only way Susan, his own mother, was able to contact him; that's how the boy wanted it. Private and stubborn struck a familiar chord with Henry and a few weeks later, with no little anticipation, he drove to Boston to find the son who called himself *Scott K. Macguire.*

To his delight, he discovered a young man in his early twenties with a reserved and quiet nature. He was living on his own, had a decent paying job, and a recently acquired girlfriend.

Henry was shocked at his good looks—tall, sandy-haired, and blue-eyed—just like his mother; nothing like his father with his short stature, gray eyes, and dull brownish hair. Lucky for him, Henry thought. The kid would have hated being short and stocky and looking forward to a prematurely receding hairline.

Scott Macguire didn't look like he was much of an athlete—only fairly trim and fit. He liked his job, his boss, and his landlord—hell this kid was nothing like me, Henry had chuckled to himself.

For a youngster, he was in a pretty serious relationship with a young woman of some means, or so he said. She too, had a job and a fine education according to Scott. Henry supposed—sarcastically—that she too, liked her job, her boss, and her landlord. They sounded like a new generation of *the Brady's*, to boot.

Scott said she was a sensitive, sweet girl and that they were taking it slow. He seemed smarter than Henry had been at his age. He probably *was* smarter than Henry was at his age. That fact wouldn't have surprised him one bit.

The young lady had had some problems and was just emerging from a long bout of depression.

"Jesus, not one of *those* gals," Henry said with annoyance. You're in a dangerous relationship for such a young, inexperienced guy; besides that, you say she's older than you are? Christ, you could end up getting hurt, and I would hate to see that. But hell, what do I know?"

Scott had remained silent. He seemed a little put off at Henry's negative attitude. "We'll see".

His demeanor was gentle as he ran his hands through his hair, shaking his head. He seemed to know more about those things than Henry did at his age. Anyway, it wasn't anyone else's business and suddenly the conversation turned to another topic which annoyed Henry.

The young man had been visiting a Christian Science Reading Room almost daily and he felt it was helping him to develop a more sincere and caring relationship with his girlfriend.

Henry was highly suspicious of anything that smacked of religiosity and wondered where a kid of *his* would get such a crazy idea.

They talked about superficial things—the boy clearly disinterested in digging into the past. Though Henry was grateful for that, he secretly wished the kid had wanted to know *something* about his father. That was not the case. They kept it all light and nicely packaged—the kid was just like his father in that respect. No messy regrets or accusations—pretty acceptable for the first encounter.

Henry spent the next three days in Boston. He met Scott for breakfast the next morning and was to meet the girlfriend and take them out for dinner the last night he was there. Scott never showed; or was it Henry who didn't show? He couldn't remember but guessed *he* had been the culprit. He always had a lousy memory when it was convenient—and a lousy record—when it came to deeply personal things like that.

He left the next morning with a firm resolve to call his son with an apology and try to set things straight; he hoped they could establish some kind of friendship before they tried to become father and son. He would need to start at the bottom and give the kid something to build on. Yes, he would start anew as soon as he got home. Henry never got around to calling and they never got around to building anything. Neither of them were surprised. *Henry could be a real jackass at times.*

As time flew by, he had often wondered how Scott's relationship was working out. His son had so enthusiastically described the young woman as a "gentle and expressive young woman with a quiet sense of humor" and Henry—much as he hated to admit it—was more than a little impressed with the kid's mature assessment.

One Sunday afternoon, Henry made plans to go up to Boston and see if he could find the young couple—though they might not have even wanted to see him—but he let slip away yet another opportunity to build a relationship with his son. If he had only known the truth he would have beaten a path to Boston to beg for another chance because…

...trouble would soon find both of the Macguire men. Scott would endure heart-wrenching guilt and pain and Henry would begin his dark journey into a downward spiral of confusion that would last for the rest of his life.

6 *The young Adams Women*

January 30, 1994
Good evening, kind friend!
    I apologize for not informing you of my activities and whereabouts for the last month or so; but I have been fully engaged in an extensive search for some new up-close-and-personal accounts that concern the lives of a few people that you have heard me mention, frequently, in my rambling confidences of the past few months.
    Deep in my spirit, shabby as it may be, I've been keenly aware of missing truths—or at best, distortions—in the information I had received concerning the lives of the two drowning victims—very charming summer residents of *Puckshaw.* **Anyway, after unearthing new contacts and more reliable information, I have a sharper awareness through which I hope to put to rest an elusive demon that has been sitting on my shoulder lately.**
    Though still preliminary, I do intend to keep going forward to confirm and validate my findings that I feel obligated to share with you, alone. I rest assured that I will be spared a harsh scolding or premature lecture on my lack of good judgment. So without further ado, I'd like you to meet the subjects of my fascination and profound affection."
    At this point, Henry prepared to insert a stack of neatly typed pages into his journal. Though of a slightly different color, the pages were folded and trimmed to fit in with the existing pages. He stapled the dated pages together with his usual precision and in the interest of credibility and continuity, jotted notes of explanation in the margins. During his six week journey, (he explained) he had typed his findings at the end of each day, on his little portable (electric) typewriter; now it was his intention that they should became part of his authentic journal entries which would eventually serve as an integral part of his auto-biographical manuscript.

Please Meet Belle and Sonny Adams!

My initial efforts to resurrect even some very basic information on the early lives of my two beloved subjects were met with failure, so, understandably, I was dogged by discouragement early on. Regaining my composure, I quickly calmed myself down and proceeded, with my usual persistence, to crack this thing open.

I hastened to get to know them first together, as mother and daughter, before separating their identities and appreciating them as individuals. Please don't think that I have gone off the deep end or anything like that; it's just my way of compiling the research—a bit unorthodox, but don't you think it's an interesting concept?

Well, anyway, thanks to a few nosey, yet, well-meaning neighbors who—through the years—watched the quiet but friendly young women come and go; I began to make accurate and speedy progress. After all, for some time now, I have considered myself to be an excellent reporter with proven finesse in ferreting information out of others, so... let me get to the point and return to my findings!

Belle was about twenty-seven and Sonny almost five when they moved into a one-bedroom apartment in a young, upscale neighborhood in the suburbs of Boston. It seemed to be a peaceful period during which they both appeared to thrive. They resided there for about three years and then moved to a larger, more luxurious apartment in the same development, remaining there until Belle's death, after which Sonny was not seen for several years. During those happy years they spent summers in a renovated cottage, right here, on *Puckshaw.*

Curiously enough, Sonny reappeared seven or eight years after her mother's death to take up residency in the same neighborhood, barely a block away from the apartment they had once shared. Having been spirited away when she was fourteen—grief-stricken over her mother's drowning—she returned as a twenty-three year-old mature and independent young woman.

Like her mother, Sonny was fiercely private and reserved about her relationships which were few and far between; the individuals involved rarely spoke of her publicly. A few gentlemen callers, who were too dignified to kiss and tell, only confirmed what I already knew: The Adams women held their male companions to the highest standards of chivalry. My search, still in its infancy, shows that both women were known to be bright and hard working, with matching short tempers that seemed to accompany their red hair and charming freckles.

As difficult as it was to loosen a single tongue, I finally charmed an indiscreet mailman who told me Belle had once given him hell for leaving her mailbox open; but the next day, she remorsefully left him a tiny present with a note attached to it, apologizing for having offended him. He said he still had the note but couldn't show it to me. I'm still working on him!

Similarly, a colleague of Sonny's confided to me that she had once been careless with her work which resulted in an uncharacteristic tongue-lasing; the very next day, Sonny gave the young lady a long-stemmed rose in an effort to make up for her outburst—"a lapse in good manners" she had called it.

Do you get the picture? Belle and her daughter were so much alike at times, it was amazing; they seem to be inextricably tied to one another by some invisible thread. I eventually encountered scores of incidences of similarities in behavior and I expect to discover even more as time passes.

I think that word has kind of gotten around that I am writing a book of some sort or at least a series of articles on the women, so I am sometimes treated with little trust and much hostility. Luckily—in some cases—cooperation has come my way. That's always a good day!

Since only twelve years had separated Belle's and Sonny's deaths, I was able to locate a number of people who were contemporaries of both mother and daughter. Close friends were close-mouthed but eventually, casual colleagues, clerks, and even an apartment manager gave candid interviews revealing the tender, private, and mysterious side of each of the woman. My search was also aided by the fact that they had both worked at the same publishing house—two decades apart.

Sonny was just a youngster when her mother worked at Scribe & Son Inc., but she knew many of Belle's co-workers.

Several years after Belle's death, Roberta Connors, one of Belle's former supervisors, hired Sonny. She found her to be as loyal and competent as her mother—though she never became a close confidant of the young woman. Age was a factor and Roberta admitted that she just didn't have the 'stomach' for it. She had adored Belle and had no desire to forge a deep friendship with Sonny. I could understand that, can't you, my kind friend?

I heard from a grieving young woman, who asked to remain anonymous, that Sonny, like Belle, had enjoyed a small circle of loyal and devoted friends with whom she spent quiet evenings around a small, but elegantly set, dining room table. Sonny was her mother's daughter and had learned as a youngster how to keep her friends close and her relationships private. Imitating her mother, she often entertained quietly—never throwing showy or loud parties. Given the private nature of both women the topics of conversation would not be likely to leave their dining rooms. It doesn't surprise me.

Tommy, the green grocer, told me that 'the Adams girls' (as he fondly referred to them) spent as much time as possible on *Puckshaw*. During the summer months, almost every long weekend, and three or four full weeks in July would find them nestled in the enchanted cottage or sunbathing in the little cove I've so often talked about. Tommy had often delivered fresh fruits and vegetables to whom he called the "best looking red heads" on Puckshaw. Tommy was quite a character, himself—I'll tell you more about him sometime.

When I ran out of sources in the city, I headed back to the island to organize my notes, trying like hell to complete what I saw as a massive jigsaw puzzle. Each time I compiled new information, I would put it in its place and head back to the island's only coffee shop that was open year 'round—Charlie's. Anything I got there could be pretty iffy, but I really didn't give a damn anymore. I'd figure out if it was fact, fiction, or *whatever* and take it from there. I was fully enveloped in this obsession of mine and I intended to see it to fruition.

Each morning I sat at the end of the counter and engaged the locals in conversation. We'd discuss the weather, a little politics, and some local gossip, after which I would eventually turn the conversation to the Adams women to see what I could shake loose from a willing tongue. The islanders didn't really see it as gossip; to them it was a discussion—an obligatory display of one's expert opinion with a sprinkling of rumor. A large sprinkling of rumor, I might add.

It was pretty well documented by some ever-observant neighbors that both women had—at one time or another—spent time with trusted lovers at the charming, cliff-top cottage. In spite of the fact that they were obsessively discreet, the locals were relentless in their observations, never missing anything as remarkable as a *romantic tryst*.

After two solid weeks of daily gossiping, I began to get a strong sense of the unique oneness the two women shared. At times their lives seemed to be so intertwined that it was hard to separate them. I found myself infatuated first with one, then the other, and finally with both as one.

Now, Kind Friend, I admit, only to you, that I am caught up in a conflict between reality and fantasy and it seems like I am always at an impasse, of some kind, with my good judgment; in many instances, my emotions are at war with my intellect. I dream of and imagine their day to day lives and actually experience vicarious joys and sorrows, including their final moments on the enchanted island of Puckshaw.

The January 30, 1994, entry was completed and signed at the bottom of the last page with Henry's usual closing.

Good night, kind friend.
HM

September 15, 1995

Kindest of Friends!

It's just me, with many apologies for not bringing you in on all that has been going on in my life. Has it been a year and a half? I can hardly believe it! Now don't presume that I haven't been writing; I have accumulated four large folders filled with bits and pieces of scrap paper and several miniature pocket notebooks whose pages are covered with my scribbling. I will insert them as I go along. And guess what? I am now the proud owner of a word processor and that, too, has a variety of notes tucked away in its files. Imagine me without a worn-down pencil and beat up notebook or noisy electric typewriter!

My, how things change! I recognize without hesitation that I, too, have changed. I think I'm less judgmental than I used to be and a much more patient fellow, now. This project has brought me face to face with so many issues that have always been swept tidily under a rug, here or there, but you know how I deal with things; in my own time, my own space, and always alone—with my truths.

Tonight I am actually giddy with the excitement of sharing my intentions with you. So much has gone on and I don't know where to start. I have felt the velvet-gloved touch of satisfaction and the searing pain of loss, but, as always, when the dragon's fire starts to get too close to my heels, I turn to you for comfort and fortitude, eventually coming away stronger—renewed in energy and confidence.

As the Highest Being is my witness, I never expected my life to take such twists and turns, but you, my dear friend—the unimpeachable keeper of my records—have always been privy to my the upending. You can see that there is no turning back, can't you? I have reached the precipice of the big black hole that has beckoned me for years, and now I choose to face its challenge.

Though weary as hell and experiencing some wild trepidation, I am finally prepared to begin the task of assembling, into a manuscript, the mountain of material I have painstakingly amassed over the last twenty five or so years. Of course, several chapters will be devoted to the tragic events that began in July of 1981, with the suicide of Belle Peterson Adams and ended with the shocking suicide of her daughter, Sonny, in 1993. Those events and my subsequent research on their lives have impacted my life to a great extent—as you already know. I couldn't possibly leave that part of my life out of my manuscript!

The manuscript! Oh, frenzied ambition!

Don't worry; I'm still the same guy who writes only about what I see with my own eyes and hear with my own ears. I have remained true to my craft and therefore feel confident that my collection of findings, both factual and clearly probable, will serve as a strong foundation for the story of turbulence and tragedy that dogged the Adams women for most of their lives. It is not my intention to be presumptuous or arrogant in describing the range of emotions that must have been present during the actual course of these events; but try to remember that I have grown to know these women well—exceedingly well! It's almost as if I was there, beside them—inside them—so how can I avoid laying my own emotional reactions on the blank sheet of paper before me?

All I can say is this is the way I see it. Take it or leave it! After all, it's the first time since I was a very young man that I've cared enough about anything or anyone to really venture out of my gloomy, self-designed prison. If I'm wasting my time, so be it. But from this night forward, the Highest Power willing, all my efforts will go into the completion of this ambitious and arduous labor of determination and love.

You, sir, have always been my truest and most reliable companion. Have you ever condemned my actions? On the contrary, you have patiently and consistently preserved them meticulously for my own regret or jubilation.

Now I expect nothing less and nothing more from you other than the patient ear, the impassive face, and as always, the uncluttered writing plane that you unfailingly and generously lay before me.
HM

7 *The Healing*

A blazing sun awakened the tiny Island of *Puckshaw*, further assaulting the dry cracks that lay helpless in the salt-eroded driveway of the Adams cottage. Even the old islanders, who had referred to it as the "Carter place" for so many years, had finally acquiesced to its status as the "Adams cottage".

The very driveway that had once wound its way through manicured grass and fall flowers, now cut a ruthless path from the clapboard summer cottage, through patches of scrubby weeds and half-dead bushes, to the slippery concrete stairs. Those once strong concrete stairs of childhood memories had slowly deteriorated from many winters of relentless salt-filled mist; but to Sonny Adams, however changed they were, time had not altered their purpose—they still led to the tiny, private, crescent-shaped beach and the foamy Atlantic surf— where her past would ultimately confront her future.

Sonny, bright and true to her name at barely five years of age, had been instantly enchanted by the seductive little cove during her first visit to the summer get-away in August of 1972. She and her mother had fallen in love with the secluded cottage and knew immediately it was the right place for them to spend long, lazy weekends and hot summer vacations. After all, it had been a difficult year for both of them. The painful marital split had taken its toll—swiftly and cruelly—leaving mother and daughter spent.

"Don't worry mommy, *I* won't leave you."

Her only child's innocent display of loyalty had caused Belle to close her eyes and fight back tears. Such tenacity and clarity of thought for a five-year-old!

They were in the giddy throes of resettling and reestablishing themselves, fully independent of the now absent husband and father. It had been a humbling experience after having been so protected in the deep trenches of the conventional, nuclear, upper middle class family--their safe harbor until the calamity had struck.

The breakup had turned them upside down. Belle, sensing the necessity to show strength and determination to survive, demonstrated a fighting spirit that was contagious; her five-year-old daughter, Sonny, mimicked her every move and mood learning to navigate the perilous road by emulation. This child was a perfect, tiny clone of Belle and if the truth was told, she possessed every bit of her mother's natural resilience. Already unafraid and strong-willed, Sonny's unfazed response to adversity often left her mother speechless and reeling in amazement.

It was 1972 and Belle was not seeking anything spectacular; she just yearned for a little privacy where she and her daughter could come to grips with the tumultuous turn of events that had struck like a raging storm in the night.

It was "lady luck", herself, who had led them to the aging and affordable ocean side cottage—the cottage that could well give them shelter from the chaos of change that they had been forced to accept. Longing for peace, Belle had whispered, "I have a hunch this just might be the place for us—sun-filled days and quiet evenings filled with story-telling and board games."

It was a good hunch.

It was a friend of Belle's who had heard that the old cottage, abandoned and in disrepair, was for sale or rent. It was frightful looking, having been left empty and unattended for years.

Mrs. Carter, poor old soul, had been long gone and her heirs—after using it for a few summers—had lost all interest in it. The place was badly in need of paint, carpeting, window replacements, and a variety of other repairs. Large stains and even some indication of small fires—probably caused by careless cigarette smoking—marred the once-lovely counter tops.

When Belle visited the cottage with a realtor, she had looked beyond all the damage; she saw only the possibilities of repairing and restoring the cottage to its original charm and beauty.

With Sonny firmly in tow and a generous rental contract in hand—allowing her to make the necessary repairs and retain first option to buy—Belle switched gears and returned to the city to finalize an apartment lease and enroll her only child in school for the fall. Filled with excitement, the two red-haired, blue-eyed beauties giggled all the way back to the small but lovely apartment in the Boston suburbs. There, Belle had her own parking space and private entrance—just what she needed.

"It was a doll house in the city!" That was what a friend of Belle's had said. The large bedroom with two single beds, matching dressers, and huge closet was a perfect reflection of the new occupants. Belle had been anxious to begin the process of *de-cluttering* her material-filled life and this was the first step. "Keep everything simple!" she whispered to herself, over and over.

The bedroom glowed with femininity, from the beautiful white quilts and curtains, to the pink pillows and rugs scattered about the room. The tiny powder room was similarly girlish and attractive. It was smaller than the one they had been forced to leave behind, but the personal touches and flowery scents made up for the limited space.

The kitchen was adequate with its built-ins and intimately-tiny counter where the soul mates would share breakfast most mornings. Place mats, curtains, and dainty china settings were all brightly color-coordinated—designed to help dispel dark moods and sad memories.

The showpiece of the apartment—Belle's pride and joy—was the octagonal dining room. The largest room of the apartment, it boasted an oval oak table, complemented by four gleaming chairs, all centered perfectly under a chandelier with tiny crystal drops. The matching oak cabinet held Belle's treasured china and crystal—the hallmark of her dinner parties. She had received many pieces as wedding gifts and considered them to be the very first objects of beauty she had ever owned. Everything was tiny, elegant, and breathtaking—the exact effect Belle had in mind.

The corner living room—with its pale blue sofa and accompanying dark blue love seat, usually shared by Belle and Sonny to watch favorite television shows or to read bedtime stories—was strewn with large pillows, strategically placed around the wall-to-wall beige and blue rug, to create a welcoming atmosphere for one and all!

A week after they had moved in and put the finishing touches on the apartment, Belle and Sonny had collapsed on the floor in paroxysms of glee and satisfaction. If this was to be their new home, they were off to a good start and all was well.

Belle had been up since dawn, greeting the sun with a short yoga exercise, preparing her day's agenda, and finally drinking her morning coffee in silence—waiting for the first stirrings of her beloved daughter. She was scheduled for an appointment at the school Sonny would attend in September. Confident that it was a modern facility—well staffed with highly trained teachers and assistants—Belle had hoped it would be "the one".

Her research showed that the institution was at the forefront in meeting the clamoring need for alternative after-school care—of prime concern for an increasing number of single parents. She had given the school priority consideration even before choosing an apartment in that area. *Kraft Elementary* had an after-hours program that offered academic tutoring or simple leisure time during which the students could unwind, snack, or even nap. It was a safe place where her daughter would be adequately supervised and engaged until a parent arrived to pick her up.

Sonny was a pretty quick study and had already reminded her mother that she wouldn't need any tutoring, though she fully anticipated the playtime and the chance to meet new friends. "I can't wait, mommy; I *need* some new friends!"

The bright and sensitive child had suffered some separation anxiety after her father's departure and since they had arrived at their new apartment, six weeks prior, she had been missing the companionship of children her own age. Belle knew what was good for Sonny and her needs would be addressed first; she would tend to her own social development at the appropriate time. "I know darling, I know." To lighten the conversation, Belle tickled Sonny's tummy till she rolled on the plush rug with glee.

Belle's new job was proving to be demanding but satisfying and that, alone, provided her with a new outlook on the future and helped to distract her from those sad moods that hung like dark clouds endlessly threatening to cast her into periods of anxiety and despair.

As the days of late summer turned to fall and Sonny seemed to be settling in successfully, Belle began to relax and do an exceptional job as a junior editor at the small publishing house that had recently become her employer. She was lucky to have landed the job as one of several paid interns at the small but prestigious Scribe & Son, thanks to a friend who had pulled a few strings.

A limited education and virtually no formal training were not going to hold her back. Belle had been an avid reader all her life and had an impressive knowledge of literature and a superb command of the English language. She often regretted her carelessness in not taking her education more seriously, but that was in the past and she made a firm resolution to come to terms with that shortfall later—maybe take a few night courses.

At this exhilarating moment in time, the newly separated twenty-seven-year-old beauty and her adorable five-year-old were entering a new phase in their quest for happiness. The adjustment would not be without bumps, but they both looked forward to making new friends and moving on with their lives.

As the first year drew to a close, it was with great joy that they anticipated a summer vacation without the burdens and stress that marital disharmony had placed upon both of their lives during the preceding summer. Finally, they could look forward to spending part of the summer away from the city and close to the ocean where they could mend in private from the wounds inflicted by an uncaring husband and father who had chosen to go his own way. The process would be tedious and they would heal slowly, like injured lambs.

But heal they would!

Belle had employed some professional help in preparing the cottage for their first vacation in it. Roofing and clapboard replacement, interior plaster and painting, new windows, and counter tops were all completed by local carpenters—to Belle's thrilling satisfaction. With praise-filled encouragement, she took to referring to the hard-working craftsmen as *"overnight sensations"*.

As the major improvements neared completion, a large, circular, braided carpet and panels of floral patterned curtains were purchased to match the small pieces of furniture that Belle had collected from estate sales. Bedrooms were furnished with wicker and adorned in matching curtains and light spreads. The feminine motif dominated the powder rooms in color and scented soaps and lotion. Lastly, the kitchen had been painted and its spotless cupboards stacked with colorful cottage china and hand painted glasses.

It had been a daunting six-month project worthy of praise for Belle's *weekend warriors*—the men and women who worked long hours without a single complaint. Maintaining respect and sensitivity towards the sparkling, soon-to-be summer residents of Puckshaw, they had won their tender hearts, thereby aiding in their healing process.

The Carter estate had been generous in accepting Belle's fine repair and restoration of the cottage in lieu of winter rental payments; in the meantime several of her new friends answered her call for help in the final push in completing the project. In spite of being turned down by some of her married friends who had aligned themselves with her husband's cause, she had dismissed the hurt feelings and gone forward with the challenge. Belle Adams would not be intimidated.

Loyal friends lent moral support and encouragement, volunteering several weekends of their own free time to do small odd jobs and work on "yard detail". Belle doled out the cash for gardening tools, disposal bags, and box-lunches from Charlie's. She was frugal at times, watching her budget and avoiding credit card overload. She never dreamed she would have to be careful about what she spent, but, as those who knew her would expect, she accepted the situation as a learning experience. "Never take anything for granted!" she advised her friends—*never!"*

By July 1st it had finally all come together. Belle Peterson Adams deeply appreciated every minute her loyal friends had donated to the project and graciously gave the one and only "thank you party" for the whole group. Twelve assorted friends and a few new colleagues were invited. The cottage looked dazzling as did Belle and her little 'hostess in waiting.'

Once the obligatory party was fulfilled, Belle promised herself that the cottage would remain a private summer retreat for her and Sonny; only a few treasured individuals would be invited from time to time in the future. Her friends understood and respected her decision. Nothing more or less was expected from Belle; her friends knew she needed the rest and privacy and they would graciously acquiesce.

The cottage had truly been turned into an enchanted hideaway; the cozy family room—an oblong-shaped room located on the North side of the house—quickly became Belle's and Sonny's favorite room in the cottage. Tan-carpeted, with a wood-burning stove and white, faux fur, bear rug spread before its forked feet—it was perfect for afternoon napping. A long window seat, running the length of three large glass panels with gleaming panoramic panes, became the special daydreaming spot for both mother and daughter on long relaxing afternoons. When sitting there, the sun shone, the birds sang, and time seemed to stand still for the healing duo.

The tiny clapboard cottage was heaven and—like angels—they would enjoy a blissful, magical trance for nine idyllic summers.

It was early in the third summer when Belle's finances greatly improved with a long-awaited settlement from her ex-husband. To her delight, she was able to buy the cottage with a reasonable down payment and make it her permanent domain. The two giddy "Adams girls", flushed with excitement, celebrated their new ownership with lemonade and chocolate cookies.

That summer was pure magic! The warm days and breezy nights had gently healed their wounds and made them whole again. They had scored a victory over the pain of loneliness and abandonment; now they chose to fill their days and evenings with loving chatter and secretive girl talk which, in the coming years, would be the subject of deep sadness for Sonny.

It had become their custom to spend spring weekends, summer holidays, and a delightful three-week vacation on the sun-drenched island of Puckshaw. They had added Thanksgiving weekend to the mix of their holidays at the cottage, feeling confident enough to invite three close friends to enjoy it with them. "Wouldn't Christmas be great here?" Sonny had enthused during Thanksgiving dinner.

Everyone had stared wide-eyed at the suggestion and Belle, unusually quiet, said she would give it some consideration.

Perhaps she thought it might be too desolate and lonely for such a festive holiday, but one never really knew what Belle was thinking. It's quite possible that some kind of loneliness was creeping into her life; after all, it had been all work and no play since the onset of the divorce, over three years ago.

Now and then, she accepted evening engagements with young men or women—mostly colleagues or contacts from the publishing house—and she seemed to enjoy the break in her routine; however, Belle was single-purposed in her devotion to Sonny's needs; her job and her own self-improvement followed—in that order. She had always had every intention of surviving, but now she wanted to do more than just survive. In idle moments, she wondered if she would ever be recklessly in love again; her first impulse was to push that thought away and remind herself that she had a child to look after. Sonny would *always* come first.

Late nights at the cottage often found the protective mother and her treasured daughter hidden away in their very own little Camelot, whispering conspiratorially about, what they referred to as, *Knights in Shining Armor.*

"Do you think he will be coming soon, mom?"

"One never knows, sweetie; one never knows. Now you get to sleep; we have a big day at the beach, tomorrow."

Belle tickled Sonny and then caressed her gently until she closed her eyes and slept, clutching her favorite stuffed animal—a teddy bear she called *Orchid.*

They vowed the cottage would always be their special place, no matter who entered their later lives. "Even when you have a boyfriend, Mom, it will still be our special place, right?" Those little bits of insight, coming from the mouth of her only child, made Belle blush and change the subject. Sonny giggled, uncontrollably and neither of them felt the need for anyone else's presence in their lives during such enchanted moments.

Some Saturdays, after having arrived late on Friday night, mother and daughter would lie in their beds under cool sheets and sleep late into the morning. Sonny seemed to forget about her father—now that she rarely saw him—and Belle, successfully recovered from the pain of separation and divorce, was just beginning to toy with the possibility of a new romance in her life.

Could her *Knight* be near?

8 *Summer Knights*

It was the summer of '74 and while Puckshaw was aglow with its expected sun-lit morning, Belle and Sonny Adams couldn't have dreamed of the surprise visit that would further brighten that memorable Saturday.

A tap on the screen door announced the caller as a friendly voice called out, "Is anybody here?

Both young ladies ran to the door with unsuppressed grins, delighted to see the tall, young man boyishly tilting his head to one side. Visibly distracted by his reluctant companion—a bashful child tugging on his hand—he apologized for disturbing them.

"Good morning! No, you're not bothering us at all; how can we help you?" Belle said smiling.

She felt herself blushing—nothing unusual for those with fair skin; it was a physical phenomenon she had learned to live with. She broadened her smile and shook the red hair away from her freckled face.

"Yes, ma'am and good morning to you! We wonder if we can use your stairs to get down to the little cove below. We caught just a glimpse of them yesterday, but we couldn't get to them because of the rocks. I'll understand if they're private; we'll just move on. I apologize if we bothered you in any way."

"Yes. I mean no. Well, what I mean is *yes*, you can use the stairs and *no*, they're not private. Well, they're private in a sense that there's no other way to get to the beach from this property accept by our stairs and...well what I mean is that no one has ever asked to use them. I guess that's because there are so many other coves and public beaches around here. Oh gosh! What am I babbling about? Of course you can use the stairs!"

With an increasing pink flush covering her face and neck, Belle continued, "Anyway, please feel free to use the stairs and the beach whenever you wish, but promise you'll ring the bell."

She pointed to the three-foot mini-bell tower with a large bell suspended from a worn rope. "...so we won't be startled or caught unaware on the stairs... or the beach."

Belle was ever mindful of being alone in the semi deserted beach area and was grateful to have kept the calling bell in the middle of the back yard when they had restored the property to its original state.

When she finally collected her unexpectedly stirred emotions, she coherently introduced herself and her daughter to the young man and repeated her invitation to use the stairs anytime they wished.

Sonny—aware of the change in demeanor that had washed over her mother—giggled at Belle's breathlessness; the flirtatious reaction hadn't escaped her child's ever-sharp eye. Although at the moment, Sonny wouldn't grasp the reason for Belle's excitement at seeing a male adult she, too, was thrilled at the prospect of a playmate near her own age—if he would only come out from behind the young man..

For the next three days they watched the strangers come and go with friendly waves and laughing tugs at the bell. Soon after, Belle and Sonny would quickly grab their towels and robes and walk, with feigned nonchalance, down the stairs to the beach. After a few days of "bumping into each other" and laughingly exchanging "surprised greetings", they felt comfortable enough to share a picnic lunch and an afternoon walk on a sunny day so filled with promise.

The children got on well—building sandcastles and playing hide and seek—shrieking as they darted in and out of the cluster of huge boulders. Sonny thought the largest boulder reminded her of an iceberg, like the kind she saw in the "big boat movies".

Reid—her newly tanned playmate—was very kind, never failing to allow Sonny to catch him before she became frustrated in a game of tag. Even at his tender age, he sensed her impatience and short temper—avoiding anything that might upset her. The shy youngster was captivated by her quivering smile and sweet voice, staying close by her side when near the water; he was as *unsure* of himself as Sonny was self-confident.

One day Reid wondered aloud, "Why is your hair so red?"

Sonny just shrugged her shoulders and jerked her thumb over her shoulder toward her mother as though taking for granted that her hair *should* be the same color as her mother's. "After all..." she made a rational conclusion that both Reid and his father had the same sandy-colored hair.

The long, warm hours at play allowed both of the children to experience a unique and peaceful bonding period that overflowed with pure delight and fierce protection of one another. It was the closest either of them had ever come to having a sibling or close companion with which to enjoy such unlimited playtime. Most of Sonny's playtime had been ticked off in minutes; in the city the busy day was long and passed quickly, leaving little time to spend with playmates.

Through the children's eyes Belle and Ryan also seemed to have hit it off quite well and were having just as much fun as they were. They occasionally joined them in playing tag or taking walks—holding hands affectionately, like children.

So *A Knight* had indeed arrived for both of them and Belle suddenly realized how easily they had cast aside the loneliness that had dogged them for so long.

They were dizzy with joy! More picnics and lazy afternoons followed and soon the happy foursome couldn't imagine the summer vacation without each other. All four of them were bursting with joy and filled with the hope that this could go on forever, or at least continue after the summer ended.

There were precious, intimate moments for Belle and the sandy-haired stranger as she became acutely aware of what she had been yearning for in the last few years—companionship of both a physical and emotional nature. Obviously love-struck, the adults were both fully aware of the stunning couple they made with their tanned and glowing faces. They proudly wore the badge of shared intimacy, openly paying homage to the mystery of fulfilled passion. Their gloriously satisfying moments were stolen when the children were napping or in for the night during a sleep-over. They rarely left the beach—lest the spell be broken.

Ryan was a head taller than Belle and would dangle his arm loosely around her shoulders and gently pull her against his warm side as they strolled along the beach. In spite of the tingling joy she felt all over, Belle still struggled with her conservative conscience. More often than not she felt some apprehension, knowing so little about Ryan. She was also embarrassed at having jumped into a physical relationship with a virtual stranger; yet, she was unable to convince herself that she might regret it.

Ryan—on the other hand—was in rapture and felt honored to be her first *serious* lover since her self-imposed celibacy following her divorce. She had begun to share information with him during tender moments and hoped it wouldn't change things. She knew how men hated it when a woman got *too serious, too soon;* but she was relieved and thrilled when he reacted with such sensitivity.

She was terrified to even think it—and she hoped it wasn't so—but Belle had an elated, yet, sinking feeling that she might be in love.

Maybe it was just the hot sun or the cool, breezy nights, but a reckless and youthful passion that neither of them had felt in several years was suddenly awakened.

The ocean became a daily delight for all of them. Ryan was a fine swimmer and confidently took the children out into the ocean on his shoulders or in his arms one at a time. He viewed his expertise as a tool to exercise his fathering role in teaching his son about the dangers of swimming in the ocean; "Safety first!" he warned sternly.

Though the boy had spent a lot of time in swimming pools; he had always been under the watchful eye of an adult supervisor, both in school and at the upscale health club that his father took him to on weekends. To his father's chagrin, the youngster made little progress; he still lacked confidence in the water—another casualty of the divorce.

Having barely adjusted to the lifestyles of his newly married mother and now-single father, Reid had emerged from the ordeal with a new set of fears—strangers, dogs, riding his bike, and water—causing his father renewed concern for the city-bred youngster.

Many of the boy's friends had two sets of parents and seemed to take it in stride, but not Reid; he was a sensitive and lonely child and it was almost a year before he had accepted the split. He would never know how hard his mother and father had worked behind the scenes to maintain a loving front without spiteful or bitter exchanges. His well-being was of the utmost priority and just as the boy had begun to take things a little more calmly—a new shock was delivered.

Three weeks had passed since his mother had gently informed him that they would soon be moving to Hawaii and he would be spending six months out of the year with each parent. He had screamed and struck out at her as the cause of *another* break-up. "No!" He wouldn't like *any* arrangement that kept him away from either of his parents for a whopping six months. The boy had a mature concept of time—having gone through the recent split—and he knew that six months could feel like forever.

So, it was with a heavy heart that his father had taken him to *Puckshaw,* for a three-week idyll, before he was to leave for Hawaii. Schooling had yet to be arranged and the boy was edgy and fearful about making new friends.

Ryan had different concerns; the thought of his son's new proximity to the ocean was a frightening prospect. He hoped that Reid would gain a little confidence after spending three weeks on Puckshaw—swimming in the ocean, daily.

Belle had feared the water for as long as she could remember and had inadvertently passed that fear on to her daughter, Sonny. She didn't know where or when it had taken root; she had spent very little time near the water as a child and could recall no specific incident that could have caused her fear.

After their first two summers on Puckshaw, Bell and her daughter, with the help of a friend, put aside their fears and were soon confidently wading along the shore, chasing large gulls into the surf and playfully splashing one another.

All in all, both adults and children were ecstatic throughout the safe and sun-filled vacation on the island.

Inevitably, the three-week summer idyll flew by and as it drew to a sad close, plans were made to keep in touch and perhaps reunite in a few months. Belle and Ryan were thrilled that they would only be a half-hour's drive away from each other, though the excitement was dampened by Reid's impending departure for Hawaii.

The boy was not due back in Boston until March 1, but perhaps a visit could be arranged after Christmas, when his mother came east to see her parents in New Hampshire.

It was with forced enthusiasm that both children and adults hugged each other in preparation for fond farewells on that sunny Saturday afternoon. Hope ran high all the way around. And why shouldn't it have?

Belle, having promised herself that she would not lose her composure at the last minute, was saying a reluctant good-bye to Ryan in the family room and only half-noticed Sonny and Reid through the window as they skipped, hand in hand, up and down the long driveway. They were giggling, and Belle, too, felt a giddiness rushing through her when she realized she and Ryan were alone for a more intimate good-bye.

Time flew quickly as they kissed with passion—trying to forget their impending separation. Clinging to each other Belle noted, with pleasure, the time on the sun room clock. It was two-forty five and their plane was not leaving until six p.m. The lovers ran hand in hand into Belle's bedroom, closing the door behind them. If the truth was told, they had fallen headlong in love with each other and their passionate outpouring felt perfectly right and natural.

When the sun came streaming across the heavily scented, printed sheets, Belle sat up in bed with a start. It was already four o'clock and she was about to playfully wake Ryan with a passionate kiss when the air was split by a piercing scream. She jumped out of bed, grabbing a terrycloth robe off the doorknob as she ran to the hallway while Ryan, jerked out of a light sleep, reached for his clothes at the foot of the bed.

Sonny was standing at the end of the hallway shaking her hands, rocking from side to side and struggling to stop her teeth from chattering. It seemed like forever before Belle could make out what the child was saying.

Startled by the sound that rose from her chest and shot out of her throat, Belle screamed out Ryan's name.

Still shivering with shock, they lined the concrete stairs as the tiny body was carried up to the top of the cliff and into a waiting ambulance. The little boy's sandy hair was matted, framing his white face and amazing purple lips. There were no visible cuts or scratches. Sonny stood staring at the serene face of the sweetest friend she had ever known, but unexpectedly his paleness frightened her. The next thing she felt was Belle lifting her gently and carrying her up the stairs toward the cottage.

When she opened her eyes and looked around. She was lying under a light blanket on the sofa, unaware that she had fainted. Blackness came again and again as she slept fitfully, her little body trying to black out the shock it had sustained. The next four days were a painful blur of unanswered questions and tears.

There was no formal farewell.

The authorities concluded that the boy had waded out into the surf a little too far while chasing a seagull.

Sonny described a medium-sized wave that had capsized the little body and sucked him under quickly. Within seconds his struggling body came crashing back to the shore and landed between two large boulders. The very boulders the children used to hide behind when they frolicked in the sun. The child lay still until a near-bye boater, having spotted the boy's body crashing onto the beach, sped to the scene. Diving off his boat to swim the last fifteen yards, he restored the boys breathing and carried him to safety—barely alive.

The golden idyll ended in chaos.

Packing was simple. Belle and Sonny left most of their summer clothes at the cottage and were soon in the station wagon on their way back to the apartment. A vacation so full of promise had ended in utter despair—nothing new to the young summer residents of *Puckshaw.*

Sonny could not remember a single time when she had even dreamed of descending the stairs to the beach without an adult.

Belle never worried about Sonny going too close to the water; she could not remember a single moment of their days and weeks at the cottage when she didn't know *exactly* where Sonny was.

Now, complacency had gone and played a cruel trick on both of them.

Back in the city, the gray days of fall descended with a sudden coolness and the joy Belle and Sonny Adams had recently known quickly dissolved into a bittersweet memory.

Deep in the dark of night, Belle relived the moments of sweet intimacy she had known and now longed for.

Sonny, contrarily, summoned an uncanny courage to block out both the joy and horror of the magical three weeks.

With characteristic determination both mother and daughter focused all their attention on the days before them. Long school days for Sonny and pressure-filled hours at the publishing house for Belle, were the norm; they welcomed any distraction that might help force the memory of that time deep into the recesses of their respective minds.

Reid was recovering nicely but there had been very little communication besides short phone conversations during which Ryan seemed unable or unwilling to discuss the frightening brush with death that Reid had experienced. Belle assumed that he and his son were going through the same thing she and Sonny were going through and waited eagerly for him to contact her.

The communications ended abruptly. Ryan no longer accepted or returned her calls.

It would not have been unreasonable of her to think that he might seek comfort in her arms after his son's near-death accident; when he didn't, she knew why. She suspected that Ryan felt the same guilt as she did: they were most likely making love or dozing at the precise moment Reid was struggling for his life. They never had the chance to discuss it and they never would.

Ryan battled his own demons for months before quietly disappearing. No explanation. No forwarding address.

Belle wondered, curiously, if he had relocated to Hawaii to be near Reid.

She could only assume what she could process.

At school, Sonny often sat with her head in her hands, believing the accident was her fault; her behavior attracted the attention of her teachers and arrangements were made for counseling sessions.

Belle was disappointed when her beloved child was unresponsive to a sensitive and caring counselor, but that's what appeared on the reports. "Intense efforts have failed to elicit the child's unwarranted guilt over her companion's terrifying accident."

Sonny knew better than to sneak down the stairs and play in the surf without an adult watching over them. They were just going to play for a few minutes before returning to the cottage without Belle finding out. The child felt confident; she had been on the island for three summers and knew more about the ocean than Reid—a novice at the dangerous game of chasing gulls into the surf. When she stumbled, toppling him into to a crashing wave, she had shouted and reached out to him but he went under quickly. The child did what any child would have done; she ran for help—then blamed herself.

Belle thought she saw something off-putting in Sonny's eyes but couldn't define it; for some inner reason she chose not to pursue it. More emotional upheaval would be too painful for both of them and silence proved to be a wise option.

As the dark, cold days of fall turned into winter, Belle and Sonny recognized and accepted the fact that they would never see Ryan or Reid again; it was just another ordeal they would have to survive.

And survive they did, with their own special brand of extraordinary courage and spiritual purpose.

9 *February, 1996*

February 15, 1996
Hello, kind friend.

Progress on my manuscript is coming along splendidly! It is filled with twists and turns and I think we'll both like the finished product.

I've recently made several trips to Boston to check the validity of some new information that came my way; my dear friend, it drastically changes the direction my manuscript is going in. Don't be surprised, but I have come to know my own son, Scott, of whom I knew so little before I began this endeavor. I have grown to love him more with each new day. God, I wish that I could have helped him through some of the bad times he was confronted with. And his mother, Susan, deserved a better hand than she was dealt—I should have helped her more. I *wish this* and I *hope that*, but the fact remains that I have been a selfish scoundrel and it has taken me all these years to discover what was right before my blind eyes all the time—a son I could have and should have loved. Who knows? He might have loved me in return. It's too late, now.

I am filled with such bitter remorse for my past actions that I need to confide in someone who won't judge me. I've judged myself—now I flee to you for cover. I am entertaining different ways of atoning for my remiss behavior, but I'm not quite ready to discuss my final decision. I have a lot to do on the manuscript and more research awaits me back in Boston. Some new discoveries have knocked me back and will definitely change things for me, but I'll check in with you to let you know how things are progressing.

Until then, will you wish me good luck on the successful completion of my manuscript? It will soon be time for me to contact Scribe & Son to see if they are interested in publishing it for me.

Good night, kind friend. HM

February 22, 1996
Good evening, kind friend,

I am very excited about sharing something with you tonight. I just returned from a small Hamlet about sixty miles south of Boston. I drove down yesterday to look up an old friend of Belle Adams'. She was probably one of the last people to see Belle alive—besides Sonny, of course. She was guarded and suspicious at first but after I begged her to listen to me and promised her anonymity, she relented and reluctantly consented to be interviewed. I promised not to use her real name or give her present location, should my research ever be published. I thought that was only fair; then she surprised me and gave me permission to use her real name. Her name is Bobbie. She immediately explained that she didn't like to be called that, but was forced to, because one of her supervisors at work had the same name as she did—Roberta—so her colleagues took to calling her Bobbie. Oh, for heaven sakes, I'm rambling.

Bobbie lives in a small apartment on the top floor of an old three-story house with a deteriorating front porch. Two large front windows, probably designed to let the sunlight shine into the tiny apartment, were covered with thick dark blue panels—seemingly, now, to keep the world from seeping in. She didn't know that I had already inquired into her private life and knew that she had become a reclusive widow shortly after her husband and four-year-old daughter had been killed in an auto accident just one year before our meeting. She had been driving the old pick-up and lost control on an icy patch of the road. I was eager to tell her how sorry I was to learn of her loss and subsequent grief.

Believe me, this woman was no stranger to pain. She was a quiet, law abiding citizen who did not judge her fellow man or have any desire to be judged by anyone other than the almighty.

She told me that the recent tragedy involving Sonny, had debilitated her for months and, now, three years later—in spite of her own recent loss—it still brought tears of anguish and grief to her dark, olive shaped eyes.

She still remembered Belle as if she had seen her just yesterday; yet, she could barely speak her name. There were so many acts of kindness Belle had showered upon her that she didn't know where to start.

Bobbie didn't know too many details of Belle's death because she had left her job at Scribe & Son shortly after assisting Belle and her daughter in settling in at the ocean front cottage, where Belle wished to spend her last days. Bobbie felt it had been a great privilege to be chosen to spend some of those precious days with her two dear friends and, yes, hardly a day passes that she doesn't think of them.

She wistfully recalled how Sonny—dear Sonny, whom she had lovingly called 'princess'—had possessed the courage of a devoted warrior when faced with her mother's terminal illness. "She was barely fourteen years old...you knew that, didn't you?"

Being a woman of deep spiritual convictions, Bobbie said she liked to think of her past loved ones as preparing a lovely reception for her own arrival in paradise at some future date; she knew Belle and Sonny would be among them, along with her husband and beloved child. This deeply spiritual woman said she had no idea when that would be; she was ready whenever *they* were.

Kind friend, this woman has confirmed what I have believed to be true all along. Belle and Sonny Adams were two ordinary women who behaved with extraordinary grace under the best and worst circumstances of their lives.

And oh, by the way, I have decided to sprinkle my manuscript with these conversations that I periodically have with you. I think it will make it so much more interesting, don't you?

Now that I have made that decision, I hope I don't get all careful and mushy about what I say to you and become an old boring windbag. What do you think? I hope you won't mind. It won't change our relationship—you can count on that.

HM

P.S. While I have my journal open and still feel like talking, would you like to hear something funny? Let me tell you about the unforgettable character that I encountered at the Heliport just as I was preparing to take the short flight across the bay to the mainland on Friday, past.

I had purchased my ticket from the new automated ticket vendor and walked over to stand in the shade of the tall, narrow flight tower, which dominates the tiny airport. It was there I met a diminutive, octogenarian intently reading the fine print on her twenty-two-dollar ticket. I know it sounds expensive but it beats driving your car over to the docks and then taking a thirty-five minute ferry ride, only to battle slow moving traffic all the way to the highway. That whole thing could take up to one or two hours on busy days—not to mention the inconvenience to those who don't drive and have to be picked up at the other end or are forced to take some sort of shuttle into Boston. It's time they build a bridge!

ANYWAY, I said, "Good morning, madam! How are you today?"

This four foot tall curmudgeon looked me straight in the eye and said with exaggerated clarity, "Don't call me Madam!"

"My apologies, Madam—oops, excuse me, uh, Ms."

She nodded a little arrogantly, accepting my apology. I took in the full picture of this pint-sized tyrant in *Nike* sneakers as she returned her attention to scrutinizing her ticket as though she might have been cheated, or something. You know how I love to study people, so I began to take a mental photograph so I could later write about her.

Her hair would have been lovely had it not been tinted such a deep shade of blue, but what do I know? She must have known what I was thinking as she glanced over at me with murky blue eyes that bore the hallmark of recent laser surgery and healing drops. She took a few steps sideways as though she might contract the plague from me and as she stepped away, I almost hooted out loud at the skinny ankles, with rings of orange pantyhose gathered around them, comically sprouting out of her oversized blue and white sneakers. And the white, pleated tennis skirt? Well that was a blessing as it hung well below the knee.

You had to give this little troll some credit; so far her hair, eyes, and sneakers matched perfectly. I turned my back to her and allowed my shoulders to quake with silent laughter before clearing my throat and straightening up to lean against the cool building again. She harrumphed me a few times as though I was a *dirty old man* trying to pick her up, so I walked around in a little circle and cagily returned to rest in the same spot I started from.

I checked out her little white double-knit Polo shirt with the neat, dark blue, monogram on the pocket—which I assumed was this fashion icon's personal coat of arms by the way she was acting. Her venous arms and gnarly hands were covered with freckles and I concluded that she was in no danger of losing that huge diamond on the third finger of her left hand—not over those painfully swollen knuckles! She threw me another withering look and smoothed down the front of her Polo shirt over a caved-in chest with non-existent breasts.

Suddenly, she cleared her mucous filled throat, loudly. Well, she got my attention, so I looked over at her and nodded; with that she spewed at me, "Mind your manners, young man!"

Me, almost all of fifty-five years old! Or am I fifty-six? I really don't know anymore, but I was becoming annoyed. I shook my head from side to side and started to hum something tuneless. After a safe amount of time had passed, I returned my gaze in her direction to complete my study of this *numbingly typical aging Islander*. After all, I *was* a reporter and it *was* my job to be observant, so how could I miss the garish gold chain that was wrapped around her thin neck and the matching heavy, gold hoops dangling from a pair of foot-long ear lobes.

I was almost at the end of my assessment of —or should I say amazement at—this most unforgettable character when I was blinded by the new coat of bright red lipstick which she was generously applying; a huge smear of red balm over those poorly disguised, pencil-thin lips would just have to do. I shook my head thinking that her face, alone, could have doubled for a stop sign that most drivers would have preferred to speed through.

I finally decided to make one more attempt at conversation. After all, she was probably just a lonely old lady who needed a friendly soul to cheer her up, but just then the Heli-Bay taxied out of the hangar and the service attendant approached with his little portable step ladder used for boarding the shiny new helicopter. We both walked toward it in silence and as we neared the step I stepped aside and said, "After you, Madam."

She glared at me with those beady, blue eyes and said—you guessed it—"Don't call me Madam!"

10 *Disaster*

It was rough making it through 1975, but the next four summers and winters passed in peace and moderate prosperity as Belle and Sonny continued to become strong and determined individuals, conducting their lives with characteristic simplicity and dignity. Belle was promoted several times at the publishing house and life was good for her. Sonny, a sweet-faced teenager, was turning into a lovely young lady. Alone, but no longer lonely, both women lived for the lazy summers at the cottage where they whiled away their weekends and long summer vacation—still naively fantasizing about the promising future. Occasionally, they wistfully mentioned Ryan and Reid, but neither of them liked to dwell too long on the subject, lest one or both of them be plunged into long sad moods of silence.

Few trusted friends and distant foster relatives played a very small part in their lives—mostly during holidays and on birthdays—but their joy at being exclusive was obvious. They trusted and loved one another not only as mother and daughter, but as best friends—two souls sharing the same spirit. They played small practical jokes on one another, hummed the same tunes, and sometimes tickled each other until one or both gave up in mock tears. In that time and place, the world was a safe and serene place to be as long as they were *both* in it.

Carena Adams had reached her fourteenth birthday and the bloom of young womanhood had transformed her into a charming replica of her mother—with the same curly-but-tamed red hair, lightly-freckled skin, and the willowy body of a ballet dancer ready to leap into life. The youngster, bursting with enthusiasm for life, was filled with newfound self-awareness.

Likewise, glowing with pride over her stunning offspring, Belle had reached a comfortable period in her life that seemed full of promise and passion; she too was prepared to leap into a new stage of life with no small expectations.

Both of these women were models of decorum and virtue; blessed with good health and spiritual contentment, they were mysteriously aglow in the time and space of their own choosing.

Only an unthinkable misfortune could disrupt their idyllic existence.

It was spring of 1981 when it arrived—a disaster of such proportion and major significance that not a living soul could have prepared for it.

Sonny Adams' seemingly charmed life was about to spiral out of control and eventually come to a brutal halt with the discovery and diagnosis of her mother's illness. The world, as she knew it, would fall apart—never to be restored to complete sanity again. Belle's beloved child would be catapulted from sweet adolescence to bitter-tasting adulthood with the speed of lightening and the roar of thunder.

Sonny hadn't sensed anything different in her mother's demeanor—maybe a little anxiety that was uncharacteristic of her—certainly nothing that was cause for any comment or concern. After all, these two individuals spent an enormous amount of time together and were attuned to each other's every mood and movement. Sonny would later mull that accepted fact over, again and again, in her confused state of mind. How did she miss the signs of such a serious event unfolding in her mother's life?

How was it that she was the last to know?

Later she recalled the quiet phone messages from a doctor's office and a number of late evening calls which Belle had received from a few close friends at Scribe & Sons—calls which she had taken behind her closed bedroom door. The youngster, feeling no sense of urgency or danger, had ignored the incidences.

Sonny was very sheltered and her world was still small; inhabited only by her mother, her teachers, and a few close friends, she had no preparation for the crises at hand. She was fourteen: what could have been more important than *that* to the youngster? Months later she would sift through the train wreck for the warning signs and wonder how she had missed so much.

Belle had picked her up from an overnight at her girlfriend's and they were headed for a Saturday afternoon lunch at Riggi's, a popular Italian hangout where they were well known.

For several years, after shopping and doing errands, they had enjoyed their favorite Italian dishes there. They were no strangers to calamari, veal Parmesan, and a variety of primavera dishes. Regardless of the meal, the Adams ladies always shared a banana split after dinner—their reward for a hard week's work.

Her mother actually broke the news quite calmly—practically in a whisper. Any other way would have been out of character for her and the only sound Sonny recalled hearing, as she relived that afternoon, was the roar of the vent on the brown, wood grain dashboard.

"I have not been feeling very well, Sonny, and Dr. Morrison is not satisfied with my test results," was all she had said. "He would like me to go to the hospital for some further testing. Bobbie will stay with you for a few days and drive you to soccer and dancing. Is that alright with you?"

It was as simple as that—no time or place for uncontrolled emotions.

The few days stretched into three weeks of hospitalization and quiet, daily, visits. Sonny spent the last fretful week of Belle's hospitalization at her girlfriend's home, until Bobbie could make arrangements to come back to the apartment and help prepare for Belle's return home.

The youngster went through the motions of schoolwork and extra-curricular activities as if in a fog. She had been shocked at the change in her mother's appearance in the last two weeks; now pale and thin—her looks had changed—her bright eyes were cloudy and distant.

There was a valiant attempt at resuming a normal routine after Belle arrived home, but she was weak from surgery and ill from the harsh medication and soon-to-be-discontinued treatments she was receiving.

With little fanfare they made arrangements to spend the late spring and the entire summer at the cottage. They were fully aware that staying at the cottage would protect them from sympathetic looks or unwanted visitors.

Based on her excellent academic record, Sonny was given permission to take her exams early; she was numbly cooperative with that arrangement.

They packed their belongings quickly; each of them obviously preoccupied with a host of complex reactions to the shocking events of the last few weeks. Skipping the usual ritual of past years—jumping on the beds with excitement and running back and forth to check on each other's packing progress—they remained silent. Many of their summer clothes were already at the cottage, though they always had new items to take. Endless books, magazines and board games—such an important part of their recreation in the evenings—had to be packed.

Later, Belle would wistfully regret that they hadn't taken the time to gather up any of the *little things*, like nightstand photos, or favorite CD's, but it was out of her hands now. She moved about quietly, as if in a fog.

Bobbie had arrived a few hours early to help with last minute errands but the absence of her usual bubbly conversation was a painful reminder of the grave situation they now found themselves in. By four p.m. they took off quietly, avoiding their neighbors.

Their departure was duly noted and documented by those who felt it was their duty and obligation to report on the comings and goings of the popular, though obsessively private, women.

Bobbie took the wheel and nervously adjusted the mirrors as she prepared to make her way through rush hour traffic. It seemed like an unusually long ride to the island but it was well worth it. The shop lights were on and hopeful owners were hard at work preparing for the summer onslaught of boaters and vacationers. Main street was swept clean and newly painted signs could be seen everywhere.

Alone in the backseat, Sonny remained stonily silent while Belle and Bobbie spoke in hushed tones.

The trio arrived at the cottage just before six p.m. and quietly spent the evening settling in after a quick take-out supper.

Bobbie, happy to bunk in on the new futon, unpacked her small suitcase quickly and saw to Belle's personal needs while Sonny turned to the chores of opening the cottage for the season; she busied herself with dusting and stocking up the cupboards with cereal, popcorn, canned goods, and cookies she had gathered from the cupboards in the city apartment.

At ten-thirty Belle and Sonny were fast asleep while Bobbie read and kept an eye on the wood-burning stove as it crackled and sparked, keeping the little cottage warm. By morning all three were refreshed with emotions well under control.

Once the cottage was freshened up and stocked with groceries, Sonny and Bobbie baked cookies and prepared some meals that could be frozen for later use. Most of the time Belle rested or gave instructions as she sat curled up on the soft, comfortable window seat. She was not feeling strong enough to do much of anything but gaze out of the triple paned window that Sonny had lovingly polished.

Though Bobbie tried hard to keep the mood light, the youngster, ever sharp, observed the deep sadness in her eyes. She had heard her and Belle talking late into the night and though she felt some resentment at being excluded, reasoned correctly that they were *just being the grown-ups*—trying to protect her.

The days flew quickly with Bobbie rising early each morning, tidying up the back yard and taking solemn solitary walks on the beach.

Ten days had passed and things seemed well under control when Bobbie shocked them with the unceremonious announcement that she would be leaving in the next few days; a friend from the office was coming for her at ten a.m., "come Friday". She was expected back at her desk on Monday.

Belle was not surprised by the news, but Sonny was stunned. Her mind raced; she knew they wouldn't have much use for the wagon—she was too young and her mother was too weak—so she asked Bobbie to park it at the end of the long driveway after which she dutifully put the keys on the little hook to the right of the kitchen door—as she had seen her mother do a thousand times..

After dinner Bobbie called Sonny outside and gently put her arm around her and led her down the driveway—silent at first, as though she needed time to gather courage to speak. She resented being the adult, having to deliver the news with such finality. After all, they had always been "pals"—kid-like.

"Sweetheart, it's time for you and your mom to have some time to yourselves now; do you understand that?"

Sonny nodded her head up and down without speaking. "I know."

"Do you have any questions I might be able to answer for you?"

Sonny shook her head back and forth with deep solemnity and acceptance for a fourteen-year-old. I don't know what to ask; there's just *so much* going on.

"I know; but at this point, it's all between you and your mom. You probably won't be seeing me again; at least not for a very long time—if ever. I hope you can understand my actions. Please try. I love your mom very much and don't want to make it any harder for her with my sad eyes and all. Do you understand why I'm leaving?"

Now, Sonny spoke for the first time in a weak and frightened voice. "No and yes, Bobbie; but I still want to thank you for everything you've done for me and mom; you've been such a wonderful friend and I don't know how we're going to make it without you. You should stay here; we need you! You're part of our family.

"Please forgive me if I'm hurting you; but I have to do this. I have to go!"

Sonny turned and buried her face in Bobbie's baggy sweatshirt and sobbed so softly that she wasn't even sure the youngster was crying.

"I have a meeting set up for tomorrow to tell your father about this situation; I've spoken with your grandparents and they will be coming up to see you and your mom in a few days—I'll call you as soon as they get here. They'll stay at the motel in town for ten days to see what they can do to help you along.

Dr. Morrison wants you to call him anytime you have a question or if you just want to let him know how your mom is doing. His nurse is going to stay in close touch with you; she plans to call you every other day and visit twice a week—right after work. Don't worry, honey; a lot of people are looking out for you; you won't be left alone. Even Tommy, from the next cove, will tend to the stove each day; he said he'll stop by after breakfast each morning and you shouldn't worry about it. It's warming up quickly anyway—you won't need to use it for long.

This is just the way your mom wants it, ok? She wants this time with you, and you alone, and she said she knows that you can handle it and so do I, sweetie."

Without any warning Bobbie was overcome with her own emotions and turned around and faced the roaring ocean below, shaking her head. "Sonny, I'll be thinking of you every single day! Stay strong and keep well, little sweetheart! My love will always be with you and my dear friend, Belle. I love you both so much!"

On Friday morning, Sonny did not miss the look that Belle and Bobbie exchanged as they tenderly walked to the waiting car arm in arm. She knew they were saying goodbye.

Bobbie had been devoted to the little family that had embraced her when she was broke and broken-hearted; she would be forever grateful.

Now, as one last act of selflessness, Belle was releasing her of further pain and service; she was to move on—her work was done, there.

They would never see her again. Sonny would find out later, that Bobbie returned to work for a month—just long enough to train someone in her place—then moved away without a word to her colleagues.

On that cool April morning, as she rode back to the city, Bobbie recalled Belle's kindness to her when she first arrived on the job—pale and thin, recovering from a collapsed relationship,and *very* unsure about her future.

Belle—though very cautious about becoming too friendly with colleagues—instinctively sensed Bobbie's desperate loneliness and invited her for dinner.

Bobbie's spirits soared when she was introduced to Sonny and her bubbly teen companions. It was an enormously kind gesture that she never forgot. Being welcomed into their little family had assuaged her homesickness and given her the courage to move forward.

Soccer games, dance recitals, and school plays were the order of the day for the new trio—Bobbie attending with vigor. She was enjoying an adult relationship with Belle and playing "Auntie Bobbie" to Sonny and her young friends; she had found joy, at last!

Now her heart ached as she parted from them. She looked down at her muddy tennis shoes and recalled ironically that it had been two years to the day since they had met. She was honored to have been asked to assist them in preparing for the final time they would have together; she just didn't possess the inner strength to stay until the end. Her frail nature would never bear up under the grief she so feared.

On her way back to the city that night, she had made the decision to start over. She had run away from her friends and family, once before, escaping pain caused by an unfaithful and uncaring partner; now she was running again. Running from the pain of seeing a good friend surrender her young life to a wretched illness and the expected devastation it would wreak on the loving child of her heart; this time Bobbie would run *toward* her family with a new determination to put things straight and start a new life.

Belle and Sonny had helped to make her strong enough to go home; only *they* understood why Bobbie couldn't be with them at the end. In all truth they preferred to be alone; *just as they had been for most of their lives.*

Once Bobbie was gone, Sonny ordered whatever groceries they needed by telephone. The *Green Grocer* delivered the goods and presented his bill. Sonny paid him the exact amount after scanning the bill for possible errors. Melvin would smile at her "grown-up" behavior and thank her for her order.

Belle ate very little—mostly a little fruit, vegetables, tiny sandwiches, and deviled eggs—favored summer fare they both enjoyed. Sonny always ate exactly what her mother ate, though she often craved French fries, pizza, or hot dogs—foods that Belle would frown upon with a little shake of her head. Both women loved desserts, so cookies and ice cream were always on the menu; a little dip for Belle and a large one for Sonny.

As the summer progressed, Sonny found herself eating alone most days for Belle had at last lost her appetite. The child was a very resourceful youngster and made the best of it by eating her lunch on the beach or sitting on the window seat reading a magazine while Belle slept away the long warm afternoons.

Every few days, Sonny spoke to her father and grandparents and touched base with the Doctor's office. She never exhibited any anxiety or fear over her situation; her mother was her strength and courage—everything else paled in comparison.

It would be difficult, but Belle's wishes were clear: she refused to have her loved ones hovering over her with solemn faces. She and her daughter would cling to each other until the end; when the time came, Sonny would be cared for and life would go on.

But fate—always fickle—had yet a crueler blow to deliver.

Early one morning, as her daughter dosed before the triple-paneled windows, Bellemara Peterson Adams crept out of the cottage and disappeared into the roaring Atlantic.

11 *The Telephone Call*

March 9, 1996
Good day, kind friend.

I was awakened at five a.m. this morning by the ruthless and persistent ringing of my telephone. Now, you've known me long enough to know that I rarely fall asleep before daybreak and when I do, it's gratefully acknowledged as a gift from a higher power. So I think I was justified in wondering who the hell was calling me at such an unreasonable hour; I assumed it might be someone just trying to get even with me for being such a carbuncle during some past dealings. I, myself, have made it a practice never to call anyone late at night or early in the morning—it's far too off-putting.

Well anyway, the voice at the other end of the wire identified himself as a Daniel Adams. I bolted straight up and grabbed my pencil and notebook, which always rest on the floor right next to my bed as I sleep. I thought, aha, another ghost from Belle and Sonny's past!

Mr. Dan Adams said he was returning a call I made to him over a year ago! Go figure that! After all this time he was ready to share some of his recollections with me as I had requested.

I said, "Jesus, at five o'clock in the morning?"

A slurred voice at the other end of the line said something about getting ready to leave Boston and wanting to get a few things off his chest to set the record straight. I remained silent and ready to write.

He startled me with his boldness when he said, "Hell, I really loved Belle, you know, but she was just too young and inexperienced for me. Dazzling yes, but she just couldn't cut it like the other wives. She lacked the *Mayflower background*, you know what I mean? A little old money—even new—wouldn't have hurt her chances either. The corporate ladder is tough enough as it is, and a guy needs an influential woman behind him to push him up a rung or two. She couldn't do that for me. The baby came too soon and we both wandered before the second year passed. It really bothered me that she had that embarrassing affair at the health club right under my nose; hell, I always thought she was happy!

Now take me; I was a guy with a great looking secretary and she wasn't distracted by a child or a home, so I just went for her. It was not unusual for someone in my position—hell it was damn near expected of me—to wander now and then. I was on my way up and I needed all the loyalty I could get, even if it was from those flashy, high-heeled, secretaries that ran the corner offices. It was fun. It was risky. But it wasn't supposed to break up my marriage.

So you wanted to know my point of view about Belle—I loved her! Did I give you enough?"

I had no chance to respond as he continued immediately with, "As far as I'm concerned it was both of our faults. I should have never even gone for Belle to begin with; but I thought her good looks and pleasing manners would compensate for her shabby, foster upbringing and limited formal education. Not that she was dumb or anything; obviously, she just hadn't gone to the right schools or seen enough operas or maybe she just wasn't willing to kiss enough asses—I don't know."

I dared to interrupt his monologue but I needed some answers. "What about your daughter, Sonny?" I held my breath. I was sweating and my hand was aching from writing. I thought maybe he had dozed off for a moment; that was possible if I was correct in my assumption that he had been drinking. Finally, the now familiar slurred speech started up again with a slight whine added to it.

"My dear, sweet Sonny—I hardly knew her, but don't get me wrong—I'm not proud of that. She was such a loving child and always so cheerful. And bright?—she was sharp as a cracker, but by the time she was three, Belle and I had grown pretty distant and I was coming home so late at night that she was always in bed by the time I arrived; it didn't take long to drift apart. Jesus, I hardly had a chance to be a father in those days. I know that later on she blamed me for the break-up. Sure, she saw her mother crying all the time and assumed I had inflicted some horrible pain, but she never saw *my* tears. I cried too, you know. I hated leaving Sonny—a hell of a lot more than I hated leaving Belle. She could choose a boyfriend or another husband, but Sonny couldn't go shopping—or advertise in the paper—for another Daddy, now could she?"

This guy was certifiable; a terrific find! I murmured something sympathetic and he continued.

"Just before the final split-up, I took Sonny to my parents' house in the country for the long weekend. I actually tried to explain things to her and say some sort of good-bye, but nothing came out right and I knew she didn't understand what I was getting at. That following Tuesday, when I arrived home from work, they were gone. Just like that. I spent a week making a little collage out of nature objects Sonny had collected on our walk and left in the trunk of my car; I put them under glass, in a lovely blue frame and sent it to her. She never thanked me. I figured if she didn't care, I wasn't going to care either.

I didn't see too much of her after her seventh birthday. I remarried, lost my job, hit the divorce trail again, and ended up selling the house we had once all lived in once upon a time. I split the money with her mother and heard—through the grapevine—that they bought a cottage on *Puckshaw* with Belle's share of the money. I also found out that she put a good portion of her share into a trust fund for Sonny. When she died, the mortgage insurance paid off the cottage and the kid was home free. I guess Belle was a lot smarter than I gave her credit for and a lot more generous than I was. A better parent all the way around, I guess. I would have never thought of doing that; hell, I was almost broke *and* unemployed—why would I? Why *should* I? They didn't care about me. I saw Sonny on and off for a while and then just let go of it all. I didn't hear anything from them until Belle got sick.

After *that* whole mess, Sonny came to live with me in a two-bedroom condo until it was time for her to go to college—where else could she go? They were four lousy years! I think she hated me, but to be honest with you I didn't know how to be a father anymore. God, I hardly knew how to be a human being! It had been so long since we had been together—or needed each other—that we just tried to co-exist, peacefully, in the same house.

It was pure hell. The kid didn't know how to deal with her grief over her mother or how to forgive me for the poor excuse of a father I had been. And you know what? Neither of us knew how to start over—we just played the survival game until her graduation from high school."

I finally cut in on his rambling. "Excuse me Daniel, but do you think you should lie down and rest for a while and maybe I could come up to Boston and see you tomorrow?"

"No, no, no, I'm just about finished. Besides, I'm off early in the morning and I don't think you'll hear from me again. Got a new job in the Detroit area; automotives, you know. And now with both of my parents gone, I don't suppose I'll have much reason to return to Boston—ever again. Anyway, let me finish.

After a few months had passed, I went to see Sonny at her dorm one night—without being invited—and she was pretty cold to me. Took her just about a minute to tell me she was on her way to break up some stupid college affair—actually she made sure she told me it was her *third* one. Damn her anyway! I could see she was pretty unhappy and I couldn't do anything about it. We parted without an embrace or even a smile. She didn't stay in the dorms long; she had enough money to get a nice little apartment near the school and I never saw her again. I don't think she ever had those affairs in college, either, do you? She just wanted to let me think she had so I could feel guilty about being such a lousy role model. I heard she had a pretty nice boyfriend just before her accident.

But I guess you know more about all that than I do, with your research and all. So, Mr. Macguire, I hope I helped you out with your book; just be sure to say what a great kid Sonny was, and yeh, what a good mother Belle was, and me? Don't write anything about me—it'll just ruin your book. Bye, now."

The dial tone brought me back to reality. I could hardly believe this nearly one-sided conversation had really taken place. I quickly added a few remarks to my notes, since I had missed some of his ramblings—even though I was writing as fast as I could. I was still in shock!

Well, trusted friend, what think you? I haven't told you nearly enough about that conversation but I'm exhausted and have to sleep now. I'll try to tell you more later on. By the time I show up for coffee at Charlie's, it will be eleven o'clock and they will all certainly think I have turned into a lazy lout since my retirement.

Good night kind friend.

HM

12 *Hate and Love*

Henry Macguire's research was coming full circle, now. Bona fide interviews and eye-witness accounts were beginning to provide him with many missing pieces of the puzzle. After speaking with Sonny's father, Daniel Adams, Henry was able to reconstruct a period of Sonny's life which had been, heretofore, missing.

Justified confusion ruled Sonny's life for an unbearable period of time, threatening her robust health and sanity.

After the shock wore off and the few close friends and relatives that were *"happy to help in any way"* had receded into the background, Sonny's shattered life became a series of unpleasant and unsuccessful public school terms, peppered with cool and uncomfortable visits to a few distant relatives on her father's side. Her grandparents were aging prematurely—due to poor health—and she barely knew her cousins. Her mother had been an orphan with only distant foster parents making up her extended family, so Sonny was left with very few viable options.

The fourteen-year-old really had no choice but to spend the next four years in her father's custody—hardly in his company. They had so little in common and were often irritable and uncomfortable in each other's presence. After all, visits to her father had pretty much ended by the time she was seven or eight years old. She barely knew him.

In retrospect, visitation was strictly adhered to immediately following the bitter divorce; there were festive holiday visits, special birthday parties, and at least one extended vacation period. By the time Sonny was seven, the novelty had worn off and subsequent time spent with her father became strained and boring—leaving one or both of them testy and itching to end the visit. Daniel's young daughter may have been a bright and intuitive child, but she couldn't be expected to understand what was going on in his head during that period.

The truth was that Daniel Adams had unexpectedly fallen out of the inner circle and was distracted and worried about his career.

By the age of eight, Sonny could sense the change in his life style but was too young to understand what was going on. He obsessed over his ever-changing girlfriends and whined continuously about his latest job. In general he had become boorish and boring.

It appeared that Daniel's successful career and active social life had consistently declined in direct proportion to Belle's fresh and promising ascent toward stability and independence. His personal life was in shambles; he had another failed marriage behind him before Sonny turned nine, and job opportunities "dried up" as soon as he applied.

In the ensuing years, while his wife and daughter were enjoying relative peace and prosperity, Daniel had lost many of his friends, most of his money, and all traces of the dignity he once proudly possessed. By 1981, Daniel's downward spiral was complete—hastened by the addition of alcohol, depression and paranoia.

Suddenly, to further complicate his situation, he was called upon to welcome his grieving, fourteen-year-old daughter into his *so-called life* under the most unthinkable circumstances—her mother's untimely death. Things could not be worse.

With Belle gone, he was hardly prepared to take on the guidance of the youngster whose well-being had been placed squarely on his shoulders. True to form, he dodged his obligations with abandon; during the day, Sonny was in the hands of teachers and counselors, while most evenings found her in the company of sitter-companions—often themselves teenagers.

Sonny couldn't begin to process what was happening; she neither understood nor cared what her father was up to. She simply reached into her deep reservoir of fortitude and sank quietly into her private world; a world which up until now, she had only allowed her sweet mother, Belle, to enter. She wouldn't dare make room for anyone else—especially Daniel Adams.

Moody and alarmingly prone to periods of self-inflicted isolation and cool silence, Sonny Peterson Adams was grew more reclusive with each passing day. She had few close friends and spent most of her time alone or arguing with her father in his comfortable, two-bedroom, well-furnished apartment in a fine area of Boston.

Daniel Adams might have been a drunk and nearly broke, but he always made sure he lived in the right part of town—*de rigueur* for the upper middle-class childhood he had grown up in.

To Sonny, comfort was not necessarily a precursor to happiness. She was obsessed with the memories of her mother and the more she thought of her, the less she liked her father. With a desperate need to place blame on someone for her deep sadness and growing unhappiness, Daniel Adams became the proverbial sitting duck—the object of her misplaced anger.

Resentment and obsessive privacy increasingly overshadowed the cheerful smile that had been Sonny's calling card since infancy. Now, it was only a matter of time before Carena Peterson Adams would sink into a serious depression and remain there until she left her father's house to attend college. For the time being, she was trapped in dark despair and loneliness—except for the time she spent in long recollections of life—as she once knew it—with her mother.

Sonny, never comfortable discussing her problems with her father or teachers, adopted the habit of writing pain-filled verses to assuage her intense emotional state. This practice allowed her to look deep into her spirit and slowly make progress in understanding her life shattering grief.

Aimless and bored, the youngster finally reached her eighteenth birthday, having had more than the usual number of highs and lows—her father and a few of her teachers being the only adult witnesses to the *unremarkable* development of a *remarkable* young woman.

Belle had taken great pains to set up a small trust fund for her daughter which was increased considerably by an insurance policy from the publishing house. Upon her death, friends and colleagues had rushed to set up a memorial education fund to be administered by a trustee selected by the board of directors of Scribe & Sons. At nineteen, the memorial account, Belle's trust fund, and the ample insurance policy—all having been carefully invested by Scribe & Son—allowed Carena Peterson Adams to declare herself financially independent of her father.

Daniel Adams breathed a sigh of relief and congratulated his daughter on her new status. He had known about her trust fund and investments and even wished he had access to them a few times, but as both fate and fortune would have it, he never had a chance at touching her money. Trusted friends, advisors, and accountants at S&S Publishing would remain vigilant when it came to this special minor's account. They later said it was a fine testimony to Belle's foresight; *or a premonition of her early demise.*

After Sonny graduated high school, she dipped into that fund and with little enthusiasm and enrolled in a small local college with no career plans whatsoever. With her father's help, she quietly moved into the dorm on a cool fall morning. Upon nodding a "thank you" she closed the door in his face and never looked back.

Daniel Adams had driven away, confused, discouraged, and disgusted over the lousy job he had done as a single parent for the last four-and-a-half years. He begrudgingly concluded that Bell had been light-years ahead of him in parenting.

He went over and over his last conversation with Sonny until tears spilled onto his ashen cheeks. He recalled how he had knocked on his only child's door the night before she was to leave for school.

"Who is it?"

That pissed him off. "Who do you think it is? It's your father."

"What do you want, Dad?"

"Can I come in to see how you're coming along? I'd like to talk to you."

Without waiting for an answer Dan Adams opened the door gently and stepped into the neat, girlish room. He winced at the memory of her arrival a little over four years ago as a frightened and grief-stricken child. Broken—the only way he could describe her as he looked back at that period. She had insisted upon bringing her own bedding, curtains, and towels. He was offended at first; having erroneously assumed that she would easily slip into the guestroom and into his way of life, but Sonny was not going to make things easy; not for him, not for herself, not for anyone. She had hysterically insisted that he make arrangements to empty his ex-wife's apartment and transport everything to storage—painstakingly packed and marked—as she was unwilling to part with anything of her mother's. Then, as a final insult, she had asked for the key to the storage unit.

She spent the first three months holed up in her room, every day after school—brooding, doing homework and talking on the telephone to a few trusted friends. Her conversations with her father were brief and to the point. That hadn't changed in the last four years and suddenly the two strangers faced each other on the eve of Sonny's departure for college.

He cleared his throat and started with, "Sonny, I know things haven't always been terrific between us, but I've done my..."

"Forget it Dad," she said with a tight smile; then she seemed to reconsider. Shaking her head she smiled in irony before the floodgates opened and the pent-up youngster exploded.

"No, wait a minute, don't forget it. You're right; things haven't been that terrific between us. As a matter of fact, nothing has *ever* been terrific between us, has it? You are supposed to be my father!   What the hell did you do, forget that little responsibility along the way? Really, Dad, what the hell have you *ever* done to make me happy? When was the last time you went out of your way for me? This has been going on since I was a kid.

Let me tell you something: When you cheated on Mom, you cheated on me, too. You know what I mean? When you left Mom, you left me, too, right? But just remember one thing: I'm the one who *lost* Mom! Not you. You threw her away. I *lost* her!"

It was quiet for a moment. Daniel was silent, but not Sonny. She was shouting at him now. "Did it ever occur to you that I might miss her, or even be lonely? Probably not; everything has always had to revolve around you—never me! First it was *your* job; then it was *your* girlfriends and then *your* new ex-wife. What is it now Dad? Feel sad because you're losing *your* little girl? Sorry to inform you, but you lost me a long time ago!"

Maintaining her composure, she stepped across the room to the tiny bathroom and, never forgetting those impeccable manners, she whispered, "Excuse me, please." and closed the door behind her.

Daniel thought he heard her crying softly but, as usual, he was without any resources to cope with such an emotionally charged situation; he couldn't think of anything to say or do that might be of any help. He walked out of her room and closed the door gently behind him. Careful not to make a sound, he fixed himself a drink in the little kitchen, totally unaware that the sound of the ice cube tray never escaped Sonny's acute hearing—not in the past and certainly not this night.

The next day Sonny did not come out of her room until noon. She had finished her packing, tidied up her room, and made a few phone calls; only then she opened her door—signaling her readiness to depart. Her father was to drive her to the dorm and carry a few heavy items up to her room for her. He was shocked at her paleness. She seemed on the verge of tears but Sonny Adams would never let that happen—not now. Any sign of weakness might be interpreted as a betrayal of loyalty to her mother. The tears would come later, in the privacy of her dorm room.

"Want some juice?"

"No, thank you."

"Well, okay, then, let's get going; I imagine there will be a lot of traffic around there today."

As he drove home Daniel Adams had a sick feeling that from this moment on, his life would be long and lonely. Sonny was probably gone forever. He was *almost* right.

That night, weeping bitter tears in a strange bed, Sonny Adams accepted the possibility that she might never see her father again. She made a firm resolution to carry on with courage and dignity—as her mother would have wanted her to.

Her college years had been nothing to write home about—had there had been someone to write to. She was an average student; bored at times, though usually cooperative and efficient. She had the usual number of boyfriends—some more exciting than others—but overall, surrendering her virginity had been no big deal. Without her sweet mother to share life's milestones with, she just took them as they came with no fanfare.

After her graduation, which she did not attend, Sunny visited her paternal grandparents for a few days and then Belle's foster parents, the Cranes; she spent only a week with them before quickly returning to the city to look for a new unfurnished apartment away from the campus area.

She had planned to stay with the Cranes for two weeks but felt strangely out of place. They were kind and gentle, but they had never really gotten over Belle's departure for the big city or her youthful marriage and subsequent divorce. Now, since her death, they missed her desperately on a daily basis—hour to hour and moment to moment. As a matter of fact, in a morbid and grief-stricken way, they assuaged their sorrow by talking about her incessantly. It made Sonny so anxious and depressed that she manufactured an excuse for an early exit, promising to visit them again soon.

Getting a job after graduation seemed the natural thing to do although Sonny never felt uncomfortably pressured to do so. She had never been a struggling student, desperately trying to make ends meet—the administrators of her trust fund had seen to that. Even after five years of college her funds were still intact. The stock market had been kind to her.

Though financially stable, Sonny remained very discreet and modest about her assets. Two accountants from Scribe & Son had continued to manage her already wisely invested portfolio that provided her with funds for many material comforts and complete peace of mind. Her money was safe. It was the big eighties—*what's-his-name* was president, and *dollar* was king.

Replacing her trendy college wardrobe with smart expensive clothes, she drove a leased, newer model car and confidently carried major credit cards—never ceasing to live by the same commandments her mother had lived by: "Don't buy what you can't pay for in thirty days and *never* borrow money from friends or relatives—*that's what banks are for!*"

Sonny had learned, early on, to act on the advice of her accountants—they *usually* knew best. At the age of twenty-four, she accepted her good fortune with grace and humility while secretly thanking her mother, nightly, as she prayed for her departed soul.

In her search for an apartment away from the campus area, she was drawn toward the same little community in which she had spent many happy years as a child with her beloved mother. Through a discreet friend, she learned of an apartment that was soon to be vacant and within weeks she was comfortably settled in the lovely bachelor apartment in an upscale and secure neighborhood of Boston. She took many of her mother's beautiful pieces of furniture and china out of storage and arranged them elegantly in her new surroundings. The miniature oak dining room table and the glittering set of crystal goblets brought tears to her eyes, but she knew Belle would have wanted her to use them joyfully. She would—some day.

Having completed her liberal arts education in five mediocre years, Miss Carena Peterson Abrams settled for a somewhat average job at Scribe & Son publishing house, working for a colleague of her mother's.

From all appearances it seemed that slowly, but surely, Sonny Adams' life was developing into a stable and contented existence. After five months on the job, she began to enjoy the company of a few new friends—accepting an occasional dinner and movie invitation from one or two suitable young men.

To widen her circle of acquaintances and keep herself fit, she joined an adult class at a local dance academy. Exercise and careful eating had always contributed to her fine figure and beautiful skin—she intended to keep them that way.

After a few warm and friendly dates, Sonny Adams began a quiet but romantically adequate relationship with a young man whom she had met at work. It was low keyed; *don't jump into anything too intense or demanding* the little voice in her head had whispered. He was kind and reserved—far from the *Knight* she had always imagined—but in any event, he was a caring companion. If he was slightly lacking in spontaneity or excitement, Sonny made up for it with her infectious sense of humor and unexpected bouts of giggling.

The young couple loved books, music, and privacy—spending spending several nights a week dining and listening to music in Sonny's luxurious apartment. Seemingly well matched and content in each other's company, they had both agreed to take it very slow and the relationship progressed without incident for several months.

Strangely, just as the relationship was on the verge of deepening, a change occurred; the young man seemed to be slipping into remote and silent moods that alerted and alarmed Sonny. Trying hard to block it out of her mind, she chalked it up to her overly sensitive nature. In a lapse of sensible judgment, she ignored the "red flag" and dismissed the creeping suspicion of *another woman.*

As the weeks passed she increased her efforts to be more devoted to Scott—now growing moodier with each day and less aware of her growing needs. She began to panic, doubling her efforts at the dance academy—working harder to appear more attractive and energetic. She just *couldn't* let this relationship go down the drain; losing him might easily send her spinning into a devilish blue mood that could take weeks to crawl out of.

It had been almost a decade since Belle's death and Sonny felt the loss more than ever in times of need. Any unguarded remembrance could still throw her into a dark bout of grief that resided just below the surface of her consciousness and could still reappear uninvited with a sudden fury. Now, under pressure to keep their wobbling relationship fresh and romantic, Sonny knew she was going to have to do most of the work;

certainly she would have to avoid burdening him with any of her emotional challenges.

She reflected on the two other relationships she had had—immature college boys that had left her empty and disappointed. Blaming herself for being *too much* for them, she had backed off quietly. At twenty, she had been looking for approval and the kind of intimacy and devotion that is rare in college affairs; now she had a glimmer of hope that she might find fulfillment in her relationship with Scott. *So, what was going on, she wondered.*

His name was *Scott Macguire*. He was different than any man Sonny had ever dated. Though moodily quiet, he could be comforting and pleasantly protective at times—especially when he allowed his guard to drop. In those unguarded moments, warmth and affection flowed through his veins and Sonny responded enthusiastically.

When he talked about himself, it was always in a brooding, self-deprecating, manner; Sonny worried about that and tried hard to dissuade him from such negativity. Whatever his faults might be, she felt herself tumbling helter-skelter into deep trust and possible love with this quiet, slightly unpredictable young man— whom she wished she knew more about.

Susan Harris, a young, single mother with very little family of her own had performed the arduous and sometimes lonely task of raising her only child, Scott. While trying to hold down one low-paying job after another she took him to a number of day care centers she could ill-afford. When the bill escalated to a danger point she would withdraw him, promising to pay it as soon as possible; inevitably she would enroll him in another center where she was not known and, there, repeat the exercise.

Late one night, in a surprisingly open and melancholy mood, Scott had reflected on his school years with great embarrassment. In barely a whisper, he unburdened himself to Sonny.

"I knew I was not like the other kids. My clothes were dirty, I needed a bath more often than not, and my mother never attended any of my school functions. I was about seven years old before I became aware of the cause of her radical behavior and physical inertia. I began to take notice of the empty liquor bottles topping the open trashcan in the curtained cabinet below the sink. So this was the enemy! God, I'm still amazed that at such a young age I instinctively knew that I had to insulate my inner self and shield my outer body from the unsavory by-products of my mother's addiction. I shut it all out—the empty bottles, the boyfriends, and the rest of the rubbish that came with it."

Scott stopped and took a sip of wine from the crystal goblet and returned it to the tiny marble coaster.

He shrugged his shoulders and said, "The next thing I knew I had fallen into puberty and was speeding towards a dreaded four years of high school. By that time I was practically on my own, though it never occurred to me to quit school. Somewhere along the way I had developed an attachment to the thrilling escapism of reading and writing and school was the one place where I could indulge myself in the newly-discovered passion."

By the time he had reached his senior year, it was no surprise that Scott Macguire had become a classic loner. He entertained dark thoughts of hatred towards his classmates and passed his days with little interest in extra-curricular activities or anything else going on around him. Never impressed with the giddiness of teen-aged girls, he avoided being in their presence whenever possible. It was difficult at times since he was occasionally the target of embarrassing *crushes*; which he fought with a vengeance—narrowly escaping—red-faced and embarrassed.

Popular and sought after high school sports activities annoyed him to no end.

"I would have rather eaten glass than play contact sports—all that grunting and spitting!"

Sonny had burst out laughing at that remark as they fell into each other's arms giggling out of control.

As Scott remembered it, by the age of seventeen, books and television were his only companions. By that time, his mother had allowed him to pretty much run his own life—as long as he didn't cause her any trouble. It was a delicate partnership: he would stay out of her way and she would provide him with a roof over his head and throw in a micro waved dinner now and then. It seemed fair enough to him.

As luck would have it, his developing passion for reading and writing had not gone unnoticed by his English teacher. Scott recalled, with fondness, that Miss Polly was the one person who seemed to care about him; at the rebellious age of seventeen, he found it quite bizarre that *anyone* could care about him or his interests. (He had already come to accept himself as a common societal reject—without purpose or talent.) At the end of the semester she handed him a leather-covered pocket notebook and encouraged him to continue his experimental writing and voracious reading. Without even saying, "thank you," he took the gift *and* her advice.

Scott Macguire's mother was only mildly surprised when he announced, with little fanfare, that he had enrolled in Metro College and was expected to report for the fall semester following his graduation. Miss Polly had assisted him with all the necessary preparations and financial aid forms—which Susan had signed without question or knowledge of their content. For the first time in his short life, Scott thought he had a faint clue as to what the hell he was going to do with the rest of his life and he liked the way that felt.

Occasionally, Susan offered her only son fifty dollars which she would deprecatingly say she had received from *him*—that was how she referred to his father, Henry. He usually mumbled a polite thank you and never entertained a stray thought of what the hell Henry Macguire was even like. He had no desire to open that crusted wound—not now and more likely never.

If the poor youngster had had any desire to know *anything* about Henry, he would have learned where his love of writing and reading came from; if he had only asked, surely, his mother—drunk or not—would have told him of his father's sullenly private nature and deep desire to be alone. In the face of unintentional deprivation, the youngster withdrew deeper into himself, becoming chillingly private and coldly insulated from the outside world—a safe existence he had no intention of changing at the tender age of eighteen.

The first thing he did was secure a job as a dishwasher at an Irish Pub just outside the perimeter of the campus. He worked from four to eight, Monday through Friday, earning a few dollars for transportation and incidentals. He was rewarded with a hot meal at the end of his shift, after which he worked another two hours hauling trash and doing odd jobs for old Duffy, the owner. At ten p.m., he hopped a bus or walked home. Routinely, he nodded to his mother, took a lukewarm shower, and did his homework until he fell into an exhausted sleep—usually after midnight.

Silently morphing from boy to man, he efficiently completed all the requirements for his graduation and found a job in the inventory department at a small but prestigious publishing house. He loved being around books and working alone—the job afforded him both. It was also a tremendous relief for him to finally take leave of his dishwashing duties at the Pub.

He had biked, walked, run, and rode the buses to the city campus for the last four years as his mother looked on impassively. She never questioned him about his part-time job, college work, or girls—all of which he considered to be of a very personal and private nature.

Like his father, shutting people out was in his genes.

He couldn't recall actually saying good-bye to his mother, but he remembered taking his few possessions and moving into a tiny studio apartment within walking distance of his new job.

Six months later he made the acquaintance of the quiet and beautiful Sonny Adams.

Scott Macguire and Sonny Peterson Adams seemed to be moving forward slowly but steadily in their quest to become mature and loving partners. By the time they were in the eleventh month of their relationship these two young people were unquestionably committed to each other, yet opting to live independently in their respective apartments. They continued to enjoy many of the same forms of entertainment yet jealously guarded their free time to pursue other interests and hobbies.

As time passed, the young couple recognized and respected the wide difference in their financial status and mutually agreed that a certain degree of danger lay in the financially lopsided relationship. Scott was of the opinion that too many material possessions could easily come between them; Sonny held fast to the lifestyle she was accustomed to—never flaunting or imposing her desire or need for the finer things in life.

All in all, to Sonny, theirs was a deep and touching relationship that she had come to rely on and there were times when she even thought she might not be able to survive without Scott in her life. He had become her lifeline to emotional normalcy and healthy passion. By any measure, she was completely in love with him.

To Scott, the relationship was at a standstill.

To close observers—it was already doomed.

She should have seen it coming but, on the contrary, Sonny was blindsided when in late June, right after her twenty-sixth birthday, the sixteen-month old relationship that once felt so right was in ruins. It was 1993 and heartache loomed ominously.

Given his quiet nature, one of Scott's independent activities had been to spend some of his free time at a reading room for Christian Scientists; it was in that quiet setting that he had met a young woman who approached him in a forward but friendly manner several times. It seemed they had a mutual friend who was determined that they become acquainted. This strange woman was attractive and carefree, quickly bringing out a lighthearted side of Scott that he hadn't realized he possessed.

His time with Sonny was, more often than not, reflective and brooding—hardly ebullient or filled with the sudden surprises that belong to young lovers.

Within ten days, Scott Macguire's new friendship literally exploded into a passionate, rollicking, relationship that left him reeling. His soft and sensitive side hated to hurt Sonny, but he wasn't made of the toughness that it took to support her during the frequent dark days she suffered.

"Sonny," he had said in his familiar half whisper, "Won't you just *try* to understand that this has nothing to do with you, personally? Please stop being so hard on yourself! There is no fault here; it *just happened.*"

She had responded bitterly to his assertion that it had nothing to do with her. Painful, heartbreaking questions tumbled from her quivering lips.

"Of course it does, you idiot! It has everything to do with me! What are you thinking? How can you be so heartless? What have I ever done to hurt or disappoint you? Can't we give it another try? Please? Can you at least think about it?"

He had answered quite simply. "No."

So now Sonny was back to square one. Sad, alone, and deeply disappointed, she fought debilitating anxiety. It had taken a few panic-filled days to get control of her emotions; days during which she was forced to summon steely courage just to report for work. Fully aware of rumors, unfurling like thick, black, smoke throughout the buzzing office; Sonny held her head up high and smiled, deflecting pathetic smiles and knowing nods from concerned colleagues.

Three weeks had passed and the unexpected ordeal had left her deeply pensive and depressed; she needed to get away from the office and its rampant gossip. On a whim, weeks before Scott had left her hanging by a thread, she had decided to keep the cottage open a little longer—maybe until the end of September. She thought they might enjoy some crisp, cool weekends together before closing up for the winter.

The ever-enchanting cottage represented one part of Sonny's life that she had refused to part with—much less share with anyone other than Scott. Often, in the past—against the advice of friends—she stubbornly fled to its comforting silence and sweet privacy, returning refreshed and focused early Monday morning. In spite of its remoteness and nostalgic history, she had spent countless peaceful weeks and weekends at the cottage, quietly passing the time writing, reading, and working through the endless confusion and disappointments of the last few years.

It was a cool Friday leading up to Labor Day and she left work an hour early to avoid the rush traffic and get to the island before dark. Concerned co-workers warned her against going to the cottage alone, so late in the season.

"It's so spooky there late at night," one of the girls, Carrie, had protested; but Sonny had a surprising urgency in her voice as she tilted her head sideways and said, "I have to go! Don't worry; there will be plenty of people around for the last week-end of the summer. I'll be closing my place up soon, anyway, you know? I just have to go! I'll be fine! Might even stay a few extra days; I have plenty of unused time."

She checked her desk over—which was unnecessary since it was always in meticulous order—placed the plastic dust cover over her bulky word processer, carefully smoothing out the creases and centering it *just so*. Finally she pushed her chair beneath her desk, once again, being careful to center it perfectly. This was Sonny, *the perfectionist*, at her best. She looked around the office a bit wistfully, deliberately avoiding any eye contact and with a light-hearted flutter of waving to those still sitting at their desks, she said, " Good-bye now, I'm off."

13 *Green Velvet*

By eight-thirty, she was curled up on her beloved velvet cushioned window seat; the one that had always been her favorite "thinking place" where she could solve problems or make weighty decisions. This particular evening, Sonny Adams relaxed, closed her eyes and rapidly descended into a reverie of her childhood. She found herself willingly reconsidering and even re-inventing certain events that had deeply impacted her young life.

First, she thought of her father and could barely remember the time when she had loved him so—jumping into his arms to smother his face with kisses as he entered a room. Now all she could retrieve were memories of the pain he had recklessly inflicted upon her when he shattered her snug family life by insisting on a divorce from her mother. That was the first dark cloud to visit the sunny skies of Carena Peterson Adams' perfect world.

She was almost four years old. Lying in her tiny, pink-quilted, bed, she clutched her orchid teddy bear tightly; she could hear raised voices—very surprising, since her parents were rarely given to loud arguments or harsh accusations. This night they indulged in both. The next day everything seemed normal—the child blamed it all on a bad dream and gave it little more thought.

A week later, her mother had arrived at her pre-school precisely at one p.m., red-eyed and quiet. Sonny had instinctively known enough not to chatter too much during their customary fast-food lunch.

It was on the way home that Belle had broke the news quietly—her emotions tightly suppressed—bravely answering the usual questions unsuspecting children ask.

"Did we do something bad to make daddy send us away? Where are we going? Is Daddy going away too?"

Belle's answers were fragmented and full of anguish as she released the flow of bitter tears she had been holding in for weeks. She drove to the nearby park where they walked in painful silence for an hour, Sonny holding onto her mother's hand tightly—as if she might lose her. She thought it must be the most dreadful day of her life, but then she was only four years old and it probably was.

As far as Belle was concerned, there had been other dreadful days in *her* life and she had no doubt there would be more.

Still curled up in the window seat, Sonny squeezed her head between her long slim hands and tried as hard as she could to conger up at least one pleasant memory connected with her father; finally a hazy scene began to take shape. It was a fall walk she had taken with him during a September visit to her grandparents' small country home outside the bustling city of Boston. It might have been shortly before the separation took place. With her tiny hand firmly tucked in his they had walked along a leaf-scattered path, stopping occasionally while he pointed to colorful leaves, wild fall flowers, tiny acorns, and a sweet, resting ladybug. He spoke quietly about things she did not and could not grasp; instead of listening, she skipped and hummed to dispel his serious mood, cleverly creating her own atmosphere of joy.

Daniel had never been good at making small talk and this was no exception.

It was only now, twenty-two years later, in this intensely reflective mood, that Sonny realized that he had been trying to say goodbye to her. He was struggling to explain that it was over between him and Belle, but he would always love this precious child of his. Unfortunately he lacked the ability to bring such a serious concept down to her five-year-old level. His attempt was inadequate, at best, and he eventually let the topic go and turned his attention to something more cheerful. In that fleeting moment the seriousness of the conversation was diffused and forever left unacknowledged.

Now, at the age of twenty-six, Sonny, slightly disorientated and pained by her memories, picked up her little silver pencil and pad that rested on the coffee table and jotted down a few words for her diary. She described her father's cold and futile efforts and the chilling effect they had had on her.

"At best, it was inadequate. In reality it was disastrous."

A month later her father had sent her a memento of that quiet walk; it arrived in a delicately framed, glass-covered shadow box. Neatly pinned under the glass, lay a few dried purple flowers, two perfectly shaped maple leaves, and a tiny plastic lady bug. There, in the simple blue frame, was represented everything her father ever meant to her. She had kept the strange gift in a "treasure box", stored under her bed for several years—never understanding the real meaning of it. Once, when she was ten years old, she carelessly tossed a heavy book into the box, accidentally smashing the glass. Pausing for only a few seconds, she pushed the box back under her bed and never thought about it again—until this night of all nights.

Today, shifting nervously on the green velvet cushion, Sonny reached deep into her soul to try to understand and forgive her father. She had to love him. She had to forgive him. As far as she was concerned, all else paled in comparison to the resolution of this fleeting moment in her life. She nodded her head; yes, she still loved her father—deeply—only now, it was a too-late discovery and a more painful goodbye.

It was Saturday morning and the rising sun found Sonny pale and exhausted from a long night of self-examination and recrimination. She had been warned not to go to the cottage alone; a few close friends noted how these lonely weekend visits, though often refreshing and energizing, lately, left a lingering scent of depression.

The previous night, sleepless, she had blamed herself for every fault and failing she could possibly think of, generously accepting the pain as some sort of private punishment that she felt she deserved, though she hardly understood why. That soul-searching marathon had lasted from Friday evening to early Saturday morning. Her only diversion was a driving rain that had strained the rusty gutters until they overflowed with tiny waterfalls cascading noisily down the hastily closed windows on the North side of the cottage.

There had been one memorable rainstorm—the one on her thirteenth birthday—when she and her mother had cuddled on the window seat for hours, waiting for the rain to stop so they could run down the stairs to the crescent beach and pick up the first of the new shells that had washed up on the sand. They would always creep softly to avoid sending the baby crabs scurrying. On one of their searches, Belle stepped on a sharp shell that inflicted a deep gash on her right foot. She was forced to lean on her daughter's shoulder all the way back to the cottage and ended up having to stay off her feet for two full days after seeing the island doctor.

The child had loved the role reversal.

She laughingly imitated her mother saying in a gentle little voice, "All right now, Mom, get off that foot; I'll do the dishes". And then with stern authority, "I mean it Mom!"

Belle in turn had mimicked her daughter with, "Okay, okay! I'm going!"

How little they knew that the time of a more serious role reversal awaited them.

Sonny had always chosen the window seat for the view of the gulls circling over the sharp cliff that dropped down to the crescent-shaped beach. One morning she had asked her mother, "What do those large birds eat when they are hungry?" She was saddened to hear that they swooped down and plucked out the innocent fish that swam too close to the surface of the water. She was glad she could not see what went on below the cliff.

And now, as an adult, she still sat at that special panoramic window with the green tufted velvet seat that, as a child, she had picked at, leaving several bare spots. She and her mother had, together, selected the fabric the second summer of Belle' tenure on the island. Now, after all these years, green velvet still worked a special magic for her.

It had been a fun project for them that summer; after Sonny's school term had ended and things had quieted down for Belle at the busy publishing house, they had spent a whole Saturday picking out the fabric and looking through magazines for ideas. They had browsed the little shops, giggling at a man that wore a large red turban wrapped around his head and carried a little puppy, hilariously dressed as a ballerina. All afternoon they had people-watched while munching on caramel popcorn and giggling.

"Do you think anyone is looking at us and laughing at our frizzy red hair and freckled arms?"

"It's very possible, Sonny; very possible. Perhaps we better stop."

In a rapture all their own, they whiled away their first two-week vacation in a state of self-induced euphoria, creating memory after memory. They sunbathed, read, sang songs, and went wading into the surf after lunch, though never very far— neither of them swam well and both had a serious fear of the ocean.

They both ate little—often tossing part of their lunch sandwiches to the busy gulls in order to save room for ice-cream.

In the late afternoons while Sonny played hopscotch on the tiny concrete pad reserved for the station wagon, Belle kept a protective eye on her while she lovingly measured, cut, pinned, and finally sewed the green velvet fabric, readying it to cover the window seat cushions.

Sonny recollected her squealing reaction when she rose one morning to find the window seat covered with the beautiful fabric. She couldn't believe her eyes.

Now she caressed the soft, worn, pillows again; she could almost smell the new fabric as it mixed with her mother's distinctive hand lotion.

If only she could think clearly. Maybe she would change her mind. In desperation she surrendered herself up to sleep.

14 *The Cranes*

April 15, 1996

It's a depressing day my Kind Friend.

I say depressing because it's tax day; the day the money grabbing IRS celebrates with great jubilation—thanks to the hard-working masses of Middle America. I guess that includes me because I surely will be making my way to the US Post Office to mail my donation before this day ends. To tell the truth, I really don't care much about money anymore. I have a little more than I used to have and a lot more than I need; I hope it will go to good use someday, after I'm gone. *That may be sooner than later—we'll see.*

So now, let me bring you up to date on the latest breakthrough I've had for my book. Sounds strange to be calling it *my book*; for so long I have only thought of it as a manuscript—always in progress—but that's what it finally has become. A real book! Soon I hope! I'm rambling, aren't I? More like stalling, but here goes.

I've been up in Sunapee, New Hampshire, for the last couple of days. I took a speedy trip up there to visit the Cranes—Belle Adams's foster parents. By the way, they called me a week ago and invited me—I would have never intruded on them uninvited; maybe in my younger days I might have—but not anymore. I have mellowed, I guess. Anyway, I had written to them several months ago and it took them all this time to respond to my request for an interview; now, I understand why.

They looked so much older than I thought they would and seemed to be in pretty rough health—Mr. Crane more so than his wife. When I arrived, Cora Crane greeted me with a cautious smile and opened the door before I had a chance to knock. I had spotted her peeking out from behind pale blue curtains as I got out of the car. My heart leapt! As I entered the narrow hallway I truly hoped I hadn't made a mistake. Maybe it would be too much for them. She was bent over and walked with a slight limp as she led me into a small, dimly-lit, parlor that made me wonder why on earth anyone would shut out a beautiful, sun-washed April day. Then I saw why: Mr. Crane was in the darkest corner of the room, seated in a wheelchair. He wore dark glasses and I swiftly deducted that he had some kind of trouble with his eyes. A fringed plaid blanket was draped over his lap—one leg suspended beneath it. I nodded and shook his hand, mumbling my condolences about his obvious poor health. He didn't speak and I wondered if he even could—he might have suffered a stroke along with his other obviously debilitating ailments.

I sat on the edge of a large stuffed armchair and as I looked across the room, I came face to face with three large photos of Belle; there she was, staring out at me from dusty oval frames. She might have been ten, twelve, fourteen, or something like that. I was struck with a terrible sadness of not having known her in those days.

Mrs. Crane broke the silence with an offer of something to drink and I said I would be pleased to have a cup of coffee if it wasn't too much trouble. While she was out of the room preparing the coffee, I looked over at Mr. Crane; I couldn't tell if he was looking at me or not, so I proceeded straight ahead with, "So this is where Belle grew up, sir?" He nodded just enough for me to catch the acknowledgement.

"Nice little house you have here; bet it was a fine place to raise a youngster."

Mrs. Crane entered the room with the coffee and responded to my statement. "Belle had a wonderful time growing up here; she loved to run around the yard, climb trees, and swim in the *crick*. She had lots of friends from school coming around to play with her all the time. Everyone loved her red hair; it came with a good fiery temper, too, you know, but she was never unkind or inclined to hurt anyone."

Mrs. Crane seemed unable to keep herself from talking—even to catch her breath.

"Belle was a fine girl and a good hard worker by the time she was twelve; she even used to mow the big lawn for Jim and help me around the house, cleaning and such. She sang a lot; did you know she could sing? She also was a terrific reader. Oh yes, my how she could read...she drifted for a moment then looked away and added wistfully, "My sweet Lord, how we loved her!"

Jim nodded silently, as if to agree with her. I wished he could speak; he looked like he might have been a real interesting guy to talk to—not that Mrs. Crane wasn't. It's just, I don't know. I don't know why I'm even writing about that.

I hated to break their reverie, but I cut in with, "Do you know much about Belle's life prior to her placement with you and Mr. Crane? I mean did the social service people fill you in pretty much?"

"Of course they did; we knew everything there was to know before she came! It wasn't anything illegal, you know." Cora seemed somewhat indignant at the question. "What is it you're looking for? I mean she didn't do something wrong before her death? Did she? Or is it about her daughter? Or should I say our granddaughter? You know we never got to know Sonny very well; when she was small she was reserved and stuck pretty close to her mother, and later on—especially after the divorce—well you know how kids are. Poor things—I remember when Belle called to tell me about the break-up; they both cried over the telephone. I don't know, I guess I just never understood about those things—probably wasn't much help.

About Belle's death; I mean after getting sick and all—she was taken so quickly we hardly knew what happened. Then Sonny came and we only had a short time with her before she was whisked off to stay with her father. She visited us after her college graduation and we had only a week with her before she said she had to go. Now tell me, what were the chances of that youngster dying so young? You know all about that right? What's wrong, Mr. Macguire, what is it you're after?"

"Nothing, no nothing, Mrs. Crane, nothing is wrong. My apologies, if I've alarmed you in any way."

I knew right then and there I couldn't tell them about the details of their granddaughter's death. If they were under the impression that she had died accidently, I thought it best to let it be. I just hoped they wouldn't read my book.

I continued with, "Someone that had worked with Sonny had the ridiculous impression that Belle had had a sad childhood—trouble of some sort. Something about being taken from her mother as a toddler and reared by an *old maid* aunt. Can you fill me in on any of that information? I hope this isn't too hard on you; just tell me to stop if it's too much. You see, I'm writing a few chapters in my book about Belle and Sonny; but I'll understand if you don't want to talk about it. You see you're not the only ones that loved Belle; a lot of people did. *Even some people who never met her have come to love her.* You might not understand that statement, right now, but maybe someday you will."

Both of the Cranes acknowledged my explanation.

I stayed for dinner that night and, afterwards, Cora showed me where Belle had slept as a child; a little corner room with a single bed and an old fashioned *high boy* with a matching night table with a little lamp sitting atop it. My heart leapt and—I swear—new confusion threatened my sanity.

"Sometimes I sleep in here when Jim is having a really bad night. On those nights I think of Belle until the sun rises and Jim stirs."

"Yes, I can imagine that you would."

Later in the evening I walked around the yard and down the street while Cora helped Jim settle into bed for the night—having declined my offer to help. Afterward, I returned to the little parlor to sit with Cora.

It was just beginning to grow dark when Mrs. Crane, speaking in a soft and sentimental whisper, described Belle's early childhood to me—as she knew it. Young Belle had told her of those five forgettable years with her Aunt Beebe. I didn't have to ask many questions; Mrs. Crane was pretty thorough and sure of herself, too. Marvelous head for details! I could hardly wait to get back to the Inn and get them on paper!

It was close to ten o'clock when I left the Crane house, promising to stop by the next day to say good-bye. I wanted to express my gratitude with a little gift of some sort. I had taken a room at a little place down the road and I thought I would pick up a box of candy and a bunch of flowers the next morning. Well you probably already guessed what followed; I never went back. I started writing as soon as I got to my room and when it got light out, I simply got in my car and headed back to *Puckshaw*—my safe harbor. Wasn't that just like me? I guess I'll never change. I'll be in touch, soon.

Good day, friend.

HM

15 *Aunt Beebe*

That night—after leaving the Crane residence with a promise of returning the next day—Henry returned to his motel in a frenzied state. He had to write; it was all right there in his head, just screaming to get out. Cora Crane had given him what he needed to describe this period in young Belle's life.

Another important piece of the puzzle!

He wrote about Aunt Beebe all night. He no longer carried his typewriter around; it was cumbersome and noisy for the other guests when he was staying in a small Inn and wanted to work all night. That night he was like an artist painting a picture on a blank canvas, giving each detail that Cora Crane had lovingly shared with him its own place and color. When the canvas in his mind was covered with every color of the spectrum, Henry was finished; the pages of his notebook overflowed with his unbridled attention to every detail and suddenly he was exhausted. He looked out the motel window and saw the sun rising. He had the urge to escape with his new knowledge of Belle's childhood before someone tried to steal it from him. Thinking irrationally—he fled.

On the drive back to *Puckshaw* he knew what he would add to his manuscript, regarding Aunt Beebe. Deep down, he knew what Bell would *want* him to write in regard to that mind-numbing period of her life. As he drove, he pictured his newly acquired information as it occurred—according to Cora Crane—in its own time and place.

****

A bright sunny day was just coming to an end as Belle sat on the front porch at Cora and Jim Crane's lovely little cape. She had yearned for her very own porch when she was a child, living with Aunt Beebe; now, close to her eighteenth birthday, she sat with unrestrained joy, shouting "hello" to passing neighbors while tossing bread cubes to a pair of sparrows twittering at her feet.

"Fifteen minutes 'til dinner Belle, dear," Cora Crane called out from the kitchen. "Better get washed up!"

"Yes mummy, in a minute."

Belle closed her eyes tightly and carefully prodded her memory to recall her childhood for just a moment. At this particularly inviting introspection she felt compelled to compare the drab five years she had spent with Aunt Beebe to the wonderful ten years she had lived in the loving care of Cora and Jim Crane.

Although Belle Peterson had never been formally adopted by Cora and Jim Crane, she considered herself lucky to have lived with the same foster family from her eighth birthday to her now approaching eighteenth milestone. She hadn't been able to recall one fond memory of her childhood before her arrival at the home of the Cranes, having never been able to forget that brief, stomach-churning period of her youth preceding the *rescue*. Her memory was flooded with pain. Buried deeply in the creases of her consciousness, Belle, often without reason, deliberately summoned the pain.

Much too young to actually remember being removed from her mother's care as a toddler, Belle had been told the story of neglect several times by a stern maiden aunt—Beebe Cummings—who became her guardian for close to five stultifying years. Beebe was her birth mother's older sister and the only surviving relative of the small Cummings family. She had sneeringly informed the child, on her fifth birthday, that her birth certificate, now lost, showed that her father's surname was Peterson. No, she had no idea who or where he was.

Aunt Beebe lived in a small one and a half story cape on the outskirts of a *typical* New England town where everybody—seemingly—minded their own business. No questions were asked, but eyebrows could be raised in unison at the drop of a hat—should the situation call for it. It was the kind of town that was filled with people who nodded rather than smiled and preferred a grunt in place of a greeting. Most of the people that Belle could remember seemed to walk with their heads held high and their noses pointing even higher. To these morally upright and god-fearing citizens, the less fortunate were considered as non-persons—routinely patronized and made to feel insignificant.

Young Belle's sharp eye and quick mind took note that she was often treated as one of the less fortunate.

Technically speaking, Belle's new environment *could* have been described as stable; sparse, safe, joyless, and adequate—not a bad place to be as far as *Madam Social Worker* could gather. Her investigation indicated that this distant relative, known as Beebe Cummings, could easily provide all the necessities for "the poor child"—with the aid of a monthly stipend to assist her in the pursuit of such a "selfless act of charity". When it came to the final disposition of Belle Peterson's case, the judge's opinion stated that, "the placement of this abandoned child, with her very own blood relative, was truly *a stroke of genius* on the part of the Department of Social Services for Children!"

Belle's haunting recollections of the stoic and bizarre standards to which she had been held would someday cause her to suspect—even challenge—the sanity of the judge, *Madam Social Worker,* and *all* adults in general; why shouldn't she?

Her new surroundings were neat, sparsely furnished and efficient—a reflection of Beebe's own character.

The kitchen—used exclusively for cooking and eating—was painted completely white and devoid of all trim or decorative knick-knacks. Large squares of white and black tile covered the floor which was religiously scrubbed every Saturday afternoon.

During the week, once meals were over, the eating area was immediately cleared of all signs of life; dishes washed, floor swept, and any scrap of trash taken out to the large can behind the tiny tool shed. There was no sitting around the kitchen table with cookies and milk or drawing pictures and telling funny stories—not in a world inhabited by Beebe Cumming!

The cheaply carpeted sitting room housed a large oak desk which young Belle was allowed to sit at only when reading or doing homework as Beebe read the daily paper by the fading light of a small window, keeping one eye on the child's progress. *Occasionally,* the stuffy little room was used for watching television—if the program was deemed "worth watching". The room was nothing like the cheerful dens of Belle's school chums; casually comfortable rooms in which they watched television, ate cookies, and played games—all while doing homework!

There was *one* room in the non-descript cape that Beebe Cummings fiercely guarded with secret pride; it was her small parlor, conveniently located to the left of the front hall entrance. Bright with sunlight during the morning hours, it boasted a faded flowered loveseat, one worn winged-back chair, and Beebe's treasured coffee table which was faithfully dusted and polished every Saturday. The window panes gleamed above wide marble sills that bore colorful china saucers—each with a different potted plant sullenly struggling to stay alive. Beebe pampered her "glum little friends" and was even heard whispering words of encouragement now and then.

The parlor was her *special* room; it was only to be used for entertaining rare visitors—the *church ladies* or *Madam Social Worker.* The room was never to be entered without permission, as Belle discovered when she had aimlessly walked into it, one day, to gaze out the front windows.. Beebe had charged in behind her, delivering a near-hysterical tongue lashing and a stern warning to "stay out of the room in the future—unless invited."

Belle's favorite room was the mud room, where she could kick off her boots, fling her coat on the bench and drop her school books on the floor. That was the one room Aunt Beebe turned a blind eye to; apparently, in her infinite wisdom, she saw the need for one little corner of the house where a child could act with abandon. Belle never understood why it was called a mud room; she once laughingly told Cora Crane that she had never seen a *speck* of dirt in that room; as a matter of fact, in that house.

Belle had spent hours daydreaming about having a front porch where adults sat and relaxed, talking through the evening, and drinking lemonade while their children ran about the yard, screeching and playing tag. It was truly just a daydream since Beebe Cummings scoffed at neighbors who enjoyed such an evening of chatter, laughter, or watching their children at play; she considered it a waste of time and an exercise in frivolity, at best.

Keeping all of Aunt Beebe's commandments in mind, Belle steadily adapted to the strangely stoic environment with forced enthusiasm while going about her daily routine without complaints or questions.

Beebe made sure the child was provided with a regimen of healthy foods, in substantial amounts, and taught her, in detail, the basics of good hygiene and good manners. Plenty of rest every night was a must and each morning, clean and pressed clothing was placed on the chair next to her single bed, ready to be donned and worn without vanity, to and from school.

From all appearances, one might assume that Bellemara Peterson was well cared for and lucky to be where she was. If, by some chance, the child *was* in need, she cleverly concealed it behind her mysterious blue eyes and curly red bangs.

Beebe Cummings was so full of confidence that all the material needs of the child were being met that she never felt the slightest obligation to provide any other sign of support or affection.

Whenever anyone asked her how her "new charge" was coming along, she would put on a brave face and solemnly assert, "I'm doing my very best."

More than a few onlookers commended her in her new status as *aunt extraordinaire* when in reality they found her to be irritating and pompous at times.

Belle could not recall a single instance when her aunt ever laughed out loud; although she did see a few suppressed smiles when the mailman, in an effort to get a rise out of her, would deliberately call her "Phoebe" instead of "Beebe".

On any given sunny day, when the village was alive with buzzing bees and flowers brilliantly bathing in the sunlight, a child might be tricked into assuming that the whole world was happy. Just then, Aunt Beebe would greet Belle with a dark frown and a quick nod of her head with its frizzy fringe of fiery orange hair. Her greetings were more like commands. "Good morning," meant it *better* be a good morning and "good night" really meant "go to bed without another word, young lady".

Belle obediently accepted her situation with all its restrictions; after all, it was not as though she were being beaten or deprived of a roof over her head. She had convinced herself that she was actually lucky—regardless of the absence of any sign, whatsoever, of affection. In fact, her aunt often declared with tear-filled eyes, that "any child would be very *lucky* to be in *your* shoes!"

All in all, Beebe had taught Belle well: "You've got to make the best of what you get!" The child took that maxim to the bank, time and time again, as an adult.

The unquestioning child lived in a house that was devoid of all compliments, lest they be undeserved or lead to *vanity*—the most *serious of all flaws.* Unable to grasp the true meaning of the word "vanity"; Belle reasoned, with some maturity, that it was better not to be complimented then to be *seriously flawed.*

Then there was that word "calamity"—she never knew exactly what that word meant, but Aunt Beebe was always saying she hoped the Lord wouldn't *rain down another calamity* upon her "already burdened" shoulders.

Through a child's eyes, God could be a very revengeful Being and rain could be a very dangerous act of nature. Whenever it started to rain, Belle would quickly make her way into the house, lest a *calamity* came raining down on her little red head.

She had once confided to Cora Crane—with fresh pain and embarrassment—that as a third-grader, she had run home with a blue satin ribbon pinned to her dress for her fine reading performance; Aunt Beebe had greeted the news with, "Hmm. Now go quickly—put that away before you get a big head."

The beaming child had hoped to put it on the refrigerator, like she had seen her friends do, but that was not to be. Instead, she was consumed with worry that she might get a big head and how she would look with one. She ran directly to the bathroom mirror to make sure Aunt Beebe hadn't cast a curse upon her. Studying her image critically, she concluded she had narrowly escaped a *calamity* and ran to put the ribbon under her bed where it wouldn't be seen.

The impassive orphan came to accept, as fact, that there would be no "pretty little girl" compliments extended to her. She had learned that she neither deserved nor needed them and could live very well without them. To this gentle and oft-silent child, life was just like a quiet rainy day: *dreary, but no harm done.*

Based on Aunt Beebe's strident rules concerning school, Belle had come to believe that education was a most serious undertaking—never to be neglected.

"Thou shalt not miss school," was Beebe Cumming's first commandment and Belle secretly believed that would probably be followed by, "Thou shalt not ask questions." In any event, everything else paled in importance to attending school. Belle was taught to read before she went to kindergarten. It was the old-fashion method of "listen, point to the word, sound it out, and repeat after me". No frills, no thrills, and no pat on the back. Teachers and classmates were very impressed, but not Aunt Beebe; excellence was the rule—not the exception.

Sunday attendance at church services was a challenging exercise in discipline as Belle recalled the demanding task of sitting still and looking pious. She understood little of what was going on, yet she was fully aware of an awe-filled presence which hovered over the breast-beating, God-fearing parishioners, as they knelt with heads bowed in deep prayer. She did eventually learn to sit, kneel, stand, and bow, with lightening speed, in the proper and demanding sequence. Aunt Beebe was impressed with that fete and had rewarded her with a terrible looking bonnet with a scratchy black bow that tied under her chin.

"Here Bellemara, wear it this Sunday. And don't go running to the mirror now."

Was the hat really a reward? When it came from Aunt Beebe, no child could ever be sure.

Belle could still remember her stunned reaction when they stopped going to church and her attendance at Sunday school was suddenly curtailed. Not a word of explanation! She seemed to think it happened about the same time Aunt Beebe's *friend,* Charles, came for a lengthy visit. All during that time, the drapes were kept drawn while *Charlie* slept on the sofa for hours at a time. Belle was served a proper dinner but, now, ate alone. When dishes were done, she was sent to bed early most nights to read or do homework. Gloom and isolation ruled her ever shrinking world.

Well into her teen years, Belle Peterson shared another shattering event with Cora Crane.

****

The day started out as any ordinary one would have. Breakfast with Aunt Beebe was fine. Quiet, but fine. School went well and the walk home was fun until the last block, when her friends turned into their respective driveways, hooping and howling with excitement and Belle silently approached the dull cape with its little mud room door ajar. She pushed the door open, put her books on the bench, and kicked her shoes off. Nothing seemed amiss.

As she entered the kitchen through the swinging door, half expecting to greet Beebe and throw a quick glance toward Charlie, half asleep on the sofa, she was surprisingly met by a roomful of icy adults—all shaking their heads and peering into her eyes with pathetic nods. With utter disbelief, she concluded from the disjointed explanations from several persons talking at once, that Aunt Beebe had run away—yes run away—leaving no instructions or forwarding address!

Not one adult had thought to hug the child or take her into their arms and reassure her that all would be well.

Thoughtfully, Beebe had called a few "church ladies" and the school principal after gaining a good running start. They would help decide what was to be done about the child's care as soon as *Madam Social Worker* could get there.

Belle was deadly calm and drew on her training from Aunt Beebe to remain cool and stoic about the whole thing. After all, she thought to herself, they can't blame *me* for it; I haven't done anything wrong and I wasn't even here when she ran away. What could they do, arrest me? I'm only seven going on eight!

No one thought to ask her if she knew anybody that she could call or if there was a single soul that might come to stay with her until things could be worked out. Certainly she would have told them how much she liked the young women with the flowing red hair who *used* to come to play with her once in a while when she was younger. She would always kiss her before she left, leaving behind the strange odor that reminded her of the rubbing alcohol that Aunt Beebe used on her sore shoulder.

She hadn't been around in years and the child could barely remember her face clearly. She never knew—or couldn't remember—the red-haired lady's name, but recalled with a warm thrill that the women had always called her "honeybun"—not Belle or Bellmara, but "honeybun". There would inevitably be a shouting match between Beebe and the *nice lady* and, more often than not, the visit would end in door slamming and name-calling—*names a child could not and should not understand the meaning of.*

The morning of Belle's eighth birthday arrived and three days had passed since Aunt Beebe had gone away. She had spent the last two nights at the home of one of the "church ladies"—very solicitous without being condescending, as Belle recalled.

A *new,* pretty, brown-haired social worker was there early that morning with a small birthday present for her. *Things had changed.* While she was opening it, Belle received the *good news* that she was going to meet some nice people by the name of Mr. and Mrs. Crane; sighing audibly she thought to herself, *great—another happy home for Belle!*

She had mastered the art of cynicism, thanks to Aunt Beebe.

The young social worker drove steadily for at least two hours, making cheerful conversation all the way; it was a kind effort to dispel Belle's gloom. She offered to stop for a little lunch but Belle declined politely, explaining she didn't think she could eat anything—not before meeting the new people called "Mr. and Mrs. Crane".

They arrived in the small town of Sunapee, New Hampshire, and drove immediately to a medium sized farm house with a lovely porch and three wide steps leading up to the front door. With a little plaid bag in her hand—a gift from the church ladies—Belle climbed up the stairs and stood resignedly, with her arms hanging limply at her sides and her little feet, in brown scuffed shoes, shuffling with nervousness. She waited, dutifully, while the young social worker rang the bell.

The unavoidable drama had filled her with such dread that her stomach had responded with a loud gurgle—announcing her urgent need. "Do you think they'll let me use the restroom?"

****

Now in their late thirties, the Cranes turned out to be a gentle couple who had been trying to adopt a Caucasian, infant female for several years—albeit unsuccessfully. Finally convinced that it was a good move for them, they applied for a foster child and were quickly offered an eight-year-old abandoned child.

Adoringly freckle-faced, with bright-blue eyes and red unruly hair, Belle Peterson was their best chance for a child and they were grateful to have her. Although she was almost grown—they had hoped for an infant—they accepted the reality that she was the closest they would come to their dream of having a child of their own. They welcomed her with open arms.

The shower of affection was a perfect panacea for the loneliness and emotional neglect Belle had endured for almost five years. Once awakened, the bubbly, warm nature that had been buried deep within her for so long exploded in sweet relief. It was exciting to be happy and *free* to laugh out loud!

Cora Crane was a little hesitant at first; she had always thought she would start out with an infant and have plenty of time to bond and grow into motherhood, instead, she was an instant parent to an eight-year-old. Good-naturedly, she took the bull by the horns and began by teaching Belle how to make muffins, fudge, and apple pie. What Cora was too shy to put into words she put into action, showing plenty of support and good humor.

As far as spiritual matters were concerned, Cora taught the child by example: kindness, respect, and compassion toward others with complete faith in the "powers above". And that was how Belle learned to tend to matters of the soul.

On the other hand, with little effort, Jim Crane was a natural father; he taught Belle how to mow the lawn and wield a paintbrush with the accuracy of an artist. He even allowed her to help him refinish some old pieces of furniture, plying her with compliments that filled her with new confidence. *Good-bye vanity—the most serious of flaws. Hello, self-esteem.*

Together they trooped through the woods, Jim carefully pointing out poison ivy, poison oak, and other harmful plants and bugs. He'd jump out from behind a tree and present Belle with a giant sunflower, just to see her face break into unabashed surprise.

She knew it pleased him.

"She's a good Buddy," Jim would say proudly to the neighbors.

Belle knew within the first few days that her stay with the Cranes would not be a repeat of those achingly-dull, stultifying years that she had spent with Aunt Beebe; her new lightheartedness was testimony enough to that truth. She was the center of their grace and favor and the happy threesome, all of whom obviously took pure delight in each other's company, thrived. Nothing else mattered.

As the years passed, technicalities prevented the Cranes from formally adopting their beloved foster child. The young red-haired woman—whom Belle believed was her birth mother—seemed to have vanished without a trace. The Social Workers had no idea *who* she was or *where* she was and did not have the resources to pursue the case. Obviously, the child in question was safe, healthy, and happy and the Cranes would "just have to be content with the *status quo*".

Belle often wished she remembered more or knew someone who could tell her about those first three years of her life, but that would never come to pass.

In spite of the insensitivities she had endured at the hands of an imperfect and sometimes culpable system, she happily remained in the foster care of the Cranes until she reached the age of eighteen. She considered it to be her good fortune not to have been shuttled around from family to family like other abandoned children she had heard of.

As fortune smiled on Belle Peterson, she passed from childhood into young womanhood with ease and joy—gently guided, fiercely protected, and profoundly loved. She was happy—very happy—but at the age of seventeen she was filled with a natural yearning to seek out her birth mother and father—if they were anywhere to be found. She was convinced that her mother was the red-haired lady that used to visit her when she was a child; after all, she hadn't failed to notice her own hair—the same deep shade of red—not orange, like Aunt Beebe's. There was a secret contentment knowing that she bore some physical resemblance to her (probable) birth mother.

She pleaded with the Cranes to allow her to return to the small New England town that she knew as a child. Beebe's neighbors and friends *must have known* the story behind her arrival as a toddler—they knew everything else. They would have asked questions back then—that's how they were. Perhaps a loose tongue might furnish a clue as to whether or not her suspected birth mother had other children. Maybe Aunt Beebe was back and would be willing to give her some information now that she was almost an adult. She also wondered if anyone had *ever* heard Aunt Beebe talk about her *father*. Maybe one of the "know-it-all church ladies" could shed some light. In any event, Belle was determined to find out who she was.

The Cranes were reluctant and feared she was making a big mistake—perhaps even letting herself in for serious disappointment and heartbreak. After serious thought, they relented and generously supported her in making the necessary arrangements to visit the town of her childhood. The Cranes were wise; they knew if they wanted to keep her in their lives, they would first have to let her go.

Belle clearly remembered the tiny village in the Township of Coleman; it was called *Whitehorse*. The large white sign that welcomed one upon entering the village often haunted her dreams; the place was hardly welcoming as she recalled.

Jim Crane accompanied the youngster just in case she ran into any difficulties, but discreetly remained at the motel when Belle drove off in the family car to reacquaint herself with the landmarks of her early youth.

She was amazed at the way the town had not changed over the years. Everything was eerily the same—as though the town, itself, was unaware of the passage of time. A few villagers remembered her and the mysterious circumstances under which Beebe Cummings had fled, leaving her *poor niece* behind in the hands of strangers.

"No, nobody remembers where you came from when you first arrived to live with your Aunt Beebe; you appeared right out of thin air!"

Belle mentioned the name "Charles" to one of the now aging "church ladies".

"Yes, her departure probably had *something* to do with him".

They were all *very* polite and *very* sorry. "After all, Miss, it was *so long ago*".

At the end of the day, the last villager that Belle politely called on was the mother of one of her best friends in Kindergarten who *"just barely"* remembered the foster child. She was cool and uncooperative. *"Ask me no questions and ..."*

The search was short and unsuccessful and the distraught teen fled to the motel to sob in the comforting arms of her father.

Jim, relieved, and Belle, deeply saddened, promptly returned to Cora Crane's anxious embrace. Filled with remorse for the anguish and pain she had caused the two people she so loved, Belle begged their forgiveness.

Shortly after the empty search for her birth parents, the youngster came to a mature realization: The Cranes *were her real parents* and she would love and respect them for the rest of her life.

16 *Love and Marriage*

At eighteen, Belle was formally released from the foster care system. It was no secret that Jim and Cora Crane hoped she would stay close to home and further her education, but she had other ideas; the wide-eyed youngster wanted to strike out on her own and see what Boston was all about. The magazine pictures of the bustling city had filled her with wanderlust and she was anxious to spread her wings. It wasn't a matter of not loving or appreciating the Cranes—she adored them—but it was almost 1963—a wondrous and exhilarating time to be eighteen and independent. Young Bellemara Peterson didn't plan to miss a thing!

Like a true fairy-tale, the sweet, simple girl met an older, attractive man and fell headlong into an incredible mismatch. After one year they were rewarded for their passion with the arrival of a lovely child. Belle had insisted they call her Carena Peterson Adams, then immediately nick-named her "Sonny", for her bright smile and sparkling eyes. After four years and some infidelity on both sides, the loving couple earned a bonus—a bitter divorce.

They never had a chance. Their passion for one another had been explosive and satisfying but they were light years apart in education and background. They were soon cast as the star-crossed lovers in a hopeless marital situation.

Belle had been the "new girl in town"—working part-time and taking a few night classes—when, through mutual friends, she met Daniel at a casual mixer. She was impressed with his *grand attitude* and obvious experience in the *grown-up* world. He was nothing like anyone she had ever met and she openly admitted to a "mad crush" on him.

Ten years her senior and besotted with her youthful adoration, Daniel thought, in time, she would make a great partner—if only she possessed a little more experience and sophistication.

"It would be great if she understood the mechanics of belonging to the "upper middle class," Daniel had confided to a friend at his club."

"Be careful, my friend; be careful. I mean it!"

Ignoring the warning signs, Daniel declared that there were times he was completely enchanted with her small town upbringing and *charming naiveté*. He was sure he could make it work.

He had been playing the field for almost ten years. Weary of the hunt, Daniel Adams was ready for a family and a stay-at-home wife who would provide him with the usual creature comforts when he returned from his arduous day at the marketing firm's office; he decided to take *la grande plonge*.

On the contrary, to be tied down in a serious affair so soon after gaining her independence conflicted with Belle Peterson's overall plan. It was her inexperience with men and a deep longing for her own natural family that had propelled her, blindly, into a premature and passionate affair with Daniel Adams.

Less than a year after a proverbial whirlwind courtship, the overwhelmed couple sealed their magnetic attraction towards one other with a lovely wedding attended by the Cranes, a few of Belle's friends from Sunapee, and an overwhelmingly lopsided number of Daniel's blue-blooded friends and relatives. Observers noted that at least ninety per cent of the guests were the groom's invitees.

In her *charming naiveté*, Belle had no idea how the wedding was paid for; she had begged Cora Crane to make her wedding dress, gratefully accepting it in lieu of a wedding gift. The Cranes were very leery of the rapid turn of events, but too respectful to interfere in her life now; she would soon be twenty years old. They attended the wedding—keeping a very low profile among so many sophisticated and prestigious guests—and wished Belle and Daniel a long, happy life together.

During the first year, life seemed good for the deliriously happy couple and no one was surprised by the blessed arrival of their beloved daughter, Carena—twelve months later.

Belle was a devoted mother and wife, but as time passed a hint of boredom and gnawing regret over her lack of education and social standing began to tarnish the sparkle of the much ballyhooed union. Belle secretly wished she had kept in contact with her old friends—at least, renewed some of the acquaintances that she so missed;, but a new husband, quickly followed by a new baby, kept her very busy—too busy to take time out for old friends or hobbies. When she did have a few hours to herself and called a friend on short notice, they usually had plans, saying regretfully, "Let's get together real soon, Belle; we sure miss you!"

The new wife and mother faithfully wrote to Cora and Jim Crane every month, detailing her "marital bliss"; if the truth were told, her intense devotion to Sonny and Daniel was a façade she hid behind to convince *herself t*hat she was doing the things that made her *happy*.

Before long, Belle waivered; lonely and tired, she chalked her down days up to a bad case of the *blahs* and not getting out and about enough. She would be just fine, she assured herself.

The deterioration process was subtle. There were no big blow-ups or long separations, but Belle and her husband seemed to grow tired of the dullness that had surreptitiously crept into their marriage. As they became increasingly cool and polite toward one another, their relationship declined into suspicious silence. The third year of their marriage drew to a close and the cooling couple stiffly celebrated the anniversary with a quiet dinner at a nearby restaurant. Belle felt it was incumbent upon both of them to try to salvage the crumbling marriage and, that night, convinced Daniel to put forth a new effort to improve the situation. Weeks passed—nothing changed. Then, something *did* change.

It had been a foolish and disastrous experiment for Belle Adams to become involved with Sharon—the stunning thirty-something whom she had met at her health club. Disenchanted and disappointed with the state of her marriage, she welcomed the adult company of the "new friend with an outgoing spirit" who seemed to understand her situation so well.

"I've been through it myself; believe me, you *will* get over it," Sharon had said sympathetically, quietly soothing her apprehensions.

They used to joke about it at first, asking themselves why in the world they connived to escape from their husbands and children only to exhaust themselves by exercising for hours. Soon Belle took comfort in the humorous and confidential conversations she had with Sharon and anticipated her thrice-weekly visits to the exclusive health club with tingling excitement.

The sexual advances were so subtle and unexpected that by the time Belle found herself in a clearly compromising situation, she was both flattered and flustered. She didn't rebuff Sharon's advances toward her in the beginning, but quickly thereafter, she explained to her that it was not a suitable option for her; she felt guilty and wanted out of the now-disturbing relationship. Sharon understood and they parted as warm friends. *"Just a fluke," Sharon laughed; "fagettabout it!"*

That evening, with Sonny in bed they had shared a quiet dinner after which Belle—embarrassed and humiliated—confessed the affair to her husband, tearfully promising to make up for her foolish and hurtful behavior. She assured Daniel that it had all been very discreet and she was sure that nobody was the wiser for it. She vowed to be faithful in the future and rose to put her arms around him only to be rudely rebuffed.

Howling in disbelief and disgust, Daniel had pushed her away, openly shrinking from her touch.

"Not that androgynous bitch; I bet everyone knows by now! You've made a fool of me! I knew I should have never married you. They all said you weren't good enough for me and I guess they were right, weren't they? Well, I've got news for you; "I wasn't going to tell you about this, Belle, but I haven't exactly been a boy scout."

He angrily confessed that he, also filled with frustration over his marriage, had become involved with a woman from his office.

In view of his wife's shocking disclosure, he was convinced that he was being laughed at behind his back and wished to end the marriage as soon as possible.

Pale with shock, Belle pleaded with him to make one more effort for all three of them. Daniel gave in reluctantly, but after a few weeks they jointly agreed that the marriage was, for all intents and purposes, over and they should prepare for a separation.

Belle reflected that the short but thrilling courtship with an older, sophisticated man—clearly out of her league—and the arrival of a new baby—dangerously soon after their marriage—had actually prevented them from developing a substantive relationship. The bleeding marriage was irreparably damaged and Daniel was *adamant* about ending it.

The truth was that Daniel had overestimated Belle and she had not been of any help to him as far as his career was concerned. He could survive *that* error in judgment, but now he feared that her indiscreet behavior was sure to make the rounds of his social *and* business circles—threatening to become an ostracizing, career-ending blunder. Haunted by that possibility, he decided, purely in his best interest, to move on without her and concentrate on damage control. He considered the impact this would have on his daughter, but only for a moment; he had to look after himself..

The separation was emotionless and swift, leaving behind three wounded souls

17 *Decision*

Sonny stirred.

As expected, daybreak arrived with pomp. The warm, lemony sun was not unusual on a September day—not on *Puckshaw*. She made a final tortured effort to physically push away any lingering guilt by shaking her head back and forth. No. No. No! Nothing would deter her from her plan. The decision had been made with the precision of a mathematician—taking into consideration every detail that might in anyway jeopardize the act that would soon be played out with a final flourish.

It had been an easy decision that, once made, had filled her with relief. The Epiphany had struck several weeks ago in a small, deserted chapel on the island; it had taken less than an hour for Sonny to assess her life as having morphed into a series of robotic executions that left her limp with exhaustion and wanting in fulfillment. There seemed to be no respite in sight from the anger and pain that haunted her night and day, day and night. She thirsted for a way out.

In the semi-darkness of the tiny chapel, she had poured out her soul and begged for assistance in sorting things out. After a variety of setbacks, seemingly brought about by the destructive, self-designed guilt over her declining faith in God; Sonny had made a resolution to stop burdening herself with such unreasonable, overwhelming demands. She began immediately to shake off one guilty verdict after another, although there were some issues she could do nothing about.

Now that her loving and most satisfying relationship had ended badly, her life had been condensed into a series of difficult choices; choices that were void of peace or anything resembling happiness—choices that only brought more pain. She had one more decision to make and she made it swiftly and firmly.

Sonny Adams chose freedom from the hell she lived in; though it would come at a very high price.

Afterwards, a few friends and relatives were left speechless by the news, recalling the exciting plans she had for the future just a little over a year ago—plans that included her newfound love—Scott Macguire.

Fourteen months ago a benevolent God seemed to have smiled on her and life was coming together for her; she had a new apartment, a satisfying job, and a loving, sensitive boyfriend. Suddenly, it was in shambles; stunned colleagues were asking what the hell had gone wrong. The shockwaves of this event would be of no small consequence. Sonny had loved deeply and was loved in return by loyal, trusted friends and both sets of aging grandparents. Not a living soul who knew her could bear to see this sensitive young woman, with an already-painful past, endure another heart-ache

Without her soul mate—the only person ever allowed entrance to her innermost sanctum—her fragile psyche could no longer differentiate between love and hate. The fear of more pain and her deep desire to face it with courage had become intricately entwined, giving new birth to a deep sense of confusion and resentment—especially over the loss of so many of her loved ones.

One by one, they had all abandoned her; first her father—whom she had only recently come to understand—had recklessly taken his leave when she was only five; then her beloved mother, Belle, who rather than succumb to the treachery of a fiendish illness, had taken fate into her own hands and chosen the time and place of her death while Sonny was still a child; finally—the deepest cut of all—the love of her short life, Scott Macguire, had coldly ended their relationship with cruel finality.

For many years Sonny was convinced that after her mother's death, she never again would luxuriate in the unconditional love she had received during her youth, but after meeting Scott, she had been fooled into thinking that, yes, once again, she was loved wholeheartedly, without strings—as Belle had loved her. Now fate had swiftly and cruelly outsmarted her again—Scott Macguire was gone.

Just in the last few years, Sonny had made great strides in putting to rest many of her childhood resentments with respect to being the center of her mother's universe. She was a child and had acted like a child. Fearlessly possessive, she had refused to share Belle with anyone else. She had driven away adult colleagues and friends and made it nearly impossible for her mother to have male companionship of any kind. She regretted such selfish behavior now that she was adult and understood the complexities of adult companionship.

It was after Bell was gone for many years and Scott had come into her life that she finally began to recognize and establish her own *grown-up* identity and its inherent needs. Now she was on the verge of becoming a whole being—stripped and cleansed of the various layers of disillusionment, revenge, and guilt. It had been a difficult climb but today she was serene and her reconciliation was complete.

She came out of her reverie and glanced at the tiny gold watch she had received from the Cranes on her last birthday. She had seen them only once or twice a year in the last few years and wished that she had developed a closer relationship with them; sadly, there was nothing she could do about that now. *The time was at hand…*

She blinked with shock and acknowledged that twelve long hours had passed since she wrapped the soft quilt around her shoulders and curled up on the lush, green, velvet covered window seat. In those lonely hours she had witnessed a bloody sunset and listened mindlessly to yet another thundering rainstorm. Toward morning she half dozed through the lazy arrival of the island's famous lemony ball as it glared down upon the faded roof tiles and water stained clapboard—so characteristic of the cottages on that side of the island.

The frail, waif-like figure shifted her position slightly and curled her legs up beneath her as she experienced the final pleasure of gazing down the patchy driveway—the path to the barely visible stairs. She loved those stairs. Somewhat reluctant this time, she gave in to yet another excruciating reverie.

She was fourteen again.

She had sat like this a hundred times in the last days of her mother's illness; always in the early morning sun, while Belle was still sleeping, heavily drugged by the medication that allowed her the only relief she could expect, by then. They had been at the cottage since early April—gloom filling most days.

Sonny recalled the gray morning dream with crystal clarity; the incandescent spirit—a lithe, robe-clad figure shining brilliantly—gliding down the driveway toward the slippery stairs. In the distance, squawking gulls screamed for attention as a mournful, plaintive voice seem to cry out her name.

Covered with fear, the youngster remained entranced—motionless—staring out the window for at least an hour before rising to tiptoe into the kitchen and turn the kettle on for morning tea. Shaking her red curls and blinking her large blue eyes, she admitted to dozing off—having had a *spooky* dream.

By now tea was all that her beloved and weakened mother could tolerate. Making the best of any situation—as had always been their practice—they had courageously continued to enjoy the quiet morning ritual of breakfast tea. They would speak in soft voices, occasionally touching and smiling with their souls—as only those with the purest love and deepest understanding are allowed to. Sonny could still make out the beautifully sculptured face behind the pale mask that ultimately becomes the trademark of those afflicted with a terminal illness. She would often reach out to smooth her mother's hair and straighten the collar of her robe; it was a tender gesture that exposed the raw compassion and devotion she felt.

Though health workers came and went to bathe and care for Belle's personal needs, she saved her faint smiles and tiny nods to acknowledge her daughter's trusted and treasured presence. The two mysteriously picturesque figures sipped the herbal brew each morning—often without comment—Belle sitting up in bed and Sonny in the soft chair beside her.

For Belle, tea and tiny pieces of saltine crackers were followed by another dose of medicine and a slow shuffle around the perimeter of the cottage—weather permitting—before retreating back to bed for the rest of the morning. This profoundly sad routine did not strike her or her fourteen-year-old daughter as unusual—but rather something they looked forward to every morning.

On this particularly drab morning, Sonny did not go to her mother's bedroom after putting the kettle on low—as was her habit. Today she pulled a hooded sweatshirt over her head and stepped out into the cool mist—allowing Belle to sleep a little longer.

Silently slipping out the door, she stepped, barefooted, onto the driveway to make her way to the stairs that led through the damp tunnel and onto the beach. Faintly aware of the morning dew and the danger of slipping she grasped the railing and counted the stairs as she had done since childhood. "One, two, three…"

She struggled with her thoughts; why on earth was she going down to the beach at such an hour—all alone? She need not have asked that question—she knew the answer.

In the past, the crescent shaped beach had always been reserved for sunny walks well after breakfast and again after dinner, the noon sun being far too dangerous for the two fair-skinned, red-haired women. Today the youngster took the dreaded early morning walk because she had to. Her heart pounded, vibrating thunderously in her ears. One more step.

As Sonny stepped onto the cool sand, she looked first to her right where the three largest boulders stood guard over the tiny beach. Then, as if in slow motion, she turned to her left and was not at all surprised to see the tiny, crumpled, terry cloth robe on the sand. It was the robe that her mother customarily wore from the day they arrived at the cottage until the day they returned to the city, at which time she would switch to the simple black silk robe she wore in the luxury apartment they had lived in since Bell's last promotion.

Sonny walked toward the robe at a normal pace and dropped to her knees—without touching it. Then, as if to breathe in the familiar smell one last time, she picked it up and buried her face in it, weeping salty tears into the sweet-smelling fabric. She whispered a tender goodbye and rising quickly, hurried back to the cottage to silence the whistling tea kettle—before calling for help.

To a small number of people, the outcome of the investigation into the death of Belle Adams brought some comfort when the drowning was ruled as accidental—due to unintentional over-medicating; still, the same group of people were convinced that Belle had deliberately taken that last step, not only to end her own suffering, but to bring to a close the painful ordeal which was being visited upon her beloved and devoted daughter.

Sonny had barely understood or accepted either theory. Both she and her mother would suffer either way—whether Belle lived or died. Through a child's eyes, it was a situation without the slightest possibility of a favorable outcome.

As a mother, Belle had acted in her child's best interest, but the grieving fourteen-year old saw it as a betrayal of sorts; her beloved mother had *chosen* to leave her just like her father had.

Sonny Adams would struggle for the rest her life to forgive her mother for that selfish act.

18 *Farewell*

Jarred back to full alertness by the noisy gulls, the reality of the day struck anew and the seriousness of what she was about to do weighed heavily upon Carena Peterson Adams.

Today, for this particularly troubled young woman, bravery would have to come with ease in the early hours of the day, when few souls might be stirring on the remote island and the familiar gulls would be circling over the cliff, preparing to dive for their breakfast. The sweet coolness of the sand would cushion her bare feet and the sun would still be tolerable without a hat. These conditions were necessary because Sonny had no tolerance for the burning sand stinging the bottom of her feet or the hot sun scorching her fair skin and hair. Ironically, she would be pleased if the gulls would keep her company on this, her last journey.

In spite of the perfect conditions of the day, courage would still need to be summoned.

A sudden rush of unexpected joy seemed to wash over the tense young woman as she rose from the window seat and quickly walked to the smallest bedroom; she had slept in that room every night since her arrival at the summer cottage—except for an occasional night when, frightened by a loud rainstorm, she had crawled into bed with her mother.

Her room was brightly papered and curtained to match the spread covering the wicker double bed that had sustained years of gleeful, childish jumping; and in more recent times, passionate nights of love-making with Scott Macguire.

She was careful not to look in the direction of her mother's room which had been kept sacrosanct since her death twelve years ago, at the age of thirty-six. Even as an adult, when she would come to the cottage with her own young lovers, Sonny always occupied her own room to avoid offending her mother's memory in any way. She smiled at her prudishness in those matters; *had she been more practical, her mother's bedroom was larger and much more accommodating for two adults.*

Unbeknownst to her daughter, Belle had observed the same propriety when spending an occasional weekend at the cottage with a male companion while Sonny was on a camping trip or spending the weekend with a young friend. Belle always closed the door to her daughter's bedroom in order to protect and preserve her privacy. It was *off limits* and her guests knew it.

Now, Sonny automatically smoothed a single wrinkle on her quilt and lovingly ran her hand over the oft-dusted surface of her dresser as she passed it.

Gingerly, she stepped into the small bath across the hall without closing the door—a habit her mother had always teased her about. Standing before the oval mirror they had picked out at a nearby flea market, Sonny did not smile at her reflection, as was her habit—albeit a vain one that she was ashamed of. After scrubbing all the color from her cheeks and lips with a soft pink wash cloth, she lovingly removed her treasured rings, earrings, and the small gold watch of sentimental value, gently dropping them into her robe's deep pocket. She left only a tiny gold band on her right hand that had once belonged to her mother.

She vividly recalled her mother's appearance the last morning she had seen her alive—pale and unadorned—and she, too, chose to go to her own death with unpainted lips or adornment of any sort.

After taking a long look around the rest of the cottage she stepped resolutely onto the warm, grey porch. How many nights had she and her mother sat in the two-seated-swing rocking back and forth, making memory after memory? Now, barely holding back tears, her eyes fell on the little table that held a few small coasters and an outdoor candle. She rolled up her black velvet hair ribbon and placed it, along with her jewelry, on the delicately flowered china coaster—the same coaster that held cool drinks in summer and hot cocoa in early autumn.

Sonny could almost taste the stinging cold lemonade that her mother allowed her to sip while she read to her on hot, sticky days and the steaming mugs of hot chocolate they drank on chilly, fall nights. When she was a child, hot chocolate often made her sad, for it signaled the impending closing of the cottage for the long winter.

For years she had honored the closing rituals: fastening the shutters, rolling up the awning, and locking all the windows. This summer things had been different and too many lonely week-ends at the cottage had left her depressed and drained of all energy. Much of those long week-ends were spent sleeping or planning. After all, to be successful, the event had to be planned.

The tiny table that held the mementos was sturdy and shielded from the elements by a large green and white canvas awning. It was very important that these few personal belongings were found easily and perhaps given to a caring friend or two. Sonny Peterson Adams had nothing left to give to her aging grandparents or her semi-estranged father; they had suffered enough. At this point in her short life, a few close friends would need a memento to get through the shock and grief more than anyone else.

It had finally come to the defining moment.

There were no more conflicting recollections or untoward recriminations to be dealt with. This poor, bloodied soul, wounded in battle far too often, had finally rescued itself and returned to its pristine origin. Sonny was ready to leave the cottage. She would walk down the sun-cracked driveway, to the weather-beaten stairs that led to the foamy, September waves of the Atlantic, and there, life would be born again.

Leaving sharp and silent footprints in the cool sand, Sonny made her way slowly toward the edge of the rough surf. Unable to stop her teeth from chattering or her toes from cramping at the shock of the chilling water, she finally had a vision of herself as she really was—in all her strength and weakness—without lip color, velvet ribbons, or any other adornment.

It was the right thing to do. *It was the only thing to do*—give her body and soul up to the ocean's rough waves and demanding undertow. Soon she would fly freely as a gull, weaving in and out of the low cottony clouds.

"Oh my sweet mother, help me!" she cried.

Close to ecstasy now, she threw her arms open wide to greet the world as the morning sun seemed to dance in the blue sky before her. She wondered vainly, just for a moment, how she looked—though it really didn't matter.

The near-perfect human vessel continued to walk with a faint frown on her pale face—a sudden visit from uninvited fear. In that unfamiliar instant she was filled with overwhelming remorse and the deep cut this act would make on her few loyal friends. An uncontrolled sob rose from the back of her throat and escaped through her lips. It was loud and frightening. She grimaced—not having intended to cry.

She thought of her friends and hoped they would understand. She *knew* they would understand. Another sob rose, like vomit struggling to leave her body; she was momentarily distracted and physically disgusted by the sound it made. She closed her eyes and planted her feet, as if to affirm her intention. Slowly, a montage of faces unfolded before her tear-filled eyes; she saw the images of those she had loved and had loved her in return, especially her sweet mother, Belle, and the love of her short life—Scott Macguire. And this time, with finality, a loud, wrenching sob escaped.

Sucking in a deep breath, Sonny let the belt to her short, white, terrycloth robe fall into the shallow surf.

Just for a second it reminded her of a scene from a movie and the drama of the moment made her blush, though no one was watching. She stared with curiosity as her tiny belt was sucked into the rough foam, quickly disappearing before her eyes. Struggling to gather the strength and courage to meet the challenge of this frightening and defining moment she prayed to no one in particular and indulged in one final moment of vanity to wonder how she would look when they found her. She had not seen her mother's body until after the morticians had restored it to the best of their ability. Now she wondered who would find her—weep for her.

Someone would.

She stepped into the surf with bold determination, scrambling to get out much further than she had ever attempted to before. She was surprised at the speed with which her body was submerged, leaving just the crown of her red hair glowing under the glaring sun. When the salty water was up to her mouth, quickly causing her to gag, she bobbed up and down in a last effort to breathe.

She was compelled to act or abort.

The mysterious void loomed while she rejected her last mortal compromise and lunged forward to deliver her convulsing body into icy darkness. For a moment she waited, somewhat impatiently, for that flashing finale of forgiveness or the arrival of cherubic enlightenment. Then, like a shimmering dagger, a fleeting second of consciousness stabbed her and at the exact moment that the light left her wide-open and questioning, pale blue eyes, a massive, gray cloud passed before the morning's sun, casting the peaceful island, called *Puckshaw,* into deep confusion.

19 *Aftermath*

There was some fallout.

The New England Times ranted and raved *ad nauseum*, suggesting that a copycat syndrome could very well grip the island as it had the Mid-west, a few years back, when a bunch of kids had thought it *cool* to jump to their deaths in imitation of a young celebrity and her boyfriend. And yes, "wasn't it a shame that the young woman had no friends or relatives"? And so on and so forth...the copy was endless—most of it false.

The Boston Daily explored the "murder on a lonely beach" theme, suggesting a campaign to beef up security throughout the island. Just what it needed—"more law enforcement on the payroll!" the *Sunny Islander* had harrumphed. (Under Henry Macguire's by-line)

The Cape News, proclaiming "new inside information", reported the presence of a suicide note, replete with all the gory details. *"More to follow..."*

It all made good copy and sold papers—right or wrong—and the *Sunny Islander's* resident reporter covered the event with his usual unbridled search for the truth. There was the possibility of an eyewitness and even a suicide note pinned to a green velvet window seat. Henry continued to follow-up on his own time.

He would eventually accumulate enough information for several chapters in his autobiography.

The young victim's grandparents, the Cranes, politely refused all requests from the media, withholding any public statement or display of grief. They wished to be left alone, but since the victim's father was unable to be located and the Adams grandparents refused to speak to the media; the shy, rural couple continued to be hounded for more information.

A young unidentified man asked if he might have the black velvet ribbon that *Cape News* had painstakingly mentioned; he was told by a distantly cool attorney that there was no such item found. Such irony! The young man, himself, had recently given Sonny a card with three black velvet bows pinned to it; it was his last personal gift to her. He knew the black ribbon was neatly rolled up on the table in the corner of the front porch, next to the swing. He knew of its presence because he had been drawn to the front door, where a tiny light was left on the very night of her death. If only he had arrived five minutes sooner. Too late—inconsolably distressed—the young man had pounded his breast in a tearful *culpa*.

Scott Macguire and Sonny had not spoken since he had stopped to see her with a small, *"I'm sorry; can't we still be friends?"* gift. She was gracious but curt and left him standing in the lobby with, "Thank you for the gift, Scott, but I have to get back to work, now."

Two months later, on a Friday evening, he had received a telephone message from one of her co-workers that she had acted curiously strange and was heading out to the beach for the long week-end—alone; could he please check on her?

He had gone to bed around midnight and woke up at four o'clock in the morning feeling restless. Unable to shake the mood, he jumped out of bed and dressed quickly, while dialing the cottage phone. No answer. After making a quick cup of coffee he left for the island.

He drove carefully, as was his habit, and arrived shortly after dawn. Sensing some sort of danger was at hand, he ran up the two stairs to the front door, looked around and knocked. There was no answer. Without waiting he began to pound repeatedly. Frenzied, he moved quickly around the perimeter of the cottage, peering through the windows with a sinking feeling; it was obviously empty. Finding the back door of the cottage ajar set off the last of the peeling warning bells. Sonny would have never left it open.

After shouting her name several times through the partially open door, Scott spun around and headed to the nearby cliff that overlooked the roaring ocean; it wasn't likely, but just maybe she had gotten up early and was already on the beach watching one of her favorite things—a glorious sunrise.

It was almost six-thirty as the loan figure stood on the edge of the cliff and peered down at the tiny crescent beach so handsomely lit by a pale halo of the risen sun. With a sinking heart he saw her as if in a dream. Her naked form was moving slowly at first—gentle waves washing up against her waist; then before the young man could move or make a sound she disappeared into the surf and was gone. Only then he screamed out her name.

If only she had heard him.

Remaining motionless for several minutes, the stumbling shadow staggered to his car in anguish. He knew instinctively that it was too late; by the time he could get down the stairs and to the water she would be out at least thirty-five feet. He had always had a slight fear of the water and was a timid swimmer.

If the real reason was known, something deep within his sensitive soul demanded that he bow to Sonny's wishes—he owed her that much.

The dark and narrow beach road could be treacherous in the early morning mist. He drove slowly, blinking and shaking his head in confusion as tears of anguish splashed onto his cheeks and lips; for the first time in his adult life he felt utter remorse. Why had he treated Sonny Adams with such cold cruelty, giving in to his lust for Lila, an obviously less sensitive and caring individual? Why hadn't he given their relationship more time and effort? Why, why, why?

Twenty-four hours later it was leaked that there had been a lone witness that had seen the drowning shortly after dawn. The young man had come forward within hours—without a lawyer—giving a full statement, providing immediate identity of the suicide victim. The file on this case would be held confidential—as agreed—until the young man could leave the area without being hounded by the press.

There were some naysayers that didn't believe there was any truth in the witness rumor; after all, who in their right mind, would be wandering about such a remote cove at dawn? It was private and, in recent years, only the Adams women and their guests had been known to walk that particularly desolate strip of the beach.

Henry Macguire had been sticking close to the case from day one and had been to the police station dozens of times. He knew that sensitive information could be held for at least ninety days and was annoyed to get the same answer every time. "No Henry, nothing new."

He was being stalled and he wondered why.

He had continued to check in now and then and it was late in December, three months after Sonny Adams' suicide, when he dropped by the damp, cold station and asked the officer on duty if he could see the most recent file updates on the Adams case. He showed his I.D. and was shown to a tiny room with a desk and chair; while he waited, he told himself it was the last time he was coming by. This case was driving him crazy and enough was enough. And besides, they never seemed to have anything new on the case and he felt stupid for bothering them all the time. He was finally prepared to go out on his own and dig up the information he felt so compelled to be privy to, by now.

The officer came in with a file and asked Henry to sign a small card attached to it when he was through reading the latest report. He nodded his head and walked toward the window to catch the natural light and began reading the report. The hand-written account gave him a jolt of excitement that resembled a mild electric shock from a badly-wired socket. The police had finally made the mysterious witness's account part of the record and not one of his contacts from the station had even called him! He was annoyed, but shrugged it off.

The witness—an ex-boyfriend who had been alerted to Sonny's depression by her co-workers—was not a suspect. His record was as clean as a whistle and he had no known motive; just in the wrong place at the wrong time. How unfortunate. The account was brief and factual and was signed at the bottom.

Henry blinked. *He blinked again.* The neat signature at the bottom of the statement read *Scott Kelly Maguire.* He closed his eyes for a moment and let out a long, withering sigh. He straightened up on rubbery legs and stumbled out of the stifling room, stopping at the small desk just long enough to slide the report under the nose of the young officer who was struggling to stay awake.

So, that was why they had kept it from him; they were trying to protect the innocent kid and keep Henry—his father and lead reporter on the case—out of it.   He nodded in agreement—what else could they have done.

Henry Macguire walked out of the station ashen and weak-kneed—a broken man.

Scott had already left Boston and had been gone for weeks, having asked the police to protect his anonymity and keep his whereabouts confidential. In return he had given the police a full account of his relationship with Sonny, along with a surprisingly short list of her friends and relatives that should be contacted. The police knew where they could reach him if necessary and that was it.

It was the way the Macguire boy wanted it.

It was the way Cramer, the heart and soul of Puckshaw's law enforcement team, would handle it.

Henry drove to his cabin and sat in the driveway howling without restraint. He reminisced about his last visit with Scott and how he had fully intended to get back to Boston to spend some time with him and his girlfriend. Tears of shame spilled down his chalky face and he swallowed hard, pounding on the cluttered dashboard, sending maps and empty coffee cups flying.

He cursed the selfishness he was born with—the evil root of the estrangement between him and his son; how could he have let that happen?

Tonight, *Puckshaw* no longer held any enchantment for Henry Macguire. His spirit sagged and the gray clouds—too often hanging over the island these days—stood as grim reminders of his downward spiral. Filled with anger and frustration he sobbed in despair. He hated himself. He hated his life. And now—once unimaginable—Henry Macguire found himself seriously questioning his love for the enchanted isle of his dreams—Puckshaw.

20 *Lila*

Lila was ecstatic and tingling with anticipated passion as she packed her small overnight bag for a long weekend with Scott Macguire. She liked the privacy of his frugal studio apartment much more than the spacious flat she shared with her two roommates. His place was quiet and intimate—the perfect setting for what she had in mind for the next two days.

Tired from her long day at the dance academy, she would forget her aching body as soon as Scott walked through the door. She usually arrived at his apartment close to eight p.m., preceding him by an hour or so. She had offered to pick him up from work, but he had refused the offer explaining that he enjoyed the half-mile walk from Boston's small, prestigious publishing house called Scribe & Son.

On the other hand, Lila had grown up in rural New Hampshire and enjoyed driving her white Toyota for hours on end. She rarely walked anyplace. After spending long days on her feet at the dance studio, she could hardly wait to get into her car and randomly drive—the wind in her hair and the radio blasting.

She dialed Scott's number and entered his extension.

He came on the line with a quiet "Hi, Lila. What's up?"

"What shall I pick up for dinner tonight?" she asked him in her distinctive foggy, private school accent, "Thai or Mexican?"

"Anything will be alright with me."

"Okay. I'll choose," she purred.

(He knew she would choose, anyway.)

"Right, see you later."

"Okay, bye, Scott."

He was the type of guy who said little; contrarily, Lila Powers enjoyed talking on the phone endlessly and became irritated when he cut their talks short. Today, she chose to ignore his curt response for in just a few hours she would have him all to herself—serving her voracious sexual and emotional appetite.

She looked at herself in the mirror and stood sideways to admire her flat abdomen; then, shaking her head she let loose her wavy, auburn hair to tumble gracefully to her shoulders.

Perfectly aware of her stunning good looks, she turned with a flourish and, using her headboard as a ballet bar, stretched a long leg over it; she held it there for a moment, until it burned and then slowly and deliberately dropped her head forward to rest on her knee. It might strike an observer as painful, but Lila Powers lived by the rule of exercise; she relentlessly worked through pain and exhaustion almost every night, vigilant in protecting herself from leg cramps that might attack while she slept—especially after a long day on her feet. Recently, her job had become particularly brutal with the arrival of several new fall students.

There was no need for anyone to worry—Lila Powers loved her job at *Madam Cherie's Academy*. She taught ballet to what she called, "Gawky, geeky teens—ages fourteen to seventeen—little talent and less hope." Most of her colleagues considered that a cruel and uncalled for assessment of her students, but they would never think of telling her to her face.

Rumor had it that Lila had shown *some* promise as a mid-level professional dancer until a few years ago, when she was diagnosed with diabetes. Having been sidelined with the flu for five days and unable to bounce back completely, her dancing teachers and parents had insisted on some testing, after which they were shattered by the news that Lila would have to change her lifestyle.

There would be no more missed meals, long work days, or punishing schedules bordering on self-abuse. In the blink of an eye she was forced to think of herself as a *diabetic*. Given her decisive nature, she came to terms with that fact unhesitatingly—more than she could say for her teachers and parents.

Under her new regimen there would be little chance of a strenuous dance career in New York or Boston which would have included travel, missed meals, and irregular hours of rest.

After learning of the severity of her diabetic condition, it was out of the question; as it was, she could barely complete a full schedule of dance lessons and auditions

Lila quickly assessed the situation and got on with her life. It was the *nineties* and she planned to take advantage of every bit of medical technology available to her.

Less than two years later, without warning, she announced her intention to move on and continue her work in Boston.

Left out of the decision and cruelly dismissed, her disappointed parents had no choice but to support her move to Boston, where she had already accepted a position as a dance instructor which included teaching four classes a day and the continuation of her own lessons—important lessons which would allow her to participate in the *Boston Community Theater of Dance*.

Lila was anxious to get out of town. Having been on the edge of independence for some time she was chafing to live on her own, be responsible for her health, and last but not least, deal with the adventurous and questionably reckless streak that had suddenly reared its head after having lay dormant since her promiscuous teens.

Lila's parents were fully aware of many thoroughly unattractive characteristics she had displayed throughout her youth. By the age of thirteen, she had become dangerously competitive and frighteningly temperamental; at eighteen, actively dating, she became inordinately possessive and promiscuous. Mr. and Mrs. Powers, so often at a loss in dealing with her uncontrollable behavior, continued to hide behind their pat statement. "She'll grow out of it".

Some of Lila's former high school classmates and more recent fellow dancers recalled her fierce desire to be the center of attraction; not one of them chose to complain about the cruel, dark side she had occasionally exhibited. As a matter of fact, most of them eventually admitted to having a deadly fear of the formidable Miss Lila Powers.

A rumored incident detailing her shameless stalking of a classmate during her senior year in high school was repeated time and again. The popular student was a young promising dancer who had landed the lead in the much sought after, *Nutcracker*. Lila had counted on getting that role, but when she was selected as the understudy—she openly seethed and pouted. Midnight phone calls and menacing messages were her remedies for the unexpected pain of such a disappointment. She made the youngster's life miserable to the point of distraction in her performances.

Much to Lila's delight, the frightened student was swiftly removed from the dance school after the production was over.

Lila was unashamed of her despicable behavior—often taking pride in it. Intimidation was her calling card and her colleagues took due notice, avoiding unnecessary involvement with her at all cost. She didn't seem to care; she was far too self-absorbed and strong-willed to notice the isolation.

A classmate once said, "If you became her friend you had to accept her the way she was; no criticism of her actions or opinions of your own were allowed. It was "love me, love my temper. Yes, you had to be *very careful* when it came to loving Lila."

After living in Boston for about a year, Lila was introduced to Scott Macguire. She had been visiting a Christian Science Reading Room on the advice of her dance advisor, *Madam Cherie,* who thought the sessions might calm and relax the high-strung, thrill-seeking perfectionist; it just might keep her distracted enough to get over her emotional break-up with *Dante, Madam's* dance partner *and husband.*

Madam Cherie was no fool.

The old diva was acquainted with the young man and was an avid believer in the Christian Science Philosophy; perhaps Scott could provide the perfect balancing factor for Lila. *Madam* had encountered him during group discussions and found him to be gentle and easy-going. She thought of Scott as reserved and shy until he began to confide in her.

Scott told her of a serious relationship that was becoming increasingly difficult for him to manage. It appeared he was involved with a well-educated young woman who was employed at the same publishing house that he worked at. She lived in an upscale neighborhood and owned a summer place somewhere on *Puckshaw*, where Scott often spent weekends.

Madam Cherie knew that the young woman was financially stable and probably much more sophisticated than Scott.

He confided that she often cried for days on end for no apparent reason and it left him exhausted and confused. Now Scott was trying to get his courage up to break it off without causing her further distress. He was like that—avoided hurting others at all cost. After expressing his frustration and apprehension to *Madam*, she thought she had the perfect solution to his problem: *Miss Lila Powers.*

Lila and Scott were introduced and mutually struck by an overwhelming attraction towards each other. Scott was somewhat needy and Lila was possessive—wildly possessive. Within days they began to see each other secretly—Scott promising to end his relationship with his girlfriend as soon as possible. He kept his promise and he and Lila quickly entered into a tumultuous, passion-filled relationship.

Lila had an hour to kill before picking up the take-out and driving out to Scott's cozy apartment; she opted for a long, hot bath rather than the depressing evening television news.

Before stepping into the tub, she stood before the mirror staring critically at her naked body. Ever the perfectionist, the image she saw never seemed good enough for her. Although she was slim, shapely and carried herself with the pride of a *diva,* she still made a disappointed face at the mirror before lowering herself into the steaming tub.

As the hot water washed over her relaxing body she let her mind wander. She carefully reviewed events that had changed the course of her life in the last few years—in particular her final few weeks in New Hampshire, where she basked in the love and attention of family and friends.

She shivered with shame—trying to summon the courage to admit to at least *one* of her demons.

God knew she had many.

She relaxed her long body in the tub of hot, scented water and closed her eyes.

She pictured *Evan Dowd*: well bred, recent graduate of the prestigious Lowell Sandhurd Business Institute, and adored son of the Dowds. The young man was spending a hard-earned summer at the opulent home of his proud and protective parents. With hopes and dreams soaring, they enthusiastically introduced their youngest son to their inner circle of social contacts—the men and women who held the keys to certain career success. If he "showed well" he was sure to be allowed access to the stable of necessary and suitable young *Phillies of fine breeding.*

Lila had recently completed an Associate Degree at a small women's college in the area of her hometown of Seneca, New Hampshire. It was a very unremarkable period in her life and some questioned whether she had actually graduated. Lila's dream was to become a dancer and the undemanding academic program of this small college allowed her to continue her lessons and perform at the *College Arts Theater.*

Among the many benefactors of the *College Arts Theater* were Evan Dowd's parents, respectfully addressed as *Mr. and Mrs. D.* They stood out as devoted supporters and it was not unusual for them to attend opening nights, complete with trips backstage to congratulate the hopeful performers. Evan had accompanied his mother on one of those nights and was casually introduced to Lila, along with several giddy, young actresses and dancers. Lila's cool and nonchalant nod of the head and tiny curtsy did not escape his attention.

She hadn't meant it to.

Evan returned to the theater later that week looking for Lila in order to ask her out for dinner; after two dates, he was hopelessly smitten with her. Consummation of their attraction was quick; glowing with satisfaction the lovers rushed to declare themselves "a couple".

In between their passionate love-making sessions, they did the usual things together: watched movies, shopped, and to Lila's delight, freely enjoyed the privileges of the exclusive *Jericho Country Club*, thanks to Evan's family membership.

It hadn't gone unnoticed that behind the scenes, their relationship was becoming dangerously volatile; it was fraught with arguments over a variety of issues with Lila regularly erupting into tantrums and Evan, endlessly chastised, capitulating to keep things from getting out of hand..

The lovers had been seeing each other for almost three months and while shocked friends and family observed with incredulity, the lop-sided relationship flourished.

Evan seemed blissfully unfazed when Lila bullied him; she often accused him of being uncaring and lazy and then waited until he begged for her forgiveness—which she would withhold for a tantalizing length of time before demanding a torrid make-up session in atonement for his "wretched behavior". It was an exercise; a game they both enjoyed playing with Lila as the victor—greedily grabbing the spoils. Evan seemed content with the status quo until late one night when he "dropped the bomb" on her.

They were saying goodnight in front of her flat when Evan sat up and whispered, "We have to talk."

"Talk about what?"

"It's my parents, honey. They're not happy with the direction my career choices are taking me in. They feel that my search for a solid position has stalled and I should be doing better; you know, making more contacts and kissing more asses. You know what I mean, don't you? Well, anyway, I promised them I would try harder."

If he had been honest he would have told her that they really didn't like the way his relationship with *her* was heating up. The Dowds hated the way she belittled him and constantly found fault with him. They especially despised the way she corrected his grammar and pronunciation; after all, he was well brought up and successfully and expensively educated. Any parent would resent that sort of criticism and yet, Lila always seemed to find something to ridicule Evan about—in front of Mr. & Mrs. Dowd and other family members. Her expected presence was soon *dreaded* at family functions—everyone remaining silent in order to spare Evan's feelings.

The Dowds were patient; he *was* their youngest son and his indiscretions were attributed to his youthful exuberance. They continued to indulge him though, secretly, the whole family wished the relationship would blow over so he could settle down with *one of their own kind.*

The last time Lila had spent an evening with them they were embarrassed and disgusted at the way she made not-too-subtle sexual innuendoes toward Evan in front of them; in their opinion, a proper girlfriend would have never committed such a *faux pas.*

Evan, on the other hand, rather enjoyed it, taking it as a sign of promised intimacy to follow later that evening.

Now, in the darkened car Lila began to wail. "Oh, for Christ's sake, are you going to let them run your life forever? Can't you tell them you can make your own decisions about your career? Jesus, grow up, will you!"

"Well maybe we could just cool it a little while I send out *résumés* and check out a few leads on jobs; you know, have lunch with my Dad and some of his cronies. It's necessary, Lila. So can we just… "

She didn't give him a chance to finish his sentence. Her voice grew shrill, "what the hell are you talking about? So now you're going to dump me?"

Evan backed down with, "No, honey. I just need to spend more time making some good contacts and getting myself set up. Don't panic, for Christ's sake."

He put his arms around her and reminded her that his brother's wedding was coming up in three days and everyone's eyes would be on them as the *next happy couple* to get engaged. She smiled to herself in the dark car and kissed him very deliberately and sensually, making sure he kept his promise and *she* kept the upper hand.

Saturday rolled around quickly, and she spent the late afternoon primping and pampering her body in order to look her best for the wedding reception. Evan was a groomsman and was unable to escort her earlier in the day, so she chose to meet him at the reception at six thirty.

And that she did.

She arrived breathless and stunning, in an emerald green, two piece cocktail dress with a postage stamp-sized velvet top—held up by two thin straps; it hung perfectly over her slim shoulders and lifted chest, barely reaching her tiny waist. Onlookers snidely agreed that just a glimpse of her flat midriff was well worth the wait. The glove-like skirt ended at mid-thigh with a slit on the right side. Lila Powers—perfectly groomed from her shiny, auburn hair to her sensually painted toenails—arrived in all her glory; she would not go unnoticed by the family and guests that had already gathered in Jericho County's largest ballroom to begin the cocktail hour.

Evan immediately strode toward her with pride, knowing that all eyes were focused on them. He kissed her on the cheek and whispered something in her ear that made her smile. Taking her elbow lightly, he led her over to greet the bride and groom who were standing with his parents.

Lila's expectations ran high, but she was cruelly brought down with embarrassment and horror when she was treated as a casual guest—not the privileged insider or family member that she saw herself as. She did not let it pass without a complaint to Evan, who was caught up in the excitement of the day and flippantly responded to her complaint with an off-handed, "Oh Christ Lila, don't start!"

Lila tilted her head to one side and opened her eyes wide in surprise as they walked toward the bar where Evan ordered her a white wine—the only alcohol she drank since she had been diagnosed with diabetes. They joined a small group and chatted politely until Evan excused himself to see why his father was waving at him.

Lila continued her conversation with Sanders, a family friend that she had met briefly, once or twice. He was only slightly drunk but openly infatuated with her and they remained engrossed in conversation, eventually opting for a tiny table for two in the darkest corner of the ballroom. When the music started they found it quite natural to get up and dance without saying a word. They danced silently—clinging to each other sensually.

Neither Evan nor his parents missed the point Lila was making. She had been treated shabbily and now the *genie was out of the bottle*. Evan came to her side several times to speak to her or guide her away to be introduced to friends, but she always made her way back to Sanders. The third time Evan approached them he was visibly irritated and asked Sanders to excuse them for a moment.

"Lila, what the hell are you trying to pull?" he whispered hoarsely. You are making a spectacle of yourself and pissing everyone off. Come on honey, cut it out. Okay? This is a *family occasion* and we should all be together tonight." Evan put his arm around her affectionately, congratulating himself for having successfully diffused a potentially explosive situation.

Lila pouted playfully for a moment and then allowed Evan to kiss her. She glanced around—secretly hoping his parents were watching as she rubbed up against him and cooed, "Will you get me another glass of wine, honey?"

Evan showed some surprise, since she always drank with monk-like restraint, but he left her side to go to the bar and when he returned she was nowhere in sight.

Visibly frustrated and mumbling under his breath to no one in particular, he waited patiently, hoping she had just gone to the ladies room. After several minutes he began to roam around the room looking for her, chatting with old friends and trying not to be too obvious in his search.

All eyes were on him. How would this little drama play itself out?

Evan was a little drunk and very tired; he was hoping they could just go back to his house for the night. He knew he could apologize for his parents' behavior—put things right; but he also had to convince her to be a little less critical and more agreeable when she was around them.

After circling the dance floor several times he stepped outside for some air and to see if she had stepped out to do likewise. He scanned the parking lot for her car; hoping to convince her to follow him back to his home and spend the night. That would be okay with his parents; they knew he had had a tough night with her. Locating her car, he quickly made his way through the crowded well-lit lot. She was sitting in it quietly and he suddenly felt guilty for not having been more sensitive when she had been treated coolly by his family. He thought of jumping into the car and taking her into his arms and apologizing. As he approached her car—feeling better already—he suddenly realized she was not alone.

"What the hell?"

Boiling with anger and disgust at finding Sanders beside her, partially undressed; he screamed an obscenity at her and ran back into the ballroom to find his parents.

Lila was too preoccupied to respond, but the filthy name he shouted had not escaped her ears.

By the time he found his parents, Evan was visibly distracted and made some incoherent apology promising to meet them at the house. He left the ballroom and ran through the parking lot blind with rage. Jumping into his flashy, blue sports car, he slammed the door and raced out of the lot—heading straight for the Dowd estate deep in the suburbs.

Lowering the window, he inhaled deeply and tried to get a hold of himself. He slowed down a little while he struggled to piece together what the hell had happened in the last few hours. He wasn't drunk; it had been at least two hours since his last drink and he never drank much to begin with.

He felt calmer; he would figure out a way to work things out. He had about eight miles to go before reaching exit twenty-two and the short dark ramp off the main highway. He drove carefully—his radio playing softly. It was just as well if he didn't have to work things out *right away*. He planned to wait until the next day—calmer emotions might prevail. Evan dropped his shoulders and relaxed as the radio continued to play.

He considered his fast-deteriorating relationship with Lila and knew, deep in his gut, that he would be better off without her. Now, for the first time, he was ready to admit it—not only to Lila, but to his family. He would take care of it first thing in the morning; maybe it wasn't too late for them to move on without further ruining his brother's wedding celebration.

As he approached the exit, he glanced in his mirror and was surprised to see headlights not too far behind him—possible wedding guests that had been invited back to the house; to be polite, he slowed down and the car behind him seemed to do likewise. He hoped the driver wasn't sick or drunk; he was not in the mood to take the responsibility for anyone else's lack of sobriety.

Relieved that there was no problem, Evan gradually resumed his speed. Within seconds, he spotted the yellow hazard lights behind him flashing, along with bright headlights. Swearing under his breath he stopped and waited to see what the driver behind him was going to do. Obviously something was wrong.

When the car stopped moving and no one got out, Evan jumped out of his car and took a few steps toward the disabled car. *"Goddamn it! What is it now?" he whispered into the darkness.*

He shook his head and raised his eyes just in time to see the vehicle lurch forward and speed toward him. He tried to back up but the crushing impact lifted him off his feet and momentarily sandwiched his body between the unknown car and his own idling vehicle. The last thing he heard was the screech of tires as he slid to the pavement with blood gushing out of his mouth. He wouldn't wake up until the next afternoon.

****

Lila's mother wasn't sleeping very soundly and answered the phone on the first ring. It was almost one a. m.

"Hi mom; I'm so sorry to wake you.   Listen, the reception is winding down and I've decided to drive up to Halston for two days and visit a friend from school; as long as I'm out this far and feel pretty good, I might just as well get a start by leaving tonight. Evan will be delayed with his parents at the reception—to take pictures and stuff—I guess…and…hey, remember the job opening I told you about? Well, I'm going to check it out. Don't worry about a thing; I'll be home late, Monday."

And before her mother could ask any questions she said, "Love you, Mom. See you Monday."

She hung up the pay phone and put in another coin. She got Evan's machine.

"Hi, honey. I'm so sorry about tonight. It's not what you think. I hope we can work it out when I get back on Monday. Nothing went right, I know, but we'll set everything straight on Monday. Okay? Sorry to leave in a rush but I have a friend in Halston that I've been promising to visit—decided to drive up there tonight and look her up first thing in the morning. Call me Monday? Love you. Bye."

Lila knew Evan's parents would hear that message. As a matter of fact, she was counting on it. She got back in her car and drove nearly eighty miles north of Jericho County and stopped at a Holiday Home. She realized she was overdressed for the middle of the night and might give the wrong impression, so she grabbed her dark raincoat out of the back seat and pulled it tightly around her shoulders as she drove into the lot. She felt dizzy; if she didn't soon eat and rest—she could pass out.

After a quick check-in she picked up a sandwich and a glass of orange juice from the near-empty case and went up to her room. She ate quickly, stretched her legs and back out, and settled her naked body between the cool sheets. She had nothing to wear to bed but, of course, that would never bother Lila; on the contrary she felt unrestrained when she slept nude. More so than any other night, her deliberate nakedness seemed to increase her defiance and determination.

She would not be had.

She slept soundly until noon; waking famished, she called down for some breakfast and the New York Times. With the paper spread out on the bed, she ate and read, barely paying attention to the news items. Instead, she looked at the employment ads and jotted down a few notes on a hotel note pad.

Maybe Boston—Madam Cherie's Dance Academy sounds good to me!

Lila was fastidious when it came to bathing, so before her long, hot bath, she ran a boiling shower for several minutes to make sure the tub was clean. An hour later, refreshed and energized, she checked out of the hotel shortly before three p.m., with her rain coat belted tightly around her waist. She started the hour and a half drive home, stopping once, at a car-wash—just in case.

She hummed a tune with the radio and smiled—relaxed and content with her *wondrous* deed. Pulling into the driveway, she stepped out of the car and removed her raincoat before running up the front porch steps. She walked into her house casually, looking her mother straight in the eye with a rested smile and a cheerful greeting.

"Lila!" her mother shouted, "Where have you been?"

"I told you, mom. I was driving to Halston right after the reception, but I felt awful after an hour so I stopped at the Holiday Home for the night. I guess I just didn't eat enough Saturday. I felt so lousy and weak that I didn't bother to go to Halston. By this afternoon I was better and decided I'd better come home and rest; so here I am! I've been doing *way too much* lately; I think I really need a good rest."

"Lila!" Her mother wailed. "You don't know? Evan was hit by a car last night. He's in a semi-coma at County General. It was all over the T.V; didn't you see it?"

Lila shrieked. "What? What? My God! I've got to go to him! Now! Where is he; at County did you say?"

She ran up stairs shouting behind her that she needed to change her clothes.

It was a short ride to the hospital and she was amazed at the tears that ran down her cheeks as she stepped off the elevator and rushed down the hall. Evan's father was standing outside the room and coolly waved her in.

She stepped inside. Evan's mother turned and glared at her—blinking back tears. She seemed distant—in shock.

Lila hesitated—caught off guard for a moment. She had to think. Think fast.

Mrs. Dowd had turned away and was looking upon her son's pale face. "He woke up about an hour ago," she said without turning around to make eye contact.

Visibly relieved, Lila moved in closer and said, "What happened? My mother said he was in a car accident."

"No he wasn't! He was *hit* by a car! They think it could have either been a drunk driver or a botched car-jacking;

187

whatever happened, Evan was left on the road *half dead!* You can see that for yourself. The doctors say he's going to be okay but he has a concussion and probably some internal injuries. They'll be doing x-rays as soon as they can move him. He's lightly sedated, right now."

With that she rose and walked past Lila, quietly excusing herself as she left the room.

Lila moved closer and looked over her shoulder before touching Evan's hand, causing his eyes to flutter opened.

"Oh, Evan," she whispered. "I'm so glad you are going to be okay. I'm so sorry about this; what on earth happened? I know you can't talk right now but don't worry; I'll take care of you. About Saturday night; I'm sorry. It was all a misunderstanding and…"

Evan whispered something she couldn't make out.

"What? What is it, darling?"

I said, "Get out of here, Lila. Get out; *now!*"

"Evan, you don't know what you're saying, honey; you're going to be okay. I'm here now. Just get well and we'll work things out."

He spoke again and this time he whispered in a very calm voice, "Go away, Lila. *Please.* Get out of here and get out of my life. Now, *go!*"

Lila shook her head and said incredulously, "What are you saying? I don't understand."

She felt someone move in the room. Evan's mother was standing behind her and had heard everything. Lila's eyes were like slits as she turned to question his mother who was nodding her head in agreement.

"Just go," she said. "That's what he wants. That's what we *all* want!"

Lila was speechless. She grabbed her purse and bolted from the room, passing other family members in the hall as they stared at the floor. She ignored a waiting elevator and headed toward the stairs trying to keep control of her emotions; this was not a good time to fall apart. She hated what she scathingly referred to as "that whole fucking family"; she wouldn't give them the satisfaction. Anyway, she wouldn't miss them. She wouldn't even miss Evan.

Her work was done, there.

She pushed open the door and stepped out into the bright parking lot, digging into her purse for sunglasses and car keys. She hesitated for just a moment—took stock of the situation and walked briskly in the direction of her car.

Lila Powers never looked back.

It was understood that her parents would never speak of Evan in her presence. At first, when they had tried, she swiftly cut them off with a derogatory comment about his being a momma's boy; if they dared to bring up the *so-called* car accident, she met the inquiry with a stony gaze that filled them with dread. At least one, but more likely both, of her parents harbored a sickening suspicion that they would never verbalize; it was just too ugly and frightening.

Two weeks later, with her suitcases packed, Lila Powers was ready to leave for Boston. She kissed her mother and father, promising to call them as soon as she got there. She calmed their fears with assurances that she would take good care of her health and drove away with a firm resolve to get as far away from *Jericho County* as she possibly could.

As Lila's car turned the corner and disappeared from view, a heavy silence hung between Mr. and Mrs. Powers.

"Who was it that Lila intended to visit up in Halston on the night of the wedding?"

Mr. Powers shrugged his shoulders and stared into space for an endless moment—"I have no idea; no idea at all.

****

The clock on the bathroom wall ticked loudly. She still had an hour before leaving for Scott's apartment. Stretching her long leg out of the tub, she slowly came out of her disturbing reverie, shivering. Shrinking from the chilly air she sank back into the lukewarm water and recalled her tumultuous arrival in Boston.

****

She had arrived at *Madam Cherie's Dance Academy* with the look of a hungry-for-success young dancer—ready to take on the world. *Madam* was as impressed as *Dante,* her dance partner and husband; they knew immediately— they were going to like her.

Lila was given her class schedule and a week's orientation to settle in. She observed some of the classes and got to know a little bit about her students, taking notes and deliberately saying and doing exactly what was expected of her. She ended most days with a one or two-hour class conducted by *Madam* and Dante; most of the instructors took the class to keep fresh and competitive for their constant auditions and hoped-for performances at the *Community Theater.* It also allowed *Madam* and Dante to revisit their youth and demonstrate flashes of their early successes. The workouts were hard-hitting and demanding, but most of the teachers enjoyed the challenge. After all, had they not all, realistically or not, aspired to stardom at one time or another? Eventually, each, for his or her own good reason, had made the decision that eventually led them—one by one—to *Madam Cherie's Dance Academy.*

Madam and Dante were the perfect caricatures of aging dancers with just a little too much circumstance and pomp, but plenty of energy and style. *Madam* was tall and thin with dyed, black hair, pulled tightly into the traditional bun. Her thin lips were always covered with bright, red lipstick that was applied well beyond her natural lip line. If she wasn't careful, a clown-like smile could be the result—especially on stressful days, when running the business, meeting with demanding parents, and inspiring her ever-brooding teachers, all caught up with her. In any event, her weekly dance demonstrations were always very elaborate and dramatic, ending with deep and sweeping bows. She would feign coquettish shock when her teachers applauded, demurely thanking them before turning the class over to her life-long partner, both in dance and marriage.

Dante always kissed his wife's hand and bowed reverentially before taking over the class. He was proud and fully aware of having maintained a very trim and muscular physique and a full head of gray, wavy hair to boot. He leaped around the polished, hardwood floor like a young stallion on the audition circuit. The only tell-tales of his advanced age were the bulging calf veins and arthritically deformed knees and feet, which he took great pains to keep hidden from his devoted staff. The long years of pounding and prancing had taken their toll on his slight frame but he was not ready—not by a long shot—to give up the boyish, free-spirited life that kept him in close proximity to young—not necessarily talented—women of the dance.

It was common knowledge that Dante and *Madam* both had a roving eye when young and pretty female dancers were involved.

The self-proclaimed *diva* and her sensual husband dwelt in a little world of their own on the top floor of the academy—each with a deep understanding and acceptance of the other's faults and failings. There *were* favorite dancers; *Madam* always praised Elaine—the twenty-six-year-old blonde, athletic dancer, whom she thought was an excellent teacher with not the slightest chance to dance in New York, Boston, or San Francisco. The young woman was already too old; her dreams were unrealistic and she had never really had a chance—it was just a little game *Madam* and Elaine insisted on playing.

Dante, on the other hand, was openly in awe of the sixteen-year-old student teacher, Tessa, who was leaving public school soon. She would *definitely* be leaving Boston, having won several competitions and the starring role in most of the local productions. The promising *prima ballerina-in-waiting* was allowed to work out with the teachers in order to accelerate her progress. The youngster possessed all the qualities of making it on the big stage, although nothing was *definite* when it came to young dancers; they could grow too tall too fast, become large and clumsy, or just lose interest and give it all up. And Madam always said, *"Beware of the dreaded, raging hormones; once they make an appearance, nothing is sacred."*

Dante had had more than a few discreet liaisons over the years and he knew this sixteen-year-old was *taboo* and that he should be looking elsewhere; so it was no big surprise to *Madam* when she saw the little flirtation being played out between Dante and the newcomer, Miss Lila Powers.

When she joined the staff class, she was severely tested by the prolonged concentration with which they did their stretches and position workouts. They took turns leaping, pirouetting—each trying to recapture the agility of their first fervor. Lila worked hard in spite of her health restrictions and was fully aware that she had caught and was holding Dante's attention. He grabbed at every opportunity to lift her, hold her, or just touch her. She was flattered by his boyish overtures and took open pleasure in his clownish attempts to make her laugh at his jokes.

Madam, though quite annoyed with the blossoming flirtation, turned a blind eye whenever possible. She continued to put some distance between them during class, but Dante always found a reason to position himself next to Lila at some point; a point being well-taken by the rest of the teachers.

Within two months Dante and Lila were meeting for a few stolen moments in a tiny motel not too far from the dance academy. She had a pleasant enough flat, but she shared it with two other roommates and bringing men to the apartment was off limits, forcing the new lovers to meet clandestinely—adding dramatically to the passion of the moment. Sometimes they came together for coffee or dinner in an out of the way restaurant, where they sat in darkened corners hardly able to keep their hands off of each other; and at other times they unceremoniously fled to the motel for a few hours of passion-filled intimacy.

Lila was quite content with the whispered title of *Dante's Girl.* Having quickly acquired a rather haughty attitude, she was definitely not a favorite among *Madam* and her teachers. In spite of the obvious negative undercurrent, *Madam* smiled sweetly while Lila responded with the little curtsy that the older *diva* had come to expect each morning.. It was a little game of chance between the two clever women. However, *Madam* held the power and had already decided the charade would not go on much longer.

The expected argument was loud and violent. *Madam* broke an ashtray and Dante smashed his fist down so hard that it cracked the glass top on the coffee table in their ornate living room. The altercation had taken place in their apartment well after dance hours and no one had heard or seen it. The monumental arguments which may or may not have occurred in the apartment above the dance school might easily have been considered the stuff of which legends are made, but no one will ever know—they always took place in complete privacy.

"But that's what makes them so delicious," *Madam* would crow when she spoke about them.

She was unusually harsh and vehement when she leveled Dante with her most recent threat. "I will get rid of that girl in one beat of your heart if you don't end this foolishness."

"*Mon Cherie*, you've had dalliances with plenty of little girls over the years and I've never interfered; what is the big *boohoo* about Miss Lila?"

"I don't like her attitude. She's downright arrogant about this *flirtation*—*Madam* would never call it anything more than that—and she has been spreading outrageous rumors that the two of you will be traveling together this summer. Is that true? Is that what you are filling this young women's head with. Tell me, when exactly did you lose your mind? She's young, foolish and dangerous; I know the type—well. I want this thing ended—immediately—and I mean it! She's different than all the others; I believe she is *trouble!*"

Dante's voice changed slightly when he said, "What the hell are you talking about? What trouble? Traveling together? We've never discussed anything so ridiculous—you're the one who has lost your mind. You're acting crazy tonight! Believe me, there are no summer plans; Christ *Cherie,* you know me better than that. God damn it, I'll get to the bottom of this first thing Monday morning. No, I'll call her *right now!*"

He went into the bedroom, grabbed the phone, and angrily rang her up. *Madam* couldn't hear what he was saying but he raised his voice time after time before storming out of the apartment without a word.

The *old Diva* ran a hot bath, poured a glass of wine, and took her Oriental silk robe off before the full length mirror, concluding with disgust that her body was either sagging or bulging in all the wrong places. She concurred with the mirror that there was nothing she could do about her body, but she *could* do something about the embarrassment that Dante had brought down upon her. She thought about the argument and congratulated herself for successfully convincing him to end such an annoying *liaison.* She smiled as she concluded that she always got her way, although she had to admit that this one was close. *Very close.*

Lila was waiting outside the coffee shop when Dante pulled up. His heart always pounded when he saw those long legs covered in a black leotard, but tonight—with her dark trench coat belted tightly around her tiny waist to accentuate her statuesque form—she reminded him of an international spy, hiding in the shadows. Her dark hair, sleek and smooth, was held back with a green satin ribbon, indicating she had taken some time to arrange her look. Her eyes were cast down and she appeared pensive and edgy as she shifted her weight in the semi-darkness of a street lamp.

Dante hadn't expected her to be so shocked at his tone of voice when he rang her up; she became extremely agitated and was very reluctant to meet him—it was the dinner hour for her.

Now, with her lithe body in his cross hairs, he could barely muster up the anger he had felt less than an hour ago; it had been replaced by the familiar excitement of simmering desire.

It wasn't hard for anyone with the use of reason to understand why Dante was so besotted with her. The fact that he was old enough to be her father further inflated his ego and added to the excitement. Tonight he had to be firm—*act furious.* He had no idea that she, too, was seething; an impromptu summons to meet him during her dinner hour was unacceptable to the in-control partner of this quickly disintegrating duo.

He took her arm, like an old friend might, and propelled her down the dark side street. Suddenly his anger returned and he tried to control his quivering voice.

"What the hell is going on here, Lila? What the hell kind of rumors have you been spreading about us? When did we *ever* discuss traveling together this summer? Christ, *Switzerland!* Are you crazy or what? What the hell has gotten into you, anyway?"

Lila became defensive and shot back with, "Jesus! What are you getting so excited about? I was only winding them up when I said that! Those goddamn, jealous teachers knew it too! They baited me and I gave them a little something to talk about. What did *Madam* say? Tell me! Jesus, I hope you stood up to her. Dante, *my love*, everyone knows she has her own little stable of girls! What about her and *little Claire*? What is she, *twelve*?"

Dante was exasperated now.

He softened his voice as though he was speaking to a child. "Sweet, Lila. Things were going so well; why on earth did you ruin everything with such foolish talk? *Cherie* is usually most understanding about these matters—now she is angry and embarrassed and demands that we end this. We'll have to bow to her wishes; she is on the verge of exploding and I can't stand by and allow this to happen. She's my wife, my partner, my...we've been together a very long time and have had a good life together; I can't let this ruin everything. Do you understand me?"

Lila wanted to scream and strike out at him, but she seemed to reconsider that action in a split second and instead began to cry, inaudibly. She walked to her car with Dante walking beside her, silently. She unlocked her car and he opened the door for her, as he always did. Pausing for just a moment to look at him—as if she wanted to say something, but changed her mind—she slid beneath the wheel and sullenly adjusted the rear view mirror. She didn't look at him and he wasn't sure what she said as she snapped her seat belt and started the car; he assumed it was either good bye or good night or...maybe it was good riddance.

He didn't know and he didn't want to know. He reached inside the car and sensually rubbed her hand, feeling himself turning to jelly again.

"Come on, you need to get home and get a good night's sleep. You'll feel much better in the morning. You're alright, then? You understand, don't you?"

She put her head down and said nothing. She wanted to return his touch and coax him into the car to make love to her but she had too much pride. After all, she had been through a lot more than this. *She was Lila Powers and no one was going to make her grovel.*

Dante would have leaped into the car if only she had invited him; instead, he waited for her to lock her doors before he walked away to his own car. He knew it was best for him to get away from her now. He had had a very close call with his wife and he didn't like the feeling it left him with. In spite of all his machismo, *Madam Cherie* wore the pants—never letting him forget it.

Lila stopped at the little Mini-mart on the way home to by a chocolate bar. She had ripped it open and taken a bite, feeling the onset of sugar level discomfort. She sat in her driveway and ate the rest of it while she regained her composure and then calmly walked into her flat with the candy wrappers in her hand, greeting her roommates as if nothing was amiss.

Once again Lila Powers had reached deep into her reservoir of incredible fortitude and deliberately put her feelings on the back burner. She had no choice—they had no idea that she had just been through an ordeal.

The girls exchanged a few pleasantries and Lila went into the kitchen to make a snack. She ate quickly—never took food to her bedroom—and headed upstairs mumbling something about being exhausted.

She ran the hot water in the tub and lowered her shaking body into it; patiently waiting for calm to come. It was over between her and Dante but she wanted to stay on at the Dance Academy—how she loved that job! She loved dancing and the freedom it allowed her; she wasn't ready to give it all up. She knew what she would do; she would go in early Monday morning and throw herself on *Madam's* mercy. She would promise to stay away from Dante. It would work. It had to work. *It always worked.*

****

The hot bath finally relieved her aching legs and Lila came out of her reverie slowly, as if completing a long journey. She looked at the little clock on the wall and was shocked to see that an hour had passed and she was now running late to pick up the take-out dinner and drive the thirteen miles to Scott Macguire's apartment.

When she arrived, she hung up her jacket, tossed her overnight bag behind the pullout sofa, and turned to setting the little dinette table. After placing the take-out cartons in the microwave, she washed her hands. This was a ritual she had observed dozens of times and she rarely deviated from it. Lila cherished two things; order and control. She strove to maintain both of these elements in her life—and Scott's—under any and all circumstances.

She also observed a strict preening ritual in preparation for his arrival; first, she changed into a soft olive green robe and freshened up her make-up; then she took her hair down from the medium-sized ponytail she had worn all day, allowing the soft curls to cascade about her shoulders in big clusters. As a final touch she sprayed a little cologne behind her ears and in the cleavage peaking out between the lapels of her modestly revealing robe. Scott was funny that way—he didn't like the obvious—so she had learned to be understated in her manner of dress when spending time with him. She quickly checked the whiteness of her almost perfect teeth and she was ready for him.

When she heard the key in the door she ran and greeted him with a warm and welcoming kiss. It was meant to be a sexual overture, so she was obviously stung when Scott didn't respond. He made light of it and went into the bathroom to wash up and change into his usual tee shirt and khakis. When he came out, feeling and looking more relaxed with glistening hair and bare feet, he apologetically crept up behind her and kissed her on the back of the neck. He confessed that he had had a tough day and a lot on his mind; he was sorry.

Lila turned to kiss him and he knew she had forgiven him.

The weekend went by quickly and by noon on Sunday Lila found herself packing her overnight bag and feeling just a little sad to leave. They read the Sunday papers together and made plans to attend a show at the *Community Theater* the following Saturday night. Lila was reluctant to leave, but she shook off the strange feeling and began to pick up the newspapers before washing the few dishes they had used. She remembered to wipe out the bathroom sink, which had strands of her long dark hair scattered about it. She knew Scott hated that and she didn't blame him; after all, she was fastidious about her grooming and toiletries and fully respected his aversion to sloppiness.

Just before she left, Lila had coaxed Scott into being intimate one last time. He had not responded at first, leaving her disappointed, but suddenly he returned her overture with a burst of passion that surprised her. She loved that rare spontaneity that inevitably left her glowing with satisfaction.

As they walked to her car and said good-bye, neither of them would have dreamed that there was a distinct possibility that they might never see each other again.

It was Saturday night and the phone rang again and again in Scott's dark apartment. Lila was furious; where the hell was he, she wondered; he had never done this before. She was dressed and ready for the theater and about to pick him up. She continued to speed dial his apartment to no avail.

By Monday, Lila had heard about Sonny Adams from a friend at the Reading Room and sped to Scott's apartment to comfort him—though she felt no sympathy for either of them. She discovered that he had taken his few possessions and disappeared without leaving a message for her or anyone else. She was consumed with deep rage and frustration as she returned to the Reading Room day after day; no one had seen Scott or had any information that they were willing to share with her.

Madam Cherie had seen to that.

Neither Scott's boss nor his colleagues responded to her messages or inquiries; inevitably, Lila would have to come face to face with the obvious truth: A concerted effort to shield Scott from being contacted by curiosity seekers, or *anyone else,* was being played out by a few of his closest friends—with his permission.

Scott Macguire did not want to be found by anyone—not even Lila Powers.

She turned to *Madam,* who had advised her to wait for a few days and give him some time to recover. After ten days had passed, Scott Maguire seemed to have disappeared without a proverbial trace. Lila was determined to carry on; she continued her classes at the Dance Academy and immersed herself in her work, eventually becoming *Madam's* right hand.

They had struck a delicate balance after Lila's affair with Dante had ended. *Madam* seemed to understand Lila—they were so much alike—now she would help her climb out of the deep black hole of loneliness she had been cast into.

During Lila's period of vulnerability, *Madam* had become very attracted to her and, inevitably, the relationship had become sexual for a short period of time. The simple truth of the matter was that Lila Powers, being a demanding and passionate woman, needed the strong arms of a man to hold her and *Madam,* in her infinite wisdom, accepted that without question.

Within weeks the two women moved forward in a close platonic relationship.

Now, Dante was on the outside looking in. He and Lila were polite to each other and each tried hard to keep out of the other's way. Dante's heart still leapt when he saw Lila working out after school and she, in turn, often yearned for his mature and skilled lovemaking. Wisely, they both knew better than to resume their affair; *Madam Cherie* might not be as forgiving as she had been the first time.

Lila had a new apartment. Things had deteriorated very quickly after Scott disappeared and she had become unhappy and impatient with everybody—often giving in to the frequent outbursts of her childhood. Her roommates were appalled—especially at the disparaging racial remarks she had uttered in front of invited guests. She was asked to leave and was gone three days later. *Everybody was better off.*

Two months had passed and Lila had finally settled into a dull but rigorous routine with one unforgiving problem: *she was pregnant.*

As the first devastating year without Scott drew to an end, Lila had two things going for her; her unconditional commitment to being a mother and *Madam Cherie's* financial and emotional support.

Recovered from childbirth and desperately clinging to motherhood, she clawed her way back to health and financial stability with a vengeance. Her father had heard of her difficulties and began sending her a monthly stipend.

She was soon on her feet—no surprise to those who knew her well.

Within three months of the birth of her daughter, Lila returned to her work at the dance academy and began to enjoy the company of a few young men, always keeping a sharp eye out for a new, eligible, and unsuspecting partner. Lila Powers desired the company of a man who not only could satisfy her craving for raw passion, but one who understood that she would remain firmly at the controls. And yes, she had become much more expensive.

Two years had passed when out of the clear blue sky Lila received a post card from Scott Maguire. He was somewhere in Maryland and said he would keep in touch with her. He continued to send a postcard now and then and finally, without warning, Lila received the long-awaited letter apologizing for the way things had ended.

Scott explained how severe depression and guilt over Sonny's death had cast him into darkness and confusion for several months; he told her of his struggles to sort it all out his own way—alone. He hoped she would understand; this time he was enclosing his address, just in case she still wanted to write to him.

He was ashamed to admit he was still trying to get a grip on things and asked her not to try to visit him—yet. He was emphatic about his desire to take things slowly—if they were to renew their relationship at all. He wanted to know if she was still interested in working things out and re-establishing their connection. He asked her *not* to call him; if she was so inclined—he would just like to correspond. Their letters were sporadic over the next two years and Lila's last letter to Scott was filled with bad news.

She had neatly clipped out the article from the *Boston Daily*, well aware that it could cause pain and sow more seeds of confusion. She was still filled with rage and resentment and if her letter was going to hurt him—so be it—he had it coming. She had harbored the grudge for a long time and now the opportunity to *get even* had finally presented itself.

She had enclosed the obituary in one of her flower scented envelopes and mailed it with a cold smile of revenge.
She didn't love Scott anymore—she didn't even like him—but that wouldn't stop her from going to the post office every day.
Deep in her heart she knew he would write again—someday.

21 *May es96*

May 20, 1996

Good evening Kind Friend.

My latest research has involved a young woman by the name of Lila Powers. Born and raised as an only child in Seneca, New Hampshire, she attended—but didn't graduate from—a small mediocre Institute. She seems to have relocated to Boston in her early twenties under some pretty weird circumstances. A relative of hers told me she had dreams of being a dancer but didn't make the big time. She may not have made the big time; but the girl is *big trouble*.

I received a long letter from a *Madam Cherie* the other day and she gave me an earful! According to her, the girl, Lila, is a *fiend of the highest order*. But guess what? *Madam* says she just *adores* her and that Miss Lila is the only one who really understands the poor old thing. Baloney! She confirmed most of what I had already dug up about Lila, but says she would deny it all if I put it in my book. I called her on the telephone and you know what I told her? I told her that I had several other sources that could corroborate the facts and her permission really didn't make a goddamn bit of difference!

"In that case," she said, "you won't make me look like an old, washed up, French Whore, will you?"

I said, "no, no, not at all, *Madam*." And that was that.

Life is such a silly game isn't it?

On a more serious note, right now I'm trying to get my courage up to write about my dearest son. I have a more than a little bit of fear about tackling that, but I plan to devote the last few chapters of my book to what little I have come to know about him.

Scott Kelly Macguire. God, I should have made it my business to find out so much more about him—especially during his childhood. I know nothing about his first steps and first words, or his first day of school, or even his first date. I often wondered who taught him how to drive a car or change a tire. I guess I should be grateful for the little I did come to know about his life and *I thank God* (yes, I'm starting to believe, again) that I met him, even if it was only once—for a very brief time. It all should have and could have been so different. I might have been of help to him and maybe we would have gotten along really well and become great buddies. Oh God, it makes me weep at times.

You know what, dear friend? I'm feeling wearier of this project with each day that passes and I must confess I am happy to see it drawing to a close. There was a time when I didn't want it to end. Really! But now things have changed. I've changed—albeit—way too late. I so hope I haven't wasted my time. Oh well, if I have, I can't do a thing about it. I'm tired and lonely and I really don't have the desire to do much more these days. Maybe I should do something about *that*. I'll think about it.

Good night, friend.

HM

22 *Scott Macguire*

After Sonny's death Scott Kelly Macguire had fled to Baltimore on a noisy, lumpy-seated Bluebird bus that smelled like yesterday's fish fry. It wasn't a particularly long ride; just an annoying one with two screaming babies, one snoring drunk, and a fat man with a bird on his shoulder. Having never gotten around to buying a car; Scott vowed, then and there, to use part of his precious savings to buy a used vehicle as soon as he got settled.

Though no one had actually taught him how to handle money or plan for a rainy day, he was glad he had been thrifty in the last few years; he instinctively knew it was the right thing to do—save a little of his paycheck every week. He could be frugal—never cheap; especially when it came to his girl friends. He stared out the grimy window and reminisced about the only two *real* girlfriends he had ever had.

Sweet and sensitive to his feelings, Sonny Adams was always satisfied and appreciative of whatever entertainment Scott chose to provide when they went out for an evening. Though more sophisticated and *much more* financially well-off than he was; she often insisted on treating with dainty little sandwiches and cocktails before they left for the theater or movies.

It didn't bother her at all that Scott didn't own a car; she generously drove—never complaining. There was no need for an expensive taxi ride when it came to Sonny Adams. To save money, she often suggested that they spend evenings at her apartment in the city, eating a home-cooked dinner, or at her charming hide-a-way on *Puckshaw*—grilling hot dogs.

He had to be careful to choose just the right moment to think about her. He knew that it wasn't his fault; after all she had been dangerously immersed in her problems long before he came along. It was just bad timing, but that conclusion alone was not enough to stop him from missing the adoring smile she always greeted him with. Never aggressive or demanding, she was just grateful for his affection and companionship; that was *Sonny*. He felt tears welling up and protectively switching gears, thought about Lila.

Passionate and excitable Lila Powers! Self-centered, and frighteningly demanding, she always preferred that Scott spend more money than he could afford. She rarely offered to treat him to an evening out with dinner and drinks or even share the expense of a pair of theater tickets. She spent her money on herself. That was *Lila*—selfish and temperamental.

Scott closed his eyes and shook his head. He could only imagine how furious she must be at him for leaving Boston without letting her know, but something told him it was the right thing to do—flee without her. She had learned of Sonny's death quickly and Scott was fully aware that she had been trying to get in touch with him. His boss and his next-door neighbor had informed him of persistent calls and visits before he had even boarded the bus out of Boston.

He paused to ponder those purple rages she could unexpectedly fly into and how they had stunned him, but shrewd and sweet, Lila always had a rational excuse for her irrational behavior. Scott had planned to talk to her about the increasing violence that accompanied her rage; he thought she should talk to a professional—and soon. Anyway, he planned to call her and explain everything—just not right away.

Scott Macguire's escape from Boston *and* Lila had been nothing short of a miracle. With the permission of the *Puckshaw Police* and the help of a handful of friends, he took care of a few bills, explained things to his boss at S & S, and boarded a bus to Baltimore—all in just a little over twenty-four hours.

The emotional trauma had shaken him to the core and left him teetering on the edge of despair. Given his obvious innocence, he had been assured by the authorities that he would be allowed to leave the area as quickly as possible—as long as they knew where to reach him, if necessary.

He had jotted a note to his mother and given it to his landlord just in case she rang or asked to come around. Always mindful of her lack of funds, Scott left an envelope stuffed with cash for her—Shep would dole it out as she needed it. Finally, he packed his belongings and took a cab to the station to board a midnight bus to Baltimore, Maryland.

Taking a deep breath, he galloped up the three steps of the unwelcoming bus and handed his ticket to the driver with a slight nod. Half-way down the aisle, he tossed his duffle bags into an empty row and dropped into the window seat. "Good-bye Boston," he whispered, with a sigh of relief.

Though darkly depressed over Sonny's death, it wasn't she that he was missing.

Scott still couldn't help thinking of the singular and passionate Lila Powers. She could light him up like a Christmas tree and she knew it. Wild and physical, she had brightened his otherwise dull life—eliciting a raw masculinity from his timid and reserved nature that secretly filled him with pride and prowess. She had continuously challenged him to meet her physical needs and he had risen to the occasion—for the most part—even though her demands often left him exhausted and bruised after a weekend together. In spite of his growing apprehension with respect to her violent outbursts, he had pursued the relationship with vigor, continuing to seek the thrill of her touch. He shook his head in an effort to shake her out of his thoughts. It worked—for the moment.

As the aging bus bounced and his lumpy seat creaked, he distracted himself by thinking about his job and his studio apartment in Boston. He had liked his work at the publishing house—it was Boston that he just couldn't bear anymore. Too much had gone on there and he needed to be alone in order to sort out his feelings. For some reason he didn't want Lila's sympathy or mothering to get him through this rough period; he'd go it alone. It wasn't the first time he had traveled this road; he had already been through a lot on his own. An absentee father and an unstable mother—hopelessly addicted to alcohol—had already forced him into manhood without a shred of guidance or affection.

In spite of everything, he concluded with philosophical maturity that though his life had been far from charmed—he Scott Kelly Macguire, could have done much worse.

Out of the blue, he wondered if he had been lucky or unlucky to have had that strange encounter with his old man almost two years ago. He promised himself to try to communicate with him again—soon.

He knew he should also try to reconnect with his mother; he'd send a note as soon as he was settled. He had been sending her a few dollars now and then, but lately he had grown disgusted. Susan, now in her forties, drank to excess and had recently taken a vagrant boyfriend. The money went for alcohol and dog food and that was enough to discourage her only son from making any effort to see her in person. He still felt obligated to assist her in some way—considering her obvious deterioration. He resolved to keep sending her a stipend through a third party; maybe try to see her in six months or so.

After all, she had never beaten or belittled him or even thrown him out of the house before he was ready to go. He guessed she wasn't so bad after all. Maybe he'd just not think about what she was doing with the money he sent her and call it a draw.

He made a mental note to send a card to his friend and former landlord to provide him with his address—as soon as he had one. If his mother needed him, she knew she was to call Shep, who would in turn contact Scott immediately.

He thought about getting a job as soon as possible; he didn't want to lie about idly—brooding all day. He had his modest savings to see him through until he could draw a paycheck, but that rainy-day money could dwindle pretty quickly.

So far, his only real employment history and experience was with books, word processing, or data-base building; he loved that work but he needed to do something different—something that was physical and distracting. He needed a job that was noisy enough to block out the buzzing in his head that had resided there since the night he saw Sonny Adams walk into the cold, Atlantic surf to end her life.

He hadn't tried to save her; he wasn't even sure she would have wanted to be saved. Somehow, he would learn to live with the choice he had made.

Before leaving Boston, Scott had stuffed a Baltimore Sun newspaper into his back pocket; he planned to look through the *want ads* later on during the bus ride—if he didn't fall asleep.

Never materialistic, he had only a few boxes of books, an aging Stereo System, and a couple of reading lamps stored in one of the numerous facilities near his Boston apartment; he was glad not to have accumulated much in the last few years—one never knew when one might be compelled to take flight. Leaving Boston, he carried only two large, camouflaged duffel bags stuffed with casual clothes, books, and toiletries. He would send for his meager belongings later on; Shep had offered to handle that for him.

He dozed on and off for hours—not bothering to leave the bus during its numerous stops. Suddenly he was in Baltimore, Maryland, in need of an inexpensive room with a hot shower. Near exhaustion, he staggered to a nearby motel and checked in quickly. Stumbling into the dull little room, he pulled the shades and collapsed—fully clothed—into the center of the soft bed. He allowed the whir of the overhead fan to put him into a deep, dreamless sleep, from which he did not stir until dawn, having slept a solid twelve hours. It was the first solid sleep he'd had since Sonny's death; he felt rested and hungry.

He needed to shower and shave; the 24-hour stubble which darkened his naturally fair skin was unbecoming. A deluge of hot water and two large towels physically restored him within minutes. A fresh change of clothes and he was on his way to the coffee shop. He ate his breakfast while looking at the *want ads* and smiled to himself when the waitress gave him a withering look that said she'd seen tons of guys like him before. He tipped her and walked quickly back to the motel front desk where he handed the desk clerk two one-dollar bills for a bunch of quarters for the phone booth.

"Jesus, this is filthy," he murmured audibly.

She rolled her eyes, shrugged her shoulders, and sighed. He slammed the phone booth door shut and turned his back to her. While staring at the grimy public telephone, he was suddenly overcome by profound loneliness; a strange city, a lousy motel, and a dirty phone booth! Had it come to that? He struggled to restrain himself from calling Lila. He almost called his landlord—just to hear a familiar voice—then decided against that, too. Call his mother? No—that would be a major blunder.

Scott Macguire had never felt as alone as he did at that moment. He focused on the newspaper ads and started dialing. He needed a little luck—right now! The day flew by. With a sigh of relief, he welcomed the darkness and headed toward the motel where, for the second night in a row, he slept soundly.

The fall morning was a little cooler and he needed a windbreaker over his light shirt. His deep sleep had calmed him and he was beginning began to feel more in control—a good feeling. The desk clerk, unlike the waitress in the coffee shop, smiled generously; Scott nodded and smiled back.

His appointment was for ten a.m. and if he got this job he would look for an apartment immediately. He desperately needed a distraction or he might be inclined to run back to Boston with his tail between his legs.

His new boss, Gus, told him he could start as soon as he got himself some proper coveralls and metal-toed work boots. Scott Macguire was going to work in a scrap metal junkyard and it had everything he'd ever imagined—including the dog.

Old Gus promised to teach him how to tear down cars, bikes, appliances, and tractors. He also assured him he would be so tired at the end of the day that he would forget all his troubles. Scott figured everybody in Baltimore just assumed that if you came in on a bus and were looking for a job, you must be brokenhearted, in trouble, or trying to forget something. *They were right on the money.*

Gus sent Scott to a small apartment building about three blocks away; the owner would be waiting for him after work.

"Bring six hundred dollars with you and tell *Gato* you want to move in right away—and don't take any *crap* from him."

Scott walked the three blocks, carrying the money rolled up in his left hand which was thrust deep into his pocket. Without showing the money, he told *Gato* he needed to move in right away. *Gato*, whose name meant *cat* in *Italian*, asked to see the money, handed him a key, and crept away, silently. One could see why they called him *Gato*.

Scott went around to the side of the apartment building and let himself in. A surprise awaited him. He had half-expected to find a shabby, less than clean, perhaps even roach or mouse-infested, flat. Wrong! It was clean, adequately furnished, and bright looking. In a state of elation, Scott headed over to the motel to collect his few belongings. He was sorry not to be saying good-bye to the day shift desk clerk for, after all, she had been kind enough to give him a newspaper at night and a wake-up call in the morning so he wouldn't be late for his new job. He thought about stopping around the motel to say hello to her in a week or so. His intentions were decent.

Time flew at the junkyard. Fall had turned into a mild winter and Scott learned to dress a little warmer. He learned how to disassemble a variety of vehicles and sort the parts into scrap piles, working with an intensity that Gus liked. In peaceful inner silence and singular purpose Scott began to heal. At times, his soul was actually at peace and his spirit soared with joyful satisfaction over his new life. He was almost whole again; he couldn't believe eight months had passed and summer was upon him.

Gus assumed "the kid" might be thinking about leaving—now that the weather was good, but Scott assured him he was happy and wanted to stay where he was—if it was okay with him.

The sweltering summer came and went and Scott worked hard through the day and read his books or listened to music at night. (Shep had kept his promise and retrieved Scott's belongings from storage and had them sent to his new apartment.) He kept to himself, still unwilling and unable to admit anyone into his quiet sanctum.

The silent young man hadn't made any close friends or given anyone his work or home telephone number; understandably, he was shocked to get a phone call at the yard. Gus had walked toward him slowly, shaking his head back and forth.

"What is it, Gus?

"I'm afraid you've got some bad news coming, son."

Gus put his hand on his shoulder and told him to sit down and take the call at his desk, while he stepped out into the hallway..

The voice on the other end of the line was a familiar one. It was Scott's former landlord, Shep. He didn't waste any time. He simply said, "Your mother has been found dead in her apartment; seems she fell and hit her head. Might have been drinking—maybe not. There was nobody there at the time. A neighbor called the police when she heard the dogs barking. Do you want me to do something for you?"

"Thanks Shep, but I gotta think for a minute. Where is she now?"

"She's at the hospital morgue," he answered quietly.

"Thanks again, but I'll see what I can do from here first. I'll make some calls and you'll hear from me soon." Scott hung up the phone and tried to sort out the conversation that had just taken place.

Gus entered the tiny cluttered office and sat down.

"What is it you need son?"

"I don't know," Scott said quietly. "I have no idea what I should be doing about this."

"I have a lawyer that can take care of things for you, if you like."

"Gus, I think I'd like that, if you wouldn't mind."

Gus's lawyer drove up to Boston with power of attorney and saw to the cremation and interment of Susan Elizabeth Kelly. She had no furniture, jewelry, or money; literally speaking, she had no estate whatsoever. Scott had asked the lawyer to retrieve photographs—if there were any—and give everything else to the Vincent De Paul people. He still remembered how good the Catholic Society had been to him and his mother when he was growing up. He could still recall the joy with which he greeted the Catholic workers when the DePaul van pulled up to the building parking lot with boxes of warm winter clothes to be distributed from door to door.

By the time he was twelve years old, he was so filled with embarrassment that he hid in the basement whenever the truck approached the building.

Scott made it very clear to the lawyer that his whereabouts were to remain confidential, no matter who inquired. There were very few people he knew that would know his mother or anything about her. He never even thought of calling his father. Anyway, he would accept condolences only through his lawyer. He would pay for any and all expenses his mother may have left behind and he had no desire to hear from anyone in Boston; not his co-workers not his neighbors and e*specially*, not Lila. (Once again, he was shutting her out of his life.)

He paid the lawyer in cash and went to work two days later with one less person in his life to care about. Still, deep in the middle of the dark nights that followed, he thought about calling Lila and even considered calling his father—*"that bastard, Henry Macguire."*

He didn't call either of them—but he did send Lila a card.

One evening, alone in his misery, he went around to the Motel to look up the front desk clerk—seeking some sort of comfort, he guessed; he was not surprised to learn that she didn't work there anymore. It was just as well; he didn't need any complications at this point.

Life would go on and so would Scott Macguire.

Almost two years had passed since Gus had hired him to "work the junkyard" and Scott had fallen into a comfortable groove of working, reading, and occasionally going to the corner bar with the guys for a drink and a few laughs. Gus continued to try to set him up with young available women, but Scott had recently observed that life was good for him and he liked the new and free Scott Macguire; he deliberately chose to avoid the complexities that would come with letting a woman into his life, again.

On a clear evening, with little bitterness left within his heart, Scott felt confident enough to write to Lila, making sure to reveal his mailing address for the first time in two years. He had asked her not to call or try to visit him but, if she wished to write back, he would be happy to hear from her. He hoped she would respect his wishes at this time. He knew it would anger her, since she preferred to be in control of any situation that included her; but if she wanted to keep in touch with Scott it would be on *his* terms, this time. This type of relationship would be a big change for Scott—and a bigger change for Lila! Anyway, she did write back and they corresponded for the next several months.

In his third year of living in Baltimore Scott thought he had made considerable progress in his quest to lay his demons to rest. He was able to put his relationship with Sonny into perspective, successfully ridding himself of the guilt that had haunted him for the first two years he lived in Baltimore. It had finally become crystal clear to him that Sonny's death was not *his* fault; then, and only then, had he been able to bury that vision in some profoundly secret place, where only he could still visit it from time to time. Of course, there were still episodes during which the tragic scene came rushing before his eyes, uninvited—debilitating him for hours. In making peace with himself, Scott concluded that the vision of Sonny's death would have to join that special place of *things unspoken*—the place that Scott would jealously guard against any reference to for the rest of his life.

He calmly recalled his mother's death and was satisfied that he had grieved properly for her. Although he had taken care of matters by proxy, he felt he had shown proper respect and had done the honorable thing. He wasn't being calculatingly cold; it was just that there had been no need to go to Boston for her burial. There was no one there that needed consoling and certainly no estate to settle.

When he looked back to that shaky time, he was glad he hadn't contacted his father—he didn't think it was the right thing to do. After all, his mother was never married to Henry Macguire and hadn't had any contact with him for years—that was his understanding. Besides, he had no score to settle with his father; he thought it was the right thing to do—just let it be.

Some nights, when he was lonely and disappointed with his decision, Scott secretly admitted to himself that he feared a relationship with his father at this point; perhaps another time and another place—maybe even another planet—just not here or now.

He was still working on whether or not he should resume his relationship with Lila. He wished she wasn't so overbearing and controlling; her bossiness still came across loud and clear—even in her letters. He quietly thanked God that she hadn't tried to see him without his permission or force his hand into playing a card he wasn't ready to play. Right now, he lived by *his* rules. Forget Lila, Henry, his mother, or Sonny—this was *his* world and *he* made the rules.

Scott's social life moved very slowly; sometimes it was actually non-existent, as far as he was concerned. He had entered into a few casual relationships with a couple of pleasant young women, but they hadn't progressed any further than a movie or bowling, followed by a hamburger. He felt he needed more time and put dating out of his head while he went about his business of working and trying to conduct his life with some purpose. He did not feel the need for complications of any sort, at the moment.

The seasonably warm day started as any other August morning. He was up early and off to work. Scott had grown fond of his job and enjoyed the mindless banter that went on between him and the guys at the yard. He always arrived early enough to have coffee with them and do a little male gossiping. They enjoyed teasing him being the college graduate with a dictionary vocabulary. Ever mindful of his desire for privacy, they never inquired about his personal life; he was appreciative of their sensitivity.

Gus and the guys had come to respect the wishes of this shy and silent young man who had arrived from Boston a brooding loner and had slowly morphed into the friendly, cheerful young man who now brightened their lives—and that of the once-irritable junkyard dog.

Scott usually broke up his day by walking a couple blocks to the post office to check his mailbox. The guys whistled and howled catcalls when he would return with a letter deliberately sticking out of his pocket—secretly enjoying the implication. He let them think whatever they wanted to think.

Another manifestation of his penchant for privacy was his preference for a mailbox at the post office rather than the box downstairs in the hallway of the apartment house. He would grab a newspaper on the way and say hello to a few vendors whose acquaintance he had made in the last couple of years.

First there was Fats, the hot dog vendor, followed by Shorty, the newsstand operator, and at the end of the block, Mr. Big—the huge Latino who owned the small car wash and always complained to Scott he would never get rich off the guys from the junkyard. Friendly, impersonal, and harmless; they completed his small, but impenetrable world.

The post office was refreshingly cool, thanks to its roaring air conditioners; yet, Scott felt an eerie chill that wasn't caused by the blowers on this particularly warm day. He trembled in a way he couldn't explain as he walked over to the bank of tiny mailboxes and unlocked number 200—immediately spotting a piece of mail that was easily recognizable. The lavender envelope with the tiny flowers on it signaled a letter from Lila. He took out a tiny penknife and slit the end open carefully. A newspaper clipping fluttered to the floor as he removed the single sheet of stationery with the delicate border of flowers. Before bending to pick it up, he pressed the scented sheet to his nostrils and inhaled the familiar scent. It was *Lila's scent*. He exhaled slowly and began to read the note:

August 15, 1996

Dear Scott,

It's been almost three years since we last saw each other, but I always look forward to your post cards and letters. Time hasn't exactly been kind to me but I'm doing okay, now. I had a really bad time when you left Boston so abruptly; you have no idea what I've been through at this end, but then you had your own problems to deal with. You must have suffered very deeply over Sonny's and then your mother's death, but I guess, sooner or later, we all have to accept such losses and keep moving forward. Alas, my darling, I'm very sorry to enclose this article. I wasn't sure anyone would call you—somebody probably would have—but I thought you should know as soon as possible. If I can help in any way, please contact me. You know where I am.

Love, Lila

By the tone of her letter, Scott figured someone he knew well or at least genuinely respected, had died—he hoped it wasn't Shep, his old landlord, or his former boss at S&S—so he bent down and picked up the folded newspaper article and began scanning it quickly.

Puckshaw ___Aug 11, 1996___

Yesterday, a local helicopter pilot reported that a white male passenger jumped out of his light commuter plane and was apparently drowned in the Bay of Puckshaw. The ticket agent—an acquaintance of the victim—reported that the older gentleman had earlier bought a ticket for Heli-Bay—the new shuttle plane that replaced the old ferry that once carried islanders across the bay. The pilot reported he and the gentleman exchanged normal pleasantries and as he began the ten-minute crossing, his passenger suddenly released his seatbelt, pulled on the emergency handle of the light plane door, and jumped without a sound. This morning, the body of the passenger was retrieved and identified as Henry Maguire, long-time reporter for the *Sunny Islander*. Ed Barton, editor of the newspaper, said that he considered Henry a good friend and an honest and thorough reporter. He noted that Henry had recently completed a manuscript detailing the most memorable events of his twenty-five years on the island and was looking forward to its publication. He said the islanders would miss Henry Macguire. One son, Scott K. survives. Arrangements are pending.

Surprisingly shaken, Scott crumpled the newspaper article into a ball and threw it against the wall. He felt his morning coffee rise up from his stomach and spurt into the back of his throat.

He hated the thought of leaving Gus, but he knew, this time he would have to go to *Puckshaw* and bury his father. Strangely enough, he wanted to. He accepted Gus's condolences and the sincere offers of assistance from the rest of the guys and realized—by the lump in his throat—that he had come to embrace them as his true friends. He was ashamed that he had been so unaware of the bond that had subtly formed between him and this group of strangers. After all, they *had* welcomed him into their world when his own was fraught with pain and confusion.

By the end of the week he found himself in a daze as he said good-bye and began to close up his tiny apartment. He wouldn't use a lawyer this time; it was not going to be that simple. Henry Macguire was a volatile, complicated, and creatively gifted individual who would not leave this world in a conventional manner. True to his nature, he would be as complex in death as he had been in life.

So now, after all the years he had battled anger and resentment over his father's absence in his life; Scott Kelly Macguire was going to *Puckshaw* to handle his estate and confront him in death.

Gus's lawyer had arranged a telephone conference with Ed Sims—Henry's long-time friend and lawyer whom he had found humorous enough to write about in his manuscript; and Ed Barton, the editor of the *Sunny Islander* and Henry's boss and personal friend for many years. Barton said that no one could be Henry's boss—"He was smarter than all of us put together and never took direction, anyway."

Ed Barton was practically a legend on *Puckshaw*. He did most of the talking—he knew everything there was to know about Henry's professional and personal business. Ed Sims would legally probate and execute the will but he allowed Ed Barton to speak freely.

Scott was not surprised to hear that his father had left a will and that he was Henry's only child and heir. He wondered, with some vanity, if he had impressed his father when they had met a few years ago; or if Henry had come in search of him to make sure he was deserving of his estate in the event of his demise. After all, Scott reasoned, you never knew how or what this driven, thorny, and creative individual might be thinking.

Henry's boss told Scott there was some property—a small house and an empty lot he had just purchased—and two vehicles.

Scott registered surprise and asked, "Did you say *two* vehicles?"

"Yes, two vehicles, son!" Ed Barton shouted.

There were bankbooks, some cash in Ed Sims' office vault, and a manuscript that Henry had dropped off just a few days before his death. He was hoping to get it published and had asked Ed Barton to have a look at it.

The bankbooks and cash were of little interest to Scott; but a manuscript? Where was it? Scott was extremely curious about the manuscript that Henry was on the verge of shopping around to a few known publishers. A manuscript! Scott felt excitement coursing through his veins.

When he inquired about the contents of the manuscript, Ed said he guessed it was a chronicle of the daily events that Henry had experienced on his ten-year odyssey across the country as a youngster; and the events Henry had covered on the island for some twenty-five years.

"Oh Yes, there is a special section on the lives of two women who had committed suicide on *Puckshaw*. I imagine that will be pretty interesting to a lot of folks. You know, he did hundreds of hours of research on the mysterious victims; I'm not one bit surprised that he would write about them."

Scott let that slide though it sent a slight shiver through him.

He was still in awe that his own father might be a possible author! Deep down, he had always suspected his reading and writing talents may have come from him—certain that they hadn't come from his mother, Susan. With a sudden twinge of guilt Scott came to his mother's defense against such an assumption. He reasoned, with all fairness, that she never seemed to have had the opportunity to explore her talents—whatever they might have been.

The conference call ended abruptly when Ed Sims announced that he had "a lot to do in re to Henry's estate". Ed Barton agreed that he too, had some work to do on the comprehensive article about Henry that he was still editing. "It'll run in a day or two; I'll save you a copy," he promised.

Scott wasted little time in packing; he still had the same two duffle bags that he had arrived with so he tossed his grimy work clothes into the trash can and stuffed the bags with his meager wardrobe of casual clothes, socks, and underwear. He made arrangements to store his aging stereo and treasured books; yet again promising to send for them later.

God, he thought, haven't I done all this before? He cursed under his breath regretting having never bought the car that he promised himself, but since he lived within walking distance of his job he—practical to a fault—had not felt the need for it. His old friend, "frugality" had never really left him.

So now, just about three years after arriving in Baltimore, Scott Macguire was on his way to the bus station—he would depart in the same fashion in which he had arrived and, of course, he would leave no forwarding address.

The trip to *Puckshaw* was a blur. Scott's mind was spinning, not only with mild grief and confusion, but with a weird sort of excitement. In a sense, he was going to meet Henry Macguire for the second time in his life!

Two days later at noon, Scott Macguire, only son and heir to Henry Macguire—the well known reporter and twenty-five-year-resident of *Puckshaw*—waited outside Ed Barton's office like a kid waiting for the principal to summon him into his office. He had more apprehensions than expectations and was struggling to keep his breathing from spinning out of control into hyper-ventilation. In one sane moment he saw his whole rational pattern of thinking as having gone impossibly haywire. "He was whispering between chattering teeth to keep calm when Ed Barton's secretary motioned him to enter his office.

He forced himself back to reality as he was ushered into the tiny, cluttered, corner office that was home away from home to the *Sunny Islander's* editor.

"What's his name again?" Scott whispered to the matronly secretary, who rode shotgun for Ed Barton in the waiting room. No one had ever gotten into the editor's office without her approval during her entire tenure and never would, as long as she was alive and breathing.

Just then the short burly editor burst into the room and thrust out his hand.

"Hello son, I'm Ed Barton—I run the paper here on *Puckshaw*—sorry about Henry. He was a good man; a bit lazy but, in my opinion—a good man."

Scott half-rose and shook his hand, mumbling his thanks for the condolences and his help in expediting the matter at hand.

For some reason he didn't like Barton. He definitely did not like the comment about Henry being lazy; he thought it was insensitive and in very bad taste.

"Ed Sims will be here soon; you met him on the phone, a few days ago."

Scott snapped back to attention when Barton tugged his sleeve to lead him into an even smaller office with a little more privacy. "Shotgun Annie" was watching and listening to everything; Scott was glad when Barton firmly closed the door. He had a sneaking feeling he was going to have to listen to a lot of crap before they got down to business, but he was pleasantly surprised when Ed Sims, the attorney-at-law who would explain the will and see to its proper execution, arrived to join them.

Scott hated to do this, but he felt he was entitled to some privacy, so he interrupted Ed Barton with, "Sorry, Mr. Barton, I don't mean to be impertinent, but may I ask why you are still here?"

"*Your* father and *my* good friend, Henry, appointed me co-executor of his will. Does that answer your question, son?"

Flushing with embarrassment, Scott murmured, "Yes Sir. I was not made aware of that fact. Sorry."

Scott figured he had the right to ask for privacy and his easy confidence surprised him. It even pleased him! He had learned a lot in the last three years—a lot more than he realized.

The next hour was a blur of *legalese* but when the meeting was over, Ed Barton declared before God and man that he had discharged his duties honorably and rose to dismiss the other two men.

Scott felt like a child again—sent to the back of the room by a stern teacher. He gathered up the large manila envelope which held the manuscript, a bunch of keys, and two bankbooks; looking around in confusion. There was so much to remember; overwhelmed, he mumbled his thanks to both men and started out of the office. He had no idea what the hell he was doing or where the hell he was going and Barton didn't seem to care—so much for someone who had insisted on calling him *son* and proclaimed to be Henry's good friend.

Barton had done his job and Scott had been less than gracious; now he would be left in the hands of a strange barrister to sink or swim; Barton didn't give a damn.

Edward Sims, the portly attorney with the shiny suit and scuffed shoes, followed him out with, "Son, you're going to need help with some of this stuff—can I be of service to you?"

Scott gave the man a grateful look and let his shoulders sag under the weight of his new and unexpected responsibilities. All he had ever worried about was paying his rent, buying groceries, and getting to work on time. This turn of events was overwhelming—an understatement to be sure.

Sims read the kid's body language and sensed his need, swiftly swinging into action.

"Okay. Good. Let's get some lunch and get down to business. Do you have a car or a place to stay?" Before Scott could answer, Ed continued with "I figured you didn't—we'll take care of that right after lunch."

With the formalities out of the way, Edward Sims led Scott out of the newspaper office and up the street toward *Charlie's*, the island's most popular restaurant. Once there, they sat in a large back booth which Scott assumed must be Ed's office by the way he made himself at home in it. Ed, still in charge, deftly ordered lunch for both of them. No one seemed to care that he had spread his paperwork all over the table and placed two oversized mobile phones, prominently, at his right hand. An overly familiar waitress gave Scott a noticeable once-over that annoyed him. He was tired and *everything* was annoying him.

While they waited for coffee and a sandwich, Scott learned that one set of keys was for the tiny house about a half-mile up the main drag and the other was for the jeep that was still parked in the lot near the Heli-Bay ticket booth. When Scott tried to picture Henry buying a ticket on the very day he was about to end his life, he shook his head and couldn't believe he was indulging in such morbidity. He heard a jingle and looked up questioningly while Ed Sims dangled the third set of keys.

"And those are...?"

Ed smiled. "It seems like Henry just bought himself a brand new Toyota Camry! You know, he was always complaining about the Jeep and how he was going to get rid of it this year. We all thought that maybe he was planning to take a trip and needed a better car. Well anyway, it's parked in the garage at the house."

Scott retorted darkly, "He was planning on taking a trip alright!" Immediately regretting the sarcasm, he lowered his head and rubbed both eyes with the thumb and middle finger of his left hand.

Sims assumed the kid was left-handed—like his father, Henry.

The truth was that his head was swimming and Scott was beginning to hate Henry, anew, for not being there to explain things to him. He even cursed him under his breath saying, "The son of a bitch."

Edward Sims never showed any outward sign of hearing Scott's remark, but entertained a privately held thought that this kid was an ungrateful little bastard. Ed had been Henry's lawyer and confidant for over twenty years and objected to the remarks. Too shrewd to lose a client and guessing that Henry would appreciate it if he prevented the kid from financially destroying himself in the first year of his inheritance, he continued—patiently.

"Here's the plan, son. I got you a room at the motel for tonight; it's a nice place and you'll need a good night's sleep. It's right down the street. Right after dinner I'll walk you over, okay? Did you take the bullet train into Boston?"

"No; some kind of a rapid transit bus with fewer stops. I don't know. I don't know. Had a long layover someplace and got in this morning. Whatever."

He was hungry and tired and sick of the whole thing. He wanted to be alone.

They ate quietly, exchanging a few words now and then, but as soon as they were through eating, Ed Sims took his arm and led him down the street to the motel. You're all checked in, son. I'll be out here at nine tomorrow morning. Now get in there and shower and get to bed."

"It's the first thing that you've said, all day, that makes any sense to me."

They both laughed and Scott turned and opened the door to a blast of icy air.

He couldn't sleep. After a long night he fitfully drifted into an uneasy slumber; it was uncomfortable and short. A jangling phone jolted him to attention; a wake-up call from the front desk clerk.

"Mr. Macguire, Mr. Sims has asked me to call you. Are you fully awake, sir?"

Henry hung up on her.

It was the first time he had ever been addressed as Mr. Macguire—or sir.

A quick breakfast at *Charlie's* and they were at it again.

"Let's keep going, son," Sims continued.

He opened a large manila envelope and took out a long envelope with some legal papers in it. "There is a little piece of property in the beach area that used to have a cottage standing on it. It was almost demolished by a storm in early June. Henry paid a bundle for that little triangle—made a few of the past owner's relatives rich. (The Cranes and Sonny's father most likely had split that windfall.) Jesus, I can't believe I just closed that deal about three or four weeks ago! He was planning to rebuild that cottage and retire there—anyway, that's what he *said*. I'll take you over to see it later. Nice little spot that overlooks a cove with a great private beach."

Scott felt that cold shiver again but dismissed it with a shake of his shoulders.

"I know I'm throwing a lot at you, son but there is still the matter of this money."

Sims slid several bankbooks, encased in thick plastic sleeves, across the booth—carefully avoiding the coffee cups and bacon-and-egg platters. One could see he was used to transacting business in the coffee shop, in his favorite booth.

Scott almost shouted, "Money, what money?" He looked at the bankbooks, not expecting anything more than ordinary savings and a simple checking account. He was secretly relieved since he had been told by Barton that he would have to pay for Henry's cremation and interment. Henry had left him (Barton) a personal note on that subject that read: *Cremation. No services. No headstone. Please, Ed! Thanks.*

Barton had obliged. He told Scott, earlier, he would show him where Henry's remains had been laid to rest just four days ago. "And by the way, son, Roberts Funeral Director would appreciate a check at your earliest convenience. Sims will provide you with the invoice."

Scott had already thought about making some charitable donations if there was any money left after settling Henry's estate. After all—the way he saw it—it wasn't money he had earned and he wouldn't feel right about taking something that really didn't belong to him. Ed Sims quickly helped to dispel that notion by reminding Scott that Henry had worked *very* hard for *every* asset in his estate and fully intended that his only son inherit and enjoy the fruits of his labors. He always told me that he owed you *something*. So…there you have it."

Scott thought of his mother and wished she were still around; he'd be happy to pass any windfall on to her. After all, Henry had pretty much ruined her life when he left her with a kid to rear. Maybe he had given her a little help over the years, but it was never enough to sustain her—or her son. He remembered his poverty with a resentful pang.

"Christ! Is there no end to this?" Scott shook his head incredulously.

Ed smiled. "Soon, son, soon; now this bankbook, here, shows a savings of $301,000.00."

Scott gulped and closed his eyes. "Jesus!"

Ed raised his eyes to the heavens and folded his hands in prayer. "You should be happy! And yes, there is more. Cash—there's a pretty big wad of it in my personal vault; fifty or sixty grand—I think. Also Henry recently reminded me that he had a large safe-deposit box at the bank that contained a couple dozen journals of some sort and a few personal papers. You know. Deeds to the house and property and car ownership papers—personal stuff. It says here in the last paragraph that the contents of the box are to be delivered to you alone. However, that box must be opened in the presence of a bank trustee so proper taxes can be levied if there is cash or jewelry in it. I don't think we'll find cash *or* jewelry in it; Henry was pretty smart that way—but one never knows!

We're moving along nicely, son, so let's head over to the bank and get that out of the way. Mr. Jordan is expecting us sometime today. Are you up for that, son? It's right down the street."

"Christ, seems like everything on this island is right down the street," Scott murmured.

And why the hell are they calling me son? I've gone through twenty-eight years of my fucking life without a father and all of a sudden I've got two fathers in one day.

Ed Sims felt a pang of tenderness; even a stranger would have noticed the similarities in the attitudes of Henry Macguire and his son. They both possessed the same no-nonsense, no-pretense attitude that Ed admired—more so in Henry than in his kid.

The safe deposit box held one surprise. In addition to the journals and personal papers, there was a worn gray envelope with "Susan" scrawled across it. It contained stacks of tens, twenties, fifties and one-hundred dollar bills, neatly banded, along with a cheap, silver-plated woman's watch. So Henry *had* thought of her; he just hadn't counted on her pre-deceasing him.

The bank trustee, using a little electric calculator, solemnly counted it. It seemed to take forever but when he was through tallying all the cash, he announced proudly that the total was $38,500.00. It was duly noted and Scott signed an IRS form confirming the amount in the box and authorizing the tax deduction on the spot.

Ed assured all present that he would expedite the proper tax forms for Scott—obviously proud to be representing him. Other than that little piece of business, Scott was free to take the contents and leave. The trustee asked him if he wanted to continue the rental on the box. Scott shook his head back and forth in a hazy state of mind.

"I really don't know." He looked at Sims, utterly confused and showing signs of exhaustion.

"We'll keep the box for now, Sims said decisively. The boy will be back for the rest of the contents later in the week…"

Scott interrupted Ed Sims in mid sentence with, "What happened to my father's manuscript? Where did it go?"

"You left it in the booth last night and I brought it with me, son. It's locked up in the trunk of my car. Not to worry; now let's get going and take a look at the house. You probably could stay in it tonight. Hell, it's yours, now. Don't worry; I'll take care of the transfer of ownership for you. We'll drop off your things and I'll take you out to see the beach lot. After that we'll pick up the Jeep and you can go back to the house and get a good night's sleep. Can you handle this? Just a couple more stops, then I'll get you something to eat and literally take you home and tuck you into bed. How does that sound."

Scott looked at his watch; it was five-thirty and the meeting had started at nine-thirty with an hour for lunch during which Ed continued to conduct business. He hadn't had a chance, yet, to collect his feelings about Henry's death. Not that he felt like grieving or anything like that; but his father was dead—and he *had* committed suicide—and that seemed to be *overlooked* by Mr. Sims.

Giving Ed the benefit of doubt, Scott guessed that the guy figured he had a job to do and just wanted to get it over with and be paid for it right away. He was aware of how Sims had eyed that cash like a cat sitting before a fishbowl.

What he *failed* to recognize were the red, swollen eyes that gave evidence that Sims had been crying on and off. If the truth was known, Ed Sims had loved Henry Macguire like a brother and he was missing him sorely. He wondered if maybe—just maybe—he could grow to love, or even like, his kid; though he highly doubted the kid could fill his father's shoes in the *friend* department.

Ed pulled up in front of the little house—barely a house—more like a cabin that sat on a lot between two small buildings at a dead end. They guessed at a key and tried the back door. The house was in perfect order; small and meticulously well kept. For a bachelor pad, it was immaculate and uncluttered. Scott took note of the expensive furniture and attractive rugs, streaked with evidence of having been recently vacuumed. Though he never gave that impression to outsiders, Henry was fastidious behind those closed doors; it was just another side of the quirky reporter that was closely guarded—more like concealed.

Ed helped Scott deposit his two bags inside the door and dropped an armful of envelopes, including the manuscript, on the dinette table. For a moment they both were silent as they took an admiring look around. Ed Sims had known Henry for years but didn't have a clue as to how he really lived behind these closed doors. He conducted all his business at Henry's tiny, cubbyhole office down at the *Sunny Islander* or in the legendary back booth at Charlie's. Ed couldn't remember having ever stepped foot into Henry's private world. Slightly distracted by the charming little house, he ushered Scott out mumbling something about getting to the beach property before the sun set.

As Ed took off and left the tiny business district behind him Scott felt cold again. He hoped he wasn't coming down with something; he had become chilled several times during the day. As they drove past the whitewashed building that housed the newspaper archives, Scott thought it looked like an interesting place to visit sometime. He would like to do that before he left the island.

The traffic had thinned out and Ed took a sharp left and headed toward the beach area. Scott had already recognized a few buildings and intersections but now he felt dangerously close to something he couldn't define. Mr. Sims had been talking for several minutes before Scott heard what he was saying. He was jabbering on about the eerie history of the cottage that used to sit high on the cliff overlooking the Atlantic and how Scott's father, Henry, had researched this property's history so thoroughly that he was considered somewhat of an expert on the cottage and its various occupants.

Scott felt light-headed and out of control. A nauseous wave filled his mouth with salty saliva and without warning he flung open the passenger door, forcing Sims to step on the break violently enough to send both of them lurching toward the dashboard. Scott could hear him shouting as if in the distance.

"What the hell's the matter with you, boy? Are you sick? Why didn't you say something? Jesus, I know you've had a long day, but..."

Scott wiped the perspiration from his face and shook his head, "Turn around, Ed. I have to go back. I'm too goddamned tired to hear another word or take another step. Please. Take me back to the house, will you? I'll come out on my own in a day or two and get back to you about the rest of this business. Is that okay with you?"

Sims was tenacious. "What about the Jeep? Do you want to stop and pick it up?"

"No, no," whispered Scott. I'll get it tomorrow. I can't do anymore today. I've had it. Sorry."

"Alright son" said Sims, somewhat perplexed, "Let's get you home right away. Maybe we overdid it today and don't forget; you've been through a lot, kid. Christ, I'm really sorry; I should have known better."

They were back at the house and Scott darted out of the car without a handshake which annoyed Sims, who was also tired. He had tried to whisper a "thank you" but he wasn't sure it was even audible. He let himself in the house, quickly locking the door behind him. The room spun as he dashed into the bathroom, slamming the door behind him. Afterwards, he felt relief to have been purged of the day's binge on so many legal and emotional issues—and Charlie's greasy fare.

He showered quickly, rummaged through his duffle bag for some shorts, and within minutes he lay between crisp, cool sheets in the freshly made bed. He wondered if Sims had seen to that bit of housekeeping—or was it Henry.

He struggled to collect his thoughts. His father had thought of everything! Scott almost wished he had known the man—a loyal friend to few and a harmless eccentric to most—but he couldn't think straight. He was overtired and close to passing out.

Maybe he was hallucinating, but Scott Macguire fought sleep—or so he thought. When he checked his watch, he had been staring at the ceiling for at least three hours. Perhaps he *had* been sleeping—he wasn't sure.

He wasn't sure about anything anymore.

Lying in the dark, hyperventilating, he began to feel nauseous again. This would have to stop or he was going to be in serious trouble. He could see a doctor—Henry must have had one—and get some pills to calm himself down. After all, he still had papers to sign, a car to pick up and he began several other legal duties to tend to as the sole heir to the estate of Henry Macguire.

He needed to take it easy and a glass of cold water seemed like a good idea. He rose from his bed like a sleep walker and padded, barefoot, into the kitchen. The new, GE fridge was well stocked and he reached for a small bottle of spring water. He sipped it and tried to avoid thinking about the last four days.

He glanced around and noticed, through the large kitchen window, that the back yard was bathed in shimmering moonlight.

Flipping the small yellow light on, he stepped out the back door and faced the silent, scarcely treed lot. No neighbors on either side—just like Henry. He had bought the place because it sat between two small businesses; no one would be around in the evenings when he was home enjoying his solitude and writing. By the light of the full moon, he spotted the lone, wooden, sun chair under a leafy tree and was instantly saddened. Henry's chair. He walked over and dropped his slight frame into it. He wondered how many times the poor guy had sat here alone, with no one to talk to.

Scott Kelly Macguire felt heavy. He thought how erratic his behavior had been in the last twenty-four hours, especially earlier in the evening when riding in Ed Sims' car. Now he felt foolish; he had almost caused the guy to have an accident. He was ashamed; after all, he was a grown man—acting like a stupid child! He planned to apologize first thing in the morning.

He was fully prepared to face the fact that he knew where Sims was taking him! He had been down that private beach road dozens of times.

Since Sonny always drove when they spent intimate weekends there, she proudly took little shortcuts that only *the islanders* knew of. Besides, she was terribly discreet and never wanted to be seen spending the weekend at the cottage with a lover. She liked to arrive after dark on Friday evening and leave at dusk on Sunday. It may have satisfied her desire for privacy, but it never stopped the neighbors from taking note of her arrival and departure—or whether she was alone or not. She even bought groceries and beverages before they reached the island, avoiding the business district where they might be seen together. Sonny wasn't ashamed of Scott or her relationship with him; she was just fiercely protective of her private life.

So Scott was no stranger to that little road; he had seen it many times—almost always in the semi-darkness, but surely recognizable. Now, he envisioned the tiny cove and the sterling crescent beach that gave them all the privacy they needed on those passion-filled weekends. And the thought of the enchanted cottage—always warm in the fall evenings and blissfully cool in summer—forced him to take a deep breath in order to control his emotions. This was not a good time to fall into paroxysms of sorrow or guilt.

He rose and stumbled back into Henry's tiny house—he had difficulty thinking of it as his very own—and sat at the shiny wooden table where he sifted through an armload of large envelopes and legal papers. He sorted the mess out and put aside a large, heavy envelope. His heart fluttered; it was the manuscript and even though he was exhausted, he was anxious to start reading it.

He guessed (correctly) that his father had seen a lot on the island in the last twenty-five years and must have been a pretty decent and knowledgeable reporter to be retained by the *Sunny Islander* for so long. At least that was the impression he got from Ed Barton, his editor-in-chief.

He stared at the envelope with insatiable curiosity. He was aching to just read a sample of his father's writing. Beside the journals that were in the safe-deposit vault at the bank, he noted at least a dozen more volumes in the book case next to Henry's bed. It would be some time before he could even think about reading them. Right now, he needed to get a look at the manuscript.

Preparing for whatever the hell it was he *thought* was in that manuscript, he took a deep breath. Why was he so afraid? So what if Henry covered Belle and Sonny's deaths and became interested in the property and its fascinating occupants? So what, if after a bad storm destroyed the cottage, Henry doled out the necessary cash to buy the strange triangle of beach property? Why was Scott so afraid of opening the envelope that lay on the desk before him like a challenging gauntlet? He closed his eyes, still fearing its contents.

His father couldn't possibly have known about him and Sonny—unless he had read the police files. He wouldn't have had access for ninety days and by *that* time Scott had already disappeared like a flash of lightening in the night. Even if or when Henry learned the truth and wanted to help his son, he wouldn't have been able to—not if he couldn't *find* the kid. He had a slight chance of finding him, but if the kid didn't want to be found, it would be twice as hard.

Sims had said it was well documented that Henry had researched the drowning victim's life for at least three years, so maybe... Scott swallowed a ball of sticky saliva and nodded to himself. Henry Macguire *did* know about his relationship with Sonny and probably just couldn't find him after he fled to Maryland. *Or* maybe he didn't *want* to find him; it could have been all too complex and painful by then. *Maybe! Maybe! Maybe!*

Scott allowed a bit of vanity to creep into his thoughts and wondered if there was anything in the manuscript about him. Had Henry regretted his cowardly flight from Boston, shortly after his son's birth? And then again, after he had promised to spend an evening with Scott and his girlfriend? Had he made any effort to find his son after becoming aware of the truth? He must have known—probably just too late to do anything about it.

Henry's journal would show that it was a *full ninety days* before he saw the police report and knew of his son's involvement with Sonny Adams. Only Henry's *Higher Being* knows what his feelings or intentions were following his discovery of the truth; certainly he must have been saddened over his son's loss and his own bad behavior.

With no little regret, Scott remembered how he had sworn his ex-boss and his former landlord to secrecy about his new apartment; he had only done that to put some distance between himself and Lila—and to keep his mother at bay. He had no intention of hiding from his father—he wasn't even *thinking* of him at that time.

In hindsight, an encounter would have required a lot of courage and probably would have been uncomfortable for both of the Macguire men, since neither of them had made any effort to see each other after the initial meeting in 1992.

Still, Scott fantasized over what it might have been like if Henry had been close by during those tumultuous times, when he could have used a caring human being to guide him through the battlefield. The point was moot; he was wallowing in the realm of raw emotion; only later would he realize how much that intense soul-searching would painstakingly cleanse him.

He wasn't sure who knew what or when they knew it. His relationship with Sonny had been very private; only one or two of his co-workers, his landlord, Shep, and, of course, Lila had known about her. When she committed suicide, Scott, deep in shock, had made his deal with Sheriff Cramer and fled *Puckshaw*.

Suspecting Scott's his relationship to the *island's* well-known reporter, Cramer, presuming the trail would grow cold and most of the media would not bother to follow the fading scent, decided to deal with Henry when the time came—if he continued to pursue the case. If not...so be it.

Although it was a matter of public record after ninety days, only a few outsiders would actually see the statement. Henry saw it in late December, after which the file was locked up in a drawer—"conveniently misplaced"—for some time.

A good reporter probably would have seen the statement late in December and tried to find Scott to confirm the document. A good reporter would have found Scott—if he *really* wanted to. Scott Macguire would never know what Henry's intentions were. He had no idea of what was going on in his life or in his head at that time. Although he *did* know Henry lived on *Puckshaw* and worked for a newspaper, he never could have dreamed that he would have such an obsessive connection to Sonny's drowning.

Scott was searching for a ghost. His father had never really belonged to him. Trying to imagine how it might have been in a time or place that never existed for him was pure fantasy. Now, their lives could only intertwine through Henry's writings and the sooner he accepted that fact; the easier his life would become.

Suddenly, in the pre-dawn darkness, young Scott Macguire experienced the first pain of loss in the profound silence of his self-induced sphere of loneliness. He wept.

Morning had sneaked in and he was still as exhausted as he had been the night before. Rising, he took the phone off the hooks, relocked the doors, and went back to bed—sleeping for several hours. He finally woke with a start—momentarily disoriented.

After a long, hot shower that was both calming and invigorating, he used a large bath towel to scrub his body dry—adrenalin coursing through his veins, restoring much needed strength to his muscles.

He dressed quickly and decided to walk over to Charlie's for breakfast before getting directions to where the Jeep was parked; *Heli-Bay airport parking garage—or something like that—as he recalled.* Maybe he'd pick up the Jeep and drive around for a while; he needed to prepare himself for whatever was in the manuscript that was still lying, untouched, in the large manila envelope on Henry Macguire's oak desk.

By the time he picked up the Jeep and stopped for a few groceries—mostly frozen dinners and desserts that he was accustomed to—he realized how hot the sun was and promised to buy himself some shorts, tee shirts, and tennis shoes, as soon as possible. As he put the groceries in the back of the Jeep, he also resolved to stop eating frozen dinners that were so full of fat and salt. "After all," he whispered to himself as he raised his eyebrows, "I *am* a man of means now! I'll have to start eating responsibly".

He stopped in his tracks for a moment and hoped he wasn't going to turn into one of those self-absorbed phonies just because he had a *half-million dollars*.

If the truth was known, Scott Kelly Macguire felt deeply undeserving of this windfall.

While he was out of the house for a couple of hours, the answering machine recorded two messages for him and one for Henry. Both Ed Barton and Ed Sims had called to see if he was getting on okay—renewing their offers of assistance. Though he assumed (incorrectly) that Ed Sims was anxious to present him with a bill, it was the third message that hit him like a jackhammer.

"Hi Henry" the voice said, "This is Joe, over at Toyota. How's the car running? You're going to love it, I promise. Call me if you need anything and thanks again."

Scott erased all three messages and resolved to change the answering machine greeting, but he couldn't do it just yet; he wanted to be able to hear his father's voice for just a little while longer. Then he thought of disconnecting the phone all together—an irrational and silly thing to do.

With errands, shopping, and small, time-consuming tasks—time flew.

Popping a frozen dinner in the microwave, he reached into his duffle-bag and pulled out a pair of khaki shorts and a worn tee shirt. He daydreamed for a moment—the warning bell on the microwave breaking into his reverie to remind him that his dinner was ready; taking one look at the boxed, shriveled-up dinner, he quickly changed his mind and dumped it down the garbage disposal. Fresh fruit and a few slices of sharp cheese were much more appealing. A deep cereal bowl with a bunch of grapes, an apple, and a banana should do the trick.

With paper napkins in hand he headed for the large easy chair near the window. The view was lovely and within a half hour the sun began to sink below the horizon rapidly—no fanfare. Scott finished his bowl of fruit and last scraps of hard cheese. He felt much better.

He threw a quick side-glance at the large oak desk and the contents strewn across the shiny surface. He was frightened for some reason; as though he should be asking someone's permission to remove the heavy manuscript from its envelope. He did it quickly, using his strong arm to lift and pull the manuscript out of the rough envelope in one swift motion. He held it on his lap for several minutes before rising and heading for the long, leather sofa; piling up three pillows, he fell lengthwise onto the finest piece of furniture he had ever laid eyes on. If this was to be his home in the future he would start by making himself comfortable. He had many new things to get used to and plenty of time in which to do so.

He was surprised at his assumption that he would be staying for an undetermined amount of time.

He fanned the telephone book-sized manuscript with its conventional double-spaced text. After all, Henry would know all about those things; having been a published journalist for so many years—submitting mountains of typed pages. But then, so would Scott; albeit low on the totem pole at Scribe & Son, he had been promoted to junior editor and it was accepted and expected that he would continue to be promoted with increasing time and experience. He noted that the manuscript had been typed on a computer or word processor and assumed there was a disc somewhere in Henry's desk, which he hadn't gone through, yet. He wasn't anywhere near ready to touch that inner sanctuary of his father's privacy.

He settled in to concentrate, making every effort to force all other noises and distractions out of his frame of focus.

The manuscript was held together with three, oversized, loose-leaf rings. The title page simply read "Untitled" and after a blank page the actual manuscript began. It was written in a casual journal-entry style with the date in the upper left-hand corner and a greeting of some sort. Henry methodically described events that he considered worthy of preserving and commenting upon.

He wrote, in wide-eyed wonder, of his youthful journey across the country during the sixties. Sometimes the entry detailed a story he was covering or an ongoing human-interest event. It could be as simple as an essay on the change of seasons or a complex dissection of opinions on gun control or the heathcare of an aging nation. After most entries, Henry would skip a few lines and meticulously analyze and reflect upon it with the emphasis on humor and irony. He spared no reproach when it came to the rich and famous or his favorite target: politicians.

Scott read for about an hour shaking his head and smiling to himself. He loved the idea that his father had been on the cutting edge of the 60's youth counter-culture. He tried to imagine him with long hair and a beard—smoking funny cigarettes!

He had no idea Henry was so adept at writing; particularly, in conveying his thoughts with such humor when it came to portraying *The Islanders*! Funny, after all those years, he never considered himself one of *them*. It was "them against me" as far as Henry was concerned, but anyone could see that deep down, *Henry Macguire loved Puckshaw with all his heart!*

After an hour or so, Scott came to a few blank pages and was surprised and disappointed to be coming to the end of the first section so soon; suddenly he was struck by the simplicity of a new title page. It read simply BELLE. That would be Sonny's mother—Bellemara Peterson Adams. She had been dead for over ten years by the time Scott had met Sonny and had heard her referred to only as "Belle". Underneath the title was the date, June 30, 1981.

Scott read the entries voraciously. He always thought that Bellemara had died of an accidental drowning—so he was shaken to read about her illness and questionable death. He tried to picture Sonny as a fourteen-year-old teenager with photographers chasing after her until relatives had arrived to spirit her off the island.

Henry had covered it as a *suicide* although the final police report stated that due to heavy medication and disorientation, the victim "was not deemed responsible for walking into the ocean" that early June morning, when she and her daughter were staying in the cottage.

Scott read on with no little urgency.

So Sonny's mother had been a foster child who, at the age of seventeen, had searched for her birth parents unsuccessfully. Another thing she had never spoken about. She had never talked about the details of her parents' failed marriage either and, since he had no interest in such sensitive information, Scott would have never pried into such matters.

He would have been shocked at Belle's affair with another woman; Sonny would have instinctively known that—steering away from the incident all together.

Scott was fully aware of how protective she was of her parents—especially her mother—and now he understood why.

Belle must have told her about the early years of her life with Aunt Beebe—years so devoid of affection. Then there was the shock that she must have endured when Beebe fled—causing her to be placed in foster care.

Sonny had always said that she hardly knew her maternal grandparents; (The Cranes) yet, she clearly remembered her paternal grandparents and spoke of them with reserved fondness. But then that was Sonny: everything locked up tightly, inside.

Scott was never a prying kind of guy—he had troubles of his own, so he just accepted Sonny as she was— melancholy, sweet, and sensitive.

As he looked back, he realized with deep sadness that she might have just begun the healing process when they met. He wished he had been more perceptive, but that was then and this was now and back-pedaling could be a dangerous sport to indulge in at *this* point.

Scott let the manuscript drop to his chest for a moment. He watched curiously, as it rose and fell with his breathing. He had once had an incredible cat that used to lay on his chest as he rested on the sofa after work each night and it, too, rose and fell with his heaving chest. He dwelled on that recollection for a moment; how he had loved that cat! His name was Cosmo—short for Cosmopolitan. He was friendly and loved throughout the whole neighborhood. Cosmo went out at night and slept, purred, and ate all day. Scott recalled with a shake of his head how that cat loved to eat chopped up meatballs with canned spaghetti sauce—often causing him to sport a red mustache on his beautiful, champagne-colored, furry face. He took his eyes off the manuscript and smiled. How that cat had style! He was a beauty—and he knew it.

Closing his eyes, Scott Macguire let his mind wander for a few minutes, trying hard to put the last week into perspective with the rest of his adult life. He asked himself where the hell *all this new stuff* was going to fit—he had no answer.

He opened his eyes and looked at his watch. "Jesus!" he whispered.

He must have fallen asleep sometime during the night because it was now four-thirty a.m.

He went to the bathroom and checked himself out in the mirror on the way out; large bags had appeared underneath his eyes. He returned to the sofa, pulling a light afghan over his feet and legs.

He began to read about the wonderful summers Belle and Sonny had spent on the island in the early years. In Belle's obituary Henry had written: **"A mother and daughter healed, found peace, and nested together in perfect harmony for almost ten years. Such a magical web of protection they did weave around their little world."**

Suddenly, Scott sat bolt upright! He was shocked to read about the near-drowning of little Reid during the summer of 1974. Henry had mentioned it very briefly in his journal—called it "a frightening summer accident involving the near-death of a little boy". Now, he thought about the pain Sonny must have endured; if only he had known some of these things. She had never mentioned the near-drowning *or* dissolution of the enchanting relationship that she and her mother had enjoyed that summer.

There were so many things Sonny hadn't told him; he had a strange feeling there was a lot more he would find out before he came to the end of this manuscript.

Henry had written about Belle's death with accuracy and sensitivity—given the circumstances of her terminal illness. There wasn't much to say once her daughter, known around town as "Sonny", disappeared from the island.

The cottage was closed for some time though it was rumored that the teenager had made a few visits with unknown adults in the succeeding summers. Sonny would not appear in Henry's journal again until September of 1993.

Henry continued—in his unique journal-entry style—for several years. He wrote of his close brushes with love and hate, while relentlessly ranting against those whom in some way had offended him or stirred his ire. In some entries he would beat his breast in anguish and guilt over his own faults and failings, but in the end, he always reverted to threatening to withdraw from his reporting career—maybe life, itself—in order to satisfy his desire for peace and privacy.

His journals reflected the *big eighties* as decade of both humorous and sobering events—two royal weddings, several notable deaths, and the usual amount of global traumas; including wars, insurrections, hurricanes, serial murders, and a few high-profile scandals. And when the eighties whimpered to a close, some lucky Americans found themselves rich while others were left wanting. Henry had been one of the lucky ones.

Scott noted that from 1990 to September of 1993, there were less than a dozen entries Henry found worthy of referencing in his manuscript; most of them were lacking in enthusiasm or detail, indicating that he was either slowing down or maybe just had less to say.

On the contrary, Scott had spent most of that same period with Sonny. It was a strange period that would eventually have a marked impact on the remainder of both of their lives.

Scott let his mind wander for a moment to the night he had actually met Henry for the first time—late '91 or early '92. His father had surprised him by stepping in front of him as he walked home from the publishing house one night. He introduced himself as Henry Maguire. Scott was stunned and had questioned the stranger. "How the hell do you know who I am and how did you find me? What is this, some kind of prank?"

Henry had put his hands up in front of him saying, "No! This is not a prank. Please, listen to me, kid."

They talked softly, but briefly, and Scott said he needed some time to think things over since this had come as quite a shock to him. They spoke of Susan, Scott's mother, and then

Henry offered to take him out to breakfast the next morning. He offered to pick him up at seven.

Scott had shot back with, "How the hell do you know where I live?"

"I'd be a sorry reporter if I couldn't find my own son's address, now wouldn't I?" Henry had retorted.

Both were curiously taken aback by Henry's use of the expression, *"my own son's"*.

They went to a small diner for breakfast and exchanged strained pleasantries at first; finally, Henry expressed the desire to get to know him and maybe develop a real father-son relationship. He wanted to apologize for a lifetime of neglect, but that seemed like an oversimplification of such a serious issue. He knew he couldn't turn into a father overnight, but he *was* willing to try to build something between them. His voice was calm but his eyes begged Scott for a chance to make things right.

Scott sensed a hint of sincerity in him though still reluctant to commit himself. In the end he had nodded his head and lowered his eyes as if giving permission—or absolution.

Scott wanted his father to meet the quiet and lovely girl he had been seeing for a while and Henry said he would like that. They made plans to meet for dinner a couple of nights later but, true to form, Henry went back to Boston early the next day. Scott never knew why and wouldn't know for years how Henry despised himself for that disastrous lapse in judgment. How was *he* to know that they would never see each other again?

Out of the twelve entries from 1992 and 1993 eleven of them mentioned his name.

The sun rose and Scott sobbed out of exhaustion.

During the next few hours, he slept uneasily; the phone ringing over and over while the machine dutifully recorded the messages.

The bank manager called to remind him that he had business to take care of—"Please reconfirm investment appointment for nine-thirty." Also, Ed Sims had left three messages about getting together to "tie up some loose ends". The fourth message surprised him the most; it was from Ed Barton over at the *Sunny Islander;* he asked if Scott might be interested in writing a few articles for the paper—since he was somewhat in the business—just sort of fill in for his father.

Scott was intrigued and honored by the offer.

After showering, he stood before the steamed-up mirror looking at his naked body; visions of Lila popped before his eyes; he was still conflicted about his feelings toward her and convinced that it was only a matter of time…before she came looking for him.

When Lila wanted something—she didn't give up until she got it and nobody knew that better than Scott Macguire. The thought of her obsessive behavior still frightened him at times and he never fully shook off the intimidation he felt during her bloodletting rages. The longer he was away from her, the sharper her flaws emerged; he missed her aggressive physicality—which brought out his finest manhood—but he wasn't sure he loved her anymore. *He wasn't even sure he liked her.*

Breakfast at Charlie's was not worth mentioning.

Ed Sims showed up with an armload of papers, a yellow legal pad, and his pair of mobile phones. Scott wondered why he always carried them around with him—they had yet to ring in his presence. He reminded Sims about his appointment at the bank and made arrangements to meet him later in the day—in the back booth—if that was alright with him. Scott was now convinced that Sims transacted more business at Charlie's than he did in his little hole in the *Sunny Islander* building. *That little hole* was important; it was home to the big, bank-like vault that still held an envelope filled with his father's cash. He made a mental note to address that issue.

At some point during his boring meeting, Scott took a moment to let his mind wander and address a mild irritation: Why was everybody on the island named Ed, Eddie or Edward? That thought reminded him to get in touch with Barton; he was prepared to tell him that he wasn't sure his talent was in writing articles or even reporting on news events, but he would be willing to give it a try. What he really hoped was that he had the guts to ask if Barton could stop calling him *son*. He had just lost one father and wasn't prepared to take on another—so soon.

He decided against offending the editor-in-chief of the island's only paper; it would have been a bad move.

Scott rested in his father's large, comfortable chair for twenty minutes and tried to absorb the morning's transactions. The coffee at Charlie's was good, but he really couldn't take one more greasy breakfast; he felt better with a lighter, healthier fare of fruit and cereal. He marveled at how Ed Sims had managed to stay alive so long on such a frightful diet! Anyway, he would meet with him again, later in the day.

Scott thought the meeting at the bank went well; the investments were out of his hands and over his head—for now. He trusted the ultra conservative, Mr. Edward Silver, to look after his financial affairs—in the short term, at least. (It hadn't escaped his attention that Sims was up on the market action —always scanning the *Wall Street Journal* for stock quotes—and pretty sharp with numbers. He might look into consulting with him on his long term investments later on.) He shook his head and smiled. The intense bank manager had rambled on while he, nodding in agreement, gave his permission for a number of investment transactions that made Mr. Edward Silver's eyes light up with relief.

Imagine me, Scott Macguire, talking investments! Oh, Lila, if you could see me now!

Henry Macguire had looked after his boy, after all.

Earlier that very morning, while shaving, Scott had tried to think of Henry as *"my father"* or *"Dad";* he just couldn't wrap his brain around it. He didn't know if he would ever be able to do that.

He tried to picture Lila, lying naked beside him and—for the first time—he couldn't. There was *never* a time, since the day they had met, when he couldn't picture her naked or otherwise, and now...*What was going on?*

He was back at the little house by one p.m. and feeling aimless, he stepped out the back door and there it was—the empty chair. He felt sad. *What now?*

An annoying growl came from the pit of his stomach and he blamed it on Charlie's. It was almost one-thirty and he thought a little lunch might dispel the queasiness. He deftly put together a lettuce and cheese sandwich and placed it on a delicately flowered plate. He had never seen such fine china except at Sonny's apartment. He was typically a paper-plate-and-napkin kind of guy, but today he reveled in the ownership of something so beautiful and expensive. He carried the plate the polished coffee table in the living room but quickly returned to kitchen in search of a place mat and a glass of milk. He had never outgrown his love for milk and he knew why—as a kid he never had enough of it. He still remembered his mother's trick of adding water to the quart as soon as it was half empty.

She would say, "See, magic!"

Scott didn't think there was anything magical about the taste. He had another word for it.

Sims called to cancel; he was headed to Boston in aid of a friend. Scott was glad; he spent the rest of the afternoon sitting in the back yard waiting for the lovely sun-set, after which he went in for a hot shower and a quiet, peaceful evening.

Clad in his faded boxer shorts, he sat on the edge of the sofa and clicked the TV on. It was the first time he had turned it on since arriving on the island. Back in Baltimore he preferred to read at night or write a little poetry; T.V. was something new for him—*everything* was new to him these days.

A half hour passed and he had no idea what he was watching—he pressed the "off" button and tossed the remote on the table.

It was Saturday night and he was determined to finish the manuscript before morning. He wanted to spend Sunday clearing his head and setting up some goals for the next few months—just prepare for a fresh start.

He had nonchalantly decided to stay for a while. After all, he had a home, two vehicles, and a sizeable amount of money to take care of—not to mention the new turn of events: as of this afternoon, the possibility of a new job loomed very real. Barton had seemed sincere and enthusiastic in his offer and Scott didn't want to let him down.

He stretched his arms over his head and did a few knee-bends. He needed exercise badly and resolved to get on a regular program of physical conditioning as soon as things died down. He was finally beginning to feel committed to seeing things through and he automatically attributed his resilience to the island's fresh, salty air and quiet atmosphere.

He felt comfortable—as if he had been invited to stay.

He settled himself on the sofa, drew his knees up to his chest, and placed the manuscript squarely in front of him. It was left open where he had stopped—on a blank page. He tried to guess what was on the next page but he was frightened. Getting to the point was the hallmark of Henry's journal entries. What could be next?

September 2, 1993
Good evening, kind friend.
"Yesterday, I met Sonny Peterson Adams, with her face framed in flames of red hair and her sparkling eyes shooting a look over her shoulder at someone who must have been pretty special."

Scott knew immediately that Henry was making a reference to the beautiful, colored, nine-by-twelve photograph that Sonny had surprised him with after they had known each other for only a short time.

Henry continued, with uncharacteristic emotion, to recount Sonny's tragic death along with a recap of her mother, Bellemara Peterson Adams' death, twelve years prior. He had pasted a few file photos of both women on the opposite blank page. Beneath the photos he had scrawled in barely legible penmanship: "striking look-a-likes, copycat suicide, possible murder, accidental drowning," and a few other short phrases that had been scratched out and rendered illegible. The whole page seemed to convey Henry's confusion.

Scott turned the page and continued reading the account of how his father had become obsessed with the Adams women and had chosen to research their lives and develop a profile of what he called the *missing years*.

He had plenty of information on Belle, but her daughter Sonny was another story. Henry had to go up to Boston several times to get a real profile on her. Yes, she was bright, beautiful and a young woman of reasonable means. She had been shuttled around from her father to her grandparents and back to her father; eventually she was tucked away safely at college to reach full maturity and prepare for her adult life.

Henry didn't waste time with the common knowledge of her whereabouts during her early twenties—everyone knew where she lived, worked, and how she conducted herself in public, but there was still a lot missing. After intense searches and a few tips, Henry stumbled upon a few friends and acquaintances that supplied him with little known events in Sonny's short life.

It was startling news to Scott, that Sonny had taken some dance lessons at *Madam Cherie's* to improve her physical fitness and round off a self improvement kick she had been on. She had gotten to know most of the teachers and found them to be dedicated and helpful. Though she was not destined for a career in dance, she was still given quality time and attention to improve her muscle tone and flexibility. One of the teachers she had met in passing, by the name of *Miss Lila,* had given her some fine points on improving her posture and balance, reducing stress and avoiding the headaches that often sidelined her.

A month later, Sonny was terrified when Lila made threatening and obscene calls to her apartment, warning her to "let Scott go or you will be sorry".

Sonny was in tears when she confided in a teacher, "How does she know that Scott is my boyfriend? She spoke as though she knew him *very* well! I'm scared to death of her; do you think Scott might be seeing her behind my back?"

Sonny left *Madam's* without notice; she simply dropped out. One of the teachers told Henry about the episode—said they all knew Lila's game and preferred not to tangle with her.

Scott felt sick when he read that. He reread it and flung the manuscript across the room. "God damn you, Lila," he cried. "God damn you!"

After calming himself down, he retrieved the manuscript, flipped the pages to where he had left off, and continued to read on:

"Today I talked to a fellow worker of Sonny's from the publishing house. She confirmed Sonny's fear of Lila and how she had tried to steer clear of her. Sonny confessed that she didn't want to be a burden to Scott and was not going to tell him about Lila's threats. She knew she was losing him and had decided to cut him loose with no more begging. She thought she was strong enough to get on with her life. Besides, if he was no longer in love with her and was already seeing another woman—whom she assumed was Lila—she didn't want to hold him back."

Scott felt sick as he read Henry's description of her last few hours at the office with her few trusted friends.

One young lady who wished to remain anonymous said, "Sonny was actually happy that Friday. It was the happiest I'd seen her in a long time. She had picked up a bunch of fruit and bought a couple packages of hot cocoa mix on her lunch hour. I begged her not to go to the cottage alone but she just shook her head back and forth and said she had to go. That was the last time I saw her. After she left, I called her old boyfriend—Scott, over in editing—and told him that I thought she needed someone to look after her this weekend. He said something about having tickets to the theater on Saturday night, but he would see what he could do. I called him because I knew he was a nice guy who still cared about her well being even though he had another girlfriend. I've heard that he *did* go out there but was too late. What a shame *that* was. We all still miss her."

Scott held back tears and tried to continue reading. He was coming very close to the end of the thick manuscript when he felt a stiff object wedged in between the pages. He turned the page and found a little green spiral notebook attached to a journal entry dated Aug 8, 1996.

Scott went to the bathroom, splashed his face with cold water, and washed his hands before returning to the manuscript. He wondered just how much more he could take.

It was a foolish question. Scott Macguire put the little spiral notebook aside and returned to the manuscript to immerse himself in his father's words—yet again.

23 *August 1996*

August 08, 1996
My dearest friend and confidant,

Is there no end to my misery? It seems that Mother Nature has played another cruel joke on me. Just a few weeks ago an early summer storm vented its rage on *Puckshaw,* visiting one last tragedy upon the unique, doll-like, Adams cottage. At long last, the cottage has gone the way of its legendary occupants—into the cold, relentless surf of the mighty Atlantic. (By the way; I purchased the cottage barely a month before the storm claimed it.)

Just in case you've forgotten, almost three years have passed since the drowning of Sonny Adams—last known occupant of the magical cottage.

Well, my friend, a summer storm raged across the island late at night, ripping the empty cottage off its concrete foundation and hurling it, with no little violence, over the steep cliff. It landed onto the crescent-shaped beach where, within hours, it was sucked up by the voracious surf.

I guess you could say the cycle is now complete: first, Mrs. Carter; then, Belle and Sonny Adams; and finally, the cottage itself—all gone to foaming destruction. Every shred of evidence of the unique occupants has disappeared. To me, *Puckshaw* is now stripped bare.

As fate would have it, an amateur photographer, roaming along the deserted beach the following morning, discovered evidence of the carnage along the shore. He was particularly interested in pieces of the water-soaked, green velvet pillows that once adorned the picturesque window seat. He waited for the sun to move overhead and snapped several pictures of the debris.

The photos were splashed across the front pages of Puckshaw's daily paper for several days, along with the reprinting of some of the old stories of the tragic women that had once inhabited the cottage and roamed the sunny beach.

My phone rang non-stop, but I didn't answer it. I supposed they wanted some kind of statement or opinion.

Some islanders are complaining that there is no end to the morbid saga; I can't blame them. I have reported extensively on the subject, myself. Many residents of *Puckshaw* go back as far as the "old Carter woman", you know. You will recall that I've spoken of her before

Friends of the last two victims who had inhabited the island for many summers are again saddened as they read the articles on the double tragedy of the private victims. They say that the summers just aren't the same anymore. No Adams women, no enchanted cottage, and some days, no sun.

Today, at Charlie's, as she rummaged through the morning papers, even *Vera*—Puckshaw's long time waitress—couldn't help but comment on the lack of sunshine the island had been experiencing for the last three summers—not that she was suspicious. She said she had had a lifetime of sun on the island and enough was enough. Anyway, that's what she said.

After I got to my *cubby-hole* at the *Sunny Islander* this morning, I stared at a stack of photos of the storm carnage for an hour before finally tucking them away in an envelope and stuffing it into my jacket pocket. I made it through the day in a deeply distracted mood and was glad when it was finally five o'clock.

Suddenly, without deliberation or cause, I began to clean out my desk by the light of the late afternoon sun, making sure to empty out my bottom drawer where I've always kept bits and pieces of notes to be put into my journal. As I reached deep into the rear of the drawer to make sure everything was removed, I felt the spiral edge of a small notebook. I hooked it with my index finger and pulled it forward. I was very finicky about anyone seeing it so I shielded it with a box of Kleenex and placed it before me, cautiously turning the pages and trying to avoid sinking into one of my meditative trances. I guess I didn't try hard enough.

At this point, Henry seems to have been interrupted or possibly voluntarily stopped in the middle of this journal entry and only later on, continued his narrative of the deep reflection and its aftermath. It was not in his handwriting and Scott guessed it was a reflection Henry completed on his computer—probably before leaving the newsroom that day.

Scott shook his head in amazement; yet another format added to the manuscript. Henry's interchanging use of handwriting, typewriting, and conventional word processing with various fonts, gave the manuscript an interesting and convincing flavor of authenticity—not to mention a hint of mystery.

Scott had already made up his mind to pass the manuscript on to the editors at Scribe & Son and let *them* decide on its format—if it was accepted for publication. He understood that it probably needed a lot of work—first books always did.

He returned his attention to the typed insert. Now Henry was telling a story about himself, sort of standing in the shadows watching his own actions and commenting upon them. This resembled his early style of deep meditative reflection that could so intrigue a reader.

It was amazing the way Henry had actually been piecing his biography together through this unorthodox and sophisticated style of writing.

Scott shifted his position and continued reading with anticipation; he had come so far in the manuscript; yet he had no idea what to expect. He read on:

Now I continue, my dear friend,

The newsroom was almost empty and no one would have found it unusual to see my graying head resting in my wrinkled, arthritic hands, as I sat at my desk at the end of a long day. Shielding my eyes from the late sun, I looked down intently and remembered—with profound embarrassment—how I had come to have the little green notebook in my possession. So now I will tell you

Back in '93, on one of those icy December days when I was roaming around the perimeter of the cottage—which I

had become accustomed to doing—I had finally perpetrated the unthinkable deed.

It didn't take much, you know. I had just applied a little pressure to the back door and dislodged the old-fashioned sliding lock right off its hinge, causing the door to fly open.

A magical two-hour tour of the enchanted cottage ensued!

I stepped onto the welcome mat and wiped my feet vigorously before entering the doll-like cottage that had recently dominated my dreams and nightmares. In one sweeping glance I took it all in and thought how lonely it must have been for Sonny, in those last dark days; I almost cried.

The kitchen was as it must have been the morning Sonny Adams went to her death a few short months previous to my intrusion. The room was bathed in early sunlight; the miniature breakfast table—draped with a pale yellow cloth that matched the still-fresh curtains on the windows—was set with a single place mat, napkin, and decorative napkin ring. To the right of the neat table setting, tiny wooden soldiers, filled with salt and pepper, stood at attention. It reminded me of a still life painting.

As I ran my hands over the counters tops, I felt the light layer of sand that the howling winds would have blown in through the cracks of the weather-beaten cottage. On an uncontrollable whim, I even looked inside the refrigerator and wasn't a bit surprised to find it clean and empty; she wouldn't have left a mess for someone else to clean.

Hand painted tulips decorated the cupboard doors which I couldn't resist opening. I stared at the rows of stacked china, glasses, bowls, and serving platters—all in perfect order—not a chipped piece in sight. I was frozen in another time. I let my eyes roam around the kitchen panoramically and vertically—wall to wall and floor to ceiling. I was mentally preserving the image before leaving it behind as I passed through the shiny little hardwood hallway toward the partially open door to my right; it revealed a half-bath—deliciously decorated with yellow plaid curtains and golden floor mats.

I didn't enter; I chose, instead, to move quickly to the north side of the house, which was dominated by a good sized sitting room with three large glass panels that were suspended above a plush love seat, covered in green velvet. My heart stopped for a moment when I saw the little pair of white terrycloth slippers, delicately embroidered with pink rosebuds, slightly askew on the floor below the window seat—probably left there the morning of her death.

For weeks I had been peering into the cottage windows, memorizing each little detail and I really thought that I had seen it all, but now I was amazed at what I had been missing. The cottage and its furnishings were all delightfully intact—just as they had been left a little over three months ago--down to the last detail. No one had come to remove her belongings. Why?

For a moment, I felt a pang of guilt over having broken the law, which is what I did by forcing the door and entering the private property. But I didn't regret it—I couldn't—not at the moment.

I proceeded to study the sitting room. The pale green walls were covered with pictures while the rest of the room was scattered with pillows, books, and puzzles—all evidence—I presumed—of long cozy evenings that Sonny must have enjoyed with her mother and, later on, her lovers. A lacquered coffee table, perfectly centered in front of the window seat, reflected a writing tablet and a slim silver ballpoint pen standing up on a silver stand. Probably a gift; the Sonny I was getting to know would *never* buy anything like that—it wasn't her style.

One sheer panel of the four-paned panoramic window was pulled to one side, as though someone had just stepped away for a moment and would be right back. If only she could! If only she would! I had to ask myself how I could miss someone I had never met.

After a long look around, I, a friendly but uninvited guest—also known as an intruder—walked in the direction of the two closed doors, separated by a full powder room, door wide open, with just a crease of light peeking through the window above the bath tub. The window was high enough to ensure complete privacy and for some reason I stopped just short of entering the private bath; I *did* remain in the doorway long enough to inhale the sweet scent of soap and perfume.

I was unsure of which door I should open first. Deep in my soul I knew that I had already invaded the privacy of Belle and Sonny Adams far beyond my wildest dreams; at this point, entering the bedrooms was just a final affirmation of my maniacal obsession.

I placed my fingers around the knob at my right and turned it slowly, letting myself into the dark, cool room. I couldn't believe I was standing in Sonny Adams's bedroom; the room in which she removed her clothes and slept naked, between cool sheets, alone, or with a lover. I knew it was her room; I could *feel* her presence.

The pulled shades kept out most of the light; and for some absurd reason I walked over to the windows and raised a shade half way up the window, letting in a the winter light.

Suddenly, I shivered; aware of a frigid draft coming in. No wonder they never stayed there in the winter—just too damn cold!

It was all there; the pink and white mirage. A double bed covered with a white, shimmering quilt alive with tiny dancing rosebuds, sheer white curtains, fastened at the sides with ceramic pink roses, and the scent of a sweet smelling woman. A magazine layout!

The furniture was older wicker, painted white—three pieces in all. A tall dresser—with a Michael Jackson 'Thriller' doll and a few framed photographs on the dusty top—stood in the corner of the room while a vanity-topped dresser with a shiny, beveled mirror and several drawers faced the bed.

I stood before the mirror and surveyed the dresser top. Neat, feminine, intimate—characteristic of everything I had come to imagine; this was the moment I saw Sonny in all her glory. If I never learned another thing about her, this image would fill the deep empty space in my heart for the rest of my life.

Almost on tiptoe, I backed out of the room with bizarre reverence and walked past the open bathroom door in order to enter the only room in the house I had not seen.

I was confident in opening this door—almost sure of what I was about to see. The room had pretty much been laid to rest. The bed was protected by a large dust cover and the dressers were draped with flowered sheets to protect them from dust and any harsh summer sunlight that might seep in. There was no evidence of anyone having slept in the room recently. The shades were pulled down and pale blue drapes were drawn tightly. An empty closet with a few silk, padded hangers confirmed my conclusion: This room had remained unused since Belle's death in 1981.

I took a small notebook out of my back pocket and jotted down a few comments. I was anxious to return to the other bedroom once more—the room that made my heart dance with excitement.

Back in Sonny's room I stood before the narrow night table; a pink, ruffled lamp left a tiny dust circle when I moved it back a little to pull the single drawer open.

I tried turning on the light but I should have known that the electricity would have been turned off. The sun was already fading and I noted that the little traveling alarm clock had stopped at ten o'clock. Allowing my reporter's curiosity to get the best of me, I wondered exactly what day the battery had actually quit.

I stared at the drawer which loomed gigantic before me; everything was out of proportion and I knew that I should be thinking of getting out of there. My mind was playing tricks on me; I had to hurry. I hoped there would be a ribbon or a comb—just one tiny personal item I could drop into my pocket without feeling as though I were stealing from the dead. I was feeling lightheaded and confused and only one thing was for sure: I was certifiable. I was *definitely* certifiable.

I yanked the little drawer open—almost tipping the ruffled lamp over—and stared at a tube of hand cream and a miniature spiral notebook with a pink ballpoint pen pushed through the metal strip. Without opening it, I put it in my pocket and left the room without a backward glance, closing the door tightly behind me.

Once out, I rested with my back against the closed door, my hands in my pockets, and my eyes closed. I relished the full impact of what I had just experienced. I had actually entered the life of Sonny Adams the way Goldilocks had entered the cottage of the Three Bears. I had experienced ultimate satisfaction.

That night, safe in his private sanctuary, surrounded by his journals, and dwelling deep within himself, Henry read the neatly written poems of Sonny Adams.

Page after page, verse after verse, she described the ecstasies, terrors, and disappointments of her first and only unnamed love. Long annotations accompanied her poetry, describing the circumstances and reasoning behind her expression of emotion. Sonny Adams had totally emptied herself onto the pages of her safe little notebook; now, Henry Macguire had become the guardian of her secrets. On and off—for three years—Henry had pulled out the little notebook to reread the poems Sonny Adams had written, from 1981, shortly after she went to live with her father, until September, 1993, just before her death.

It was Henry's last day at the *Sunny Islander* and the sun had set early; the office was quiet and he was fatigued. He had made some serious decisions in the last few weeks—decisions that would affect the people he loved most in this world and those who chose to love him, flawed as he was.

Now, drained of energy, he reached for a large manila envelope and squeezed his manuscript securely into it. Only as an afterthought, he took the tiny book of poetry out of his pocket and placed it deeply within the pages of manuscript. He would drop that off in Ed Barton's office as planned.

Henry felt profoundly relieved as he took a white envelope out of his breast pocket and made sure it was sealed. It contained his will, naming Ed Barton as co-executor with his attorney, Ed Sims. Somehow he knew that when the time came—both men would do right by him. *They would find his only son, Scott, and present him with his father's legacy.*

Easing his chair back, he rose wearily and nodded silently to a few colleagues who were working late. Drawn and slightly bent, he headed toward the rear exit, stopping in Ed Barton's office. as planned. He deposited the envelopes on his editor's desk and exited the building, pausing to take a long look around before swiftly heading toward the parking lot.

Having come to the end of the manuscript without any warning, Scott felt disappointed and cheated. He wanted an ending of some kind, but he didn't know that Henry would have said, "Say what you gotta say; nothing more, nothing less!"

He turned to what he assumed would be a blank page and was ready to close the thick manuscript when he was jolted to attention by yet another entry. Actually it was a letter. It read:

August 10, 1996
My dearest son, Scott,

I hope reading this manuscript hasn't been too much of an ordeal for you. Maybe I've been a little unfair in saddling you with all this baggage, but I *so* want you to know how sorry I am for the pain I've caused you all these years. I should have been there for you—especially in the last three years, when you must have suffered so deeply, all alone. I hope that someday you'll find it in your heart to forgive me for my cowardly behavior, but first I want you to know the truth about me; it is all here, within the pages of this manuscript—pretty much my whole life.

I know you never meant to hurt Sonny Adams, so don't blame yourself for her death. Your only fault was that you were a vulnerable and inexperienced young man who didn't understand about love and its complexities. In your naiveté, you didn't know that people like *Lila* even existed. You were taken in by her charm—and by the way, you weren't the first to fall under her spell of passionate daring-do. I checked her out, myself, and discovered that she was quite enchanting—but deadly. I followed her to a restaurant once and witnessed, first hand, her beauty and poise, but I soon found out that she was involved in some pretty frightening behavior before she even came to Boston.

By the time you met her, she was on the run; she was searching for someone to control—using her unbridled passion as bait. And she caught and reeled you in. Believe me when I tell you that she is a cruel, violent woman who used her sexuality to control your every move. She is terribly flawed, son; but how were you to know? It's too bad that I didn't find that out until *after* it was too late. If I had only had the courage and good sense to reconnect with you, I would have warned you about her kind, but that's all in the past.

Now, you must be very careful; *Lila* can still destroy you! That's what people like her do. So protect yourself; you deserve better than to spend your life with a person like that.

Scott, please forgive me, for what I am about to do, but I am at peace. Now that I have chosen to conclude my life on this earth, on my own terms, and on my beloved island of *Puckshaw*—don't feel sorry for me. I've been a pretty selfish bastard all my life and have done exactly as I pleased. I don't even deserve to make this choice.

I should have done *more* for you and your mother, Susan; I truly regret my careless and cruel behavior. I wish she were still alive so she, too, could enjoy some of what I'm leaving behind. (Yes, I was informed about her death by a sleazy boyfriend who was looking for some money in exchange for some ridiculous piece of information.)

You see, my possessions, my writings, and even my friends—here on the island—are no longer of any joy to me. I have seen and experienced the worst kind of sadness imaginable—the sadness that comes with the loss of identity and purpose. I feel deep shame for having even taken up such precious space on this planet! I don't know who I am or what my purpose in life is, anymore. I recognize my drastic decline and wish that I could have done better. So now I just want to be rid of myself—move to a higher plane—one without conflict—perhaps some kind of eternity—if there is one.

I should face you in person—admit my mistakes—but you see, I'm weak and I might lose my nerve to leave this world behind. But you, son; you are strong and purposeful and you *will* succeed.

I know that material possessions cannot make up for my failure to provide you with a stable home and family life, but I just didn't have what it took to be a good father or husband. I only did what I could with the little character that I had. Now, enjoy what I have left you in good health. You earned it. And as for *Lila,* you'll have to figure out how to solve that problem yourself. Don't wait too long or, surely, she will hunt you down and ruin you.

I hope you'll find yourself a good woman and build a fine home on the empty lot above the cove—see Sims about that—you deserve it all.
Your Father,
Henry J. Macguire

Scott pulled the afghan up over his head to block the light from his eyes and lay still while the tears flowed. He felt regret, rage, and anger for not having known the comfort of a father. He shed tears of grief for having lost a father he didn't even know, but the most unexpected of all was the wave of sadness that moved in to remind him that he never had the pleasure of feeling one ounce of love for his dead father.

Hours later he rose from the sofa. Stripped of all emotion he walked across the room to his father's desk;

searching for a sheet of paper, he wondered whether or not he should write a letter to *Lila*.

24 *Lenora*

Ten event-filled years had passed since Scott Macguire met and married Vicky Campbell and comfortably settled into a way of life he never dreamed could become so clear-purposed and fulfilling. Sometimes it was hard for him to believe that he and Vicky were the deliriously joyful parents of eight-year-old twin boys and a four-year-old daughter. Scott liked the idea that the boys were born first; they could act as *protectors* for their little sister, Amelia. He had observed, with no little pride, that they were already quite good at it.

Scott had worked hard to create the tight-knit, loving family and he and Vicky were working even harder to preserve it. It was something he had missed—growing up the way he did; now he was determined to give his wife and kids every opportunity to enjoy a healthy, family atmosphere. He made sure they spent ample time together, participating in all the island's activities; they loved swimming, boating, and attending the local events—of which there were plenty.

His children were thriving and extremely lucky to be among the first kids to attend the new *Puckshaw Elementary School* that was only two years old. Education was a priority that he and Vicky whole-heartedly promoted, supported, and agreed upon.

Scott often reflected on how the island had developed so rapidly since his arrival in 1996. He had never really *planned* to put down any deep roots on *Puckshaw*—he had only come to bury his father, which unexpectedly took on a life of its own. One thing had led to another and he found himself fully engaged in settling his father's estate—unable to leave the island for months at a time.

His father, Henry Macguire, had left a number of requests in his will that Scott was determined to carry out. There was money, property, preferred charities, journals, editing contracts, *and* the future publication of his sought-after manuscript—a detailed account of his colorful and tragic life of which twenty-five years were spent as a reporter on *Puckshaw*.

Since Scott hadn't been in any hurry to get anywhere, he thought it was as good a place as any to put his own shattered life back together and do some serious thinking.

His father's attorney, Ed Sims, had put it squarely to him. "Hell, son, you have a house, a car, and more than enough money to live on; why not take your time before jumping into anything. What's the big hurry, anyway? You just got here—stay a while!"

Not unlike his father, Scott had never been a spendthrift and had a few dollars of his *own* saved; Sims was right—money was *not* a problem.

Once the estate was settled and he got his bearings, it seemed that the island might suit Scott just fine—for the short term. Hell, if it was good enough for his father it should be good enough for him, he reasoned.

There was plenty to do that first five years; he was especially interested in completing the task of getting his father's journals published—right *after* his autobiography went to press. That pair of challenges, alone, had eventually led him down the path to an exciting career he may otherwise have missed. He worked hard making friends and contacts that would eventually be instrumental in his successful debut into the world of author representation, editing, and eventually, publishing.

He determinedly carried out his father's last wishes—one by one—without time or monetary constraints. He was young—time was on his side.

Today, he observed how he had come full circle; he had grown to love the island and his life had taken on a tranquil and satisfying glow—all too obvious to his friends and business associates.

He noted, with possessive apprehension, how the local city dwellers had poured onto *his* and many of the other tiny islands on the cape, fleeing the ever-increasing violence in the mainland cities. The country his father so loved, had been through a major terrorist attack, a few Gulf wars, a lousy economic downturn, and an explosion of violent crime. There had been so many school shootings since the millennium that you had to ask, "Which one?" when someone referred to the "student massacre".

Scott was glad that he and his family were tucked away on *Puckshaw*; to remain on the island turned out to be one of the best decisions he had ever made in his life. It had offered him and his growing family a measure of tranquility and protection—due to the fact that access to the island was very limited and *strangers* could easily be spotted and closely monitored by *certain concerned locals*.

Unfortunately, such exclusivity would soon be coming to an end with the completion of the *Puckshaw Bay Bridge*—a direct response to the increasing population and the need for speed that hordes of commuters had cried out for

It was understandable; the traffic had become such a brutal challenge—even to the most seasoned city drivers—that the citizens of Puckshaw had reluctantly given in. A bridge would be built to facilitate the flow of traffic to and from the mainland. The new generation needed to get on and off the island as fast as possible and the ferry was considered a *dinosaur* as the first decade of the millennium was drawing to a close.

The high tech, stainless steel, twin span bridge was almost finished and the residents of Puckshaw were *almost* proud of it. There was *one little problem* that was causing alarm.

Crime had arrived on Scott Macguire's precious island.

Now in the final stages of construction, the twin span project was being blamed for disruptions in the once-serene lifestyle of the islanders.

In the past summer, the islanders had gone into a state of panic when a local college student—peacefully renting the apartment up above *Charlie's*—shot three young men. It was during the *Level Regatta*—one of the biggest events of the season—and the shooting had started out as a typical bar altercation: too much alcohol had been consumed by too few patrons. Unavoidably, argument ensued.

No one expected young David Kenny—quiet nephew of the Superintendent of Education—to have a gun under the front seat of his car.

After downing half a bottle of *Jack Doberman*, the twenty-one year old sat patiently in his expensive sports car and waited for his targets. When the three men stumbled out of the bar and—as expected—began to berate him and his flashy car. Kenny opened fire.

One of the victims died and young David—after recuperating for eighteen months—went on trial to face a jury of his peers.

It was a free-for-all.

Scott Macguire thought the kid was lucky to have been rescued by Puckshaw's experienced EMT's; their dramatic testimony revealed that when they found him, unconscious, behind the wheel of his car, he was so severely impaired by alcohol that he was "without a doubt, debilitated both mentally and physically".

"The kid could not have *possibly* been responsible for his actions," a Boston Metro Doctor testified. "He was unaware of his surroundings for days after the accident—*the poor kid*!"

With the help of a fine attorney, known around the island as Ed Sims, the boy, having narrowly escaped capital punishment—was sentenced to thirty years behind bars. *He would be eligible for parole after seventeen years of served time.*

Ed Sims said he thought the boy might even be out sooner. "*Maybe the liquor company was to blame...or the bartender...or... the auto maker—for making such a flashy car that the boy had to protect himself from the drunken hecklers! You never know!*"

The shooting was one thing, but Scott still worried about the knifing incident that had occurred barely three months ago and the ever increasing break-ins—all neatly kept under wraps to avoid upsetting Puckshaw's lucrative summer economy. Security was increased—temporarily mollifying the *alarmists*.

Some residents continued to rationalize that construction workers had infiltrated Puckshaw and the *little problem* would soon end with the departure of the *outsiders*.

Henry Macguire would have condemned that kind of thinking as "typically naïve, island mentality". Violent Crime had reached epidemic proportions throughout the country and most of the world, decades ago—Puckshaw's residents had just failed to notice.

According to the police records, some of the island's very own youngsters were now rumored to have gotten into newer, harder drugs and other unsavory activities. Though unmentionable in genteel circles, guns were playing a larger and larger part in the crime spate; the truth was that the gun problem was not going away in the *US of A*.

So far, the last three presidents had been unsuccessful in stemming the tide of public opinion to "keep and bear arms"; now, with the growing availability of hand-guns, a new president was struggling with the same problem. It was Scott Macguire's opinion that *Madam President* was up against it and if she didn't do something soon, she probably shouldn't count on being re-elected.

The islanders had just voted favorably on the new Middle and High School project that would begin in six months. Scott had been in favor of it all along, since it would, once again, benefit his children directly—they would not have to leave the island every day to attend the over-crowded central school on the main land. He and his beloved wife, Vicky, were thrilled.

Sweet Vicky—she had been Scott's soul mate from day one. The couple met while attending a conference for agents and editors at The Boston Literary Forum. They were almost the same age and both rising in the agent/editor business. Scott was attending the conference at the invitation of Scribe & Son, who had been happy to take on the project of Henry's autobiography and—later on—the daunting task of deciphering and publishing his journals.

The autobiography was a run-away success—popular among journalists, aspiring writers, and—of course—*The Islanders*, who searched the pages, line by line, hoping to spot a sneaky reference to themselves or one of their neighbors.

Much of the inside humor—sidesplitting fun that Henry Macguire poked at himself and the print industry—had been edited out, along with his depressing dark side. But not so his infatuation with the Adams women; that plot was expanded to include several sexually explicit fantasy scenes. Scott still vividly recalled his anger at the distortion, though sternly reminded that if the book was to sell, it had to have "something for everyone". The senior editors at Scribe & Son knew the buying public and had reasoned that Henry, in all probability, *had* experienced sexual fantasies about the Adams women, choosing not to reveal them in his journals. Scott had given in; though he found the whole concept *creepy, he* finally agreed that it *could* have been possible.

Though finding it distasteful, Scott had come to understand how publishers played hard ball; if he wanted his father's manuscript published he had to give in on several demands—so he did.

He was quite pleased with the delicate treatment of his own character and that of his mother's, but he could do nothing about the way *Lila* was portrayed. She was the shrew—the sexual dominatrix from hell with bloodied hands—which, as he recalled, was true.

He was never a revengeful guy and wished it could have been different; but Henry knew too much about *Lila*—much more than Scott could have ever dreamed. The publishers had read between the lines and taken some liberty with her cruel and sometimes savage behavior toward Evan, Sonny, and even Scott. *Lila* was portrayed as a shameful predator to be feared at all times.

Scott still shivered when he thought about the dozens of venomous letters he had received from her; letters filled with threats and condemnation. He was relieved when the frightening missives had eventually stopped and the demonic sender faded into his past. The image of *Lila* had finally been laid to rest like a slain dragon, never to be revisited—so he thought.

When Scott met Vicky, she was working for a large company that boasted twenty-eight junior editors and interns, each searching for the "big one" that would propel him or her to senior editor status; until then they were content to slave over submitted manuscripts—good, bad, and not a chance.

Vicky had recently shown some promise on several difficult projects and her achievements had not gone unnoticed by her supervisors; her enthusiasm had been rewarded with an invitation to attend the conference. She was justifiably excited; as a young woman with strong, intelligent opinions, she looked forward to expressing them in nurturing, professional discussions. Goal-driven and determined to survive the boom of self-publishing and its *disastrous* impact on the industry, Victoria Campbell attended the conference with no little enthusiasm.

Through his involvement with the publication of his father's auto-biography, Scott easily reestablished his relationship with Scribe and Son. Familiar with his previous work at the company he was assigned, under the supervision of a senior editor, to work with a few promising writers. He was lucky to assist in a university professor's climb up the best-seller latter and was presently working with an up-and-coming science fiction writer. Ambitious and a quick study, he was also working diligently on his own writing projects while continuing to make strong contacts in the industry..

Two years passed and Scott quietly emerged as an energetic, highly motivated agent/editor. His dreams were growing larger with each day.

He felt in a very good place as he attended the first lecture of the conference.

Scott Macguire was far from unknown; he had risen steadily, marketing his father's work and exhibiting his skills with sharp editing. Smart, confident, and financially stable, he had developed a little swagger that did *not* go unnoticed. He arrived at the conference with a cool but friendly attitude—fully aware of the little buzz in the air.

More than one literary executive was waiting for Scott Macguire to make his next move—start his own company.

That very morning he had assessed his good fortune by noting that a few industry executives knew him on a first-name basis. He was proud of his success and recently began to thank his father, Henry, for having passed on some of his literary talent to his only son. Still not wanting to ignore his mother's genetic contributions, he gave her credit for his determination to survive—especially in the tough and sometimes bloody profession he found himself, slowly and surely becoming entrenched in.

Scott Macguire recognized that Susan's opportunities had been very limited and he was growing more understanding and protective of her image as the years passed. Wanting his children to respect her memory, he would often tell them of her gentleness and the compassionate kindness with which she had always treated animals. He never told them of her drunken binges; he didn't think it was necessary for them to know that aspect of his life.

It was a different story when it came to his father; Henry Macguire was actually turning into a legend on the island and it was only natural—and unavoidable—that his grandchildren would be very aware of *that* part of their legacy.

As the conference hour drew near, Scott reflected on his swift ascent into the print jungle in just a little over three years; as far as he was concerned he was about as content as he would ever be. He had no idea that the satisfaction and serenity he was experiencing in his life would escalate to euphoria after his chance meeting with the beautiful, dark-eyed Vicky Campbell.

Seated at the same discussion table, they had clicked immediately and started seeing each other right after the conference ended and the rest, as they say, was magical.

Scott was comfortable with his life now; his wife and children came first and dedication to his career came second; needless to say, his life was made much easier by the fine sum of money and exclusive property his late father had left him.

He had listened to his advisors and parlayed the inheritance into a tiny fortune and now lived as a so-called *wealthy islander*—well-respected, champion of civil obedience, and staunch watchdog of the island's environment.

Though contrary to his nature, Scott Macguire learned to wheel and deal with the best of them—earning a well-deserved reputation for toughness.

However charmed Scott's life had become, there was an unavoidable downside: like the family of any prestigious islander, his wife and children had been cast under the harsh glare of public island opinion and criticism. They had learned—the hard way—to be on guard against any type of behavior that might bring bad press upon their father. They were trained early on that it was a trade-off—your privacy for elite island status and VIP treatment.

They were "Macguires" and they had a lot to live up to.

It was a lazy summer day for most islanders but Scott had an unusually large work load for this particular Monday morning. He needed to stop at the bank and sign real estate documents, pop in at the paper for a marketing meeting, and call the landscapers about the shrubbery that was not doing too well around his new oceanfront home. He had been forced to give up the warm, tiny cape home that Henry had left him; three children, two dogs, three computers, and the need for private office space for both he and Vicky had necessitated the move to a larger home.

The new home sat on the beautiful triangular lot high atop a cliff overlooking the private, crescent-shaped beach and the roaring Atlantic. Henry Macguire would have loved it!

The mini-mansion was five times the size of the old cottage of Scott's youthful passionate trysts. Those sometimes sweet, but more often painful, memories made it difficult for him to refrain from instructing the builders to incorporate some of his favorite features of the tiny cottage into the new structure. He insisted that the long window seat and panoramic glass panels be meticulously reproduced and become part of the family room. Also the restoration of the tiny bell-tower and the old tunnel, housing the concrete stairs that led down to the beach, would be carried out as part of the finishing touches. Scott had seen to his mother's and father's legacy; now, he saw to it that a part of *his* past was preserved and seamlessly joined to his new life.

Vicky knew the whole inside story of the Macguires, which she found absolutely fascinating. Her curiosity and interest were not unusual; she *was* in the business and she was *not* about to let Scott's past disturb her—in the tiniest way.

She read Henry's journals over and over and knew every word of his auto-biography; the irony of it all was that she—the love of Scott's life—was turning into Henry Macguire's biggest fan!

And Scott loved Vicky, on that busy Monday morning, as much as he did on the day of their wedding.

He switched gears and thought about stopping for a cup of coffee at Charlie's before starting his round of appointments and errands. He could save himself about an hour by skipping a big breakfast at home where one thing always led to another and an unanticipated phone call or a scraped knee could rob him of precious time. So it was settled—he'd go to Charlie's. A big hug for Vicky and the kids and he'd be on his way.

It was mid-July and the Macguire children were excited about attending a boating event being held in the *Bay of Puckshaw*. Vicky was downstairs with *cook*, making sandwiches, while Scott shaved and reviewed his day's agenda. She loved the revered summer events as much as the children did and was grateful that her manuscript reading duties allowed her to do most of her work at home, late in the evening. She spent most of the hot summer days as many of her friends did—at the club or at an event with the family in tow. Scott was proud of the devotion and generosity she with which she was raising their children and never doubted that she deserved every bit of the fine life he could now afford to give her.

After a quick shave, he grabbed his appointment book and hurried downstairs to the kitchen to kiss Vicky and the kids, good-bye. He planned to drive up to Boston around two o'clock in the afternoon to discuss a new project *he* had recently completed (a workbook of some sort) *and* to test the waters on a little book of poetry by *Sonny Adams*.

All in all, life was good for Scott Macguire. As he knotted his red, white, and blue tie before the foyer mirror, he recollected with some sadness that he had not always coped well with the difficult periods in his short life.

He had only recently fully accepted and understood his father's final actions. After a period of introspection, he had called a truce between his resentment and his father's memory; Scott hoped it would someday evolve into forgiveness or even warm affection. So far, he still could not think of the words *love* and *Henry* in the same sentence.

In the last thirteen years Henry Macguire's son had come full circle; now he fully appreciated his good fortune, successful career, and—above all—the love of his wife and children.

He had no idea what had precipitated this uninvited reflection and shook his head vigorously to dispel the mood. At times he felt that he was behaving more and more like his quirky father with each passing day. He checked the whiteness of his teeth and resolved to stay upbeat and on task; it could be a profitable day! It was in this frame of mind that Scott greeted the warm, promising day of July 22, 2009, on his beloved, sun-washed island of *Puckshaw*.

He jumped into his Sand Jeep, still carrying the scent of Vicky's perfume; it would keep him company on his round of appointments. He headed toward Charlie's, full of peace and reasonable expectations.

He pushed open the heavy aluminum and glass and welcomed the rush of cooled air while glancing around quickly to see who he might join for breakfast and the rigidly required morning banter.

The single thud that landed in the center of his chest caused excruciating physical pain followed by a series of shivers which left him sweating and reeling. That old familiar acid rose up from his stomach and shot into the back of his throat like a newly activated volcano and he tasted his orange juice for the second time that morning.

He had dodged the bullet of fate once or twice, but at this moment he had the sickening feeling that he had been hit right between the eyes.

She was instantly recognizable. Tiny waist, straight back and that long neck, still arrowing straight up into a chiseled profile crowned with beautifully clipped, shiny hair. She was still a breathtaking vision as far as Scott was concerned. He stood still—his feet anchored in cement. His trance was only broken by the sharp New England accent of *old Vera,* the morning waitress.

"Good morning, Mr. Macguire; wasn't sure you'd be around this morning but there's a young woman sitting at the end of the counter; she says she's an old friend and would like to see you. Quite the looker, she is." The old-timer winked as she rushed off, juggling three cups of hot coffee.

Vera hadn't changed since the day Scott first saw her at Charlie's in 1996. She was working a few hours less these days, but hadn't lost an ounce of spunk or sarcasm. He nodded and began to walk, lead-footed, toward the end of the counter.

Clearing his throat and trying to look nonchalant Scott whispered, huskily, "Is that you?"

He actually felt ill as that beautiful and familiar face turned slowly to glance over her shoulder—her sparkling eyes riveting his with piercing confidence. She spun her body around on the chrome-plated swivel stool and rose to face him. Only a second passed before they embraced stiffly, with guarded familiarity. Tall and slim, in beautifully pressed khakis, sandals, and a lime green tee shirt—so unchanged—she faced him squarely and smiled.

It was *Lila*. Her hair was shorter and she now sporting a few very stylish gold highlights, but there was no denying it—she was still gorgeous.

"My God, what brings you here? You're looking quite well. Sit down. Sit down."

She sat, gazing at him with her laser-beam eyes.

Scott was shaking as he lowered himself onto the empty stool next to her.

Vera brought him a cup of coffee with skim milk on the side. It was his usual—he would ask if he wanted breakfast. He could see that Lila had already eaten some breakfast; she would have, with her health risks.

When she finally spoke, he thought he might pass out right then and there. Her voice was pure velvet. He physically ached and assumed that he must be mad because, after all, he hated this woman.

"How goes it old friend? You're looking quite well, yourself. Life must be agreeing with you—yes?" She didn't give Scott a chance to answer but continued with, "It's been over thirteen years, you know? I thought 'What the hell, it's as good a time as any to look you up!'. Jesus, I hear you're almost as big as *God* on this island."

Scott sensed the sarcasm and was not surprised by the gruffness in his own voice when he responded with, "What the hell do you want, Lila? I thought I had heard the last of you when you wrote me those charming letters a few years back. Goddamn it, you know better than to come here. What do you want?"

There was a moment of silence and Scott decided to seize it before she did.

"I know what you're pissed at; those were my *father's* journals—publishers *always take liberties* and make changes. I did what I could and you shouldn't have taken it the way you did. Only a few people would have known it was you. You made my life miserable with those letters and threats; I had only been married a short time and you scared the hell out of my wife; that was a real treat—thanks. I really hoped I would never lay eyes on you again; but anyway, what the hell *do* you want?"

Lila took a deep breath as she sat up with her usual detail to striking a good pose and slowly opened her expensive, *something-or-other*, designer catch-all. She felt around on the bottom of it for a moment and then withdrew her hand to reveal a small snapshot. She turned it around and held it up in front of Scott's face without saying a word.

Scott looked at the picture of a young girl and shook his head.

He held his arms up as though it was a stick-up. "Okay, I give up. Who is it? Come on, Lila, don't play games with me. I'm not the guy you used to know."

"Meet *Lenora Powers Macguire*. Your daughter—she looks a little like you, don't you think?"

"Oh, no you don't," Scott snarled as he pushed his coffee cup away and started to get up.

She put a slim, pale hand over his tanned arm and as her manicured nails dug ever so slightly into his wrist, she whispered gently, "Not so fast, cowboy. You've had your way once too often.

You left me hanging in Boston, refusing to give me your address or even a fucking telephone number until you were goddamned good and ready. How do you think I felt? My parents and friends and everybody at *Madam's* wondered what the hell was going on. Some of them knew Sonny from the dance school and put two and two together after reading the newspaper articles about her death. And, oh, by the way, it was *over three months* before the police reports became public and I realized that you were the lone witness. That was a real picnic! Then, on top of everything, I was pregnant! I had a pretty bad time—with my health and all—it wasn't easy going it alone."

A moment's silence seemed like an hour to Scott and just as he opened his mouth to speak Lila continued.

"By the time I heard from you, I had already had the baby and was back at *Madam's*—teaching dance again."

Her voice quivered and she actually looked and sounded vulnerable. This was a *Lila* that Scott had never seen.

She continued in a strong, determined voice. "I loved you so much, Scott, and you knew it. And then I hated you. What was all that bullshit about writing and hinting that we might get back together again? Suddenly your father died and then his book was published and I was out of my mind with anger; I just wanted to get back at you. But you know what? A part of me was still wanting to see you again to make things right. By then you were either married or just getting married—I don't remember which...but...I was angry and wanted to punish you—that's why I wrote those letters. If they made you miserable, that was my intention; now I'm sorry. I mean that; you got over it, didn't you? Look at you; Mr. Big Shot! Anyway, what's important now is *Lenora*. We need to talk about her. Nothing else matters."

She shifted slightly, allowing most of her old confidence to come roaring back.

"Don't even *think* of fighting it, Scott. She *is* your daughter. Christ, look at her!

Go ahead—take a DNA test if it makes you feel better, but I was never intimate with anyone else when I was with you. Never! And we were together almost a year. We were together the last night I saw you. Remember that night? Do the math, *genius*."

Somehow, Scott believed that part of it. Lila might have been a lot of other things; but during their time together, she was always satisfied and her fidelity was unquestioned.

"Christ! We were so good together! Why did you take off like that? I could have helped you. You disappeared and everything was ruined in the blink of an eye. Let's not ruin it for *Lenora*—not now! Don't let her grow up like you did, Scott. Please."

Scott couldn't remember the last time he had felt this sick. He tried to stand up and couldn't. He wanted to scream at her but didn't. He thought of strangling her but his strength would have failed him. It was the first time he had ever felt such disgust and disdain for any human being.

He'd have to go straight to the Yacht Club and find Vicky before calling his faithful lawyer and personal friend—Ed Sims. He was a good man who had befriended and served him from the day he arrived on Puckshaw. He'd know what to do. His thoughts were scrambled. He couldn't think straight. He knew Vicky wouldn't give him any flack—hell they had been so crazy in love since the day they met, something like this wouldn't turn her against him. Now he had to get a hold of himself—be rational. *He needed Vicky for that part.*

He leaned on one elbow and shaded his eyes with his right hand. Out of the corner of his eye he saw Lila write something down on a piece of paper and slide it over to him. Just like her! She was staying right on the island—not far from Charlie's—playing hardball.

"*Lenora* is staying with my mother and I have four days to take care of things. I'll supply a sample of her DNA just tell me where to take her. Let's get it done. Okay?"

Scott didn't look at her; he swung his legs around the counter stool, stood up, and mumbled, "I'll get back to you."

Lila never turned to watch him walk away; she just picked up her coffee and whispered into the cup, "You'd *better.*"

Within hours, Scott, Vicky, and Ed were huddled in Scott's neat little office in the corner of his mansion. Their voices were low and they could hear the kids laughing loudly as they watched a *Charlie Brown* marathon. At the moment, Scott couldn't think of anything in the world that would make him laugh.

Vicky's face was ashen and drawn; she had taken it bravely—almost sympathetically—but that's how she was—all heart.

Ed was breathing loud—his mouth partially open—as he stared at his trusty cell phone as though he were expecting a call at any moment. He wiped his face with a clean white handkerchief and blew his nose while he shook his head from side to side with closed eyes. That kind of drama always irritated Scott, but he knew his rituals well; now he sat quietly while Ed figured things out. He was very close to a solution. At last, he flipped open his yellow legal pad and began writing.

The first thing he recommended was asking Judge Carol Kenny for an injunction against Lila Powers.

"Take the offense—be pro-active!"

She was to stay one hundred yards away from Scott, his wife and children, *and* his place of business.

"*No!*" he could *not* keep her out of Charlie's; Scott would have to just stay out of there for a while. Ed had read Henry's book and journals; he already knew a lot about Lila and her type. Judge Kenny would be sympathetic; she was the daughter of celebrated parents and had been the victim of more than one stalking since she was a child. They'd have no trouble there.

His second recommendation was to order a DNA test to be conducted at the prestigious Boston Metro Clinic. Once those arrangements were complete, he thought Scott should demand to actually *see and meet* this child who was called *Lenora Powers Macguire.* While Ed Sims' version of the wheels of justice was being set in motion, he would work on the formal document designed to deal with the latest crisis of his prestigious client and esteemed friend: Scott Macguire.

At times, Ed liked to think of Scott as a son, since he was a confirmed bachelor with no known wife or children of his own; he openly adored Scott and Vicky's children as if they were his very own grandchildren.

Scott felt kind of sorry for the devoted attorney he'd grown so fond of over the years; he often wished he had a partner or children of his own. He seemed so alone all the time. Anyway, it had been quite a while since Scott had needed Ed so desperately and now his *barrister*—as he fondly referred to him—would rise to the occasion to serve him gallantly.

Ed stood up, shook hands with Scott and nodded sympathetically toward Vicky—assuring her that everything would work out—before he left by the little office door that exited to the side driveway. Tonight, breaking with his routine, he didn't stop to tell the children one of his corny stories. *He couldn't think of anything funny.*

Scott and Vicky stared at each other blankly as they headed towards the family room to prepare the children for whatever might happen. They held hands on the way and Scott was comforted by the genuine vote of confidence and obvious affection from Vicky. She'd *never* let him down.

As was expected, the kids were solemnly wide-eyed and—like their mother—non-judgmental and cooperative. They were also thrilled to be going to their grandmother's house for a few days. They could watch TV, sleep late, and eat French fries.

Scott and Vicky needed to focus on this crisis; they would do it much better if they knew the kids were tucked away in North Boston with Vicky's mother and their cousins.

The kids went up to pack their little bags and Vicky made some phone calls to her sister and mother. To spare the children any discomfort or worry, they would drive them first thing in the morning. They had a driver and Ed had also offered, but Vicky thought it best to keep calm in front of the children and put them at ease—She and Scott would drive.

Dizzy and overwhelmed by everyone's kindness toward him, Scott felt as though he had failed them by having done something stupid and irresponsible.

Vicky went to talk to *cook* about feeding the children early as Scott stepped out onto the patio and dropped, heavily, into his worn wicker chair, burying his head in his hands. He looked down at his feet and was surprised to see he was still wearing the dress shoes and silk socks he had put on early that morning. It was a little after eight p.m.—almost twelve hours since he had left the house for Charlie's, so full of *joie de vivre*. He took his shoes and socks off and pressed his aching feet into the cold flag stone of the patio floor. It felt good.

He let his mind drift back to the first few encounters he had had with Lila. He was still dating Sonny, but that didn't seem to matter at the time; he was totally besotted with her and that, in and of itself, should have been a red flag. It was unlike him to be unfaithful. It was unlike him to be attracted to a flashy, demonstrative and dominating young woman.

Do this, don't do that, and don't ask why—that was Lila's mantra.

The affair had begun almost immediately and was recklessly passionate. When Scott finally came down to earth, he got up enough nerve to ask Lila if she was on the pill after a no-condom, passionate evening.

She had laughed incredulously, "Oh my God, Scott, of course."

Tonight, with his head in his hands and his bare feet pressed to the flagstone, he thought about Lila's fanatical attention to taking her birth control pills and wondered how the hell she had became pregnant. She never went anywhere without them—reminding Scott that she was not *ready* for a child and more emphatically—not ready to be a *single parent*. She *was* diabetic and had heard horror stories about difficult pregnancies; having a child was the one thing that could further complicate her condition. She assured him that she was prepared to wait for motherhood.

Scott slowly lifted his head and his eyes widened as though he had just discovered the law of gravity.

"That bitch!" he whispered.

She had meant to trap him all along; she just hadn't counted on Sonny's suicide or his sudden disappearance.

Now, he assumed it must have happened during the last weekend they had spent together, when she had insisted on intimacy over and over. He had been exhausted and annoyed at first; but, inflamed with passion, he had succumbed—*over and over*.

She was trying to get pregnant! He was disgusted by his conclusion and renewed his hatred for her, *yet again.* His affirmation of new hatred didn't change the facts. He was most likely the father of the child and planned to fully support his daughter—financially and *...whatever else was necessary.*

Scott's mind was spinning out of control. *What about having any kind of a relationship with this child—called Lenora? He'd never want her to go through the same neglect or rejection he had endured when he was growing up. He knew he wouldn't behave as Henry Macguire had; but how much contact would Lila ever allow? And what kind of a mother had she already been and what was she like now? Who could say? Maybe she had already poisoned the kid's mind against him. That would be just like her.*

He began to panic; *what if the kid already hates me. What will the kids and Vicky think about meeting her? What if I don't even like the kid? What if, what if, what if!*

Lenora was about fourteen or fifteen by his calculations. It had to have happened in September, or maybe sooner, of 1993 and she would have been born around June of 1994. It was now July 2009; she was a young woman already. Scott's mind was swimming in an ocean of lopsided emotion and lapsed time. He would have to calm down and take one step at a time. Ed would keep him from veering off course—that was his job.

He could hear Vicky giving the kids orders about behaving properly at their Grandmother's house. They were giggling with excitement as they packed, donning somber expressions whenever Scott walked into the room to see if he could help. They knew their father was in some kind of trouble and wished they could help. They had been taught that kind of compassion and loyalty early in life.

On the drive back from Vicky's mother's house, Scott and Vicky stopped for breakfast and held hands across the table in a quiet booth in the back of a truck stop. Vicky's calm strength renewed Scott's confidence in negotiating a peaceful resolution to this crisis. The one word neither of them seemed to be able to utter was *Lila.* Her name alone filled both of them with dread.

Lila sat on the edge of her single bed and ate chicken and frozen peas out of the Styrofoam carton which was carefully placed on a tiny table set with a paper napkin and plastic utensils. *She was tired.* Her hands were shaking slightly and she knew she had to eat quickly. She gulped down a small carton of *Sun Maid Orange Juice* to level off her blood sugar, admitting to herself that she had been careless the last few days—not sleeping well or eating properly.

She had thought this was going to be easy, but things just weren't going the way she planned. Scott was not the same meek and mild young man she had known years ago—the guy who would have, by now, been falling at her feet to agree with her quick solutions. She never expected that he would have matured into a solid, clear thinking, family man *and* entrepreneur. The whole thing was being handled in a professional and legal manner and Lila was not in charge—not by any stretch of the imagination.

Ed Sims had risen to the occasion to serve his master and was doing an exceptional job at orchestrating the whole scenario. As a matter of fact, only Ed was communicating with Lila through pages of legal briefs that gave left her with the frightening impression that they could go on for months. It definitely wasn't what she had planned! On top of everything, she just *wasn't feeling well* these days.

Of course, she had lied about having only four days to spend on Puckshaw—she had a three-week vacation scheduled.

As the *Director of Claims Management at Mutual Inc. of Mass HMO,* she ran the front office like a drill sergeant. Her two assistants would be handling the fleet of twelve clerks—all having breathed a collective sigh of relief upon hearing the good news that *Miss Powers* would be gone for a three-week personal leave.

Lenora was not visiting her grandmother—another lie—but was attending an exclusive summer camp on a little key right off Puckshaw. Lila made sure that her child had the best of everything--regardless how she got it for her.

She had always had a job; even after *Madam's* school was sold she had stayed on with the new owners for three years, saving every penny—including the fifty dollars a month her father was sending her to help with expenses. She never went out in the evening if it was going to cost her anything; it was cheaper to accept dinner invitations to restaurants or private homes. She had been very lucky to find a reasonable child sitter—flexible and dependable—whom she never overpaid. Wisely, Lila was careful not to mistreat her lest she be forced into a long search for a replacement and missed days of work—resulting in a short paycheck.

When *Lenora* was four, Lila was having a relationship with an older man who was kind and generous—she wouldn't have had it any other way—and had a management position with *Mutual Inc. of Mass HMO*. Before long, *Lila* joined the staff of front line claims operators and from there, literally badgered her way into management. Her mentor was transferred during her climb, but that didn't stop her. She was making good wages and enjoying company benefits, by then. *He left, she stayed—mission accomplished.*

She continued to teach a few dance classes at night, earning a little extra money and free lessons for *Lenora*; Lila was proud to be providing a stable and quality environment for her daughter. After all, getting pregnant had been her idea and not an accident; it was losing Scott that had been so unexpected. Her plan derailed, she had vowed to give her child a good life even if it killed her.

How surprised she had been to realize just how much she loved that child. She knew herself well and would have never expected such maternal devotion to a child that had brought such turmoil into her selfish life. At times, when the day had been long, her health problematic, and she thought it might soon kill her; only her devotion to Lenora kept her rooted. It was the one and only time she would ever put anyone else before her own selfish needs.

In all other aspects, Lila really hadn't changed. She had used any means to survive single motherhood whether or not it involved lying, back stabbing, or any other form of conniving. She had tried to keep some of her unsavory behavior from *Lenora*, often shrugging off questions with, "It's a tough world out there, *Lennie*—you'll have to fight for everything you want and it's not going to be easy. If you have to cut corners—*cut 'em.* "

Lenora was aware that her mother had cut a few in her time for she had taken her share of irate phone calls—co-workers, neighbors, babysitter, and even an irate wife or two. All told, *Lenora* had been treated with great care; she was fed, bathed, clothed, and educated; *and* she had been taught impeccable manners along with the supreme importance of meticulous, personal grooming.

That was the world according to Lila.

The child was naturally bright with a mild but moody personality akin to Scott's—or even Henry's. She hadn't missed much or wanted for anything so far. Life was extremely good for the youngster the day she left for her exclusive summer camp for girls near the island of Puckshaw.

Lila ate quietly, reviewing the countless stages she had passed through since her fiery departure from her parents' home, so many years ago. Today, in her own eyes, she concluded that she had been only *mildly,* successful. After fourteen years, she felt that she had given her best years to raising a strong and confident child. Now she was ready to revive the ghost of Scott Macguire and do battle with the dragon, one last time.

She picked up the phone and dialed Scott's number. Slamming it down, she whispered, "God-damned answering service!"

Before she could finish the thought, the phone rang with a loud jangle that made her jump.

"Yes?

"Miss Powers?"

"Yes. Who is this? She knew who it was, but made Ed Sims identify himself anyway—just for the fun of it.

"Miss Powers, arrangements have been made for Mr. Macguire to have the DNA test, but you know these things *do* take time. It could take several weeks; however, in the best interest of the child—who may or may not be Mr. Macguire's—we are willing to proceed under the assumption that *Lenora is* his daughter. How soon can we set up a date to meet the young lady?"

Now her daughter was "the young lady." *Things were looking up.*

"I understand, yes, of course I can set that up immediately. I have decided to take additional time off from my job and *Lenore* is not far from here, at her summer camp. I'm sure I can make some arrangements. Thank you, Mr. Sims."

Ed made a mental note of how slick she was—lying to him about her daughter's whereabouts. The kid was supposed to be at her grandmother's—someplace in New Hampshire or Maine. This kind of cool could be very dangerous. He decided to keep it short.

"Then, thank *you*, Miss Powers. May I call you again tomorrow?"

"Yes. Good-bye."

He shook his head and swore under his breath at the way she had cut him off—"Bitch!"

That was so unlike Ed Sims, but he had to fight fire with fire.

Lila was feeling dizzy and attributed it to her erratic eating and sleeping habits of the last three days. She had to be careful with the disease that had dominated her life-style for the last twenty years or so. She needed to call *Lenora's* camp. She picked up the phone book and looked under summer camps. No good. Day camps? No. She slid off the edge of the bed with uncharacteristic sluggishness and grabbed her purse; she had a business card somewhere that she had received from the camp administrator. The number for *Summer Holidays for Young Ladies* was on the card and she breathed a sigh of relief.

Lila was exhausted and needed to rest before calling the camp to inform them that she would be up to see her daughter early the next morning. She had been given a special ID number to use when calling the camp and she remembered now; that was her reason for tucking the little yellow card in the corner of her wallet. They were very careful these days and she appreciated the security, even though it could be a nuisance, at times. She propped the card up against her little cell phone, intending to call after a short nap.

She was going to lie down for just an hour, she told herself, so she wouldn't need to get undressed or even remove the little make-up she wore. A sharp, cold, chill shot through her as she pulled the flowered coverlet up over her feet and yanked the heavy pillow out from under her head.

She set the clock radio to go off in one hour, even though she knew she wouldn't sleep that long. She lay flat on her back and felt the tension leaving her back and legs. The overhead fan was whirring softly as she closed her eyes and took a deep breath; letting it out slowly she gave herself up to the peaceful darkness.

That was how they found Lila Powers late the next afternoon.

Ed had been calling from nine a.m. in the morning until three in the afternoon. The clerk told him that the rental car was in the parking lot, but she had not seen Miss Powers since the afternoon before, when she had walked through the tiny lobby with a take-out container in her hand. Ed had asked them to knock on her door or at least listen for any noises that might indicate that she was in her room. He thought she might be pulling a stunt just to give him a hard time.

He waited, sweating and impatient, until the clerk came back to inform him that she could hear what sounded like a radio playing. He thanked her and called Scott to tell him Lila wasn't cooperating and maybe they should go over in person.

Within the hour they arrived at the hotel only to find Sheriff Cramer and Mike Stafford, the coroner, in the parking lot checking out Lila's rental car. It seemed that Holly, the desk clerk at the *Puckshaw Hotel*, had called Cramer with a little tip that she *just knew* something had gone wrong in that room.

The Sheriff had arrived within five minutes and Holly had used her master key to let him in. No foul play was expected. Lila Powers may have gone into a diabetic coma and slipped away in her sleep sometime during the night. Later, her daughter would say that she had been suffering spells of some sort, but she didn't know exactly what they were.

Scott thought it was very unusual of Lila not to tend to her health; there must be something he didn't know. He was right. Later, her medical records showed that in the last three months she had been suffering from severe high blood pressure and symptoms of kidney failure. In Lila's case, the "silent killer" had finally struck.

Once again, Scott, Ed, and Vicky huddled in the little corner office; this time in utter disbelief of what had transpired in the last twenty-four hours, not to mention the last four days.

It was decided that Ed would drive Scott and Vicky to the girl's camp the next morning. The administrator and counselors had been notified of the change and the reason for it. Everyone would do their level best to help this poor child who was about to be informed of the tragedy that had occurred.

It was a bizarre twist; early tomorrow morning, *Lenora Powers Macguire* would be informed that in one cruel but lucky stroke of fate, she had lost her mother and found her father.

Complete mayhem for any child.

In the back seat of the Chevy, Scott and Vicky literally clutched each other's hands until they ached.

Ed drove slowly through the narrow roads and onto a little traveled key where the camp was nestled behind trees and foliage. As the car approached the camp, Ed Sims' heavy breathing was the only sound to be heard by the threesome. Sims had behaved like a military tactician—planning every move that Scott was to make.

Scott was deeply appreciative of Ed's efficient assessment of the situation and obeyed his every command. But today, he thought that he would never again do anything harder than what he was about to do.

Vicky's maternal heart was pounding with anticipation as she rehearsed what she might say or do to console this bereft child—her husband's child.

Ed felt more confident than he had ever felt knowing his good friend was counting on him to facilitate the ensuing situation. He had taken full command of all communications and had already spoken with Lila's parents, who were in full agreement that Scott should be wholly involved in every decision concerning this child, who, in all probability, *was* his very own. Mr. & Mrs. Powers, who, up in years now, saw the child only a few times a year, lent their full moral support.

Ed had pulled every string he had to convince the Boston Metro Clinic to push the DNA test to a priority level. They could know the results in less than ten days. What Ed didn't know was that Scott Macguire was fully convinced and prepared to take this child into his life even before the results of the testing were in. He had a deep conviction that she was his daughter and nothing would change that feeling. Lila would never have come looking for him if he wasn't the child's father. She was guilty of a lot of cruel and cunning acts, but she would have wanted *Lenora* to be with her biological father—not just any past lover of hers.

The car rolled solemnly up the long drive toward the main building of the camp. Scattered about the grounds, small groups of girls in shorts and tee shirts were engaged in various activities, giggling and squealing as they began another sun-drenched day. The car slowed and then came to a complete stop, with Ed jumping out of the driver's side to open the rear passenger door.

Scott and Vicky stepped out and glanced in the direction of the main house just as two middle-aged women started down the stairs. They shook hands all around and spoke in hushed voices.

Lenora was sitting in the reception room alone and aware that something of major importance was about to happen; she assumed it involved her mother.

Maybe she was in the hospital or had gotten sick.

It was up to Scott to deliver the missing information and as far as *Lenora* was concerned, it would forever brand him as the messenger of the blackest news she would ever receive.

With a sinking heart, Scott approached the entrance, followed by Vicky; Ed remained outside with the camp directors. As he made small talk with them they glanced in the direction of the increasingly loud and uncontrolled sobs of the young voice from within the main house.

Scott and Vicky had entered the small visiting room, cleared of all staff and students, and were amazed at the tiny figure that rose politely from a folding chair to stand bravely behind the visitors' long table.

Scott made his way around the table to speak to her while Vicky remained standing across from them—ready for whatever it was she would be called upon to do. She had children of her own and she would use every skill she had to spare this child unnecessary pain.

"Hello, *Lenora*. I'm Scott Macguire and this is my wife, Vicky."

Vicky nodded her head with just a trace of a smile. "Hello."

This is going to be hell, Vicky thought to herself as the three of them remained standing.

Lenora broke the silence with, "Who are you? What's wrong, is my mother sick? Has something happened to her?"

Her voice rose higher with each question and the real fear she had been holding back began to break through her controlled front. She was struggling to regain a calm exterior. "Please, sir, will you tell me what's wrong."

With every bit of courage that Scott could muster he drew in a sharp breath and then said quietly, "Lenora, I am an old friend of your mother's and I've been asked to deliver some dreadful news to you. Your mother died in her sleep in a hotel here on the island the day before yesterday."

Vicky swallowed a sob and stepped away.

Scott extended both arms to the youngster, whom he thought of as *his* child, but she did not respond to the gesture; instead she put her hands up to cover her face and screamed.

It was ear shattering and both Scott and Vicky cringed for just a second.

"What happened? Why are you telling me all this? Are you sure about this? Has anyone called my grandparents? Please, please let me call them. They need to know about this. How come they aren't here to take care of me? I need to see them. They'll tell me the truth; if what you say is true, let me call them and speak to them. I want to talk to them now; please let me call them."

Then the sobs of a child came; they were loud, confused, and full of rage.

It seemed like an eternity before *Lenora* stopped sobbing. She had turned away from them at first, but now she pulled out the folding chair and limply dropped her slight frame into it. Vicky sat down facing her squarely and Scott sat down next to Lenora, closing his eyes and pressing his fingers against his throbbing temples. He shook his head back and forth as he looked across the table at Vicky. He suddenly was sorry for putting her through this—she didn't deserve it. He was brought back to the present by the child's whimpering voice.

"Please sir, can you tell me what happened? I can handle it now."

"Your mother came to Puckshaw a few days ago to see me and to take care of some business which I will explain to you in a minute. She took a room on the island while we were working some things out. She had spoken with a family friend of ours at three p.m. on Wednesday, and when we couldn't get through to her room on Thursday we informed the hotel manager. By the time we got there they had entered her room and found her lying on the bed. She had been dead for several hours according to the coroner. We've heard from your grandparents and her doctor that she was showing signs of end stages of kidney disease. I'm not sure if you knew how seriously ill she was."

Lenora started to protest, but Scott raised his hands and said, "Let me finish or I'll never get through this. Please! The coroner said she died quickly and painlessly.

Now, the reason your mother had come to Puckshaw was to tell me something. She must have known how sick she really was and needed to see me before it was too late. She came to tell me about you, *Lenora*. You see, I never knew about you. You were born after I left Boston and your mom chose not to tell me.

Scott's voice broke when he finally got the words out, "But I am your father and I hope you'll let me help you get through this."

There was dead silence at first and *Lenora* put her head down in her folded arms and wept—this time silently. Vicky came around the table to stroke her hair and gently pat her back. *Lenora* responded by sitting up and looking first at Vicky then Scott with a pathetic, imploring look.

"You know, we have no relatives except my grandmother and grandfather up in New Hampshire—they're are not too well—and I'll be fifteen soon, but I don't know what I'm supposed to do. Who will tell me what to do? Who will take care of me now? Where am I supposed to go? O God, someone please help me."

With that pathetic cry for help Scott and Vicky reached out to embrace *Lenora,* both talking at the same time, assuring her that they would care for her, promising to do whatever was necessary.

Scott took a deep breath and looked *Lenora* straight in the eye. "Let me tell you something, *Lenora*: your mother loved you so much that when she realized how sick she had become, she knew she had to find me and let me know about you. She wanted you to be taken care of by someone who could love you like she did—a real parent. You might say that she gave up the last few days of her life here on earth making sure you would be taken care of. That is a wonderful way for you to remember your mother for the rest of your life."

Vicky dabbed at *Lenora*'s eyes and kissed her tenderly on the cheek. The child sobbed again with the fresh realization of her mother's death. Vicky stepped back and Scott stood before *Lenora* with his hands stretched out and whispered, "Now, it's my turn to take care of you—if you'll let me."

Scott and Vicky spoke softly and compassionately about what would take place in the next few days. *Lenora* was not to worry about any of the details; she would need all her strength to see her mother one last time to bid her farewell. She would have a voice in the plans and Scott would see that all her wishes were carried out.

He would have taken on this youngster's grief if it was possible, but that was not an option, so he would just stand at her side and be ready to support her when she needed it. He and Vicky would do whatever it took to shield his eldest daughter from further pain.

Ed was waiting outside with the car doors open when the three of them stepped out into the brilliant sunlight. They stood on the front stairs of the main house for a moment while *Lenora* looked around at the lovely treed lot of the campgrounds.

Only a little over a week ago she had arrived at camp a bubbly teenager without a care in the world; today, she was leaving as a motherless youngster, with a long road ahead of her. She sobbed quietly and looked from side to side—first toward Vicky and then toward Scott; finally the three of them hesitatingly walked toward the car.

Once they were comfortably settled, Ed looked in the rear view mirror and met Scott's glance with raised eyebrows.

"We're ready to go home now, Ed."

Ed smiled to himself and headed South, toward Puckshaw and the waiting mansion—a safe place for all of them on this most unforgiving day.

puckshaw

BOOK TWO

Death on the Island

puckshaw

25 *The Party*

Most of us who turned sixteen under normal circumstances—during a painful acne outbreak or a bad hair day—will most likely be happy to let that "special birthday" fade into obscurity with relief—whether it was good, bad, or just plain annoying.

Today, Scott Macguire reflected that although light years had passed since his own sixteenth birthday, not much had changed when it came to the time-honored tradition. Even after the sexual revolution had run rampant for decades, it was still considered coquettishly sweet of young girls to lower their eyes modestly and giddily accept "sweet sixteen" congratulations while their male counterparts—crimson-eared, frog-voiced pubescents—still looked forward to being pounded on the back by their fathers and given the male bonding, double entendre, ritualistic wink.

Macguire, now in his forties, reflected dryly that some things never change.

Yet, for Harry and Eddie, his twin sons, fondly referred to as "The Double Mac", this time-honored bash was one they were sure to remember for the rest of their lives.

This year, Scott had enlisted the help of Vicky's sister, Thea, and his relatively new assistant at the publishing house, Francesca Covel, to help him carry out the *bash for the boys*. Although he had received various offers, he had turned most of them down and now regretted his arrogance in thinking that just three adults could handle twenty-five hormone-driven teenagers. By eleven p.m. the party had taken on a life of its own and was beginning to take its toll on him.

Nothing was easy for Scott Macguire these days; it took a great deal of effort for him to complete any task—be it large or small, important or trivial. All he wanted to do tonight was keep this party from getting out of hand. So far so good—but the night was not over yet.

He glanced at the calendar and noted that it was not yet a year since the unconquered global enemy—cancer—had taken his beloved Vicky from him. Her great love—the sun—had cruelly betrayed her and she had gone the way of all other incurable cancer victims.

Some days, when the kids were out of the house and off to school, the pain of her absence forced the grieving widower to sit down and cry out loud

He had been so lovingly dependent upon her good judgment and expertise—especially when it came to matters concerning the children; now he often felt totally inadequate to meet the challenge of successfully raising the two boys and their younger sister, Amelia. Islanders, friends, and business associates agreed, with a shake of their heads, that since Vicky's death, Scott's loneliness had been so horrific that it bordered on the destructive. He seemed to always be on the precipice of defeat—his devastating sadness reflected in everything he did.

It was no secret that Scott Macguire had been wildly in love with Vicky Campbell—having never passed up an opportunity to admit that she was the best thing that had ever happened to him. He candidly spoke of his loneliness since her death— even to perfect strangers. It was an accepted fact that he had lost a part of his very being and his life would never be sane or orderly again.

Throughout the last eleven months, he had struggled to put on a brave front for the kids; vowing to try even harder today—the boys' sixteenth birthday. He could only imagine how terrific the party would have been if Vicky had had a hand in it—now he would just be glad when it was finally over.

Or maybe he wouldn't.

From the family room, he had watched Francesca—whom he respectfully called Frankie—throughout the day, quietly moving about the patio and back yard, seeing to the decorations and the placement of tables and chairs. She was quiet, unassuming, and unbelievably efficient. Scott and Vicky had hired her only two years ago to coordinate the assignments of the five junior editors they had working for them in the small but thriving publishing house. She was bright and productive—unflinchingly focused on her career and devoted to her job at the publishing company.

Since the onset of Vicky's illness Francesca had stepped up without being asked—becoming Scott's administrative and personal right hand. She had kept him on track; preparing his weekly agenda—as Vicky would have done—to remind him of his executive committee meetings, the children's school functions and his up-coming social commitments. Since Scott had neither the energy nor the desire to devote himself to his work, Francesca had offered her assistance on every level and Scott had gratefully accepted.

He was happy that Vicky had lived long enough to see the grand opening of the neat, white building which was constructed on the large lot behind his father's original house. The tiny house that sat at the very end of the business district had been Scott's home when he first came to the island and during the first few years of his marriage. It was now incorporated as part of the front entrance to the publishing house so fittingly called *H. Macguire and Son*.

The new company was a bustling hot bed of young, creative, writers and editors; along with the necessary fleet of computer wizards hired to negotiate the electronic landmines of the new age. Scott liked to refer to these young people as his very own army of *"socially conscious, hard-working, American literary geniuses"*.

It was almost 2017 and this new wave work force had experienced a lot in their young lives. They were no strangers to terror attacks, global war, and shameful poverty and bigotry within their own country. These young brilliant minds of America were not only burdened with the fallout of a nuclear explosion; they were saddled with the chaos of *technology run wild*. These were the kids that had witnessed their parents' retirement plans in ruins and the final agonizing destruction of the once-valued American family.

Now, in spite of the new or recurring incurable diseases that continued to rage across the globe, these young people struggled for a place in the new world where they could live, work, and dream their dreams of a peaceful, healthy planet.

Scott and Vicky loved these kids; they worked hard without complaining except when the air-conditioning system broke down or the coffee machines were empty—making it difficult to complete a thirteen-hour day. Scott jokingly promised that his next business venture would be a coffee vending service and judging by the amount of coffee they drank he predicted he could get *very* rich, *very* fast.

Basically, they were a great bunch of young people that Vicky and Scott had culled from dozens of workshops and conferences. Among the bright, young, summer employees one stood out in particular; Scott's eldest daughter, *Lenora Powers Macguire.* She had narrowly escaped obscurity during a terrible period in her young life—thanks to Scott and Vicky, who had accepted complete guardianship of her remaining minor years after her mother, Lila Powers, had died.

Lenora hadn't always blended in with Scott's close-knit family, but there were some remarkably tranquil periods during the four years she spent at the mansion on Puckshaw. There were many weeks and months when she had actually enjoyed a taste of normal family life, before packing her belongings and joining hundreds of other young people on the beautiful campus of Massachusetts's popular inter-state college.

Scott looked at his watch and allowed himself a moment to think about her with unexpected emotion.

His eldest child!

He still didn't know her very well, having gotten such a late start, but he marveled at the resemblance between his own fatherless upbringing by an unstable mother and Lenora's similarly fatherless childhood—under the influence of an unconventional mother. He sadly recognized that she had lived a lifetime far before reaching her eighteenth birthday and he and Vicky admitted that there were times when they had no control over her. More than once they feared there was no stopping the run-away train she could become in the blink of an eye.

Settling in with Scott and his family had not been easy for the defiant fifteen-year-old who, up until then, had been an intensely independent youngster. With Lila Powers as her main role model, a frightening degree of duplicity and selfishness had rubbed off on her. Her mother's devotion to her well-being was unconditional, though her devious and suspicious methods were questionable—most of the time. Lenora was the end product. She would have to live with her demons as her mother had—hopefully with less anguish and more happiness.

Lila had played by her own rules and wits and the end *always* justified *her* means, regardless of who got in the way. She left many bloodied footprints behind her as she quested after economic and social stability. That tough and driving attitude had influenced her daughter's development, often over-shadowing the sweet and soft side of her that struggled to make it to the surface so often.

Vicky and Scott had survived a wild rite of passage as parents of the teenager—making more than the usual number of trips to the principal's office in the youngster's last two years of high school. Truancy and general insolent behavior were cited over and over, but Scott and Vicky—working closely with counselors—never considered giving up on her; on the contrary, the more *guff* she gave them, the more affection they returned.

Lenora vacillated between accepting and rejecting her new family; she was determined to keep them in a high state of alert and anxiety—cruelly successful at times.

The couple had been most upset by her rampage of promiscuity in the middle of her senior year—clearly diagnosed by trusted and competent counselors as symptomatic of despair over the loss of her mother. She had grown up without a father's love and then was cruelly stripped of the comfort and care of her mother's devotion; she had every reason to feel insecure and without self value.

It didn't matter that she was finally in a safe and loving environment; she still needed to act out her resentment and anger and often came down on the peace loving Macguires like a twister. And like her mother—she took no prisoners. Her twin brothers and sweet little sister, Amelia were often startled into speechlessness by her uncaring responses to their overtures of kindness. It was going to take a lot more than a few kindnesses to win Lenora Powers Macguire over.

By the time she was eighteen, the Macguires had grown apprehensive about Lenora's departure for college; they had done everything in their power to make up for her missed opportunities and the only thing left was to give her assurances of their support and let her fly. They encouraged her to work hard and make the most of her college education; the door to the ocean side mansion on Puckshaw would always be kept wide open for her.

Scott and Vicky breathed a sigh of relief as the first semester drew to a close and the independence of campus life seemed to have agreed with Lenora. She appeared to be on a normal path to adulthood and at the end of each semester a kinder, more appreciative, young woman seemed to emerge.

Holidays and summer vacations took on a new meaning for the Macguires; festive preparations became the order of the day to celebrate Lenora's return from college for each new semester break. In her own time and space the young woman was growing to recognize and appreciate her good fortune while Scott and his family continued to shower her with genuine affection.

Blocking out the noise from the party, Scott reflected with profound gratitude and relief that *someone* had done *something* right. He wished Vicky could be around to see how lovely *Lennie* had turned out, but he wasn't leaving out Lila; she, too, would have rejoiced in her child's good fortune—if she were here.

Scott ached when he thought of how hard Lenora had taken Vicky's illness and death—crying for days when he had called her at school to tell her of the grave diagnosis.

Refusing to accept the inevitability of her death, Lenora had sunk into sadness; she doubted her strength to accept another adversity.

Still, Scott observed how much stronger young people were today than in past decades; Lenora was living proof that—with some help—an endangered kid's life could be turned around. She emerged from Vicky's death stronger and more caring of her younger brothers and sister.

All the Macguire hearts would eventually mend—some faster than others.

Scott continued to be moody and introspective. His grief was overwhelming—outlasting that of all the others who had so loved Vicky. He thought about her day and night; from their first meeting to their loving marriage, through the birth of their children, and the launching of the small publishing house.

It only made sense that they would work together at the thing they both loved—books.

The young couple had used their talent, time, and money to open a small publishing company; it was the ideal vehicle for Vicky and Scott to showcase their own work and that of young writers whose skill and desire to be effective in the print industry had grabbed their attention. They employed local writers, sharp and aggressive agents and editors, and a several PR people; never missing an opportunity to advance dedicated employees by pointing them in the right direction or mentoring them in their career efforts.

The Macguires were acquiring wealth and influence—assets they never failed to share with the residents of their beloved island—*Puckshaw.*

It had been a difficult climb. The publishing industry was not without its challenges—*Major challenges.*

It was 2015 and in the last five years the market had been glutted with books by whimsical, amateur, and untested writers. The ruthless invasion, led by the availability of electronic self-publishing services, had inflicted enormous pain on many of the powerful publishing empires. Some of the giants had stumbled and fallen; as a result, small publishing houses were cropping up all over the country in an effort to restore the industry back to its original state: *ruthless, elite, and legitimate.*

It was a huge undertaking and required a large sum of up-front money and a lot of courage, but the young Macguires were enthusiastic and financially secure enough to take the plunge.

Of the two, Vicky had emerged as the strong organizer; she personally selected each employee for a specific task and saw to their effective training and orientation. She radiated a work ethic that included loyalty to the firm and devotion to detail—a very fundamental philosophy which became the backbone and spirit of the growing company so bursting with camaraderie and motivation. As the independent firm flourished, success seemed to be lurking around every corner. Scott and Vicky trusted their employees implicitly and were trusted in return.

Scott's forte' was in soliciting young wordsmiths with viable manuscripts in hand. He was meticulous in his selections and brutally honest with new writers. If they showed promise, he drove them relentlessly to reach for the brass ring without fear.

He was no less demanding of himself; he had high expectations for both personal fulfillment and financial success. At the end of particularly long, hard days he often assured Vicky of their future success. "Someday, we'll make some money; just you wait, honey."

They would make some money—a lot of money—*eventually.*

The young couple made a great partnership with their combined talents. Fearless and driven they constantly tested the markets and networked their way into the circle of some of the most influential individuals in the business.

The *young Macguires of Puckshaw*—hardworking and ambitious—were on the march; they honed their skills relentlessly, learning to judge the reading public and forecast the tricky numbers of each demographic's supply and demand. They soon crunched numbers and predicted the mainstream readers' tastes with the best of them.

Some of his competitors were convinced that Scott Macguire could miraculously see the future; that being said, he should have been able to predict the visitation of an incurable illness upon his beloved Vicky.

The youngsters began arriving about eight-thirty p.m.—and arrive they did—dressed to the "nines" in designer clothes and golden shades of tan; a virtual parade of stunning young boys and girls resembling runway models and budding heart-throbs.

Scott stood at the patio door with his assistant, Francesca Covel, watching incredulously as they assembled in small clusters, jockeying for a position of power where they could both see and be seen. The girls screeched and hugged each other while secretly trying to distinguish themselves as singularly remarkable among a sea of look-alikes. On the other hand, the boys—fully aware that they were being critically eyed and measured against the other players—strutted their stuff in an effort to give the solid impression that they weren't even aware of any competition.

"God, I've really forgotten what it was like to be that age!" Scott whispered to Francesca. "Why do the boys look sixteen and the girls twenty?"

Francesca made a mental note that Scott was about forty-seven—just ten years her senior. Happy to see that his mood had improved since earlier in the day, when he seemed to be brooding and missing his beloved Vicky with dangerous intensity, she giggled and nodded.

Scott continued to mumble. "Isn't it amazing? I wonder if we looked like that when we were teenagers. Oh my God, get a load of the orange hair on that one."

They both tried not to laugh and brushed against each other ever so slightly—hands, hips, and shoulders touching. Neither of them spoke but held on to the feeling until a loud burst of laughter broke the sensually charged mood.

"Dad, over here a minute; say *what's up* to Jenkins!"

Harry was at the top of his game tonight; his sandy hair was spiked up with a reddish gel and his clear blue eyes were devilishly alive with excitement. His attire was classy and expensive: silk shirt, navy deck pants, white scuffed tennis shoes and a new *Rollandi* watch—a gift from his father. To Scott, Harry seemed to have become a real human being in the last year or so; but tonight he was particularly impressed with this self-assured child who had grown mysteriously tall overnight.

He thought—with no little pride—how well the boys had come through everything with such flying colors. He resolved then and there to be more attentive and accessible—now that they had safely reached the much-anticipated age of sixteen. He wondered, just for a second, what his own father—*Henry Macguire*—would have thought of his kids. He probably would have admired the twins' tough independence, but Scott guessed he would have been more inclined toward his youngest—the silent and brooding Amelia. Amelia, with the tiny, under-aged frame and huge, dark, questioning eyes; Henry would have loved her.

In any event, with Vicky gone almost a year, the boys were needing Scott more and more as a father *and* a friend. He vowed to concentrate on doing a better job; try to do what Vicky would do—if he only could.

"Dad, this is Jenkins!"

Scott paused with a long incredulous look at Jenkins. His head was completely shaved except for a blonde ponytail loosely hanging over one shoulder. It was hard to see exactly what he was wearing because of the long, white, silk duster which covered his body from neck to toe. The kid deserved an A+ for flair; he wore a bright, yellow chiffon scarf casually draped around his neck and gave the impression he was totally unaware of his appearance or the impression he was making; at least that's what Scott thought.

No surprise there; Scott had totally missed the point.

"Jesus Christ, how do they do it?" This time he spoke through ventriloquist lips that only Francesca could hear. She shook her head from side to side and shrugged her pointy shoulders as she stared up at the ceiling with questioning eyes. Scott was enjoying her coquettish responses to his comments; he hoped she just wasn't trying to flatter him.

Just then, out of the corner of his eye, Scott saw his youngest child, Amelia, peak around the corner of the patio as though she were searching for a friendly face. She looked more and more like Vicky everyday and it literally made his heart ache to catch a glimpse of that wide-eyed curiosity that so resembled her mother's trademark look. He guessed it was a learned thing since Amelia had been glued to Vicky's hip until the time of her illness and subsequent death.

302

She had turned eleven shortly after her mother died and seemed to have stopped growing as a result. She had a tiny body, translucent skin, and large, dark eyes that too often seemed on the verge of tears. She stood in the doorway for a second and suddenly, as though summoned by a higher power, Vicky's sister, Thea, materialized and linked arms with her to help ease her entrance into the crowd. Amelia was getting prettier every day and Scott scolded himself under his breath; he must be careful about underestimating her needs just because she was so quiet.

The child said very little these days—hollow-eyed and shy, she moved like a tiny sprite in the long shadow of her flashy twin brothers.

Vicky had kept a close eye on that potential problem and would have handled it appropriately before any damage was done to Amelia's self confidence. Unfortunately, it was no surprise when she became the first casualty of Vicky's illness and subsequent death.

She had been sent to her grandmother's during the initial surgery and medical treatment—roughly six weeks. Once there, she spent her days in the company of her cousins and her doting grandmother. In her later years, all she could recall about that period was the wrenching loneliness that had replaced the joy that past summers had held for her and her brothers on their beloved island of *Puckshaw*. (Scott couldn't recall who made that decision to send her away, but he regretted that the child had been shut out of that important period of adjustment.)

As Amelia dawdled over breakfast, missing her ever-watchful brothers and the sweet smell of her mother's neck, her grandmother announced, nonchalantly, that she would be going home the next day. Filled with excitement and apprehension, she packed her things and prepared to return to the island.

She had never been away from home for more than a weekend and the sudden six-week separation had taken its toll on her. She had grown pale with great dark circles lurking underneath those wondering eyes.

The next morning she appeared at the breakfast table wringing her little hands—anxious to get going.

It was early September and she was worried about entering the sixth grade; all the other kids would probably be so much bigger than she was—they always were. She needed Vicky's soothing assurance that everything would be "just fine".

As Ed Sims pulled his big car into the mansion's long driveway, Amelia cast her apprehensions aside and smiled broadly. Though he had told her silly knock-knock jokes all the way from Boston to Puckshaw; she hadn't cracked a smile. Now she seemed to leap out of her gloomy mood at the sight of her palatial home.

By the time he stopped the car and "popped" the trunk, Amelia was out of the car and running toward the imposing oceanfront mansion where Thea awaited with the large front doors flung open to welcome her. She hugged her aunt and ran through the foyer calling out for her mother. She was met with an eerie silence.

Something had changed—everything had changed. It was quieter than it had ever been and the boys, coming down to welcome her home, seemed withdrawn and secretive. Scott came in from his office to hug her and held her for only a second—cool and dismissive. She had become an outsider—missed something—she wasn't exactly sure what it was.

The boys had already been told all that they could understand and process regarding their mother's illness; they were fifteen and had already had a little time to get used to it.

The thought of going back to school in a week or so filled them with anticipation and they had—as only the young can—prioritized the unfolding events in an order all their own.

This was not the case with Scott—so inconsolable and shaken by the situation that he had hardly noticed Amelia's comings and goings. If it hadn't been for Vicky's sister, Thea, Amelia might have gone totally unnoticed—further worsening the already disastrous situation.

Only Thea seemed the same; loving, cheerful, and soothing, she remained Amelia's only lifeline to her mother. She had taken the child by the hand and walked her to her mother's large, sun-lit room. Amelia, filled with an intensity that she had never before experienced, stopped, lead-footed just a few feet from Vicky's bedroom door—unable to move another step without her aunt's support. Thea read her fear and with a firm grasp of her icy hand she gently tugged at her.

"Sweetie, there is nothing to be afraid of; your Mom can hardly wait to see you. Come on, she's fine; see for yourself!" She tapped on the door lightly and opened it without waiting for Vicky to answer. "Guess who's here to see you, Vic? You have a little visitor."

She gave Amelia a little push and stepped back to allow the ailing mother and her daughter to reunite at their own speed. The youngest Macguire took baby steps until she reached her mother's bedside and gazed, wide-eyed, at the change that had come over her face. Everyone else in the house had had a chance to get used to the pale face and forced smile; this was the first time for Amelia and she needed to catch her breath.

"It's okay, honey; I'm really fine. Get over here and give me a big hug. Oh how I've missed you! Tell me; what have you been doing all the while I've been lying around in this big bed like a lazy cat?"

That made Amelia laugh and she leapt onto the bed and covered Vicky's face with kisses. Tasting the salt from Vicky's tears, she wrinkled her nose and made a face that caused them both to burst out laughing. Thea backed out of the room and walked to the end of the carpeted hall before flopping down on the top stair and dropping her head into her hands in a rush of relief.

Thea had been divorced for three years and considered it a mixed blessing; she had suddenly found herself free to pitch in and help take care of Vicky while looking after the children's needs during this dreadful crisis. She wouldn't have it any other way and neither would Vicky.

Thea and Vicky were only two years apart and had enjoyed a fun filled, carefree childhood. After attending the same schools, summer camps, and dancing school; they had grown into inseparable young women whose lives were relatively free of sibling rivalry. Thea had gone on to college but returned home a semester later. It was a bold move, but she deeply missed her high-school sweetheart and they made plans to marry shortly thereafter.

Vicky was saddened to lose her soul mate but ecstatic to be chosen as Thea's primary wedding attendant; looking forward to that honor she had reluctantly released her big sister.

The following June, it was no surprise to anyone when Vicky took several top honors at her high school graduation and basked, giddily, in the kudos that accompanied each award.

Successes came with speed and frequency throughout Vicky's whirlwind collegiate years and during her meteoric academic rise she failed to notice any decline in happiness that Thea, her cherished sister, was experiencing.

For some unknown reason Vicky never saw it coming.

Late one night, as they chatted easily on their cell phones, she was stunned to learn of her sister's plight.

The turn of events was a deep cut into Thea's dream. She was unable to have a child and adoption was out of the question for her proud and disbelieving husband. Two years would pass before a peaceful resolution, via an amicable divorce, freed them both from the impasse.

As Thea looked back, the pain of denied motherhood, separation, and divorce was nothing but a tiny inconvenience when compared to the devastating news of Vicky's illness. Without hesitation, she offered to care for Vicky and the children and, of course, Scott.

By the end of September, with Vicky far too ill to spend time with Amelia, Thea had taken a very smothering interest in her; she crafted the child's every move and protected her from every untoward situation. She saw Amelia as a little bud; cruelly frozen in time at the very moment she was about to bloom.

Tonight, just barely one year after Vicky's death, a dark cloud was once again poised to descend upon the Macguires of Puckshaw.

Scott was brought to reality when Eddie awkwardly approached him to introduce a lovely youngster who instantly intrigued one and all with her cool confidence and polished poise.

Eddie was not as flamboyantly self-assured as his twin brother Harry, but he could hold his own, especially with his penchant for great looking girls—of which this one was no exception.

Tall, raven-haired, and fully mature, she wore a gold lame` halter-top that fastened behind her neck and hung down just far enough to cover her stunning breasts.

Scott couldn't avoid their presence and politely lowered his eyes only to feast on at least twelve inches of flat midriff that suddenly disappeared into a pair of half-zipped, faded blue jeans. He swallowed hard and dragged his eyes back up to her face, which was just as thrilling as the rest of her body. In his mind's eye he pictured shades of a young Lila Powers, quickly dismissing *that* dangerous thought just in time to hear her throaty voice.

She thrust a long, tanned hand with professionally manicured nails toward him. "Hi, Mr. Macguire, I'm Cassie Albright! Geez, you've got a great place here! Thanks for the invite. See you later, yes?" And having said that all in one breathless sentence, she simply breezed away leaving Eddie standing like a stone statue. Eddie shrugged his shoulders and mumbled something to Scott and disappeared into the little crowd, chasing after her.

"Oh my God!" was all Scott could say.

Francesca shook her head—speechless. Grabbing Scott's hand conspiratorially she whispered without moving her lips, "We better put our eyes back into our heads, close our mouths, and act normal or these kids are going to get the satisfaction of knowing they are shocking the hell out of us."

Thea was watching everything from the kitchen doorway. It was a favorite observation post from which she rarely missed a thing. She had sent Amelia upstairs to retrieve a camera and while she waited she never let her eyes stray from Scott *or* Frankie. She had so hoped to be Scott's right hand tonight, but he hadn't once looked at her the way he had been looking at Francesca on this night of all nights.

Scott appreciated *everything* Thea did and told her so, time and time again. There was no sexual traction on his part and he only ever thought of her as family.

Quite the contrary, Thea saw Scott as a little boy who needed someone to look after him. Since ridding herself of her ex-husband's overbearing nature, his type of neediness was very appealing to her. Most of the time she did an adequate job of keeping her feelings under wraps with only Amelia noticing; the child's wide, haunting eyes never missed a thing when Aunt Thea and her father were in the same room.

Now Amelia placed herself directly in front of Thea; handing her the camera, she asked in her tiny voice if she could pose for the first picture. Light years away—Thea was watching Scott and Frankie and never heard her request. Confused, Amelia shrugged her shoulders and turned her attention to the loud shout that erupted outdoors; it came from the area of the stairs that led through the concrete tunnel and down to the beach.

The twins were fully aware of the rules for their party—they simply turned a blind eye to normal amounts of pot, beer, and laced chocolate sticks that were coming in via $600 designer handbags that the girls were carrying.

They would later reason, "It was just chocolate with…I don't know…something in it that makes you feel pretty good—a lot better than beer!"

The music was loud and they all seemed to be thoroughly enjoying pizza, *Buffalo* wings, and a large variety of party dips and chips. From all appearances, the party was turning out to be a smashing success—so far.

Some danced on the patio while a few couples strutted their stuff on the grassy lawn, but most of the teens had congregated along the electric lantern-lit stairway that led down to the tiny, silver-sanded beach where more partying was going on. Though they had all seen the signs that said "absolutely no swimming after dusk," there was talk of the usual *skinny dipping* that could bring this party to a swift close—just as it had other birthday parties that took place during the hot a summer months.

Swimming in the ocean at night was strictly forbidden and enforced by all parents who allowed teens to congregate on their property for any and all after-dark activities. The only illumination emanated from a dull half-moon and it would be a foolish and reckless act to swim on this particular night.

Though it was a ban that all parents and teens agreed upon; every couple of years some youngster, with the aid of alcohol or drugs and an adoring crowd, flaunted his or her swimming prowess and tragically disappeared into the surf—yet, again, to everyone's surprise and horror.

In spite of the elbowing crowd, Amelia maneuvered her little body into a position near the top of the stairs and focused her sharp eyes on *Cassie Albright*; she was at the bottom of the stairs shaking the water out of her dark, wavy hair and pulling on her clothing. The rest of the kids lined the stairs—hooting and howling as they feasted their eyes on the slim, partially clad vision. How lucky could they get? They didn't pay much attention to the young man behind her, steadying her with his hand on her hip; he was fairly well hidden in the dark shadows, but Amelia took the time to make out who it was.

Eddie came pushing his way through the crowd just in time to see *Cassie* running up the stairs to loud applause. He wasn't quite sure what had happened, but he felt his ears turning red and instinctively knew—whatever it was—he wouldn't have liked it.

He feigned nonchalance as he shouted with a contrived degree of abandon, *"Cassie! C'mon, let's dance!"*

She put her arms around his neck and kissed him with a warm, deliberate touch, drawing a burst of applause that made him feel luckier than any other guy at the party. The night was beginning to hold real promise for him.

Cassie leaned in hard against him and whispered, "Happy birthday, Eddie. God, it's crowded in here, isn't there anyplace in this whole house where we can be by ourselves? What about upstairs? Can't we go up there?"

She smelled like the ocean and felt cool in his arms as she snuggled her face against his warm neck and purred like a kitten. "Please?"

"No, upstairs is off limits! You know that. Christ, my father'll kill me."

Eddie was facing Harry who was giving him the thumbs up sign and mouthing the words, "Go for it."

Eddie smiled and tried not to move lest he disturb the terrific physical charge he was enjoying with *Cassie* in his arms and every other guy in the place envying him—even his twin brother. He *did* know where they could go to be alone—the small, unfinished storage area right under the family room where they were presently dancing. The shed was one of those projects that had never been completed. When they were younger, it was a fun place to hide and store their treasures in, but as of late, the boys used it to keep a few magazines that shouldn't be seen around the house—along with other items of interest to growing boys. The hiding place was off limits to Amelia and the twins resting assured that their little secrets were safe.

"We really can't go upstairs, but wait here for a few minutes, then follow me. I'll be waiting outside the door on your right. Just walk by me and duck into the little opening—it's right under the family room windows—don't make a big deal out of it either. You know what I mean? Just sort of wander out like you were looking for someone."

Eddie walked through the crowded room nodding and grinning and stepped outside to join a small group who were quietly passing around a couple of joints. He accepted one and kept his eye on the door—waiting for Cassie *to* come out. He listened to a few dirty jokes, quickly losing track of time. He would later recall that he had no idea how long it was before he went looking for Cassie. Maybe fifteen or twenty minutes or longer—maybe even an hour. He would never be able to pinpoint the exact amount of time, thanks to several heady puffs from the *magic stubs* being passed around.

The night seemed to stall for Thea. Scott and Frankie had spent the last three hours glued to each other—walking the beat to discourage smoking, confiscating a can of beer here and there, and in general, discouraging any other lively activity that might land one of these youngsters in trouble. Scott had done his level best to instill fear into anyone who might have entertained the thought of bringing in alcohol or drugs, but he wasn't so naïve as to think that both hadn't made a healthy appearance more than once throughout the evening.

He assumed, correctly, that all conventional party vices were still alive and well.

At last, a few parents had pulled up in the driveway to pick up some of the happy partygoers who dutifully thanked the adults "for the great fun" as they ran to waiting cars. No one would be walking home—the beachfront house was off the main road and the secondary road was pitch black once you left the long, brightly lit, *Macguire* driveway.

There were still at least a half dozen youngsters draped over the sofas in the family room and on the patio; several more were stretched out—in two's—on the lounging lawn furniture. Only a few brave couples were still dancing very slowly—actually standing still, as far as Scott could make out.

It was well after midnight and Amelia was curled up on the loveseat with her head on Thea's lap.

Scott and Francesca were carrying empty trays and plastic glasses into the kitchen seemingly flushed with a secret excitement of their own. Something had happened between them tonight—Scott couldn't count the number of times he had taken the opportunity to touch Frankie's hand or shoulder during the course of the evening and each time, she seemed to welcome his touch with a tilt of her head and a knowing smile. His heart pounded with the realization of what this could mean. He hadn't intended it; earlier that very day he had been mourning Vicky anew and wishing she could be there for the party—see how great the boys were turning out. Now he actually welcomed the familiar feeling that had crept over him throughout the evening. There seemed to be a magic fluid warming his body and he embraced the long-absent excitement with the abandonment of a teenager.

He realized that he didn't want the party to end, but it was getting late—time to put the main lights on and encourage the last dancers to call home for their rides. Everyone lived within a ten or fifteen minute ride and he assumed things would be wrapped up by one-thirty.

"Well, what do you say kids—ready to pack it in?"

His intrusion was greeted with a loud, collective moan.

He looked around for Eddie and Harry and saw them standing outdoors with a couple of kids. They seemed to be immersed in some pretty serious conversation; Harry kept glancing over his shoulder with a look of fear—at best a trace of worry.

Scott had a strange premonition that sent a shiver up his back.

Hell, it's probably nothing; someone drunk or puking somewhere out there. What the hell could have happened—a teen-age break-up? Not on this festive occasion! This was the Macguire household! What could possibly go wrong?

Scott raised his eyes toward Francesca and Thea and nodded his head in the boys' direction. Maybe they could help him figure it out. Frankie held back; she didn't think she knew the kids well enough to get too involved. Scott took a deep breath and walked over to the twins and a youngster he knew as Mollie Simon. He had convinced himself that either someone was puking drunk or a great romance had disintegrated during the course of the evening.

"What's the problem, boys; someone sick?" He didn't wait for an answer. "Do you need a ride home, Mollie?"

The little group remained silent.

"What's the matter, Eddie?"

"Dad, we think we got a little problem. Mollie is supposed to spend the night at *Cassie's* but we can't seem to find her. She must have gone home with someone else."

"*Mr. Macguire*, I hate to call her house because if she isn't there her mother will *kinda* freak. So what do *you* think I should I do, sir?"

Mollie had a whining voice that *kinda* annoyed Scott. "Well, let's find out *who* she left with, first; then maybe we can drive you over to meet her and get the two of you home to her house. How's that sound?"

"Oh, okay *Mr. Macguire*. Sorry to be so much trouble, sir." Mollie whined apologetically.

"No problem."

Thea had seen most of the kids to the door, efficiently checking their departure arrangements as they left; the house was quieter now.

Scott nodded toward Eddie's cell phone and told him to start calling the kids who had left earlier; maybe they could trace down someone that Cassie might have gone home with. He instructed Mollie, who was staring at her cell phone as though she might will it to ring, to do likewise. An hour had passed and *no one* had seen Cassie after they left the party.

It was time to call her parents—ask if she had arrived home.

Thea volunteered; she thought it would go over better if an adult did the calling; *it would show that they were on top of things—in charge.*

Mrs. Albright's initial agitation immediately turned to fear.

"She was supposed to call *us* for a ride; her father is still waiting up for her call. Are you saying she left with someone else? Do you know whom? What exactly are you saying, Thea? What's going on there, anyway? Wasn't anyone watching those kids? Jesus!"

Just the reaction Scott Macguire was dreading.

Thea explained, in a very calm voice, that they had called everyone who had been at the party and, so far, Cassie had not gone home with any of them. She explained that Mollie was planning to spend the night at their home on Cassie's invitation, but was still at the *Macguire* home—waiting—they would soon have to call *her* parents to come and pick her up.

And it was getting late.

"Mrs. Albright, have you any idea *where* Cassie might have gone? Do you know of anyone else she may have called? Has she done this before? You know, sometimes these kids get a little rebellious and go their own way. What do you want us to do at this end? I hate to alarm you, but we could call the police station and get some help; you know, nip this in the bud."

Thea was fishing for help but Mrs. Albright was not helping. She was beginning to panic and her husband was in the background talking to her in an impatient, hoarse tone. As Thea waited, they began to shout at one another and she looked to Scott for some help, holding the phone toward him to hear the shouting. Mollie was right; they were beginning to *kinda freak.*

Scott grabbed the phone from Thea.

"Mrs. Albright, this is Scott Macguire; we are concerned about Cassie's safety and we are going to *have* to call the police. While we're waiting we'll keep the floodlights on and search the grounds. Maybe she has fallen asleep or gone for a walk or... something simple. She could be just strolling along the beach with a friend. In any event, we don't want to waste a lot of time here. I'm going to hang up now; if you would like to come over, you're welcome, here."

Harry silently beckoned his father to step out on the patio; freshly alarmed, Scott followed him with a questioning look on his face. The youngster related Cassie's skinny-dipping exhibition earlier in the evening. He didn't know what it had to do with anything but he thought his father should know.

"Dad, don't say anything okay? You don't think she went down to the water again, do you?

"Jesus, I hope not; I really have no idea son; we'll take some flashlights and go down there right away."

He returned to the family room visibly shaken; he had to take charge.

"Frankie, you come with me. Thea, you wait for the Albrights and the police and tell Eddie to call Mollie's parents and see that she is picked up. Harry, wake up Amelia and get her upstairs to bed."

"I'm awake, Dad. I'll stay right here if it's okay with you," Amelia answered in her eerie little voice. *"I'll keep company with Auntie Thea."*

Scott nodded his approval and began to get the large flashlights off the patio shelf. He handed one to Francesca and they stepped out through the patio door and headed toward the lighted concrete stairway that led to the beach—*eerily black dark at two o'clock in the morning.*

Thea was on the phone speaking to the police in a quiet voice but her eyes were following Scott and Frankie. Why had he asked *her* to go with him? After all, she knew the grounds and beach so much better. The message was clear—he wanted to be alone with Francesca. She would deal with that later, but right now Thea would, again, prove herself to be efficient and irreplaceable.

Mollie's parents came to pick her up and smelling a potential scandal, began asking questions. Thea irritably asked them to leave; assuring them it was probably all a big mistake. One of the girls had probably forgotten to tell her parents she was sleeping over a friend's house after the party. Case closed.

Sheriff Cramer and Deputy Johnson arrived within ten minutes and began to look around. Cramer went down to the beach to join Scott and Francesca while Johnson took the opportunity to pull Eddie and Harry aside to get the names of everybody who had attended the party. Names, addresses, and telephone numbers of teens, adults and children; he wasn't fooling around—not tonight.

It was three a.m. and the mansion and its surrounding grounds were brightly lit. Word had gotten around and some of the parents had come back to help with the search. A young officer asked that they sign in with Johnson and search with a partner; no one was to *go solo*. Also, no teens were to be allowed back on the premises.

Cramer had his reason.

The Macguire household seemed to be in shock. Scott was sickened at the way the police were treating the whole thing—as though a crime had been committed.

"They're overdoing it, Harry," whispered Eddie. "*Cassie* is just one of those wild girls who'll probably turn up in the morning—after spending the night with a bunch of virtual strangers. That's the way she is. *What the hell else could have happened to her?*"

Amelia was half-dozing on the loveseat in the family room with a light afghan covering her little body. She stirred occasionally while Thea, openly annoyed with the amount of foot traffic inside the house, hovered over her every movement.

Having returned from the beach on Cramer's orders, Frankie remained at Scott's side, occasionally resting against him lightly. He was amazed at how right it felt. He was glad she was with him tonight, but he felt sick every time he looked at the twins—pale and frightened—sitting on the patio across from Officer Johnson.

Thea broke the silence. "Scott, shall I make some coffee or tea? Everyone is just exhausted and it's almost light out. What do you think?"

He shrugged and looked around not really answering her directly.

She saw no excuse for his off-handed dismissal.

"Maybe I'll just get Amelia up to bed and get an hour or so myself. Call me if anything comes up."

Scott ignored Thea's exit, his eyes glued to the scene now playing out on the patio. Johnson was being unfairly rough on the boys with his relentless questioning. They looked so shaken and exhausted that he felt he had to do *something* to help them.

"Excuse me, Johnson; can the boys go to bed now? They need to be up in a couple of hours to take down the tables and chairs; they've got a pretty big clean-up ahead of them. What do you say? Will you let them go to bed?"

Johnson nodded without any change of expression. He didn't appear to feel sorry for them—not at all; he had his visions of what they might find when it got light out. His gut feeling was that a drowning had occurred. He based that on the skinny dipping story, but "you never know what the hell these youngsters are up to these days; hell, it could be anything," he mumbled in response to Scott's request to take it easy on the boys.

Visibly irritated, Scott walked away.

The Albrights, having every reason to be upset, had arrived in tears, noisily joining the Sheriff in the family room. After an hour or so he told them they could go home and wait for his call or, if Scott didn't mind, they could sit in the family room and wait for the sun to rise.

He gently advised them that two of his men would search the small beach as soon as it was light out and the local security people were already in town checking out the public beach and the usual after-hours places the younger kids frequented around the island.

The Albrights, insulted, assured him that their daughter would "never be found in *one of those awful* places" and "they shouldn't even waste their time".

Cramer nodded respectfully, agreeing that he knew Cassie was *a good girl.*

They shook hands all around before the Albrights left and Cramer dismissed the small group of volunteers; they were to go straight home. He discouraged one and all from roaming around the property any further.

Hopefully, the young lady would turn up in town with an excuse that only a parent would accept.

Cramer closed his eyes and rubbed them hard. Experience had taught him that if *Cassie Albright* didn't show up within the next six hours, it was going to be a long, hot summer on *Puckshaw.*

26 *Francesca*

Francesca stepped into the kitchen for a moment to put the teakettle on. Weary, she leaned against the stove and wondered what she was doing in her boss's house—making tea at five o'clock in the morning. She had trouble sorting out her feelings; it seemed like only yesterday that she had cried at Vicky's funeral, now she was holding hands with her husband, Scott Macguire.

The Scott Macguire!

"This is impossible," she whispered into the steam as it curled out of the spout only to be greedily sucked into the overhead fan.

Was her mind playing tricks on her? She reviewed the events of the evening.

This is not my style; he's my boss, the father of three, and still grieving over his dead wife. I shouldn't be doing this, yet it seems so comfortable.

She thought of her warm, welcoming apartment on the mainland and wished that none of this had happened. It was all too complicated. She would rather be curled up under a soft comforter—watching one of her favorite reruns.

In the last few years, Francesca Covel had created a tightly-structured and most satisfying world for herself. She kept up a small circle of friends, worked hard, and enjoyed the fruits of her labors. She was classified as a single career woman that was devoted to her job and her own self-fulfillment. The end of the first decade of the Millennium had spawned thousands of them. These women were educated, self-sufficient, well adjusted, and interested in the arts as well as sports. They were at home at a small dinner party or a large cocktail bash. They enjoyed both male and female company, would get married if the right guy came along, and would *probably* opt against having children. They were highly sought after by corporate headhunters. They made first-rate executives, directors, and administrators.

The problem was that there weren't enough of them; by 2016 many of them had started their own companies with generous, government, start-up money.

Francesca's education was in business and finances and she had never turned down an internship or an opportunity that might open the door to an introduction or a new position of advantage in her chosen field. She was determined to make the right contacts and learn the ropes. And that she did—exceedingly well.

Due to Vicky's passing, a re-structuring was due at *H. Macguire & Son* and rumor had it that Francesca Covel would soon be named as one of the two new vice-presidents. She had made it known to Scott from the very beginning that she would stay with the young company as long as she was considered for advancement on a regular basis. She could play hardball if she had to, but it wasn't going to be necessary at *Mac &Son.*

A&M Inc. was still reeling from Francesca's graceful departure. The large chain of booksellers was prone to holding women *in their place* and by the time they saw the light, Francesca Covel was gone—along with more than a few sought after corporate accounts. She had devoted nine loyal years to the company and was caught off guard by their unfair treatment as she approached the executive level. She made herself a promise that she would never let it happen again. If this was *still* a man's world, they were going to *have* to make room for her. She hoped she didn't have to fight the dragon every day; but she would if she had too.

After two years, her loss was still felt at A&M Inc.

A whistle of the teakettle and the touch of a warm hand cupping her elbow broke her reverie.

"Hi, how are you holding up? I'm sorry all this has happened; I never dreamed it would turn into such a cluster..."

"Shh; it's okay. It's not your fault. How can anyone predict what these damn kids are going to pull? Have you heard anything yet? I thought I heard a phone ring."

Scott shook his head back and forth, "No, nothing."

Frankie suddenly realized that they were alone for the first time since she had arrived at his home early on the night of the party; it made her blush for some reason.

The police were outside milling around now that it was light out; everyone else was upstairs sleeping. She opened two cupboards before she spotted some cups and saucers. She took them down and looked at Scott to get his approval. He nodded.

She placed them on the table and looked around for the teabags. Scott half apologized and retrieved a box of teabags from the cupboard. He dropped a bag in each cup and she poured the hot water over them as they sat down across from each other at *cook's* small wooden breakfast table. They were silent—both lost in the stillness of the moment.

"What do we do now?" she said in a whisper, tearing the edges of her paper napkin. "I guess I should have said what are *you* going to do now? I know what *I* have to do. I have to go home, take a shower, and get some sleep! We have a meeting with the new web-site people first thing on Monday and a working lunch with John Moss at one-thirty. If you can't make it, I'll cover. What is today, anyway? Wait; the party was Saturday night, right? Today is Sunday, I guess. Don't worry; like I said—I'll cover."

Scott loved the way she was so matter-of-fact about it.

"Thanks. Thanks a million. I'm sure we'll get this thing cleared up long before that. I'll call you as soon as I hear something, okay?

"Sure. I just need to catch a few winks and I'll be as good as new in a few hours. How about you? You better get some rest; why don't you just lay on the sofa down here? Thea and the kids will be up soon and they can clean up—can't they?

"Yeh, sure they can. Come on, I'll walk you to your car."

Frankie drained her teacup and the warm liquid felt good. Scott stepped aside to let her pass through the kitchen doorway, smiling at her as she passed him. The sun was blazing and Johnson was sitting in a chair on the patio. He was typing furiously on an *A-pad*, occasionally stopping to whisper into the tiny microphone located at the top of his latest electronic device.

320

It all looked so official—he never said a word to them; just raised a distracted hand to say goodbye. It was chilling; they walked to Francesca's car and she paused for a moment before getting into the driver's seat.

"Are you going to be alright? You look awful!"

Scott laughed. "Listen, thanks again; I don't know what I would have done without you."

He touched her shoulder and Francesca put her hand up and covered his. "You're welcome, *Boss*. Good morning. Talk to you in a few hours."

Francesca slid into the front seat and started her car before turning to look at Scott.

"It'll be alright Scott. Don't worry so."

"Thanks. I'll call you later."

"Good. Do that."

Scott was resolute. "You bet."

Francesca drove away—*smiling*.

Barely an hour later, while Scott was on the couch in a deep sleep, Amelia tiptoed past him and stepped onto the patio where Johnson was still sitting in the same chair; only now his head was thrown back and his eyes were closed. His mouth agape, he made a sound like a slow steam engine. The child thought it was comical though she found very few things to be funny these days. She stood before him, studying his features intently before looking down at his large leather belt and buckled holster that held the impressive shiny gun. Her eyes moved down to inspect his high boots—caked with a thin layer of mud. She assumed he had been walking around on the wet grass and sandy beach most of the night and felt kind of sorry for him.

Amelia jumped back when Johnson suddenly opened his eyes.

"Hi there, chicken. How are you this morning?"

"Fine; why have you been here all night? Is there something wrong?

Johnson stood up and stretched. He peered through the patio window, scratched his head, and raised his arms high above his head. As he stretched noisily, Amelia caught a whiff of an unpleasant odor that forced her to step back as he removed his cell phone from its little harness on his shoulder. He excused himself and stepped outside.

She watched him through the window as he talked and shook his head. He raised his voice and gesticulated wildly; she wished she could hear him. She opened the patio door and walked out to stand behind him. He spun around and startled her.

"What's wrong, Mr. Johnson?"

"Nothing for you to worry your pretty little head about, Missy. Now run along into the house so I can get my work done."

"Are you looking for someone?"

Johnson knelt down in front of Amelia and said in a low voice, "Why do you ask me that question?"

"Because I know you're looking for somebody. I think you're looking for *Cassie.*"

Now Johnson was fully alert and didn't know if he should continue this conversation with a child without any witnesses around. He stepped a few paces away and took his cell phone out again. He talked into it so quietly that Amelia couldn't make out a thing he was saying. When he was through he walked over to her and asked if she minded coming back into the house until the Sheriff arrived.

"Did you have to wake up Sheriff Cramer? I hope he doesn't get mad at me. Maybe you'd better wake up my Dad; he's right there sleeping on the sofa."

Johnson held the door open and Amelia walked in under his arm, wrinkling her nose and ducking unnecessarily low to avoid the expected odor. She thanked him and headed toward the small sofa where Scott was in a sound asleep. She moved in to stand very close to his face. His eyes flew open and he sat up.

"Hi, honey. What's wrong? Are you all right?"

He looked at Johnson through squinted eyes to avoid the harsh sun that was streaming into the family room. The drapes would have ordinarily been drawn as a protection from the hot, early morning sun; but today, nothing was ordinary.

"What is it? Have you heard something?"

"No and yes, *Mr. Macguire*; I think I'd like to talk to you alone, sir."

"I know where she is."

It was Amelia speaking in a strange, conspiratorial tone. She moved closer to her father and repeated, *"I know where she is, Daddy."*

"What? What the hell are you talking about, Amelia?"

Johnson raised a hand in front of Scott's face and put a finger up to his lips to tell Amelia not to say anymore.

"Let's wait for Sheriff Cramer. Please, don't you say anything else, *little cutie.*"

Now Scott was wide-awake and leaping to his feet. "What the hell is going on here? Johnson! What is it? What is Amelia talking about? Christ, she's only eleven, you know."

"I'm eleven, going on twelve, Daddy."

Cramer arrived in a screech and bounded out of his patrol car, barely turning the ignition off. He entered through the patio with a large white handkerchief in his hand, wiping his forehead he began abruptly.

"Okay, what have we got here?"

Johnson took Sheriff Cramer into the kitchen and told him that Amelia had accurately named the missing girl and was claiming to know where she was. Cramer knew he had to be careful with Amelia being a child and all. He'd have to ask Scott if he could talk to her informally, otherwise things could get very sticky from the legal standpoint. He was dealing with *The Macguires* and didn't want to cross any lines.

The sheriff hoped Scott would cooperate. Actually, there wasn't much of a choice. In a couple hours Boston PD was sending down a van with the dogs and if that girl was *anywhere* on the premises she *would* be found. He hiked up his belted trousers, adjusted his gun, and strode back to the family room with Johnson behind him.

Cramer looked at Scott and waited for his permission. Scott nodded his head and whispered, "Go ahead. Don't forget, she's only a kid—eleven, right Amelia?

"--going on twelve, Dad."

"—so don't go scaring the shit out of her. She's been through a lot already. She's our baby, you know. Wait. Maybe I better call Sims—no, go ahead and say what you have to say; then I'll call him. Christ, go ahead!"

Cramer ignored the coarse language and faced Amelia squarely. "Okay, Amelia, if you *think* you know where someone is hiding how about showing us? We'll just make a little game out of this okay?"

Amelia didn't answer Cramer; she just looked at her father for reassurance and stepped closer to him. The sheriff interpreted that as a *yes* and said, "Okay, folks, let's go."

The three men and Amelia formed a little caravan and walked from the family room, through the patio, and out the screened door. They stepped into a blinding sun, shading their eyes.

With one hand tucked securely in her father's large, sweaty hand, Amelia used her other hand to point to the right. The sheriff and his little posse turned to the right and walked a short distance along the outside of the family room's raised foundation. Amelia pointed to the small, unfinished storage shed that was located below a three-paneled window.

The sheriff and his small *posse* approached the rough opening and stood before it, staring blankly.

It had two wide wooden planks pushed firmly against the opening. Both officers of the law shrugged—they had reached a dead end.

It was Cramer who finally spoke—albeit impatiently. "You know what? We might as well remove them, prove the kid wrong, and get on with the job." He was just about to say something to Johnson when Amelia spoke up in a timid voice.

"She's in there."

Cramer and Johnson both knelt, reached for the planks, and yanked at them. Not hard to remove—they popped out.

Scott pulled Amelia back and watched intently as the officers pointed their flashlights and crawled into the storage area.

"You two stay back. Get back! Do you hear me?"

"I hear you, Sheriff." Scott answered, as he stepped back further, pulling Amelia with him.

Scott was staring at the back of Johnson's high, dusty boots when he heard Sheriff Cramer let fly a four-letter word that he hoped Amelia wouldn't understand. He heard the men exchange a few words and then Johnson backed out and walked away without saying anything. It was a few minutes before Sheriff Cramer backed out and wiped his face with his ever-present white handkerchief.

He looked Scott Macguire squarely in the eye. "She's in there alright." Then his voice broke as he said, "She's dead. Appears to be strangled; she also has a nasty blow to the side of her head. We won't know what killed her until the autopsy is completed. Now get the hell out of my way!"

Then he stopped for a moment and tried to soften his voice a little. "Amelia, I want to thank you very much because you've been a great help to me today. Now you go on and get away from this shed. There's nothing for you to see. Okay? Now go on!"

All hell broke loose. The Sheriff made several calls in succession and within twenty minutes at least six official vehicles were lined up in the *Macguire* driveway—including an ambulance and the Coroner's official SUV.

Thea and the boys had heard the commotion and were downstairs begging for answers. When Scott told them what he knew they turned white with shock—Eddie sobbing out loud.

Johnson had quickly carried the news to the Albrights who arrived in a police vehicle within minutes screaming with uncontrollable anguish and grief.

Cramer and Johnson continued the flurry of calls and received news within the hour that *Tom Lavin* of the Boston PD would conduct the investigation. In the meantime, virtually everybody who was anywhere near the *Macguire* oceanfront home the night of the party was a suspect; every adult, teenager, and child—male or female—no one was exempt.

The police were busy getting names and addresses of those who had been omitted earlier. That meant Scott, Thea, and Francesca would be considered suspects. Parents who had come to pick up their children under the cover of darkness were suspects. The guy who delivered the chicken wings and pizza was a suspect.

"Amelia?"

"Yes, *even little Amelia!*" Cramer had roared at his deputy.

The day's findings rendered Scott speechless. He and his children were now part of the most inconceivable scenario that even *Henry Macguire,* in his often wild dreams, could have ever conjured up.

Everyone had been ordered to stay off their cell phones and *smart pads* until the body could be identified and removed. The party area was declared a crime scene and sealed off; no one was allowed to enter the backyard area or stairs that led through the renovated tunnel and to the beach.

Scott, Thea, and the twins sat huddled in the family room. Scott used his *cyber-phone*, with permission, to call Ed Sims and also Francesca—she had to be told what was going on. He hated to tell her that she was a suspect, like all the others, but he felt better putting it right up front to her. Thea was visibly impatient to call her mother before she saw it on television, but was unable to get her hands on a phone—not to call her mother. Cramer had warned, "No phone calls *in or out*; you folks hear me?"

The boys were silent and frightened, taking little comfort in each other as they sat at the bottom of the carpeted stairs leading up to the second floor bedrooms. With little fanfare, Amelia had lay atop the love seat and was almost asleep, yet, again.

The cell phone next to Francesca's bed startled her out of a fitful sleep that had barely lasted two hours.

"Is that you, Scott?"

"Sorry to wake you up so soon, Francesca. Christ, there's terrible trouble here."

"What's the matter?"

"They found the girl—*Cassie*—she's dead."

"Oh my God, what happened?"

"They're not saying much; they think she was strangled. Listen, I can't stay on the phone too long but will you be coming down?"

"I'm getting dressed as we speak; I'll be there inside the hour."

"One more thing, Francesca, you should know you're a suspect; Thea too; so am I. Christ Almighty! We all are! Cramer said even Amelia is! Can you believe this?"

There was a long pause and finally Francesca whispered, "*Christ*. Alright then, good-bye, Scott."

Francesca disconnected quickly and suddenly Scott felt lonely; he couldn't wait until she was at his side again. She, like Vicky, gave him needed confidence and strength.

Just as he put the phone down on the coffee table Thea appeared at his side—like a ghost. He knew in a flash that she had heard his conversation with Francesca. Her dog-eyed look of sadness was really starting to irritate him; she seemed to be doing it more and more lately—mostly Francesca was around.

His sister-in-law had been terrific when Vicky was sick; truly, she was a lifesaver when it came to caring for the children—especially Amelia.

Thea had assumed that she was the only woman in his world. They took the kids to the movies, on picnics, and had dinner together almost every night of the week. Thea willingly planned the meals and did some of the green marketing, although most of the cooking was done by *cook*.

"Auntie Thea" saw that the house was efficiently maintained, insisting that the kids keep things neat in between housecleaning sessions by the outside cleaners. In short, Thea had become the mistress of the *Macguire Household* and that included raising Scott Macguire's children for him. Not that she objected, but several times, out of courtesy and curiosity, she had broached the subject of going back to her apartment once the kids were back in school. Scott had shown surprise and panic. There was always the question of who would care for *poor, little Amelia*—and the subject would be dropped.

Just last month she had accompanied him to a few cocktail parties, considering those evenings at his side as a good sign, but they had never ended romantically.

"Are you waiting for the phone, Thea?"

"Cramer said I could call my mother," she said dryly. "Thanks."

Scott was distracted by a loud commotion on the patio and ran out to see what it was all about. Cramer and Johnson were pulling the boys away from each other. The usually placid twins were red-faced with anger.

"What the hell were you two doing? Fighting? Why?"

Johnson broke in with, "Okay, let's everyone settle down here. You two boys best keep those tempers under control, you hear? You're all in shock and need some sleep so just calm down, all right?"

He looked from side to side, first at Eddie and then at Harry.

They both pulled away nodding moodily.

Scott was shocked; he couldn't recall the last time he had seen the boys actually get physical with each other. He had heard them argue, even seen them throwing clothes and books at each other, but they hadn't laid an unfriendly hand on one another since they were seven years old.

He heard all kinds of alarms and sirens going off in his head and hoped they were reacting normally, considering the circumstances they found themselves in on this unbelievable Sunday morning. He tried to approach them for an answer to his question of why they had been fighting, but there were too many people around and too much confusion; he couldn't seem to get close enough to talk to them. Having perfected the routine of breaking away in different directions every time their father approached them; the opportunity to talk to them together kept slipping away.

Scott was *livid.*

With Cramer on his heels, he stepped into the kitchen at his bidding.

"What is it, now? No, I don't know why they were fighting. They haven't fought in years. Is it against the law, now, for brothers to argue or fight?

Cramer planted his feet, pulled up his pants and appeared to be preparing to say something very difficult. Scott stood before him with a blank stare. He had no idea what the hell Cramer was trying to say but he knew that he wasn't going to like it; not by any stretch.

To his complete shock Sheriff Cramer took a little piece of plastic out of his right front pocket and began with, "You have the right to remain silent..." and delivered the rest of the *Miranda* spiel in a quivering voice that faded to blackness as far as Scott was concerned.

Scott's head literally spun as he put his hands out in front of him as if to say, "No you don't," but Sheriff Cramer put his finger to his lips and continued reading.

When he was finished Scott said, "What the hell was that all about?"

"Scott, I've known you since the day you came to *Puckshaw* to bury your father—always a good friend to me. I hold you in the highest esteem, as I did your sweet little wife—God rest her soul. And hell, I love your kids as if they were my own and I know, first hand, that they've never given anyone on this island a lick of trouble. Today I've got a really difficult thing to do; please don't make it any harder than it has to be."

Scott thought he saw genuine tears filling Cramer's eyes but he persisted. "Jesus, you don't think *I* had anything to do with the accident, do you?"

"Goddammit, it *wasn't an accident*, Scott. Can't you get this through your head? *It was murder* and don't you or anyone else around this goddamned house forget that. That girl didn't strangle herself and she didn't bash the side of her head in by herself, either. Some son-of-a-bitch did it for her; so don't go calling it an *accident!*

Now will you help me round up everyone into one room? Nobody is going to be arrested or charged, right now, but everyone in this house is a suspect and I need to read them their

---

329

rights so they don't go off half-cocked giving statements they'll later regret and want to sue me for. By the way, you should be calling Ed Sims; don't you think? He'll tell you what to do about the children and your sister-in-law, since they live here. And, oh, the young lady who works for you will need some advice, too.

I know it sounds like a frightening ordeal but let me tell you something, *Mr. Scott Macguire*; someone has been murdered here, on *your* premises, under *your* supervision, and it wasn't pretty, either. Now I need and expect your full cooperation—is *that* going to be a problem?

Then he seemed to soften his voice and his attitude, as he put his hand on Scott's shoulder. "Deputy Johnson is in charge of collecting all the information about the kids and parents who were on these premises last night; he might have to ask you who dropped off and picked up some of those kids. Actually, he has most of what he needs—just a little left to take care of. Your boys were very helpful about it all. I'll be in charge of the situation here until the body is taken away and the yellow tape is taken down. That's going to be a few more hours."

Scott didn't like the way Sheriff Cramer had addressed him as *Mr. Scott Macguire.* It seemed arrogant and confrontational and it really pissed him off—enough that he sullenly stepped back and let Cramer's hand fall off his shoulder without acknowledging it.

Cramer got the message and went right on talking.

"There will be a lot of people around to collect evidence and take photos, so tell your family to stay in the house and avoid talking to anyone until things settle down. You know son, some of the *old-timers* around the area knew your father pretty well and are hoping that, as *Henry's kid*, you'll give them a great scoop. Don't talk to any of them! Be patient and wait until we get some answers to a few questions around here. Sometimes these things go real fast and other times it takes months. Whatever happens, I want you and the family to stay close to home. So I don't have to tell you to keep them out of the driveway and off the beach, right?"

Scott stared into space, furious.

Cramer searched Scott's face in an effort to make eye-contact—unsuccessfully.

"Now you go ahead and get your family and that *little woman friend* of yours and anyone else that was around here last night; tell them all to be in the family room in half an hour."

Then he made one last effort at being compassionate.

"This is just as hard for me as it is for you Scott, but think of the *Albrights*; they had a daughter Saturday and today they don't. Think about the terror that youngster must have felt last night as she fought for her life at the hands of a goddamned, cold-blooded murderer—and believe me she did fight! Now you go on and do what I told you; everything is going to be all right."

Scott looked out of the kitchen window and saw the flashing lights of an ambulance. The thought of that lovely youngster being taken away for a gruesome autopsy made him physically sick. He tried to picture her as she looked when he was introduced to her not even twenty-four hours ago. He couldn't help his recollection and he was ashamed at the vision that invaded his consciousness; it was how she looked when he met her and he couldn't change that.

It had become eerily quiet in the Macguire mansion; everyone was standing on the patio, awe-struck by the scene unfolding in their once serene world.

Scott looked for Thea to check with her about food, the kids, and so many other things that she automatically took care of in the running of his house. He didn't see her anywhere. "Where the hell is she?" he inquired of no one in particular. When he was trying to avoid her, she was always under his nose or breathing down his neck; now when he needed her, he couldn't find her. Someone touched his shoulder from behind and he jumped.

"I'm sorry; I didn't mean to scare you."

"Oh God, I'm so glad you're here. It's unbelievable; I don't know going on."

Scott reached out and gently pulled Francesca towards him and kissed her softly on the cheek. "It's so good to see you. It seems like last night was so long ago and I still don't know what the hell is going to happen. I'm just sick about... everything."

Frankie did not rebuff his gentle tugging or surprising kiss on the cheek; she just turned bright red. "I just can't believe it! Are they sure? I mean...are they sure she was murdered? Maybe it was an accident. I saw her parents on the way in; God, I felt sorry for them!

The sheriff knew who I was right away and waved me in. Wow, he knows everybody who puts a foot on this island, huh?"

"Yes, he sure does."

Francesca noted Scott's mounting irritability whenever Cramer's name was mentioned; she wondered what the hell that was all about.

"Maybe if you can round up the kids and Thea, we'll find out why the sheriff wants to see us all together."

She deliberately avoided mentioning him by name—she possessed that kind of tact.

"Right, I'll get started!"

Thea and Amelia were not present in the family room and that, too, visibly irritated Scott anew.

"Where are Thea and Amelia?" he asked the boys who seemed to stare into space every time he tried to talk to them. He paced around the room mumbling under his breath.

Cramer's face remained calm—the blank expression of a good poker player. "No need for that. Just take it easy, now."

He knew he had spooked them all by jumping the gun and reading Scott his rights, but he wanted to cover all the bases before the Boston people got there. He couldn't take any chances; he was dealing with a homicide and wasn't going to make any stupid mistakes. Better to have erred on the side of reading him his rights unnecessarily, rather than not reading them at all. This position would keep him in control and also forewarn anyone from shooting his mouth off without thinking. *After all, they were his friends.*

Thea arrived with Amelia trailing behind her with one hand lightly holding on to the back of her sweater. That's how the child was; always touching—needing that contact for

---

332

assurance. Her face was unusually flushed and she lowered her head in embarrassment as Thea whispered the reason for their tardiness. It seemed to be of a personal nature and no one in the room questioned it.

"Well, I guess that's it. Looks like everybody's here, so I'll get started with what I've got to say." Cramer was all business, making eye contact with each person in the room, including Amelia.

"I'm gonna start out by reminding you that no one's going to get arrested and be carted off to jail—at least not today—so let's wipe those frightened looks off your faces. It's true that last night, someone who was on these premises committed a terrible crime against an innocent girl who just happened to be a guest in your home, *Mr. Macguire*; now that doesn't necessarily mean that someone, here in this room, is the murderer. As a matter of fact, I highly doubt it; but of course, I can't be sure. After all, I'm not a psychic with a crystal ball."

Allowing a slight smile to creep across his thin lips, he made a motion as though he was looking into a crystal ball—rolling his eyes and waiting for the desired effect. Only Amelia smiled and Cramer appreciated her quick response to his attempt at humor, nodding toward her in acknowledgement it. The others in the room remained impassive—they no longer trusted the man whom they had called *friend* up until a couple of hours ago.

"Now, Scott Macguire, here, is going to take care of any legal advice this family will be needing; have you contacted Sims yet, Scott?"

Scott moodily nodded his head up and down without making a sound. He really didn't think it was any of Cramer's business to ask him that question in front of his children and the others. He thought it made him look stupid, or at best, negligent.

"Good. I just want to remind all of you to write down anything you think Ed Sims should know—just in case you get nervous and forget what you want to tell him. But I don't have to tell you that; he's a good man and he'll tell you what to do."

Scott glared at Cramer. It was none of his business what his family discussed with his private attorney. He was about to explode and ask him get on with it just as Cramer continued with his little speech.

"The Boston Police Department will be conducting interviews with everyone that was anywhere near this place last night; no doubt some of you will even be getting called to go down to answer a few questions. A guy by the name of *Lavin* is in charge of all the questioning and like I said; *that don't mean nothin'*. He's just a detective doing his job. Now, if you think you might be saying something that could make you feel uncomfortable—they call that self-incriminating information—then you should be talking to Ed Sims because it's his job to tell you what to do and what to say. Hell, he can even advise you not to answer any questions at all—but that's none of my business."

He panned the room with his arms extended—palms up—and asked somewhat dramatically, "Do you have any questions? Now is a good a time as any to ask me 'cause I'll be gone in a couple hours—not much left for me to do here. I'll be working out of my office after today. You can still call me anytime. Anyone around here can give you my number.

Thea shook her head from side to side as though she couldn't believe what she was hearing and the boys looked at each other with what a trained observer might have interpreted as a touch of panic—at best, a red flag. Amelia predictably hid behind Thea, hiding any reaction she might have and Scott stared down at his unlaced tennis shoes.

The room was silent.

Scott looked up in a daze, noting with admiration that Francesca was the only one returning Cramer's gaze—with plenty of confidence. He thought it unnerved the Sheriff and for some reason he liked that. Cramer probably didn't.

The twins rose and started to execute their departure act with perfection. They really had it down pat; only they weren't going to get away with it—not this time.

As each boy headed in different directions, Scott literally roared, "Harry! Eddie! Where the hell do you think you're going?" He didn't wait for an answer. "What the fuck is going on with you two?"

Thea gasped in horror and Francesca jumped up off the sofa to calm Scott down. "Take it easy, Scott. You're dead tired. How about getting some rest and then talking to the boys?"

"Frankie, don't tell me what to do with my kids!"

Frankie was struck into dumb silence as a flash of pain and embarrassment crossed her face.

Scott knew that his outburst had stung her pride; he regretted it immediately.

"Sorry, Frankie, I don't know what the hell I'm doing or saying, anymore."

He walked across the room and affectionately embraced her. She put her head on his chest and nodded her acceptance. Amelia stared in awe. The boys were pleasantly shocked—smiling at each other; if their father finally had a girlfriend maybe he would get off their backs. Only Thea failed to react. She rose and quietly left the room without any expression, keeping her disappointment to herself. The scene she had just witnessed confirmed what she had suspected right along; this once professional relationship was definitely turning into an "affair of the heart".

"Okay boys, upstairs. I think it's time we had a good talk before Mr. Sims gets here."

Eddie didn't comment—only Harry mumbled, "Sure Dad, okay."

27 *The Players*

Tommy Lavin was the obvious choice to head the investigation; he possessed incomparable experience and a solid reputation for cracking some of the most difficult cases in the Boston area. If the truth was known, he had hoped to dodge this one—pass on it as the ranking detective on duty that morning—but a little alarm went off in the back of his head when he got the *bullet* from his chief.

A teen-aged girl was murdered while attending a birthday party for the twin sons of *Scott Macguire*, the young publishing executive residing on the fashionable island of *Puckshaw*. The victim was found in a rough shed on the grounds of the ocean side mansion.

It was a savory piece of bait; Lavin's curiosity for the lifestyles of the rich and famous in and around the Boston area was legendary; no one was surprised when he accepted the challenge with enthusiasm.

He stood and whistled loudly to get the attention of his partner, Detective Mel Abrams—fondly referred to as *Cherry*. Categorically not fond of rookie partners, Lavin impatiently waved her into the chief's glass-surrounded cubby-hole.

Abrams responded with a look of panic as an unexpected release of adrenaline shot through her system. She rose hesitantly and stumbled toward the office—ignoring the catcalls of her colleagues who sat at their desks bursting with anticipation.

Lavin was never anything but direct. "Sit down and listen," he said to the young detective.

The chief proceeded, somewhat impatiently, to retell the sketchy facts he had just received from Sheriff Cramer; finishing dryly, with, "That's all I got folks."

Lavin leaned back in his chair without comment but Mel Abrams, unaware of the little farce that was being played out, began to ask a question, only to be cut down in mid-sentence as Lavin thrust a finger in her face. "Be still!"

She knew enough to obey his order; he could be hell on wheels with a new partner and rumor had it that Lavin had it in for the new kid. Somewhat cowed, she watched in amazement as he tapped and swiped the garish screen of his tiny *A-Pad* with legendary efficiency, feeding various clues into his personally-designed, twenty-five year old database lovingly called LDB; it never failed to assist him in a search.

The name of the victim, *Albright, Cassandra,* turned up zilch so he went on to the *Island of Puckshaw* itself, which suggested twenty or thirty links to other possibilities. One link stood out in particular—the surname *Macguire.* He knew the murder had occurred at the ocean side mansion belonging to the popular resident, Scott Macguire, son of the island's long time reporter and author, *Henry* Macguire. Yes, he had heard of him. He recalled the day old Henry had jumped out of a helicopter over the Bay several years ago while he was still a rookie on the streets of Boston. Lavin heard he was a cranky old son-of-a-bitch at times, but he was a great newspaperman and quite an author—as was discovered posthumously.

Like most of the islanders and residents in and around the Boston area, Lavin had read the book. He was fully aware that Macguire's kid, Scott, had remained on the island and made it his home as a charitable, law abiding businessman with a lovely wife, now deceased, and three equally lovely children. He shook his head in disbelief, acquiescing to a deep premonition that the *Macguires* would soon be in the headlines again.

He typed *Scott* Macguire's name into the database and was linked to several abbreviated stories—including his eyewitness account of his ex-lover's suicide in 1993.

Lavin was still answering phones and fetching coffee in those days, but he had a good memory.

Sonny Peterson Adams—who could forget *that* three-ring circus? Lavin let out a long, low whistle without looking at his chief. "Yes, sir." He would definitely take this case.

Mel's heart was racing; her first murder case and she had the luck of the draw in spades—Tommy Lavin as her teacher. That was good and bad.

All the old-timers were familiar with his philosophy. They referred to it as *Lavin's Law of Averages*. His behavior never varied. First he would react with disgust at the senselessness of the violence—prowling the office and ranting and raving about man's inhumanity to man. After exhausting himself, he would don the mantle of compassion and visit the victim's home to convey his singular brand of sympathy to the grief-stricken—making mental sketches of each unsuspecting family member.

Lavin would then work around the clock, laying a solid foundation for the success of his investigation; often depriving himself of food and sleep—never alcohol—until he reached a level of self-induced euphoria. After that it was a crapshoot. Days might pass without incident while everyone in the department held their breath until the moment when Lavin would finally become infuriated and impatient with the snail-paced progress of the red taped justice system; at that point he would erupt, thereafter becoming the most feared investigator in the Boston Police Department.

Cherry was in awe of her new partner though she too had every reason to fear him. He never cared much to share information with anybody—not even his partner—making it pretty tough for her to learn anything. He sent her on senseless errands and gave her bogus telephone numbers to call—hardly listening when she tried to report back to him. She hated it but was smart enough to know that he was trying to test her metal and at some point would eventually let her into his world. She could only hope.

Unexpectedly, he had finally given her a real task of questioning eight giddy teenagers who had been invited guests at the ill-fated Macguire party. They weren't *A-listers* among their peers—having been invited because of Scott Macguires business or social connections with their parents. They were more commonly known as *fringe and filler* guests that had no other viable role to serve than to show up and fill the empty spaces.

As Lavin saw it, this second tier of teens would not likely be privy to *inside* information. In addition to interviewing the unimportant kids, he threw Mel a bone: she was to interview one adult by the name of *Francesca Covel.*

Mel had a system of her own that she liked to stick to when playing the *elimination of suspects* game. She was aggressive and thorough; using a pretty reliable database of her own called MDB (*my data* base). After all, she was a young thirty-something and had worked like a dog to get where she was—on the elite homicide squad of a prestigious precinct—and she wasn't about to blow it.

The young woman hadn't reached the elevated rank of detective by sitting on her thumbs; she had proven time and again to be observant, shrewd, and lightening quick in emergency situations. After only five years on the force she had distinguished herself as a respected markswoman. She also had the conditioned body of an Olympian; she could run faster, jump higher, and take down a suspect quicker than most of her colleagues. Although she was proud of her physical prowess, she maintained an admirable modesty about her successes. Her colleagues, never underestimating her worth, knew they were in good hands when she was in the back-up seat.

As far as Mel was concerned, every detail she pulled was important; she gave it everything she had without ever taking her eye off the next rung of the promotional ladder.

This particular day, in spite of her Titan qualities, Melanie Abrams viewed Tommy Lavin and his unpredictable temper as a formidable enemy; with that in mind, she doubled her efforts to prove her worth by adhering to his arbitrary rules without question and maintaining his rigid standards without cracking.

The first thing she had to do was stop eliminating people from being suspects and implement *Lavin's Law* which went something like this: "Everyone remains a suspect until we have a confession, a trial, a conviction, *and* a sentence. When the lousy bastard goes to jail—that's when the case is closed and *only then* do we eliminate the rest of the suspects."

Lavin was dead serious about his overstated policy and Mel wouldn't think of questioning it—yet.

The first kids would start coming in at nine and given their wealthy status, Mel prepared herself for an army of testy parents and pricey lawyers. She closed her eyes and covered her face with both hands. She would stick to her game plan and hope that she didn't screw up. Fear of Lavin's reprisal was the big motivator in this instance—not personal failure.

At the Macguire mansion, Scott followed the boys up the carpeted stairs and past his bedroom—the room he had shared with Vicky—the love of his life and the mother of his three children. She had spent her last night on earth in that very room. He felt a pang of guilt when he realized that for the first time in almost a year, he hadn't thought of her more than three or four times in the last twenty-four hours.

Everything had changed since Francesca Covel had arrived at the ocean side mansion for the boys' sixteenth birthday party.

"Hey, Dad! Hey Dad, what's going on with you? Harry was actually shouting by the time Scott finally snapped to attention. "Jesus, we've been talking to you, Dad. Didn't you hear us?"

Scott shrugged his shoulders and entered the doorway of his boys' room. Resting his foot on a chair he shook his head and said, "Funny, I was just thinking the same thing. You guys are acting a little crazy yourselves and frankly, I'm a little pissed about it!"

Scott smiled—trying hard to conceal his irritability.

"I know things have been wild, but I've been trying to talk to you alone since early this morning, but you seem to be avoiding me. Why the hell aren't you talking to me about what's going on. What is it with you two? Tell me about it—now."

Eddie cut in defensively. "We've been trying to talk to you all day, Dad, but you seem to be so tied up with everything else, we *kinda* thought you just didn't have time for us; *ya see,* Dad?"

Scott didn't like his tone at all and mocked him with a disrespect that he would have never dreamed of in the past. "Well maybe you're just *kinda* wrong; *ya see,* Eddie? Who the hell do you think you're talking to, anyway?"

Harry seemed to be the braver of the two and spoke up after an awkward silence. "You were *chasing* after that *Francesca* every time I tried to see you, Dad. You *kinda* left Aunt Thea and us to figure things out for ourselves; that's what we been trying to do. *Ya see*, Dad?"

"No! I don't see that at all. You don't know what the fuck you're talking about. I've been trying to look out for *all* of us and Francesca happens to be involved because she was here *doing us a favor*. (Scott was shouting, now.) I owe it to her! Christ, she only came to help with *your* party; not to get involved in this mess! By the way, did either of you even bother to say 'thank you' to her? She's shocked as hell, but she is the one who is running the business in town in between trips to the island. Now if you don't have any further comments concerning *Miss Covel*, let's talk about last night—and this morning. You were fighting. Why?"

The twins looked at each other with belligerent looks and shrugged their shoulders.

"Go ahead, tell 'em, Eddie."

"It's no big deal, Dad. I was going to tell you about this as soon as I had a chance. We were all smoking pot and drinking a beer and I lost track of time."

"And...?" Scott was trying to be patient.

"I lost track of time and I forgot to meet *Cassie* where I told her I would."

"And...? Jesus, come on, Eddie. Say whatever it is you need to say. We'll work it out—whatever it is."

"Dad, I'm scared. I told *Cassie* I'd meet her in the shed, but I never got there, Dad. Honest! I never went near the place because I started hanging with the guys and telling dirty jokes and I forgot about what I told her—that I'd meet her. That's the truth, Dad. You gotta believe me. You believe me don't you, Dad?"

Scott grabbed Eddie by both shoulders and hugged him tightly. "Of course I do, son. Of course I do. There's nothing to be afraid about. Just tell the truth. That's all. Now calm down; we'll be talking everything over with Mr. Sims before we talk to the detectives. Don't worry; everything will be okay."

"See, I told you, Eddie. There's nothin to be scared about. Harry put a comforting hand on his brother's shoulder.

"Dad, we were fighting because Eddie didn't want to tell you about it; you know, the pot and all and I told him if he didn't, I would. He got really mad at me and said I was a big mouth. I hit him. I'm sorry, Dad. Sorry, Eddie; really, I am."

"Well, you're going to tell Ed Sims and his two lawyer friends exactly what you said to *Cassie* and exactly what you were doing the rest of the night. Jesus, Harry, what about you? Where the hell were you when your brother was smoking that shit and drinking beer? You're supposed to look out for each other, you know. You could have come to me then and there!"

"Dad, I was doing the same thing *he* was. Only I was sitting on the stairs down near the beach. Hell, everyone was smoking and drinking."

"Christ, Francesca and I were walking around all night, trying to keep you kids from doing anything *too* stupid; why didn't I see you?"

"I don't know, Dad. Maybe you were...you know." Harry's voice trailed off as he looked away into space.

"I was what, Harry? Finish whatever the hell it is you were going to say."

Eddie felt a sudden surge of courage and loyalty toward his brother. "I'm not trying to be an asshole or cause trouble, Dad; but maybe you were kind of paying more attention to *her* than to us."

Scott's hand involuntarily flew passed Harry and landed with a crack on Eddie's cheek. The three of them were stunned into silence—neither of the boys had ever even been spanked, but today they weren't about to back down.

Scott felt a sickening remorse. "I'm sorry, Eddie. Everything is getting to me. I'm sorry. I'm very sorry! I don't know what the hell I'm doing anymore. I had no idea how you were feeling about Miss Covel. You should have said something. I'm very sorry. I hope you'll..."

"Yah, me too, Dad," Eddie said—less convincingly."

The slight did not go unnoticed by his father or his brother, Harry.

Scott composed himself. He needed to come across strong and calm in front of the boys, so with forced confidence he said, "Okay. You were both smoking pot and I assume you both drank a beer or two?" He didn't wait for an answer. "Eddie, I hate to ask you this but did you uh, you know, have anything to do with *Cassie*? You know what I mean. Did you have *sex* with her or anything that was *close* to sex?

Harry, what about you, did you have anything to do with *any* of the girls at the party, last night? We've got to get this out in the open right now because all kinds of questions are going to be asked and we don't want any surprises."

Both of the boys shook their heads as if it was the silliest question they had ever heard.

"Come on, Dad, not right here in our own house, what do think we are, jerks?" Harry groused.

Eddie was silent; he knew how close he had come to getting lucky last night but that was just a bad dream now and he didn't want to bring it up.

"Do either of you have any information or ideas that are going to help the police? You do know we'll all be called down there to answer questions sooner or later. Listen, just tell the truth and everything will be just fine. Tell the truth; that's all I can say. Okay? And by the way, I'd like to remind you to thank Miss Covel *and* your Aunt Thea for helping with your party. It's the polite thing to do. Got it?"

Scott's lecture was met with stony silence at first; then both of the boys said there was nothing to tell and mumbled their apologies for smoking and not paying attention to what was happening. They agreed that they had both been irresponsible in general. And yes, they would both make it a point to thank Miss Francesca Covel *and* Aunt Thea for helping. Harry stonily reminded his father that he and Eddie would thank Amelia, *also.*

Scott got the message. He would deal with that whole situation later on. He hoped the boys weren't going to object to his seeing Frankie, but right now he had more pressing matters to deal with.

Sims was due to arrive any minute with two young attorneys that would assist him in handling the legal procedures regarding his immediate family and Thea—*and Francesca*—unless the women chose to call their own attorneys.

As he walked out of the boys' sprawling bedroom, he noticed out of the corner of his eye that Eddie had thrown himself across the bed—face down—*probably exhausted.*

Eddie pressed his face into the brown plaid quilt and closed his eyes—unaware that Harry had already told his father and Deputy Johnson about *Cassie* and her skinny-dipping exhibition. The truth was that he had only come in on the tail end of it and didn't know who else was involved. He hoped one of the other guys would "spill his guts" and then he might not have to say anything about it; maybe he'd only have to confirm the story. For some reason he was scared about that incident, but decided to keep it to himself—as long Harry didn't start carping on him again. For the time being, he just wanted to be left alone. With tears welling, he tried to remember what day it was and exactly when everything had fallen apart in his world—and he couldn't.

Tommy Lavin was quiet and brooding in the early hours of Tuesday morning. Just a little over forty-eight hours had passed since the murder and as far as he was concerned, too much time had already passed and he wanted to get started.

The body had been discovered on Sunday morning and most of the day had been taken up with identifying, retrieving, and transporting the victim's corpse; shortly after, the massive crime scene was designated and the collection of evidence was organized by a team of gloved CSI officers.

Bits of gum wrappers, a bikini top, endless beer cans, cigarette butts, and a couple of odd sandals and sneakers had all been carefully scooped into large plastic bags. Young lab workers, having been called in for a Sunday morning shift, snickered as they carefully handled discarded condoms.

Every single item would be numbered and logged into a fancy A-Pad and backed up somewhere in cyber-space—there to reside for all eternity.

Electronic paper work and protocol between the Boston PD and *Puckshaw's* law enforcement staff would be fully observed in order not to offend any of the prima donnas from either department—tricky, at best.

Lavin had roared at his small staff of two that there were to be no errors, leaks, or oversights—under any circumstances. Phone calls were to be documented, messages delivered within minutes, and the backgrounds of all walk-ins, with *so-called* information, thoroughly checked. Nothing was to be shared with *anyone* or there would be hell to pay. Lavin was almost at his boiling point—*well ahead of schedule.*

On Monday, a list of party goers, parents, gardeners, delivery persons, and the four *Macguires* was drawn up and divided between Lavin, Mel, and Deputy Johnson. Lavin made a mental note that Johnson could be a valuable player since he was on a first name basis with just about *everyone* involved.

Lavin had met with Mel and Johnson at eight-thirty a.m.; interviews would start at nine and the three of them would meet again at one p.m. to have a light lunch and compare notes. Lavin emphasized "light lunch" because he had seen the effects of heavy lunches on his staff's productivity once too often; if there was anything he couldn't stand it was *torpor.*

Anyway, he would hardly give them enough time to eat between his questions, lectures, and possible scenarios; along with unsolicited advice and veiled criticisms. He was itching to get started and this was the period that he hated most—*waiting.*

His list consisted of Mollie Simon, Jennifer Holmes, Eddie Macguire, Scott Macguire and the youngest of them all—Amelia Macguire.

Three private offices had been secured on the third floor of the old library which now doubled as the Sheriff's Department and was situated not near *Macguire & Son Publishing Co.* Lavin had chosen the room at the end of the hall—it afforded the most privacy. At exactly nine a.m., there was a timid knock on his office door.

"Yep!" Lavin shouted in response to the knocking.

Mollie Simon entered with her father and a young man who appeared to be their attorney. They introduced themselves to Lavin and waited uncomfortably to be invited to sit down. Lavin walked around the desk slowly and deliberately to pull the chair out for Mollie, while nonchalantly motioning toward her father to sit in the other one. He pointed toward a small table and chair in the corner of the room and as the young lawyer walked over and began to pick up the chair, Tommy boomed, "Stay right there, my friend—please—this is just a friendly conversation. I'll tell you when it gets legal." Lavin looked out the window—blatantly ignoring the exasperated look on *Mr. Attorney's* face. He could never pass up an opportunity to wind up one of the island's ivy-league graduates.

"Hello, Mollie! I'm just going to ask you a few questions about the party you attended the other night. You can answer them with a 'yes' or 'no'—even an 'I don't know' will do. You're not under any kind of oath here; just answer the questions as truthfully as you can. Maybe *you* can help me get an idea of what went on at the big bash over at the Macguire place."

Mollie interrupted him in her whiny voice with. "Don't I take some kind of a pledge or something with a bible… and say 'I do'?"

"No. Not right now." Lavin tried not to show his growing annoyance. "I know a lot has happened in the last few days and I'm sure you are very upset, but just do your best here and we'll be finished in no time. Okay? Good."

He rarely waited for an answer to that type of question; anyway, he didn't want this kid to start asking *him* the questions. This was his gig and he was going to be the main attraction. That's how sure Tommy Lavin was of himself.

"Now, Miss Simon, did you spend much time with *Cassie Albright* during the evening of the party on Saturday night?"

"I, no, I didn't."

"Did you spend *any* time with *Cassie Albright* the night of the party?"

"No."

"Did you arrive at the party with *Cassie Albright;* I mean in the same car?"

"No."

"Would you say that *Cassie Albright* was one of your good friends?"

"No."

"Is it true, you were supposed to sleep over *Miss Albright's* house the night of the party?"

Mollie Simon looked first at her father and then at the young man sulking in the corner of the room. She didn't answer. Lavin repeated the question in a calm, clear voice.

This time Mollie was adamant.

"No!"

"Why do you suppose I've been told that you were looking for Cassie at the end of the evening because you were going to spend the night at her house?"

"I don't know, sir."

Mollie was cool as ice and Lavin met her gaze with a wide smile as he stood up to dismiss them. "Thank you so much, Miss Simon. That wasn't so bad, was it?"

They were—all three—caught off guard by Lavin's curt dismissal and rose in unison to leave—each chair making its own grating sound as it dug into the polished, hardwood floor.

Only Mollie's father spoke. "Thank you, detective; if we can be of any help, don't hesitate to call us, again."

Lavin didn't respond. He sat down and began writing before they even left the room. In his distinct scribble he wrote: *Why would Mollie lie to Scott Macguire about her plans to spend the night at Cassie Albright's home? Was she planning to stay somewhere else—if so, where?*

He checked his watch and waited for the next young lady on his list: *Jennifer Holmes.* A young officer rapped on the door and called out Lavin's name at the same time.

"What?"

"Sorry, Tommy, but the Holmes kid is sick—can't come in."

"Jesus Christ! Thanks. Say, call the Macguire place and see if you can move them up to noon, will you? Let me know if they can make it or not."

He wrote the number two and a dash next to it. That bothered him. He wrote himself another note to have Mel call and verify Jennifer Holmes' illness.

Tommy Lavin still erroneously assumed that he had to keep Detective Melanie Abrams busy.

Mel looked at her list and took a deep breath; Lavin had changed his mind and given her a mixed bag—an indication that he might be in the mood to trust her a little more. Timmy Jenkins, Thea Schults, Harry Macguire and Francesca Covel were on her list now.

Jenkins was first and had shown up early—much to Mel's delight. She was further surprised to discover that he was alone—no parents or attorney. She had not had the pleasure of seeing him at the party—attired in all his glory—and today he was dressed just slightly less flamboyantly. He sat down without waiting for an invitation or introduction. He was running true to form, but he was not going to run Mel's show.

"Might you be Timmy Jenkins?"

"I might."

Great—a wise mouth!

She knew she should have been a little more formal with her opening, but she wasn't about to change her approach. "Hello, Timmy, my name is detective Mel Abrams and I've got a few questions for you. Hope you can help me out."

"Sure thing; I hope I can."

"You were an invited guest at the Macguire party on Saturday night. Is that correct?"

"That's a fact. I was an invited guest at the Macguire party on Saturday night. It was a blast. At least while I was there. I don't know what the hell happened after I left; pretty nasty deed, I heard. Wow!" He shook his head compassionately.

He was at his best—a classic, *new-money Islander*. He was dressed impeccably in a silk shirt, designer khakis, and brown moccasins; he also wore an expensive *Rollandi* watch. Rich, smart, cocky, and not too bad to look at, either. Mel turned to her left and looked out the window wistfully; what a shame—if only he hadn't shaved his head.

"Okay, Timmy, do you remember what time you got there?"

"Yes."

Mel was getting just a little pissed off. "And that was?"

"It was eight-thirty. Pretty early actually, but it was one of those 'kid parties', you know? It was going to break up early so I figured I'd better make an appearance before it was over. You know? Get there on time—sort of. I wouldn't have even bothered to go if it hadn't been for Harry. He's a great buddy of mine. Not too crazy about Eddie, his twin, though. So what was the question again?"

"That's just fine, Timmy. You got there at eight-thirty. How'd you get there, anyway?"

"Drove; I have my own ride now. Why?"

He seemed a little defensive but she pressed him anyway. "Oh, so you're a little older than Harry, aren't you?" She didn't wait for an answer, but continued with, "Do you recall what time you left the party?"

He responded to her first question with, "I'm eighteen, just had a birthday last month." Then he went on to answer her second question by pointing to his fancy watch. "I always know what time it is, *ma'am*. I had the alarm set because I wanted to get out of there by midnight to hit another party at the other end of the Island. The alarm went off just as I was pulling out of the driveway. Great timing, I'd say!"

"And did you go to another party?"

"Nah, I went home; I was too tired. Went home and went to bed."

"Were your parents home when you got in?"

Timmy finally lost a little of his cool. "Of course; well, my mother was home. My Dad was out of town. In the city overnight; you know—Saturday night?"

"Hmm. Okay Timmy, nothing more for now. By the way, is your Dad home yet?"

"Of course; it's Tuesday!"

"Oh, right! Thanks again, Tim. You can go now."

Mel flipped open a notebook and made a note to find out if Mrs. Jenkins had heard Timmy come in and what time it was—if she had heard him. She also wrote: *Nothing unusual; just a little cocky.*

In the meantime, Johnson was having the time of his life. He had moved himself down to the first floor of the old library and was interviewing most of the parents who had come and gone sometime during the course of the evening of the party. No one seemed to be intimidated by this red tape; maybe a little inconvenienced, but for the most part they all seemed to be cooperative and calm.

A few testy parents, dragging their frightened offspring along with them, said how ridiculous it all was... everyone had to know that some *stranger* must have come onto the grounds and grabbed *Cassie* before she could make a sound...probably shoved her through the rough opening and into the tiny shed. Maybe even attacked her somewhere else and threw her in there while the music was blasting and no one was looking...surely someone would soon describe some creepy *outsider* that was seen *lurking* about the perimeter of the Macguire estate.

Johnson greeted all the islanders by their first names, smiled, and did a little gossiping while taking down the required information. Put simply, he saw it as an opportunity to *catch up* with old friends; after all, he had known most of these people for at least fifteen years and had faithfully assisted them with a variety of problems from car trouble to run-a-way dogs and on occasion, a run-away-kid.

Today, he knew in his heart of hearts that none of these good people had had anything to do with the murder of Cassie Albright and with that in mind he poured their coffee and assured them that everything would be "just fine". An impartial observer might think his behavior was strange—considering the seriousness of the task; after all, a girl was dead—crudely assaulted and bludgeoned by a cold-blooded murderer.

Johnson knew he had not yet met the killer; when he did, he would methodically document the evidence, make the arrest, and deliver up the perpetrator to the justice system for a speedy trial.

Deputy Johnson had been underestimated by Boston's PD several times in the past because of his homey, easy-going approach to solving crime, but Sheriff Cramer knew of his deputy's shrewdness first hand. Johnson, in his own unique style, had produced the definitive evidence *and* suspect time and time again in tough cases.

Still on the case, but in the background, Cramer was quietly observing as Johnson did his own thing. He alone knew that Johnson had already checked out Jenkins' father's whereabouts on Saturday night, or Mollie's so-called sleeping arrangements—or lack thereof. The wily sheriff was also curiously aware of the Thea Schultz-Francesca Covel situation as it gathered steam on an hourly basis.

True, Cramer and Johnson had a *leg up* because they had been on the scene almost twenty-four hours before *Boston's* Lavin and Abrams had arrived. Also they were obviously on a first name basis with all who were involved in the case. What *really* made the difference was that no one knew Scott Macguire and his family history the way Cramer and Johnson did.

Both men had grown up in Boston and spent summers on *Puckshaw* before it was fashionable for *non-monied folk*; they were thoroughly familiar with its history and that of one of its more colorful reporters and prolific journalists—*Henry Macguire*. They were fully aware of the legacy he had left his son, Scott; including a solid investment portfolio, ready cash, an unpublished manuscript, and some prime pieces of property favorably located in the business district *and* on the oceanfront.

Using his inheritance, Scott Macguire built a mansion on the oceanfront property—so well documented in Henry's book—and used the business property to build a small, but prestigious, publishing house—the first and only *green* project on the island.

Scott Macguire had honored his father's memory by seeing to the publication of his precious manuscript into a well-received full-length novel—fondly known to the islanders as the *"book you'll love to hate"*. Picking up where his father had left off he was eventually propelled into the publishing industry to become one of the island's most productive and innovative residents.

There wasn't anything that Johnson or Cramer didn't know about the *Macguire Clan, the Albrights, the Jenkins'*, or any other well connected family on the island; it was *that* kind of local trivia expertise that gave them the edge in this murder investigation.

If Tommy Lavin or Melanie Abrams thought, even for one minute, that Puckshaw's Sheriff and his Deputy were just fulfilling tin badge courtesy positions, they were in for the ride of their lives.

In times past, Puckshaw had earned the reputation for grossly mishandling high profile and politically-charged cases, but that was over twenty years ago and things had changed. Due to the growing number of year-round residents and a rapidly growing tourist industry, the police department had been beefed up and more than a few old-timers and useless appointees had been retired to make way for a younger and tougher force to protect the island's residents and maintain law and order.

Cramer and Johnson had withstood the *bloodletting* and were still standing when the department moved to the old three-story library. Soon after, they were rewarded with a landslide election to hold the rank and title of Sheriff and Deputy Sheriff, respectively. No one questioned their combined experience when it came to the complex workings of the island's inner circle.

No one accept Lavin.

Tommy, Mel, and Johnson met at one p.m., as planned; they dispassionately reported on their progress—each protecting their little treasure trove of information. Lavin was not interested in any hunches, opinions, or projections; he just wanted to hear cold facts. He made no comments—just stared straight ahead while Mel and Johnson reported on their interviews.

When they were finished they looked to Lavin for his report and he returned their questioning look with, "What?"

Johnson was not afflicted with the same fear that Mel was, so he spoke up first. "Who'd you see this morning, Tommy?"

"The Simon kid—Mollie Simon. I suppose you know her."

"Yep; sure do. Know the whole family. Good people. Did she have much to say?"

Lavin hated to share information with anybody and was stunned that Johnson dared to press him for more. He was getting the drift that Johnson was not intimidated by his reputation and he didn't like the way that felt.

Johnson gave it one more shot. "Well, did she say anything helpful?"

"No, not really," Lavin said dryly.

"Hmm, might just go around and pay a friendly call later on," he said, *sotto voce.*

Tommy ignored the slam.

Mel breathed a sigh of relief when Lavin concluded the meeting.

"Okay. Finish your lunch and get back to work. Meet here at five. Each of you will be getting a few more names, but right now let's take care of the big fish. I got a few *Macs* coming in shortly, so get the hell out of here and let me get my work done."

Johnson and Mel retreated from his office while he glared at their backs and shook his head. For the first time in years, Tommy Lavin had an off-putting moment; he didn't feel like he was in control. He just didn't trust Johnson and Mel could be tricky if she threw her support over to him—of course, that would be *unthinkable.*

"Oh, piss on it!" he hissed at the closed door, "Now where the hell are those goddamned *Macguires?*"

There was a light tap on the door and it opened slowly, as if the person on the other side was stalling in order to be invited in. Lavin never said a word; he liked to keep everybody off balance—it strengthened his own position. When the door was fully opened the entrance was filled with three *Macguires*: Scott, his son, Eddie, and his under-sized waif of a daughter, Amelia.

Lavin made a quick assessment. Scott looked worn out—dangerously close to the edge of exploding as he impatiently nudged his son in front of him. The nervous teenager was jumpy and looked back at his father for direction. Lavin gazed at the father and son with a slight nod and dropped his eyes to rest on Amelia, concluding that the little girl looked as though she belonged on a milk carton. Skinny and wide-eyed, she reminded him of Anne Frank.

"Oh! Come in, come in," Lavin boomed, faking surprise at their arrival—all part of his act. "Please sit down."

Only Amelia had seen his lips form the word, *Christ*, as they entered the room; she had quickly lowered her gaze and tightened her grasp on her father's hand. After they were comfortably seated, Scott said simply, "These are my children."

Lavin's distaste for the rich came rushing into the back of his throat like yesterday's onion sandwich.

Shit! My children—like they were the only ones who ever had kids.

He hated those sporty khakis and white, monogrammed polo shirts so casually tucked in. The scuffed tennis shoes without laces and tanned bare feet made him want to burst out laughing or puke. They wore their *Island arrogance* well. The sun-bleached hair and dark glasses respectfully hanging from open collars pissed him off just enough to make him just a little arrogant himself. He fired his first question without looking at any of them. "Good day for boating, huh?"

To Lavin's amazement only Amelia showed any reaction to his sarcasm and answered with a shake of her head, "No! It's way too windy."—to which Scott and Eddie agreed, with hidden pride at her moxie.

That was round one and the eleven-year-old kid had opened with a right cross.

Lavin immediately concluded that he should break up this little trio, thus diminishing their combined power and support of one another. His questioning was simple and brief before he asked Eddie and Amelia to step out of the room. They obediently obliged.

"Tell me, Mr. Macguire, how well did you know *Miss Albright?*"

"I met her for the first time the night of the party."

"Really; you never met her before Saturday night? How well do you know her parents?"

Scott answered only the last question. "I have met them socially over the years and I know Mrs. Albright a little from her volunteer work at the new library; we do not frequent each other's homes or socialize on a regular basis. Our children were friends. By the way, call me Scott."

Nice touch!

"*Scott. Sure.* Tell me *Scott,* what was your impression of the young lady, as you say, you met for the first time Saturday night."

"What do you mean by that? I told you I met her—was actually introduced to her by my son Eddie—the evening of the party. She was sort of his date. What did I think of her? Was that your question?" This time Scott did not wait for an answer. "She was a perfectly stunning, poised, and lovely young teenager—nothing more, nothing less."

"There were other young ladies at the party. Were you introduced to each of them? What did you think of them?"

Scott was a shrewd businessman. He ate tough competitors for breakfast and closed big publishing deals before noon; he might be tired and a little out of his element here, but he was not afraid of Lavin—in any way, shape, or form. He decided in the moment to answer those questions in the same order he was asked.

"There were several young ladies at my sons' sixteenth birthday party, but I was not introduced to each and every one of them; probably because I had known most of them for most of their lives. I remember commenting to a friend of mine how drastically the teenagers had changed; the girls looked and dressed so much older than their years, while the boys looked and acted younger." Scott rested in the completeness of his response.

"Mr. Macguire, do you know how many times you saw Cassie Albright during the course of the evening?"

"No. There were about twenty-five kids in and around my home; I wasn't really paying attention to anyone in particular. Just walking around to make sure they were safe and staying out of trouble. I can tell you, right up front, that there was some pot and beer on the premises that must have been brought in on the sneak, but, basically, everybody seemed well-behaved and having a good time until the end of the evening; that's when Mollie Simon reported that she couldn't find *Cassie.*

She said she was supposed to sleep at her house after the party; it was about twelve-thirty a.m.—after that everything fell apart."

Lavin was taken aback by Scott's forthright perception of the situation and was convinced that he wouldn't lie unless he had to. And he probably would only choose that road if he had to protect *one of his children*. He was quiet for some time and then snapped back to the present with, "Okay. I'd like to talk to your son now. Did you bring a lawyer, *Mr. Macguire?*"

"Yes." Scott felt a sick churning in the pit of his stomach. "He's out in the hall—Mr. Ed Sims—he will accompany my son when you question him. He's only sixteen, you know; he's pretty shocked. You never know what he might say. Is that okay with you, Mr. Lavin?"

"Sure, fine."

Scott sat out in the hall with Amelia for over an hour; then, rising abruptly, he began pacing back and forth, looking at his watch and shaking his head. Amelia looked at her bony wrist, shook her head, and rose to imitate her father. He never seemed to notice her childish emulation—but then, he never seemed to notice anything when it came to Amelia. In reality, Scott Macguire kept forgetting that she was eleven years old—*going on twelve*—maybe because she looked and acted so much younger.

Sims came out first, huffing and gasping for air; he really *had* to lose some weight soon. "Eddie's on his way out. No problem."

Eddie came out momentarily and looked none the worst for the ordeal. "I'm okay dad."

Lavin stepped out into the hall and walked toward Amelia; she immediately took a step backward.

"Hey there, little girl, I'm not going to bite you. Would you like to come in with your dad or Mr. Sims and talk to me a little bit more?"

Amelia shook her head from side to side. "Uh, uh; I only want to talk to Mr. Johnson or Sheriff Cramer. Mostly I want to talk to Mr. Johnson. He doesn't scare me."

"Do I scare you?" Lavin said with a big smile.

Amelia dropped her head onto her chest.

"Okay. I guess that's it. I'll be talking to you all again, and I'll see what I can do about getting Mr. Johnson to talk to the little girl. We'll work on that."

The Macguires and Sims walked away without further conversation and Tommy Lavin stepped back into his office. He was definitely pissed by the situation. Grabbing his yellow pad he jotted down the date and time. He closed his eyes and pressed them deep into their sockets with the sweaty heels of his palms; he had to think about this for a moment. Finally he wrote: *Father and son passed basic questioning with flying colors. Probably had nothing, whatsoever, to do with the crime. Eddie pretty shook up about keeping the skinny-dipping episode from his father. Normal. Ask Mel to discreetly find out just how stunning Cassie Albright really was. And why the hell does that little orphan Annie want to talk only to Johnson? Sims very clever—keeping an eye on him.*

Lavin's sharp observations would not go into his A-pad. His notes were private and the yellow pad he wrote on would never leave his possession. It was *FHEO*.

While the three Macguires were upstairs in Lavin's office, Mel had questioned the fourth one: Harry. One of Sims' young assistants sat at his side throughout the questioning, *after* Harry had surprised Mel by opening the conversation with a question of his own. He wanted to know why he wasn't upstairs with the rest of his family. Mel never bothered to answer him; unimpressed she moved forward. She had seen the yearbook and heard about his charming personality, but in the end, found him to be truculent and lacking in basic communication skills.

Harry, too, was well heeled and tanned like all the other youngsters on the island at this time of year. He was good looking and he knew it, but today he was defensive—repeatedly confessing to *smoking a little pot and drinking a few beers*, and *yes, his father knew about it.* He said he *thought* someone had gone skinny-dipping but he wasn't sure who it was, and, after all, *that was no big deal was it?*

"What do you think?"

Mel didn't wait for an answer but continued with, "We'll probably talk again, okay? You can go up and join the rest of your family, now."

Harry shot back with, "Why will we be talking again? Don't you believe what I said?"

Mel smiled and thought to herself, you little bastard! But out loud she said, "Have a good day. See you soon."

She closed her office door and flipped open her notebook. *"Harry Macguire was uncommunicative and I'm not sure I believed anything he said. He could be covering for someone—that's only a maybe."*

She picked up her phone and rang the Macguire home to set up an appointment with Thea Schultz, later in the day. She wasn't available; some cleaning lady said Thea was *off to the market for fruits and vegetables* and would be back in a couple of hours. Francesca Covel was not in her office either, but Mel didn't want to tell Lavin that she didn't have any more appointments so she decided to follow up on Timmy Jenkins and Harry Macguire and make it back by five o'clock to meet with him and Johnson. She was hell-bent on making an impression—being pro-active.

As she left the building, the first floor looked like a class reunion of sorts. Everyone was smiling and drinking coffee and Johnson was holding high court. Mel wondered if they had forgotten that a young girl had been brutally murdered and swore under her breath. Irritated and distracted, she never noticed Johnson's gaze as she walked through the jovial crowd—stone-faced.

As she started her car, Johnson casually walked to the window and noted the direction in which she drove while checking the time on his watch. He concluded, correctly, that she hadn't been able to reach Thea or Francesca and she was getting out of Lavin's path.

Mel drove over to Timmy Jenkins' house which was located on the opposite end of the island that the Macguire home sat on. She was impressed with the white, two-story, waterfront home with its deep blue shutters and awnings. It was well protected from the sizzling sun of summer and the sandy winds that blew from November to April. A jeep and a newer model sedan were parked in the long pebbled driveway. A lone lawn tractor was resting in the middle of the sweeping lawn—the gardener off to lunch or having a coffee break.

Surely, Timmy Jenkins had not been mowing the expansive lawn.

Mel smiled sarcastically as she parked her older Toyota off to the side, on a little pad, and walked up the long driveway that led to the rear of the big house.

No one seemed to be around—not even the expected barking dog. Mel was waiting for someone to approach her and remind her she had wandered onto private property, but no one seemed to care that she was there.

The swift water in front of the Jenkins estate was not the Atlantic Oceanfront, but an inlet of some sort where boating was the recreation of choice. She could see by the rear of other homes in both directions that she was probably in *nouveau riche* territory. Since most the Oceanfront property was in the hands of long-time residents, the *newcomers* had been relegated to buying up inter-coastal property on the other end of the island. It was all so breathtaking and quiet that Mel had the urge to stretch out on the grass and collect her thoughts—until a grating voice interrupted her sweet daydream.

"Young lady, what are you doing back here?"

The voice came from behind a bank of screened windows surrounding a huge sun porch.

Mel couldn't see the person behind the voice but she immediately raised the flap on her shoulder bag to expose her detective's badge.

"Excuse me, ma'am, I'm detective Melanie Abrams; can I speak to Mr. or Mrs. Jenkins or maybe Timmy?"

After a little movement on the sun porch, the screened door opened and an unsteady woman balanced herself in the entrance.

"Come on up. Get out of the sun and visit with me a while, Miss Abrams."

Mel approached the snappily dressed woman with her hand extended, politely re-introducing herself and presenting her

ID. The middle-aged woman hardly took notice but held the door for her to come into the skillfully decorated sun porch, offering her a cool drink at the same time. Mel was quickly alerted by a familiar odor. She smelled alcohol and the stranger was rocking back and forth, struggling to keep her balance. Politely, Mel refused anything to drink—dying for an iced-tea or coffee she got right to the point of her visit.

"Are you Mrs. Jenkins?"

"Yes, dear; what can I do for you? I suppose this is all about that terrible thing that happened over at the *Macguire's* the other night. I was going to go to the police station with Timmy this morning, but he told me to stay home and not worry about it. You know, you just can't worry about everything these young people get involved in these days. You know what I mean? He told me not to worry, so I'm not," she giggled.

"Yes, it must be difficult raising a teenager today. Mrs. Jenkins, were you home on Saturday night when Timmy came home from the *Macguire* party? Do you recall what time it was?"

"Well, I went to bed about twelve-fifteen, right after midnight. I go to bed about that time when I'm home alone. I watch the boats and listen to the partying; then I just sit here and have my own little party. Mr. Jenkins, my husband, was in Boston on business—why they have those business meetings on the weekend I'll never know—so I was here alone. Timmy had gone to the *Macguire* party. I can't believe those twins are sixteen, can you?"

"Mrs. Jenkins, did you hear Timmy come in?"

"Oh, no, I go right to sleep once I get upstairs! I'm pretty busy all day running this big house, you know; when it gets to be around midnight, I have a nightcap and go to bed. I don't hear a thing. But Timmy did tell me he came in around twelve-thirty or one o'clock in the morning. That's too late for these youngsters to be out. Don't you think so? But you can't tell them what to do now, can you?"

Mel walked over to the screened window and looked out toward the long driveway. "Which one of those vehicles is Timmy's, Mrs. Jenkins?"

"Neither. I drive both of them, now. I drive the one parked closest to the road when I come out. Our handyman uses one of them to go back and forth from town. He likes the bigger one. I really don't care—I don't drive much anymore. But Timmy; he has a brand new "something or other". You know; it has numbers in it. Very flashy—his his father said he could have it for his eighteenth birthday; what could I do? He used to drive the jeep but now he says he wouldn't be caught dead driving it. What can I say? We gave him too much, I think, but he's a good boy—*most of the time*."

"Well, Mrs. Jenkins, I'm sorry if I bothered you today, but I'll be leaving now. And thank you so much for taking the time to talk to me; I'm sure it takes a lot of time to keep up a big house like this. It is very lovely. Well, thank you."

Mel rose and made her way across the light green carpeted porch and pushed open the screened door to leave.

"Oh, by the way, is Timmy around?"

"Oh, listen, you were no bother at all, and you're right, it does take a lot to keep up this big house; I thank God for all the help I have. You asked if Timothy was here. No, he packed up his car just a couple of hours ago and said he would be gone for a few days. I think he went up to Boston for a visit with some friends. I think it's a girlfriend, but of course, he wouldn't tell *me*."

Mel froze. *I told that little bastard to stay close to home.* "Thanks very much. You said *Boston,* right?"

She didn't wait for an answer—just started walking towards her car when she really wanted to run. She had to avoid rousing any suspicion in Mrs. Jenkins; she might not be as drunk as she acted. Somehow, Mel believed she just might not be as drunk *or* uninformed as she seemed.

Detective Mel Abrams just couldn't believe she had misjudged Timmy so naively. So he had fled to Boston and she hoped she was wrong; maybe the kid was just on a toot; too much pressure might have gotten to him.

The speedometer was well over the forty-mile-an-hour limit on the island and Mel would have hated like hell to be stopped for speeding; she slowed down to forty-five and entered the business district, nonchalantly cruising into the parking lot of the old library, now serving as the police barracks. Now she could move quickly without causing any attention; after all, it was the police station and everyone was either rushing in or out. She ran into the building and raced to the third floor, her heart pumping and her brain racing toward overload. She hoped she wasn't over-reacting; Lavin would have her ass in a sling if she was wrong.

Lavin's office was empty though the door was open and the lights were on. She bounded down the stairs and checked Johnson's office; no one was around. She wondered what the hell could have happened in the hour and a half that she was gone. She wasn't sure where to go, so she stopped at the front desk and asked a young police officer if she knew where Lavin and Johnson were.

"Christ, they flew out of here like the place was on fire."

"Do you know where they went?"

"I think they were called to the *Macguire* place. Something about a break in the *Albright* case; they left about five minutes ago."

Mel was in her car and on her way before the young rookie finished what she was saying. Five minutes. Hell, she could catch up with them in no time. Mel was mumbling incoherently as she took off.

"That God dammed Lavin; why the hell didn't he call me with the news? Goddamn him!"

She struggled to calm down, wondering if she had been deliberately left out of the final take-down. Was she up against the "good ole' boys club again?"She hoped not.

She wasn't going to call or text; that might make her look stupid—as though she didn't know which end was up. She estimated the ocean front property to be about seven or eight miles away from the station. Just about six minutes passed before she pulled onto the long concrete driveway and spotted Johnson and Lavin talking to Scott Macguire and two women.

Hmm...the aunt and the girlfriend.

She hopped out of her car and trotted up to the little group and directed her question directly to Tommy Lavin. She wanted an answer.

"What the hell happened?"

"Amelia wants to talk to Johnson; says she knows who did it."

"What? You gotta be kidding."

Lavin looked at Mel with a disgusted look. "We're not kidding."

Johnson was quiet. He was hanging his head and digging a booted toe into some loose sand along the driveway. He was waiting for his good friend, Cramer, to arrive before he went into the house to talk to Amelia. He wanted to consult with him about something, first.

For sure, Lavin was on the outside looking in and he was just about ready to blow up. It was a comical sight; Lavin watched Johnson and Mel watched Lavin watching Johnson.

Johnson finally spoke in a soft, almost sad voice. "I had a feeling that kid knew something; just the way she was talking to me on Sunday morning."

"And how was that?" Lavin asked sarcastically.

Johnson turned his head toward the road as Cramer came wheeling into the driveway. He had heard the car coming and never bothered to answer Lavin's question. He walked over to Cramer and was having a quiet talk with him.

Mel had a sick feeling that this case was being run according to *Johnson's book of rules.*

Lavin's Law didn't work on Puckshaw—shocking!

She tried to talk to Lavin but he was sulking inconsolably. He hated being left out. He kept walking away from her.

"Tom?" She didn't feel comfortable calling him "Tommy" in such a serious and dramatic moment. "Listen to me a second, will you? I have to tell you about the Jenkins kid. He's left the island for a few days. Packed his car and took off for Boston; his mother told me. I'll tell you all about her, later, but I think we should jump on this right now. I mean, why would he leave town in such a hurry? Something is *very wrong.* That's what I think; how about you?" Mel was learning to play Detective Lavin like a violin.

"What happened? Talk to me for Christ sake!"

"I *said* the Jenkins kid has left the island and I think that's a little creepy!"

By the time Mel was through, Tommy Lavin was on his car radio getting a make on the car that Timmy Jenkins was driving. He jotted down something and called Boston Highway Patrol, telling them to pull the kid over and hold him if they found him. Lavin called his chief and told him he would be in the city in about an hour.

The city police would cruise the streets and the hotel district; keeping an eye out for his flashy car. They would hold the kid until Lavin got there—if they picked him up at all.

"Read him his rights if you have to, but don't give him his phone call before I get there," he shouted, as he slammed the car door.

"*Cherry!*" he roared. "Let's get the hell out of here. Can't you see we've got a murder to solve?"

Johnson and Cramer turned and watched them as they started their engines.

Lavin was in an obvious state of excitement. "See you in the office early in the morning, boys; you can fill us in, right? Call me on my *private device* if you need me. Later!"

Both cars roared away leaving Johnson and Cramer in a cloud of sand.

"Now I wonder what the hell that's all about. You know, Lavin has had his nose out of joint all day." Johnson pushed his nose to one side with his index finger as he shook his head.

"Well, let's go in and see what my little chickadee has to say. By the way, did her father give you a hard time?"

Cramer nodded his head up and down slowly. "Yep, but he finally gave us the go-ahead."

"Well, let's do it, then!"

The officers of the law politely wiped their feet as they entered the family room through the rear patio that faced the ocean.

With a full view of the driveway and a partial view of the ocean framing her thin shoulders, Amelia sat on the loveseat reading aloud from her sixth grade literature book while Thea Schultz nodded her approval.

Scott talked on the phone—probably to Francesca Covel—while keeping a watchful eye on the boys as they sat in the kitchen and devoured a pizza in silence.

Johnson caught sight of a day cleaner scurrying through the hallway; other than that, the house appeared to be free of *outsiders*.

The late afternoon sun was streaming through the side windows with the torching solar heat of mid-day and the *Macguires of Puckshaw* were about to assemble to hear their youngest member deliver yet another bombastic eye-witness account concerning the death of *Cassie Albright*.

Scott ended his call quickly, promising Francesca to keep her informed of the turn of events now involving Amelia. He was anxious to know how her interview went with Detective Melanie Abrams, but she hadn't been summoned to the station for questioning—yet. He wondered about that as he placed the house phone back on the hall end table.

He motioned to the boys to come into the family room and walked over to greet Cramer and Johnson. He no longer had any desire to shake hands with them or engage in any of the usual backslapping small talk. He didn't like the way Cramer had jumped to conclusions and how Johnson had been treating him coolly—as if he didn't trust him anymore. The boys had been terrified of Johnson's aggressive questioning the night of *Cassie's* disappearance and now tried to steer clear of him whenever possible. The only one who seemed unafraid of Johnson *or* Cramer was the barely whispering, wide-eyed child—*Amelia*.

Scott recalled the irritation he felt earlier that day when, on the way home from the police station, Amelia had said in a conspiratorial whisper, "Dad, do you think I could speak to Mr. Johnson?"

"What? Jesus, Amelia, we just passed him in the hall; why didn't you say something to me then?"

"There were so many people around him; I thought he was too busy. Will you call him and ask him to come to our house? It won't be scary that way."

"What do you want with that ass-hole, Amelia?" Eddie growled from the back seat.

Harry chimed in his agreement with his brother's description of the deputy Sheriff.

Scott hated to hear the boys talk that way about Deputy Johnson; after all he had never been anything but kind and friendly towards the *Macguires*. He actually had been considered a friend of the family until Sunday morning when the world had come crashing down around them.

"That's enough, boys. Amelia, what do you want to see him about? Can you tell *us*?"

"I want to tell him what I saw the night of the party. I think I saw who might have hurt Cassie. I *know* I saw something that I should tell Deputy Johnson about."

Amelia's calmness stunned them into silence for the duration of the few minutes that it took to get home. Scott checked his rear-view mirror to glance at the boys who were gazing in opposite directions out of their respective windows, finally resting his eyes on the vehicle directly behind him. He felt a wave of relief to see that it was Sims, steadily following him. That was good; he would want him there when Amelia talked to Johnson.

Cramer walked to the kitchen doorway, stepping aside to let the boys through. They both nodded respectfully to the Sheriff but kept their eyes from meeting Johnson's quick glance toward their presence. Amelia moved closer to Thea who was staring straight ahead with one arm around the child's familiar bony shoulders—*Thea the Protector*.

"Well, I guess we could get started if it's alright with you, Scott."

"Hold on a minute, Johnson. Ed Sims is coming up the driveway right now."

Scott wondered what the hell had taken him so long after he had been right behind him all the way. Ed came in huffing and puffing and sat quietly at the little telephone table in the hallway. He could hear and see everything from that vantage-point and no one could see him. He liked that strategy.

The room was quiet and Johnson was preparing for what he thought might be one of his finest dramatic moments.

"Okay, I'd like to ask Amelia if she minds if I come over and sit next to her."

He really wanted to get her away from Thea who could so easily influence her answers by the touch of her hand or any other bodily movement.

Thea looked around and smiled at Amelia to assure her that it was okay. To make room for Johnson, she rose and walked across the room to sit next to Scott on the small sofa. She felt a jolt of excitement as she realized she had not been this close to Scott since before Francesca Covel had appeared on the scene.

Scott seemed to shift just slightly away from her; she hoped no one had noticed. *Of course, everyone had.*

Now, Johnson was looking around for a good spot on which to perch his tall frame and start such an important conversation with Amelia without frightening her. He walked across the room and pulled a footrest over in front of the child and began to settle himself, but not before pushing a bunch of newspapers to the floor. The Macguire kids were not used to careless clutter and all eyes went to Thea, who would have ordinarily given a gentle but firm reprimand; to their surprise, she remained silent.

Johnson had a little notebook and chewed-down pencil in his hand as he smiled at Amelia and prepared to ask his first question. He checked his tiny shoulder microphone, looked at his cyber-phone, and finally settled in, nodding to the others in the room.

"Amelia, your father called me and told me you wanted to see me about something; is that true?"

Amelia nodded her head up and down. "Yes."

"Good. He says he thinks you might know something about what happened here the other night. If that is true, I'll tell you what we'll do. We'll all be very quiet and just let you say everything you want to say and I promise I won't ask any questions until you are all finished. If you should feel tired, frightened, or even a little mixed up, you just stop and tell me and we'll help you out. Is that going to be okay with you?"

"I think so."

Johnson liked the conviction and calmness this kid was showing and thought this could be the beginning of the end of this case; in fact, he was counting on it.

"Well now, you just go ahead and start whenever you're ready, little girl. I'm listening."

Amelia sat in the center of the padded window seat where Thea had left her with the toes of her untied tennis shoes sliding back and forth making abstract patterns on the family room rug. The window served as a sun-lit frame in which she was perfectly centered. She took a deep breath, looked at her father and started.

"I was lying right here, almost falling asleep, but kids kept coming in and out of the family room to use the bathroom or get something; I just couldn't fall asleep like I usually do. Aunt Thea always lets me fall asleep here then she picks me up and takes me upstairs to bed. But anyway, the music was loud outside and the patio was very noisy, too. Some kids were dancing or eating and they were yelling and laughing sometimes. Aunt Thea was busy in the kitchen and my dad and Francesca were walking around the patio and back yard. I think they were checking on the kids—that's what Aunt Thea told me. I sat up for a while and looked out this window like this."

To everyone's surprise, Amelia hopped up on the love seat, landed on her knobby knees, and turned her back to them, demonstrating how she had put her hands under her chin and glanced out the windows up and down the long driveway.

Just beyond that partial view of the grassy lawn that ended in a steep cliff high above the beach, she had watched the party goers under the torch lights as they danced or banded together in little knots. Amelia could hear the bursts of boyish laughter and girlish shrieking. The stairs to the beach were well to the left, but if she leaned in close enough to the triple-paned window and pressed her face against it, she could see the upper lanterns that lit the stairs even though the area was crowded with teens.

No one but Scott would have recalled at this dramatic and awkward moment that *Henry Macguire* had described this beautiful panoramic window and loveseat in his book about the old cottage that sat on this property. Scott had been sure to keep that special feature when the new home was built on the site of the legendary cottage, devastated by a summer storm in 1996.

Now he watched as his youngest child re-enacted her position in front of a room filled with awe-struck observers. He forced himself to pay attention to what Amelia was saying although his mind involuntarily kept returning to Sonny Adams and the many hours they had spent in long intimate interludes, daydreaming before the great glass-paneled windows. He shook his head and blinked back unexpected tears, hoping the others hadn't been aware of his uninvited reverie.

Amelia returned to her position on the loveseat, but not before she smoothed and patted the indentations she had made with her knees and brushed away the few blades of grass that had fallen from her tennis shoes.

"You know the little shed where they found *Cassie?* Well, that's almost right under where we're sitting. Right about there." She pointed to her right and down to the floor.

Johnson nodded his head up and down. The child was right but he was getting impatient and now he wondered where the hell Lavin and Mel had gone in such a hurry, and why. He also wondered if he was on a wild goose chase with this eleven or twelve-year-old kid. He was suddenly aware of a break in the action and whispered, "Go ahead Amelia."

Quite surprisingly, Thea interrupted. "Amelia, honey, are you getting tired? Do you want some milk? What about the bathroom, do you have to go to the bathroom?"

Everyone in the room showed exasperation in unison. Scott's irritation was angrily audible. "Christ, Thea!"

Amelia ignored everybody.

"Then everybody was clapping and cheering. The noise was very loud so I got up and stood by the door for a while. I saw Eddie and *Cassie* through the screen door and they were kissing and dancing." She pointed to the patio door.

Eddie felt his face and ears getting red. That must have been when *Cassie* had come running into his arms, insisting that they go someplace where they could be alone—right after she had *skinny-dipped for one and all to see*. That's when he had told her about the shed. When she had kissed him with so much promise, his heart had pumped a *million* gallons of blood per minute. He remembered with sadness, how his brother Harry had given him the thumbs up sign and some of his other friends had cheered when *Cassie* kissed him so shamelessly on the little dance floor. Now he was ready to cry and wished to God that he had never sent her to the shed to wait for him. He wished he had never stopped to smoke a joint and drink a beer with his buddies. At this moment, he wished he had never been born.

He was stunned back to the present when he heard his name being called. Amelia was trying to get his attention.

"I'm sorry Eddie, if you didn't want dad to know you were kissing *Cassie*. I know you didn't do anything to hurt her. Don't be mad at me. Please."

Eddie mumbled his forgiveness. "Forget it, Amelia."

Now Cramer put his two cents in from the kitchen doorway where he had been standing like a statue for the last ten minutes. "Okay Amelia, can you move along and tell Mr. Johnson what is so important. We have so much to do; I hope you won't mind hurrying it up a little."

Johnson gave Cramer a surprised look and put his hand up to stop him from interfering further. Then he turned to Amelia and said in a soft voice, "Go ahead; just take your time, honey."

The patio was almost empty so I went out there to get some chips and *Cassie* said *hi* to me. She was so pretty and her hair was a little wet and she was giggling. She touched me on the head as she went out the patio door. I just kind of watched her as she went outside but she didn't go where Eddie was standing with his friends; she walked around the side of the house. I went in and jumped up on the love seat and watched as she disappeared under the window—that's where the shed is. There were a few parked cars in the driveway and a bright red one was right near the shed. The boy with the long coat was getting something out of his car and then he came close to the window and disappeared under it; a while later he passed by the window again and went to his car and then to the back lawn where the kids were. I was waiting for *Cassie* to come out but she didn't and I fell asleep.

I woke up when I heard a car start up. It was so loud! Some kids were saying good-bye and then it got quiet. The car didn't move away but the boy in the long white coat got out and took off that long scarf and wrapped something up in it and threw it in the trunk of his car; it made a noise. Like a clunk—like my dad's tools do sometimes when he fixes something and throws the tool down. I heard it right thru the screen. Then the boy with the long coat walked near the shed for a minute and looked up and I thought he saw me. I got scared and hunched back down on the love seat. I think he came in the family room to see if I was awake but I kept my eyes closed until I heard the door slam. When I peeked out of the corner of the window, he was getting into his car. When he drove off I wanted to tell someone to check on *Cassie* but I was scared; anyway my Dad was starting to tell the kids that the party was almost over.

I figured *Cassie* would come out pretty soon but she didn't. I was real scared when they couldn't find her, but I thought Eddie would get mad at me if I told about the kissing so I didn't say anything until the next morning. You remember, don't you, Mr. Johnson? When I told you I knew where *Cassie* might be?"

"Yes. I remember. I want to thank you for all your help today, but I wonder if you would mind giving me just a few more minutes of your time. I want to ask you just a couple of questions and we'll be on our way, Amelia. You said the boy near the shed had a long white coat on. Is that true?"

"Yes."

"And what color was that car again?"

"Red." Amelia was very matter-of-fact, now. "The overhead spot-light in the driveway was shining on a red car."

"What did he do when he got out of the car, just once more; please, Amelia. I want to get this right so I don't have to bother you again."

Amelia sighed and took a deep breath. She got off the love seat and walked over to Scott and put her arms around his waist. Her chin was puckered though she never made a sound. Scott was overcome with emotion as he bent down and swept her into his arms to hug her tightly.

"Amelia, Amelia, my sweet baby. I'm so sorry you've had to go through all this. It's too much for you. You don't have to talk anymore if you don't want to. I'm so sorry."

He felt Amelia quiver and he held her even tighter. Now all the guilt of the past year rushed over him and he realized that he loved her more than ever. He hated himself for not being more attentive to her, having left it all up to Thea. Now he had hurt them all—Thea, Eddie, Harry, and most of all, dear, sweet Amelia.

Thea observed the emotional scene between Scott and his youngest child and knew that her tenure at the mansion was inevitably drawing to a close. It was time to give Amelia back to Scott. She would do the right thing—and soon.

Scott stood upright and Amelia loosened her grasp and dropped her arms to her sides turning to face Johnson and Cramer once more.

"I can finish now, but I want to stay here—close to my dad—if okay with you.

The boy who was wearing the long white coat got out of the car after the other kids said good-bye and walked toward the window. After a while he....

The child accurately repeated her observations, word for word, which made her all the more credible.

...took something off his neck; I think it was that long yellow scarf, and he opened the trunk and threw it in there. I thought he wrapped something in it, maybe not, but it made a noise when he threw it, like a thump or a clunk. I could hear it through the screen. She pointed to the screened windows which were only opened in the evening. He walked toward the shed and then he looked up and I was in the window and I think he saw me. I got scared and threw myself down on the sofa and made believe I was sleeping. I think he came in to check because I heard the door open and close. When I got up and peaked out of the corner of the window, he was getting in the car. Then he drove off. That's all."

Amelia turned to face her father and he put an arm around her shoulder and walked her out of the room and onto the patio, bending to whisper something in her ear. He then stepped out onto the manicured lawn—still strewn with a few paper napkins and party hats—and did something he hadn't done in a long time: he took her hand and began to walk across the lawn—stopping now and then to point out the cloud formations like he used to when she was a little girl of four or five.

Everyone in the room was silent.

Johnson and Cramer swung into action. This time it was Cramer at the helm.

"The kid's name is Timmy or Tommy Jenkins. Let's get a make on that red car. He lives on the other side of couple of car dealerships. The kid has been picked up a couple of times for speeding. Let's go! By the way, where the hell are Lavin and his partner? We've got to let them know what's going on."

Johnson tipped his hat to Thea, thanked the boys, and walked out the door to have a word with Scott and Amelia. Suddenly he was speeding out of the driveway and the *Macguire household* was left to its own wits to cope with a new, dark silence.

It was almost six o'clock by the time Lavin and Mel reached the outskirts of Boston. They had spoken to each other several times in the last forty-five minutes and they really seemed to be clicking; traffic was moving slowly, they were on the kid's heels, and Lavin was well past his boiling point.

He had received a call on his cell phone from Johnson about half way to Boston while he was on his car radio talking to Mel. She could only hear Lavin's end of the conversation and it wasn't pretty. Lavin was valiantly attempting to withhold information from Johnson in an effort to keep him at bay for a few more hours.

"You're saying that you think it's the Jenkins kid. Why? Now are you really going to take the word of a ten-or whatever year-old? Jesus! Well, I'll tell you what. Mel and I are on our way to Boston to finish a follow-up report on another case, but we'll radio Boston Highway Patrol to be on the look-out for a red Orbiter 16X. Is that right on the type of car? Okay. You got it. I'll get back to you."

Lavin returned to his car radio; "You still there, *Cherry?*"

"Yeh, I heard your end of the conversation. What a snow job! You sure you want to handle it this way?"

"Don't question my judgment, kid. I know what I'm doing. Got it?"

"You bet." Mel hung up her radio and muttered, "*Bastard.*"

She drove steadily behind him as he wove in and out of traffic erratically until they reached the off-ramp and hopped on the expressway toward downtown Boston. She assumed they would work out of the station until something broke. Unexpectedly Lavin's breaks flashed and she followed his quick move into the right lane and eventual turn onto a service road.

"Shit! Now what?" she shouted at no one in particular.

By the time she pulled in, Lavin had jumped out of his car and was waving wildly at Mel to hurry up. She hated that, but released her seat belt, cocked her gun, and jumped out of the car—all in one movement.

"What the hell...?"

Lavin didn't let her finish. He just cut in as if he had never heard her.

"I think we got him! Highway followed him into the city limits and Corky and Doberman picked him up and tailed him downtown to the *New W*. His car is in the parking lot and my guess is that he's in the process of checking in. The little son-of-a-bitch has expensive taste."

"So what do you want to do?" Mel was cautious now. She correctly assessed Lavin as being very volatile at the moment.

"Let's get to the *New W*; Doberman is eyeballing his car and Corky is outside the hotel lobby as we speak. I told them to keep out of his line of vision; the kid's liable to freak if he sees uniforms. They'll let him check in and wait for us to get there before they advise him of his rights. *As if the little fucker should have any!* The *Albright* kid didn't have any, did she?

We can take him back to the precinct, book the little bastard and start the questioning—if he'll talk. If he uses his phone-call to call a lawyer, we'll have to wait until *Mr. Ivy League* gets there; I want to delay transporting him to *Puckshaw* as long as possible. The kid might be ready to talk—you never know; maybe we'll even get a confession out of him before the night is over."

Mel felt a little sick. A confession! Lavin had accused, tried, and convicted this kid. Now she knew what her colleagues meant about *Lavin's Fucking Law of Averages*. Right at this moment he was deadly and she hated him.

"Jesus. What about *due process* or *innocent until proven*? What the hell's the matter with you, Lavin?" Mel was a little shocked at her fearlessness but she wasn't going to back down—not now. "You said yourself that it's only the word of an eleven-year-old. Maybe there's more to it than meets the eye. Christ! Don't hang the kid. Let's just take it easy and have a little talk with him in his hotel room. From there we take him down town and book him—if he's our guy. But whatever we do let's calm down. Okay?"

Mel truly feared his wrath but kept her gaze fixed on his eyes—waiting for a response. If he was going to blow, then so be it; she was sticking to her guns.

In a surprisingly calm and quiet voice Lavin said, "I'll follow you to the *New W*; you know the way don't you?

Mel nodded.

"Good. Let's go."

Crisis Diffused.

Mel let out a long sigh of relief and whispered, "*Fuck his law of averages!*"

As they entered the *New W* lobby a strong smell of chlorine hit them, indicating their proximity to the legendary "party pool".

Lavin spotted Corky and made a beeline for him. There was no sign of Doberman anywhere but Mel didn't plan on looking for him; she needed to keep a close eye on Lavin. She really hoped he would keep his word and not do anything rash or stupid.

Mel jerked to attention when he spun around and held up five fingers indicating the floor of Jenkins' room. She joined him at the elevator as Corky split across the lobby to stand near the front door. Three squad cars had arrived to guard the perimeter of the hotel.

Mel felt an eerie calmness; she was convinced she had done the right thing in slowing Lavin down. What she didn't know was that no one had ever bucked Lavin in the past and survived his wrath to tell about it; inadvertently, she had just made history.

On the other hand, Lavin could be right. The kid could be heavily implicated even if it was an accident and he was just too scared to tell the truth. Then again, what if Amelia had missed something important—like another person who might be involved?

Mel focused on the facts; she just wanted to be fair and avoid scaring the kid to death. After all, she reasoned with her adrenaline-charged alter ego; if he panicked he might try to harm himself or some innocent hotel guest.

She had entertained this whole reflection during the elevator ride from the lobby to the fifth floor—about eight seconds in all. She saw Lavin check his gun and she did likewise.

"Are you ready? He might have a gun," Lavin explained. He acted like a caring teacher or partner for a moment—very much out of character. He motioned to Mel to step aside as he knocked on the door with the gold numbers *501* nailed to a shiny, brass plaque.

"Come right in."

"What the hell?" Lavin whispered to Mel. He knocked again and this time an older man opened to the door.

"Oh, I thought you would be room service. Can I help you?"

Lavin was apologetic. "Sorry, sir; I thought this room was occupied by a Timmy Jenkins."

"You're right. Timmy is my son and he is staying here with me for a few days while I'm on business."

Lavin was impressed with the large two-room suite. He craned his neck a bit and looked just over the older man's shoulder and saw that Jenkins was reclining in a plush chair, watching television. Timmy seemed undistracted by what was going on at the door. He too, may have thought it was just room service.

Lavin gave Mel a hand signal to follow him and stepped inside the suite saying, "If you could quietly step aside, sir, I'd like to speak to the young man there. He walked toward Timmy with his jacket flapping open to expose his gun.

"Timmy Jenkins?"

The youngster looked up and in a startled slow motion moment leaned forward in an effort to reach for some kind of a canvas backpack that was crumpled at his feet. The oversized, reclined chair inhibited his attempt.

"Don't do it, son." Lavin was calm and moved forward, kicking the green bag to one side. "Just stay put for now. We're going to talk a little bit. Now, you promise me you won't try to leave that chair and I promise you that I won't beat the shit out of you. Is that a deal?"

Timmy Jenkins ignored Lavin's question and cocked his head to one side and greeted Mel with a friendly nod.

"Hello, Miss Abrams. Maybe you can tell me what this is all about. And please, don't involve my father. Dad, why don't you just go on ahead to your meeting and I'll meet you in the dining room for dinner later on. Okay?"

Mel wondered, incredulously, if this kid was for real. He really had balls or at least he was a hell of an actor.

"No, no, Mr. Jenkins; why don't you have a seat somewhere in here where we can see you."

She backed up a few steps where she could comfortably keep an eye on Timmy and his father—and Lavin.

"Kick that bag over, Tom. Let's see what the young man is carrying."

Lavin actually obliged—to Mel's surprise—and she pulled open the multi-pocketed, *San Romei,* designer backpack and began to rummage through it.

"Wow!"

"What?" Tommy was an impatient guy and walked backwards to see what she was fussing about. "Jesus Christ! Who does this gun belong to? He didn't wait for an answer.

"Mr. Jenkins, what do you know about this? Your boy, here, is in a little trouble; actually he's in a lot of trouble. Do you have any idea why we're here?"

Jenkins senior just stared with his mouth open.

"Well, let me tell you, sir," Lavin continued. "We're here to talk to your son about the brutal crime that took place at the *Macguire place* while he was attending a party there. It seems that someone saw him milling about the area where the *Albright* girl was found murdered". He turned and looked at Timmy. "You got anything to say about that?"

"Don't say a word son. If you don't mind, Miss Abrams, I'd like to call our family lawyer. He's right here in Boston; I should be able to reach him in a few minutes."

Mel followed Mr. Jenkins to the bedroom while he used his fancy *cyber phone.* The call only took a moment and as they reentered the living room, she was surprised to see Lavin writing in his little book.

"What the hell are you doing? Did you read him his rights?"

"Yes. Be quiet; I know what I'm doing. Go ahead, boy."

"Tim, don't say another word; Bob is on his way. And don't worry, he said they can't do a thing to you—just keep your mouth closed. We don't want you charged with anything *or* spending a night in jail. He's on his way, son."

"It's too late, Dad. I know I'm in trouble and I'm going to have to tell the truth sooner or later. Please let me go to the station with Mr. Lavin and Miss Abrams. I've got to tell them what really happened. And listen, I would hate to have everyone in the hotel see me in hand cuffs; it'll be embarrassing for you. Why don't you wait up here 'til Bob gets here? He'll drive you down town."

"No! Shut up now, Tim. We'll get this cleared up in few minutes—you'll see!"

The kid was on the verge of tears when he croaked, "I have to go with them *now*. Come as soon as you can, okay?"

Mr. Jenkins nodded his head and began to pick up things that were lying around the room. He picked up the backpack but Mel stepped in front of him and retrieved it without saying a word. She was thinking that he must be pretty well known among the lobby staff according to Timmy's concerns of embarrassing him. Maybe this is where he stayed on a regular basis.

She stopped herself from indulging any further in idle curiosity; his private life was none of her business.

Lavin's cell phone rang as they left the room and he stepped away and turned his back to Mel and Jenkins while he answered it. Mel couldn't make out what he was saying, but he resembled a poisonous snake ready to strike this kid with a venomous fang. She moved toward the elevator, holding on to Timmy's elbow.

He lowered his head and asked Mel if she would wrap his white coat around him to hide his cuffed wrists—the kid thought of everything.

Corky met them as the door opened and the little caravan snaked its way through the busy lobby and out to Lavin's car. Doberman had already let himself into Timmy's locked Orbiter, disarmed the alarm, and was browsing through the trunk with his knight stick.

Timmy surprised them all when he let out a wail. "What about my car? I never let anyone drive it! What's going to happen to it? Maybe you can just leave it here and I'll come for it in a day or two. Or let my father handle it, okay?"

Mel thought the kid showed a lot of moxie to predict his own freedom in the next day or so. She tried to calm him down. "Don't worry about it, kid. We'll need to check it over; we'll get it back to your father or mother in a couple days. It'll probably be towed and I'm sure the guys will be careful; it looks like a great car."

Mel felt bad to be softening him up for the kill, but she was just doing her job.

Mel assisted the kid into the back seat of the patrol car where it was decided that it was safer to get him downtown that way. Everyone knew of Lavin's propensity for "*a terrible accident*" occurring during the delicate transport of a suspect, so Lavin was gently convinced to drive his own car—though adamant about holding the kid in the police station parking lot so he could personally escort him into the station.

Then he faced Mel. "The phone call; it was Johnson. He knows we're on to something. I told him we had a terrific break here in Boston but that I couldn't talk right then. I promised to call him back within the hour. Let's get going. I want to talk to the kid before getting back to Johnson *or* Cramer."

Lavin smelled a confession and he was not going to let anyone stand between him and it.

Fifteen minutes later he was closing the door to the stuffy little room whose only furniture was a scratched up wooden table and a bunch of folding chairs—casually stacked against the wall. A day-old pot of coffee sat on a metal serving table in one corner of the room along with an empty trash can. Lavin picked up the pot and lifted the top to sniff the black liquid; he made a face and a disgusting noise as he kicked open the door and roared out to no one in particular to bring in a fresh pot. He looked at Mel to see if she was ready and she nodded for him to get started.

She looked at the pathetic form of Timmy Jenkins numbly stripped of all flamboyance as he sat like a crumpled rag doll in the hard wooden chair. He was in for the scare of his life, but she reasoned with little emotion that it had to be done—especially if he was the snake in the grass they were looking for.

Mel had done this dozens of times before and it still made her a little sick. It was so irrevocable and once completed could never be reversed. She took the two-inch-square electronic recorder out of her large leather bag and checked the settings before placing it on the table in front of Timmy Jenkins. She felt sorry for him for some odd reason; *sans bravado* he was almost likeable.

Lavin was impatient. "Okay, let's get started. Suppose you tell us exactly what happened on Saturday night while you were at the Macguire party—then we'll ask you a few questions. We'll also let you know when your father and his lawyer get here."

There was a light tap on the door and Lavin closed his eyes impatiently while an officer brought in the pot of coffee and a bunch of paper cups. He never acknowledged him; he wouldn't even think of saying *thank you* at a time like this.

Timmy began to speak with a hint of his previous confidence. "I got to the party at about eight-thirty, like I told Miss Abrams, and I just started hanging out with different kids I knew. They were a little younger, so I was really kind of bored. You know what I mean? I wouldn't have gone to the party at all except Harry was a real good buddy of mine. I never cared much for his brother. I already told some of this to Miss Abrams, so you probably know some of this."

"I really don't give a shit what you told Miss Abrams; just tell it over again if you have to, but don't keep reminding me that you already told her. Keep talking."

Lavin looked at his watch and Mel had the feeling he was thinking of Johnson.

"I hung around for a while and had a few beers down on the beach; it was pretty dark by then and we headed up the stairs to the back yard where the lights were on and the food was set up. We danced for awhile and..."

Mel put her hand up to stop Timmy. "Who did you dance with, Timmy?"

"Uh let's see. I danced with Mollie Simon, Jenny Holmes, and then Mollie Simon again—*A-Listers*."

"How about *Cassie Albright*, did you dance with her?" Mel was gentle in her questioning and it pissed Lavin off, so he closed his eyes, indicating his impatience while he waited for an answer.

"Oh, no; I wouldn't dance with *Cassie;* she was Eddie's girl and that wouldn't have been cool. Anyway she was having quite a time for herself without dancing with anybody."

"Why do you say that?" Mel continued in the same quiet voice.

"Well, you know, she was one of the kids involved in the skinny-dipping. She was running down the stairs to the beach as I was coming up, um, she was already half undressed when she passed me."

Lavin cut in before Mel could continue her soft line of questioning. "Who else was with her?"

"Harry."

"Harry? Eddie's brother?"

"Yes sir."

"What did you do then?"

"I went to the top of the stairs and stood with a bunch of kids who were watching; even though you couldn't see anything you could hear them laughing and sort of making out—I would guess. Then *Cassie* appeared at the bottom of the stairs where there was light from the electric lanterns, drying her hair and pulling on her jeans and some gold top thing and then everyone was cheering. I don't know why—maybe because she had the guts to do what she did or maybe because she had such a great body. I mean you could see her top—her bare breasts. A couple of minutes later she came running up the stairs and Eddie appeared asking why everyone was cheering, but *Cassie* just grabbed him and started hugging and kissing him and I watched them go onto the patio and start dancing real close. I was jealous as hell, but it was no big deal. I was happy for Eddie if he was going to get lucky; I knew it was going to be his first time. But me, I'm two years older—I've been all through that."

There was dead silence for a few minutes and Lavin deliberately took his time pouring a cup of coffee. Just as he was bringing it to his lips he stopped and offered it to Mel. She shook her head from side to side—she hated paper cups that had been sitting around and handled by everyone. Lavin then made the same offer to the kid who reached up and took it without saying anything. After sipping it, he thanked Lavin.

"Go on Timmy; tell Mr. Lavin and me what happened after that. By the way, what time do you think it was when you saw Eddie and *Cassie* dancing in the family room?"

For some reason, Lavin thought it was a stupid question and shook his head, taking the opportunity to take a sip of his coffee. He made a face and made a circular motion with his hand as if to hurry things up.

Timmy tried to answer Mel's question without showing any distraction from Lavin's showboating. "You mean dancing on patio? I'd say about ten-thirty or eleven o'clock, ma'am."

Mel wasn't finished yet. "You said you were down at the beach smoking a cigarette and having a few beers. Who was with you down there?"

I wasn't smoking. I don't smoke; just a little pot occasionally, but I had a couple of beers with Mollie and Jennifer. I think Jennifer had too much to drink—she couldn't stop puking. Not Mollie though, she was cool and promised to go to another party with me at midnight. I knew we'd have fun. She just had to make sure *Cassie Albright* would cover for her and say she had spent the night at her house. This way we could stay out all night and head for the beach at dawn for a swim and some breakfast Then she said she couldn't find *Cassie* and it was almost eleven thirty and I had planned to leave around midnight."

Lavin broke into the conversation at what Mel thought was a crucial time and was shocked and irritated when he said, "Where did you get the beer?"

"The beer, sir? Oh, the beer on the beach? Someone had brought a big tub of ice and put it at the bottom of the stairs and it was filled with canned and bottled beer. I think Harry smuggled the beer down in some big beach towels during the day."

"Great," Lavin said dryly. "So what happened when Mollie couldn't find *Cassie*?"

"I told her I was getting ready to leave and if she couldn't find *Cassie* by midnight she would have to find her own ride to the party, although I would still take her home in the morning. She didn't live too far from *The Inlet*, where I live. They live *mid-island*, you know—a real nice place!"

"Keep going."

"I started to say so long to a couple of people and headed toward my car in the driveway. Just as I reached my car, I thought I heard a funny noise. I thought someone was crying or whining. It was a strange noise coming from the side of the house. I walked along the driveway toward the little shed, you know, where Harry and Eddie keep their magazines and a little pot stash; I noticed that the wooden slats were lying on the ground. I figured someone was in there. Hell, probably someone was sick or drunk or *whatever,* but it *did* occur to me that somebody might be in there making out with a girl so I figured I should mind my own business.

I could see there was a little light of some sort in there; it looked like a flashlight was left on the ground just inside the opening, so I hunched over and picked up the flashlight and started to move into the shed, holding the light in front of me. About half way thru the shed I flashed the light on a guy and one of the girls lying on a beach towel. The girl was crying and trying to push him off of her. I yelled, "Hey! Leave her alone!" and Harry turned around and told me to get the hell out. He was trying to hold up the back of his khakis as he talked to me. He started to laugh and said they were fooling around and just having a little fun.

"Really Jenks, go on, get the hell out.

"I backed out and walked over to my car."

Timmy Jenkins cleared his throat, coughed, and began to look for a handkerchief; he was clearly close to collapsing and Mel thought they should let him stop and get a hold of himself. The last thing she wanted was for this to turn into a case of coercion. She reached over and turned the tape recorder off and told Timmy to stand and take a few deep breathes. He obeyed her. She called out the door for a pitcher of water and waited silently, handing him a wad of clean tissues.

Lavin was furious and facetiously asked Mel if she wanted to hold his hand while they waited for the water.

She didn't bother to answer—just poured the kid a cup of water and watched while he downed it. Color seemed to come back to his cheeks and he sat down, indicating that he was ready to continue. Mel reached over and turned on the tape recorder.

"Go ahead."

"I walked over to my car, but then I decided I should try to find someone and tell them to check on the girl—maybe tell them what I saw—but when I got to the patio just a few guys and their girlfriends were sort of dancing and making out on their feet so I figured it was none of my business if someone was in the shed getting lucky. I stuck my head in the family room and all I saw was the Macguire kid sleeping on the sofa. You know, Eddie's younger sister. I really wanted to tell someone that maybe a girl was in trouble, but then I figured, hey, it's *Harry Macguire!* I didn't want to tangle with a *Macguire* or anyone else at that party. Hell, I really hate all of them; they're just a bunch of *oceanfront snobs!*

It was getting late and I was getting bored. Mollie couldn't find *whoever* and I decided to leave. On the way back to my car, I slowed down in front of the little shed. I didn't hear anyone crying and it didn't sound like there was any kind of trouble, so I figured Harry was in there—getting lucky. I still had the flashlight in my hand so I threw it in my trunk, thinking I might need it to find my way to the cottage party I was going to. I would need it if we went down to the beach again before dawn, anyway. I got in my car and it was twelve o'clock. I know that because my watch alarm went off. I had planned to leave that party by midnight and had set it—in case I lost track of time."

Mel took command of the empty moment. "Timmy, do you have any idea who the girl was in that shed with Harry Macguire?"

"Of course I do."

"Tell me who you think it was."

"I think it was *Cassie Albright,* no, I *know* it was *Cassie Albright.*"

"What makes you say that?"

"Her gold halter was lying on the beach towel next to Harry's leg. I know it was *Cassie's* top because she was the only one at the party with one like that. Everyone could tell you what she was wearing—you couldn't miss it! Also, I had heard Harry say, '*come on, Cassie—calm down*'."

Lavin shook his head in disgust and said, "So you got in your nice new car and drove away without telling anyone what you saw. You are a goddamned liar and I don't believe one word of what you just said, you little son of a bitch! You better tell me what *really* happened or...." Lavin was red-faced and bursting with frustration.

It was a dangerously explosive situation and Mel walked around the table to act as a barrier between Lavin and the kid. She didn't want Lavin to do what he was accused of doing in the past—smack him or even worse.

"That's not quite exactly what happened. I backed up my car and waved to Eddie Macguire. He came over to say good-bye to me. He was pretty high and smiling and acting silly, but I just said, 'listen, you better go in your little playhouse and see what your *brother* and *Cassie* are doing; I think they might be playing *doctor*'. Eddie tried to focus on what I had said and sort of let my words sink in. I just roared out of the driveway laughing my head off. It was a cruel thing to do to Eddie, but he was so stupid and maybe I just wanted Harry to get caught in the act and get his ass kicked by Eddie; or maybe his father might even get wind of it and give him a good boot. They all deserved it—every one of those *snooty Macguires*—so I just rolled down my window and took off."

"What about the party you went to from there? Tell me about it." Lavin was speaking a little softer now, but he didn't believe one word the kid had spoken so far.

Mel knew the answer to this one.

"I didn't go to the party. I was too tired and besides that my dad was out of town and my mom was home alone—I went straight home. It was about twelve thirty when I got there. I checked on my mom, like I always do, and went up to bed."

"So tell me why the hell you packed a bag and came to Boston today?"

"The next day I got scared after I heard about what happened and I wanted to talk to Eddie and Harry about it; hell, when I drove by the next afternoon, the driveway was blocked off and the Sheriff's car and a whole bunch of other cars were parked all over the place. I called my dad and told him what happened and he said he would be home Sunday night. I waited all day. He didn't make it. On Monday I got a call from Miss Abrams to come down for questioning on Tuesday and my dad couldn't come with me because he had another meeting. I was supposed to call him at the New W as soon as Miss Abrams was finished with me."

"Why didn't you get someone to go down with you, like maybe your mother or one of your father's lawyers?

Mel asked this question although she already knew the answer.

"My mother is an alcoholic and she is not able to do the things that most parents do. That's one of the reasons why my father spends so much time at the New W with uh, friends.

Then he turned his attention to Lavin. "Mr. Lavin, you said you didn't believe one word I've said, but I have told you exactly what happened at the party. I'm sure the girl was *Cassie*. I'm *positive* the guy was Harry; hell, he even called me by name and I'm sure I told Eddie about it, even if he was *half baked* by then.

Excuse me, but I think I'm ready to see my father and his lawyer. They are here, aren't they?"

"Well, son," (Lavin's sudden fatherly approach made Mel sick.) I'll have to talk things over with Miss Abrams and my chief—he's sitting in his office down the hall. Then we will decide whether we are going to hold you here and press some kind of charges—in which case you *will* need your lawyer—or whether we should take your word for it and send you home in your father's custody. An officer is going to come in and sit with you while we make that decision. I've got to talk to the people on *Puckshaw*, too—see what they think."

Lavin started towards the door and then spun around, startling both Mel and the already shaken, kid. "I have one more question for you."

"What the hell were you doing with a gun in your bag in the hotel room?"

The original swagger that Mel had witnessed earlier in the morning returned and she felt she was in the presence of that snotty, little rich kid—yet again.

"That gun belongs to my father and he has a legal permit to carry it. He didn't want to leave it lying around the hotel room when he went to the meeting so he dropped it into my backpack; I was to leave it at the desk vault when I went to meet him for dinner later."

"Would you know why your father would have to carry a gun?"

"My father is a businessman who often carries large sums of money from his offices to the local banks. He also travels late at night on deserted roads from Boston to *Puckshaw*. He feels it is necessary to be prepared for the unexpected. He has been carrying a gun for many years; I suspect you could check that out quite easily."

Timmy Jenkins stared unabashedly into Detective Tom Lavin's eyes.

"You're good, kid," Lavin said dryly. "You're *real* good. We'll get back to you."

He stepped out into the hall to get an officer and looked over his shoulder at Mel. She picked up the digital recorder and dropped it into her purse. She couldn't look at Timmy Jenkins. She didn't know if she felt sorry for him or despised him. She didn't know if he was lying through his teeth or telling the unmitigated truth. For the first time today she agreed with Lavin. *The kid was good.*

It was late evening in *Puckshaw* and Johnson and Cramer were sitting in Charlie's having a burger. The familiar haunt of the islanders hadn't been owned by Charlie Shaw for at least ten years; that lucky soul had retired a millionaire and sold the restaurant to a couple of college professors who in turn immediately called it a *Coffeehouse*. They had poetry readings and 'open *mik* nights' and stuff that made Cramer and Johnson shake their heads. They still served pretty good food and kept the place open almost all night in the summer—the first restaurant owners to take that chance. It was a smart move; that fact alone made Charlie's the top cop-stop of choice and kept potential trouble-makers away.

Johnson jerked his head up from the newspaper when his tiny cell phone rang. He whipped it off his shoulder and pressed the green button. It flashed the time. It was ten p.m.

"Johnson."

"It's Lavin. We picked up the Jenkins kid and I think he's our man. We've got it all on a recorder. You want to drive over tonight? If not, we can come to the island first thing in the morning. We'll probably charge and hold the little bastard if his lawyer doesn't get a judge to pull a string or two."

"You saying you got a recorded confession?"

"Hell, no; he's denied the whole thing. Wow! What an actor the kid is. He's blaming the *Macguire kid. Harry.* He says he saw him on top of *Cassie Albright* and that she was crying and trying to fight him off. He says Harry yelled at him and threw him out of the shed. He claims he thought they were just fooling around, so he backed off. Oh, yeh; he also says he told Eddie about it before he left, but Eddie was stoned or drunk or something. It looks like the kid, what's her name, *Amelia,* was right on the money."

Johnson was close to exploding. "Wait. Let me get this straight. You don't have a confession. You don't have a weapon. Hell, you don't even have a motive! Now what the fuck is wrong with your brain, Lavin, has it gone soft or something? You are going to have to let that kid go. I'll be at the Macguire house at eight a.m. tomorrow morning to check his story out."

Johnson lowered his voice and shook his head. "You know, the Jenkins' are fine people; don't go messing up their good name." He disconnected the call and slammed his phone down on the counter.

He looked at Cramer incredulously. "That guy is fucking out of his mind!"

Both men finished their burgers and drank coffee late into the night. They discussed every twist and turn the case had taken, so far. They both disliked Lavin and agreed that he was full of shit. But the young woman, Mel, was another story. They didn't dislike her; but they were careful about what they said around her.

Cramer agreed to accompany Johnson to the Macguire place first thing in the morning. He knew Scott would be pissed and the boys would be scared. He would just try to keep everyone calm so Johnson could do his job. They both knew it would be tricky and neither of them wanted to destroy the many years of friendship they had enjoyed with the *Macguire Family*. If that were to happen, nothing would ever be the same.

The weary officers of the law parted for the night and agreed to meet at the station by seven-thirty the next morning to drive out to the Macguire home together. Cramer didn't think it was a good idea to call ahead. His opinion was that *surprise* was about the best card they were holding at this point.

Lavin and Mel huddled in the chief's office and discussed Johnson's stunned reaction and clear opinion about letting the kid go. They all agreed that for a "small potatoes" deputy, the guy had balls and wasn't afraid to stand up to the Boston *crowd*. The chief was impressed and secretly pleased to see *Lavin's Law of Averages* openly questioned and defied. It made him chuckle.

"Okay, it's almost midnight," began Sully, an aging and visibly burned out Chief of Detectives. "Let's go over the facts and make a decision; I don't want to be here all night."

Mel wanted to speak but she held her tongue and let Lavin take the first shot. She knew her place in *this* trio.

"Well, we can hold him for forty-eight hours for questioning and treat him as an adult; he's just passed his eighteenth birthday. His father is already downstairs with two fancy lawyers and they want him charged so they can get a judge to set bail; or released on the spot. Either way they want to take him home as soon as possible. Judge Kenny is not available until tomorrow at four p.m. and she's *our* best shot at *no bail* for this little bastard."

Lavin was strangely excited.

"Of course, his lawyers are going to seek an arraignment before a more lenient judge from their list of political connections; if we stall them long enough tonight they won't have a chance to do anything until morning. That'll level the playing field. What do you say we let the kid see his father and then we all sit tight until those two clowns on *Puckshaw* get out to the Macguire house; it is possible they might be able shake the two boys up enough to blow some big holes in this kid's story."

Mel felt more comfortable in speaking up now. She would carefully dissect Lavin's cock-sure discourse and finish with her rookie opinion and suggestion.

"We should try to get a five o'clock hearing commitment from Judge Kenny's people—right now. I know Harriet Town, her personal assistant—I can call her and get on the docket. I think I can deliver that."

She let that sink in as Lavin and Sully looked at each other as if she was kidding but she wasn't going to give them a chance to respond—she had learned that tactic from Lavin.

"Once the time for an arraignment is announced to his father and to the press, tomorrow morning, it will stop Jenkins' lawyers from trying to get a judge who is one of their own. That gives us all day to work the recording to our advantage and meet with Johnson and Cramer after they finish at the Macguire place. Don't count them out; they're a lot sharper than you think."

Mel threw a quick glance at Lavin. There was no question—she was gently chiding his low opinion of their expertise.

"Then what we do is merge the twins' account with Jenkins' story, line by line, following a specific time sequence to see whose story is stronger. I think we have to be extremely careful here. Like Johnson said, *no motive, no weapon, and the testimony of an eleven or twelve-year-old kid*—we could get caught with our pants down."

Mel was pleased with her performance and looked from Lavin to Sully at least three times while she waited for a response.

Sully shrugged his shoulders with a hint of agreement and waited for Lavin to acquiesce. "What do you think?"

Lavin was stunned and looked away in a brooding silence. After a few awkward moments he said, "We can *try it*. Let's go."

He shoved his chair back and avoided making eye contact with Sully or Mel. I'll talk to the kid once more and tell him he is going to see his father. Maybe he ought to wash up a little—the little bastard is liable to say we abused him or something."

"We can almost count on that," Mel retorted, dryly. "I'll go with you and then make my call."

She still didn't trust Lavin alone with the kid.

Sully turned off his desk light and announced his departure, leaving strict orders to be called if anything changed before nine a.m. the next morning. As he was locking his door he asked no one in particular, "by the way, when is the autopsy report due?"

"Not for another forty-eight hours, sir. The Tox and DNA Lab is somewhere in Buffalo—they're moving as fast as they can. They pretty much know the cause of death, but traces of skin under the victim's nails, pubes, and other bodily fluids, will take another day."

Mel was matter of fact about that information.

Lavin was cowed again. "Where did you hear that shit?"

"Got a friend in the Coroner's office. The results can change everything—that's what I meant about getting caught with our pants down. No pun intended."

"Yeh, that's right."

Lavin stopped to get a drink of water and deliberately waited for Mel and Sully to pass him. For the first time in years he felt insignificant. Mel waited for him at the end of the hall and joined him as he headed toward the *interview room* where Timmy Jenkins was being detained. He never acknowledged her presence.

It was already passed midnight.

28 *After Hours*

Johnson showered, took out fresh clothes for the morning and was in bed by two a.m. He was wide-awake and restless; something was missing in Amelia's account of what she had seen the night of the party. After all, there was noise, music, and a lot of kids were milling around and she *had* admitted she was almost asleep by midnight. She could be wrong or even might have been dreaming; she could have missed something pretty important. *She was just a kid—a very fragile one, at that.*

Scott had refused to let him get the child on digital, so he had to rely on his and Cramer's notes and although they were helpful and accurate, he wished he could hear the inflections in her voice again. Sometimes that alone could indicate the level of confidence, stress, or veracity of one's recollection or testimony.

Johnson was still pissed with himself for letting Jenkins slip off the island and right into the Boston PD's hands. Now he was totally out of touch with a kid who might tell *him* the truth a lot faster than he might tell perfect strangers, like Lavin and Abrams. Everything was wrong with this case and he felt a sudden longing for Ginny, his one and only love.

He recalled how she would rub his shoulders, fix him a warm dinner, and lay out his clothes for the next morning. He could tell her anything and find only encouragement and patience in her response. In intimate moments, she alone could comfort his spirit and soothe his anxiety during a trying night like this one. She had loved him unconditionally and he had taken advantage of her. Their marriage was too much about him and nothing left for her. It was nights like this one that had eventually broken up their marriage and left him to his own wits.

They still spent many warm and intimate nights together; only now, the relationship was on her terms. Tonight, when Johnson had felt a deep and desperate need for her presence, he had phoned her. Could she come to him?

She was sorry; but she just couldn't make it.

He tossed and turned all night; now he was turning off his ringing clock with a numbing lack of enthusiasm. He counted on Charlie's coffee to help him get over himself and focus on the situation at hand.

Cramer looked at the clock on his office wall and was relieved to see it was finally seven a.m. For the last four hours he had slept intermittently at his desk with his head cushioned in his massive hands, propped up by stiff, sore elbows. He had not gone home from Charlie's; he had slept at the office.

Since his youngest had moved off the island after graduating college, he had no desire to spend lonely nights in his tidy little home, not too far from *Henry Macguire's* original house—now serving as the front entrance to *H. Macguire & Son Publishing House.*

Cramer had spent most of his adult life on *Puckshaw* and had seen droves of kids grow up and leave for the big cities of the Northeast. Even his own son had opted for New York, leaving the well-known widower to live alone, with an occasional holiday visit from the kid.

Still groggy, he reached into his desk drawer and pulled out his battery-operated shaver and deftly ran it over his lightly shadowed face. He never used a mirror to shave anymore—just didn't see the need for it. He rose, stretched his arms and legs and strode across the room to step into his little lavatory to wash up and change his shirt. He unbuttoned his day-old shirt with wet hands as he gazed at himself in the mirror.

"What the hell is wrong with this case?"

He and Johnson would go over every single shred of information before heading out to Macguires oceanfront mansion; if something had been overlooked, Johnson would be the guy to flush it out. He counted on it. With that firmly in mind, Cramer felt comforted as he grabbed his wide-brimmed hat and headed for the parking lot. He couldn't believe it was Friday, almost one week since the *Albright girl* was found dead; it seemed more like a year. He looked at his watch and noted the time. It was seven-twenty a.m.

Time was hard to keep track of these days. To Melanie Abrams today seemed like yesterday; tonight should be tomorrow and tomorrow was *whatever*. Everything was going so fast that she always had the feeling she was a day behind.

Mel was staying at her mother's home for the weekend, since it was her turn to help out with the care of the Alzheimer-stricken, seventy-year old. She and her two sisters dutifully helped their father out every Thursday, Friday and Saturday with shopping, house cleaning and cooking. They visited with him, encouraged him to go out for worry-free walks, and talked him into indulging in his favorite activities—bowling, gardening, and driving his beloved car.

Mel, noting her father's handiwork in the beautifully tended flowers surrounding the house, wistfully reflected on how her mother would have loved them.

Though the care of his wife had become an arduous task, he had wholeheartedly accepted it with the help of his generous daughters. He never failed to acknowledge how important their help was in making this personal level of care possible.

Melanie let herself into the house well after midnight and tiptoed to the kitchen to see if there was anything to eat. She wasn't surprised to find the fridge bare and nothing to nibble on. Her father was religious in following the menu his daughters posted on the refrigerator each week and he would use every scrap of food up by Thursday afternoon. It was Thursday night and Mel knew she needed to shop at an all night supermarket in a busy Boston plaza in order to prepare Friday's meal.

The timing couldn't be worse—she would be gone all day, every day, until this case was cracked. She thought of asking one of her sisters to trade weekends with her but she had done it so often since making Detective that it had caused friction between them and she wanted to avoid further tension at any cost. She grabbed a small bottle of diet-Pepsi and practically drained the bottle before recapping it and putting it back on the shelf.

She was startled by her father's soft voice as he whispered her name. He had waited up for her. She spoke with him for a few minutes and told him she would be back in half an hour. She didn't tell him she was going to the supermarket to do the shopping. She didn't have to.

Before she left, she stopped in the laundry room and started a load of wash. She never resented these chores; she loved her parents far too much; they had made everything possible for her and she appreciated it. Tonight, if she wanted to ponder the *Albright* murder, she would have to do so while carrying out the duties of the devoted daughter that she was.

First stop was the all-night diner—they knew her there. She ordered something to eat to revive her physical sense of balance and well being. She sat in a little booth and glanced at the day's paper with increasing distraction. Putting it aside she tried to put the facts of the case in some kind of order. The problem was that she couldn't think straight. Melanie was a strong, healthy woman and being deprived of one night of sleep never bothered her before. No—it was something else. She bit into the tuna sandwich and took a sip of bitter coffee.

"Well, at least it will keep me awake," she smiled at the waitress.

She took out a small notebook and pencil and wrote a priority list for Friday. 8 a.m.—Meet Lavin at precinct

9 a.m.—Informational meeting with press/announce 5:30 p.m. arraignment before Judge Kenny

10 a.m.—Connect with Johnson and Cramer/compare Harry Macguire's account to Jenkins' recorded interview

Suddenly Mel ripped the page out of the little book and crumpled it in her palm. Unable to finish her sandwich, she left the diner and walked across the well-lit street to do the necessary shopping. If she hurried, she could put the groceries away and throw another load of clothes in the dryer before she showered and prepared for bed. She might be able to do it all by three a.m. and she wouldn't forget to sit with her mother for fifteen minutes and kiss her goodnight before hopping into bed for a few hours of sleep. She had done it all before.

Although some days were more difficult than others Melanie Abrams still considered herself to be very lucky.

Luck was something that Tom Lavin was used to—until a couple of years ago. Now he had trouble adjusting to what most people accepted as the norm.

Under a starry sky he drove out to the suburbs with a warm breeze gently teasing his thinning hair and fanning his tense face through the wide-open window. He needed the air tonight—not the usual blaring radio that he was noted for. At the end of a most mind-boggling day, he felt uncharacteristically left out of the loop; he was deeply disappointed in the way things were shaking out in the *Albright* case. He seemed to be missing all the red flags and felt like a damned fool to be so outclassed by a rookie like *Cherry*. She was proving to be a hell of a handful although he was secretly impressed with her deviousness. She probably wouldn't think of it as that, but he knew *dumb like a fox* when he saw it and she definitely was.

He pulled into the long curved driveway of an impressive looking colonial new-build deep in a brand new gated development. Police work had been financially kind to him. The long hours had allowed him to make enough money to stay married just long enough to raise three children and see them safely through the perilous expense of higher education. He also built a new house and bought a flashy boat—all before the expected collapse was complete. He was not quite forty-four.

It was no secret that police work and marriage didn't go together. In cruel and predictable patterns, Tommy Lavin had woven a patchwork quilt of marital horrors. Infidelity, emotional abuse, alcoholism, and cold detachment towards his wife and children were all well documented by friends, colleagues, and relatives.

When the showdown came it could hardly be called such. His wife was fully prepared with money, lawyers, witnesses, and the desire for revenge. The cut was quick and deep. Lavin never had a chance to put up a fight; he had no case. She *didn't* want the house, the dog, or him; but she'd gladly accept every bit of cash and alimony that the law allowed. Now, the best Lavin could hope for was a quick remarriage on her part to save him from *The Forever Alimony Blues*.

Around the office or anyplace else for that matter, it was forbidden to mention or refer to Tom Lavin's marriage in any way, shape, or form; that is, if you didn't want to incur his wrath. He confided in no one, asked for nothing and never shed a tear.

Nobody was privy to his family affairs or the pain he suffered. The only thing that had sustained Lavin throughout the private hell that he had created was his police work and the legendary desire he harbored for *the chase* and *the kill* that came with crime solving. Tommy was known to have a solution to every problem. His colleagues always said if you gave him enough time he would figure it out.

Yet, tonight he felt the once-satisfying thrill of crime-busting slipping away from him; he'd have to find a solution to that when this case was over.

29 *Benediction*

Scott and Francesca Covel had just enjoyed their first intimate moments and were quietly drinking coffee in her little breakfast nook. He, in his print shorts and Frankie, in a tiny green teddy, sat side by side in a perfect rapture of physical satisfaction.

When Scott had pulled away from his house at six in the morning he thoroughly expected to go directly to the publishing house of *H. Macguire & Son*. He had even gone through the motions of leaving a note on the kitchen counter explaining to Thea that he needed to get some invoices from the office and check his *snail mail*. After all he hadn't been in the office for almost six days and there were many things that only he could handle. Although Francesca had been carrying the load with remarkable efficiency—keeping him informed on a day-to-day and hour-to-hour basis—he still needed to touch base with his department heads and commend them for their good work.

He was shocked to realize that he had not left the house since the party—except to go to the police station for questioning or to walk up and down the tiny beach with Francesca.

Now that the pressure was off he was feeling a touch of *cabin fever* and didn't see any reason why the kids couldn't be left at home with Thea for a few hours. He hadn't heard from Cramer or Johnson and didn't expect to meet with them without advance notice. Through Sims, he had heard the rumor that they were close to arresting *some kid* and that it was a probable smoke screen to flush out new information.

Today, Scott Macguire felt pretty safe in assuming that he and his family were cleared of any suspicion. It had all been a nightmare and he thanked God that it was almost over. He dressed light-heartedly and prepared to go to the office.

Sorely missing each other, Scott and Francesca had been phoning, e-mailing, and texting each other several times a day.

Francesca had been out to the mansion for his signature at least every other day. They tried not to call attention to their warming attraction, but they saw no reason to hide it either—except maybe not to hurt Thea who always seemed to be in the wrong place at the wrong time. Scott and Francesca both lived for any moment when they could brush hands or elbows or—if they were lucky—exchange social kisses on both cheeks— European style.

Scott had every intention of going to his office early that morning, but as he came up to the highway he took a right and headed for Boston. He checked Francesca's address in his personal electronic date book and slowed down when he came into a small development of town houses. He didn't know what he was going to say—maybe something like, *"Good morning! Can I buy you some breakfast?"*

Thinking that phrase to be pretty corny, he rang the doorbell and looked at his watch. It was six forty-five; *too early,* he thought. He wished he hadn't done this, but he changed his mind as soon as Frankie opened the door after a quick check of the security camera embedded above her door frame.

"Scott! Hi! Come in. What's wrong; has something happened?"

"No, no. I was on my way to the office, but I, I just decided to come here. You're not angry are you?"

"Oh no, come on in and sit down. I'll make some coffee right away."

Scott was staring at her short silk robe and wondered what she had on underneath it, if anything. He felt foolish and embarrassed since Francesca was talking to him and he hadn't heard a thing she said.

"Okay? Excuse me for a minute while I freshen up."

And she was gone. Scott waited for a minute or so and looked around the modern townhouse that so reflected its owner—neat, warm, and filled with expensive pieces of furniture and art. Without thinking he rose and walked to the partially closed door and tapped lightly.

"May I come in?"

"If you wish..."

Francesca was standing in front of the mirror, brushing her hair. She looked at Scott and her face turned bright crimson.

"I'm sorry Frankie; if you don't want to do this I'll understand, but I just can't stop thinking about you."

She turned and walked toward him. "I do want to do this, Scott; now."

They were lost in each other's arms—carried away by their fierce passion.

When she opened her eyes to look at her watch, it was close to eight thirty.

"Scott, where are you?"

She jumped out of bed and went into the living room and found him sitting on the arm of the chair gazing out the window.

Barefooted and wearing the light green teddy that had been concealed under the robe that she had answered the door in, she tiptoed behind him and put her hands over his eyes. She kissed him lightly on the back of his neck. "Let's have that coffee now."

The annoying buzz of Scott's e-phone shocked both of them out of their dreamy mood. He had conspicuously placed it on the counter when he walked into her house because he never seemed to be able to find it when it rang. Now, Scott grabbed it and checked the number—it was his home. He returned the call with, "Hello, who's calling, Amelia?"

"It's Thea. Her voice grated dully in his ear. You better get over here; Johnson and Cramer are here to talk to the boys. They say Lavin and his partner have some new information. Some kind of mix-up from what I can gather. I had no idea you had left the house so early. I called the office—you weren't there...you'd better hurry it up."

Thea hung up without further comment.

Scott didn't have a chance to respond. He whirled around, almost tumbling Frankie to the floor.

"Trouble again. Jesus!" He ran into her sweet smelling bedroom and grabbed his clothes—ducking into her bathroom to dress. He was out in a minute and stopped to scoop her up into his arms—conflicted with emotion. "We haven't made a mistake, have we?"

"No."

"Are you sure?"

"Yes, I am sure."

"Are you positive?"

"You can count on it."

Scott kissed her again, hating to leave. "I'll call you in a little while."

It was almost nine a.m. and Mel was pleasantly surprised by her partner's light mood as they had a cup of coffee together. He was uncharacteristically civil as they headed toward the small pressroom in the basement where they planned to meet the chief and a few members of the media.

"Oh, by the way; we're on the docket for five-thirty tonight; Judge Carol Kenny."

"I never doubted it, Mel chirped."

Lavin winked and smiled as he held the door open for her.

Mel sidled over and whispered in Sully's ear, informing him that the arraignment time was set and the chief, in a rather pleasant state of shock, began his briefing with renewed confidence. He couldn't give out much information yet; he explained to the waiting press that it was too soon, but yes, someone was going to be charged later in the afternoon and they'd have to wait a few hours for more information.

Mel was glad she was riding with Lavin though his offer had taken her by surprise; he had made it quite clear in the past that he liked to drive alone. Today they drove in comfortable silence until Tommy noticed that the members of the press were on their heels. He blatantly drove into a car wash. At first, Mel was shocked—then she found it humorous.

On the last leg of the wash, Lavin signaled to the attendants to move out of the way and literally drove off the moving rails, right past the waiting press. Mel concluded he was either being irrationally devilish or trying to impress her with his driving skills; in either case, they were in hysterics as they cruised over the bridge into *Puckshaw*—no sign of the press behind them.

Jenkins had been detained overnight in the downtown precinct holding center and Mel had checked on him before meeting Tommy for coffee. He was still sleeping. His father and a couple of lawyers had been allowed to see him the night before and would be bringing him fresh clothes to appear at the arraignment in.

The timing was perfect; with the chief's press conference behind them, Mel figured she and Lavin would be back from the Macguires in a couple of hours. She just hoped that things didn't explode before they got there. She was well aware that any situation involving volatile youngsters could erupt into chaos at any given moment. She and Lavin had to stay on their toes and avoid the over-confident pit falls.

"So what do you think, Tom?"

"What do you mean what do *I* think, *Cherry*?

"Just what I said; what do *you* think?"

"So you're not so tough after all, are you? I think you still have doubts about the kid, right? And don't give me that 'innocent until proven guilty crap', either. I think Jenkins killed *Cassie Albright*. No, let me put it this way. *I know* Jenkins killed *Cassie Albright*. Now, maybe it was an accident— rough sex and all that crap—or maybe she resisted and made him angry and one thing led to another. But you know what? It could have been cold-blooded murder, too. Maybe he just didn't like her—he already said he didn't have much use for the Macguire's and *their kind* and she *was* Eddie's girlfriend and he *had* seen her half-naked and fooling around on the beach with Harry. A lot went on that might have led this kid to act out his hostilities on the girl. So *that's* what I think!"

"Bravo maestro!" Mel clapped her hands together. "Encore!"

Tommy bowed, basking in her praise while keeping his eyes on the road.

"Wow, that's a lot of *maybes*, sir. Try this. *Maybe* he did walk in on Harry and *maybe* it did get out of hand and Harry killed the girl *accidentally*. *Maybe* Harry was jealous of his brother and wanted to get back at him by making out with his girlfriend. *Maybe* Eddie and Amelia are covering for him and Amelia is outright lying; she could have seen her brother, not Timmy Jenkins, going in and out of that shed; how about that theory, *sir*?"

Tommy was enjoying this somewhat flattering and flirtatious attitude that Mel was exhibiting. It was out of character for her, but he was loving it.

"No. The kid left the island, which indicates he was running scared. If he was so innocent and sure of himself, he would have never called his father and took off for Boston the way he did. Besides, he lied to his mother. I don't trust anyone who lies to his mother. You see, he may have feared his father's wrath, but he feared the consequences of what he had done even *more.* Also there is the question of the gun. *Why the gun*? You don't believe it was there because his father was carrying it do you?"

Mel was silent for the next few miles and then she changed the subject.

"I hope we get a crack at those two boys. Johnson has a lock on them now. Hell, we should have split up yesterday. I could have kept a closer eye on him *and* Cramer. I have the feeling they know something that we don't—something to do with that little girl."

"Don't sweat it Mel; you said yourself, there's the autopsy and the report on the car. If everything matches I think the kid is going to shoot himself in the foot. Just you wait."

Mel giggled. "I thought you were going to break into a song; "Just you wait *Henry Higgins...*"

Lavin howled.

Mel wondered what this new, explosive camaraderie was all about

Tommy liked the way he was feeling around Cherry this morning.

When they pulled onto the long concrete driveway of the Macguire home, there were already several cars parked on each side. The Sheriff's car was an obvious indication that Johnson and Cramer were there. The jeep that had been checked out two days ago was registered to Scott though usually driven by Thea, his sister-in-law. A new, white Camry pulled in directly behind Lavin and Mel. They had early on determined this car to belong to Scott Macguire. Actually, Lavin had ordered a tail on him since last Sunday and knew exactly where he was coming from today. Mel didn't, but she probably would have said, *"Touché Monsieur Lavin"*!

"Why are we here, Tommy? What the hell are we looking for? What the hell do we do if we find it? I am fucking confused, Tommy; help me out."

"How you talk; shame on you!"

Tommy sighed condescendingly, "You said it yourself; we should compare Amelia's, the twins', and Timmy Jenkins' recorded account on a line by line basis and question the discrepancies. That sounds reasonable to me. In between, we can question the twins' whereabouts in the timeline to corroborate both Amelia and Jenkins' story. Got it?"

"Got it, let's go!"

As Mel and Lavin got out of the car they greeted Scott Macguire who seemed irritated and just this side of exasperation.

"Now what is it?"

Lavin ignored his edgy mood and continued his greeting with, "Hello, Mr. Macguire, I guess we're back again for another conference. I hope this isn't a problem for you. I'm sure you want nothing but the best outcome for your children and your good name; please just try to be patient with us. I know we're not the most pleasant sight first thing in the morning and I'm *sure* you've seen *better*—just be patient."

Lavin knew he had made his point with Scott Macguire; he wouldn't have to say anything else.

He was on top again and he loved it.

Without even being aware of the double entendre, Mel whispered, *"Brilliant."*

They all walked up to the house and entered through the back patio and were reminded of the recent tragedy by the yellow tape across the little section of the opening to the unfinished storage shed. A young police officer had been standing guard for the last five days. All of the evidence that had been collected would soon be returned from the lab and made available to Lavin and Abrams; they had not even been allowed into the shed for a personal look at the scene. Once the body and the evidence had been removed, Macguire would not let anyone else near it.

On the other hand, Johnson and Cramer had already seen it all, having been on the scene a full twenty-four hours before the mainland detectives had arrived. Scott made no secret of his plans to fill the shed with gravel and seal it up with concrete as soon as possible. At this point, guarding an empty shed was a boring, rookie job. Mel noted that a bored rookie was doing it.

Scott entered through the patio and stepped into the family room nodding to Cramer and Johnson.

Thea was hovering in the kitchen doorway with Amelia cowering behind her. Scott did not greet her—still aggravated by her call, earlier. He had a creepy feeling that she knew where he was when she called him.

He walked around her and bent down to kiss Amelia just as Thea whispered, "Scott, the boys are upstairs. I didn't know what to do when Johnson and Cramer appeared; I just told them to stay in their room until I got a hold of you. I hope you didn't mind my calling you."

Scott never looked at her. "No problem, Thea."

He ran upstairs to see if they were okay and told them to stay put until he sent for them. He felt sorry for them. They looked scared and tired. He really hoped this bullshit would soon be over and told them so.

Scott came downstairs and faced all four of the law enforcers.

"Okay, tell me what it is you want."

It was Johnson who spoke up.

"We want to speak to the boys. It seems that someone may have implicated one of them in *Cassie's murder.* Just want to clear it up, Mr. Macguire. It's the right thing to do; we need to nip it in the bud and clear it up. Also, we might have to talk to Amelia again since we don't have a digital recording of what she said. Sorry about that, but if we are to clear the boys *and* your good name, we have to do this."

That's all Scott had to hear. "Thea, will you go up and get the boys?"

Tired and barefoot, the boys came down and stood sullenly without greeting anyone.

Cramer was sad and his face showed it; he had known the kids their entire lives and now he felt like a traitor. In his friendliest voice he said, "Hello boys, how are you doing?"

Both boys mumbled some form of greeting—sounding far from friendly.

Lavin and Mel were still silent and hanging back a little; after all, this was Johnson's territory and he was doing just fine—so far.

Johnson, in a most gentle manner, elicited Amelia's account again and skillfully covered all the most important points while looking over his shoulder at Lavin and Mel to see if they had any questions.

"So far so good," Mel whispered to Tommy. "The guy has talent—knows what he's doing."

When Johnson was finished he turned the questioning over to Lavin and Mel. Lavin asked Amelia a few perfunctory questions and then turned his attention to Harry and Eddie. "They tell me you boys are pretty close. Is that true?"

The boys nodded and looked at each other, shrugging their shoulders and half smiling.

"Both of you have quite a few friends, right? I guess that's pretty important when you're sixteen, isn't it? I hear you're both pretty popular with the female population of your school, too—lucky for you!"

Lavin had employed his old trick of not giving them a chance to answer or comment, thus keeping them off balance and playing catch-up. Then he cut right to the important question that he really wanted an answer to. Tell me Eddie, how about you and *Cassie;* did you like her better than all the other girls? What I mean is I bet you two were close, right?

"Sort of."

"Did you like her enough to get mad at her for fooling around with Harry down on the beach? Or didn't you know about that?"

Eddie looked at Harry and then at his father.

"I don't know what you're talking about. Harry didn't fool around with my girlfriend. And she wasn't down at the beach either. Was she Harry? Was she on the beach? You didn't fool around with her, right?"

Without a moment's notice Eddie exploded, leaping on top of his brother and taking him down.

"You bastard, you; why didn't you tell me you were down there? I was so worried about anybody finding out *Cassie* went skinny-dipping and you never told me that you were down there? I hate you! You're a rotten son of a bitch."

Scott jumped forward to separate the boys—he looked at them in utter astonishment.

"What the hell are you talking about? I thought you told me *everything*. This is it; tell the truth, Goddamn it! Right now! Harry, were you fooling around with the *Albright* girl down on the beach? Answer me right now!"

Then he turned his anger on Eddie. "And why the hell are you so worried about telling the truth about *Cassie* skinny-dipping? If she did, she did; so what? Anyway, I already knew about it, so you've been worrying for nothing.

Harry looked at Eddie and put his hand up saying, "Please, let me tell you what happened; just listen."

He proceeded to describe the scene at the bottom of the stairs, where the tub of iced beer was. "I was having a beer and smoking a cigarette when *Cassie* came down the stairs laughing and shouting that she was going skinny-dipping. She kept pulling on my sweatshirt, trying to get me to go in with her. I said, 'hell no, my dad will kill me; I'm not even supposed to be down here. It's bad enough that we got beer and pot down here. Sorry, but thanks, anyway.'

I saw her move closer to the water, kicking off her shoes and untying her *top thing*, her halter I guess you call it. I yelled to her, 'you're not going swimming, are you? Jesus, it's too dark, come on'. She kept right on pulling off her clothes and...and all of a sudden she was naked and running into the surf, screaming and laughing. That's the truth and I did *not* go swimming with her. Someone *else* did."

Lavin had that old feeling that he was getting close. "Then, tell me son, who went swimming with *Cassie Albright*?"

When Mel heard him call the kid 'son' she knew he thought he was within striking distance. She hated him again—for the moment.

There was a long empty silence and Harry finally answered in a very quiet voice.

"Timmy Jenkins. It was Timmy Jenkins who went swimming with her."

Lavin looked at Mel. She nodded. They both recalled Jenkins describing the scene in which he was smoking a cigarette and drinking a beer while *Harry* and Cassie went swimming together. Lavin let out a long deep sigh and swore under his breath.

Only Amelia flinched at the swear word before being ushered out of the room by Thea.

Mel respectfully asked Lavin if she could talk to Harry for a moment. He stepped back and let her have the floor.

"Harry, do you know Timmy Jenkins very well?"

"Not really. He goes around telling people I'm his friend and then he says he hates me and my brother, but I don' know him that well and what I do know of him, I don't like."

"What do you mean by that?"

"I don't know. I just don't like him."

"Do you think he likes Eddie better than you?"

"I don't know. Right now I don't know who the hell he likes or doesn't like and I don't care. This is stupid; I don't know what's going on any more!"

Mel ignored his ramblings and continued. "Timmy said *you* were his friend, but he *did not* like your brother, Eddie. Do you think Timmy would ever do anything to make trouble between you and your brother?"

"Sure, he would...probably. He's a troublemaker."

Surprisingly, Eddie came to Timmy's defense. "He would not Harry, you don't even know him. Don't go getting him in trouble with your big mouth. Jesus Christ!"

"That's enough," Scott roared. "Now cut it out!"

Mel put both hands up in a peacekeeping effort and tried to calm everyone down. "Okay. Let's get back to Harry. Harry,

did Cassie ask you to meet her later in the evening to make out
…or something like that?"

"No! She never asked me anything like that! Anyway, I
would never do that to my brother. I know how much he liked
her and I would have never done anything to hurt him."

"How about you, Eddie, did you have any plans to meet
up with Cassie later in the evening. I mean, I heard the rumor
about you and Cassie getting together later to…have sex?"

Eddie was livid. "Who the hell said that? Harry? I did
not have sex with *Cassie Albright* that night, or *any other night*;
no matter *what* you heard."

Mel lowered her voice and locked her sights directly on
Eddie.

"Eddie, I didn't ask you if you had sex with Cassie
Albright. I think you misunderstood my question. I'll ask you
again. Did you have *plans* to meet *Cassie Albright* to make out,
or be alone…for any reason?"

"Cassie and I did want some privacy but there just
wasn't any place where we could be alone."

"So what did you do about that?"

"We danced and kissed and she wanted to go upstairs
but my dad had warned us that the bedrooms were off limits—no
matter what."

"So?"

"So I told Cassie maybe we could meet in the little shed
under the side of the house, but I never got there. I was smoking
pot and drinking a few beers and I hung out with some of the
guys and never made it to the shed. I lost track of time; that is the
truth, no matter what anyone says. I lost track of time. Didn't I
tell you that, dad? Harry?"

Eddie was dangerously shaken and his voice was rising
to a new pitch every time he spoke.

"Okay son, take it easy. Just calm down, do you hear
me? Calm down."

Scott Macguire stepped in and put his arm around Eddie
and glared at Mel as he whispered angrily, "Are you through,
now?"

Just then Lavin spoke. "I need to ask Amelia just a few questions; is that alright with you Mr. Macguire?"

Scott looked around the room and called out for Amelia to come and sit by his side. She stepped into the room like a little ghost; she had been standing in the kitchen doorway during Eddie's outburst.

"Jesus Christ!" Scott whispered as Amelia appeared. "Is it okay, Amelia?"

Amelia nodded her head up and down.

"Good."

Lavin wasn't wasting any more time.

"Amelia, tell me one more time; who did you see near or around the shed the night of the party when you were looking out the window that faces the driveway. You know, the window above the little shed that the boys use as their secret hideaway."

"I saw the boy with the long white coat and yellow scarf."

"What did he do?"

"He came out of the shed and walked over to his car and threw something in the trunk and then came around and looked into the family room. Then he stopped on the patio and went outside and stood near the shed for a minute. I was scared because I thought he saw me looking at him, but then he got in his car and left. That's all."

"Did you see Harry or Eddie anywhere around the shed?"

"No. I didn't see my brothers anywhere near the shed."

"Amelia, this is very important, you know. Are you sure you did not see Harry or Eddie—either one of your brothers—*anywhere near* the shed at the time you saw the boy with long coat?"

"No, my brothers were not around at all."

"Thank you, Amelia. You have helped us very much."

"You're welcome."

Johnson came forward and whispered something to Scott and the boys and shook hands with each of them. Then he turned and said to his colleagues, "Okay folks; let's give these people some rest. Why don't we go over to Sheriff Cramer's office, make a pot of coffee, and make some sense out of all of this? We've got an appointment with a Boston judge later on and then we'll just have to wait for the autopsy report and the car contents. Until then, let's leave *The Macguires* to themselves for a while."

No one disagreed with that suggestion. Everyone left the house in silence to head for the *Puckshaw* police station.

When they were safely in Lavin's car Mel spoke first.

"What do you make of it, Tom?"

"I think we have our man safely in custody. All we have to do is formally charge him and convince Judge Kenny to deny bail. I'll lay odds that the kid will break after twenty-four hours. He's ready. What about you?"

"I don't know. I don't know. Amelia could be covering for her brothers—at least one of them. My money is on the results of the autopsy and the contents found in the car. My guess is we'll be heading towards DNA hell as soon as the results are in. If Cassie Albright was sexually assaulted, they'll undoubtedly find semen, pubes, and probably blood. If she fought as hard as Timmy Jenkins says she did, there will be skin under her nails. If she had sexual contact with more than one boy at the party, that's going to be a *real* problem. Cramer says she had a nasty gash on the side of her head, in addition to being strangled, so there *should* be a weapon. Christ, I heard they've stripped the little shed bare, including the first three inches of top-soil."

"Where'd you hear that?"

With unemotional nonchalance Mel answered, "A friend."

"Boy, they didn't make girls like Cassie when I was sixteen!"

"Sure they did, Tommy; sure they did. That's one mold they'll *never* break."

"Hmm, well, let's go see what conclusion the *Island Boys* have come to."

As they got out of Lavin's car, Cramer and Johnson pulled up beside them. Cramer had a little trouble getting out from behind the wheel of his patrol car and rested against the driver's side door after pulling himself out. He looked tired and drawn underneath his deep tan.

"What did you two come up with?"

Mel laughed. "Stalemate; how about you guys?"

"Johnson, here, thinks one or both of the boys could be lying; and let's not underestimate the young girl—she might be protecting one or both of them. Anyway, we'd better take another listen to the Jenkins recording."

Cramer seemed confused as he kicked up a little cloud of sand with the pointy toe of his worn boot. "This creepy situation with Harry and Eddie…Jesus, I don't know. I personally think the kid, Jenkins, is the culprit. I guess you might say we're in a dead heat, here."

"Yeh," Lavin laughed, "Might even have to wait for a photo finish. Let's go in and listen to the Jenkins account, once more. We're going to look pretty stupid in front of the judge if we aren't convinced we have the right kid in custody. Am I right or not?"

"You're right." Johnson unceremoniously entered the conversation again.

The sun was beating down on the four of them and finally Mel said, "Let's get out of this heat before we start foaming at the mouth".

They all laughed, seemingly letting their guard down for the first time since they had met—barely a week ago.

Got a quiet spot in there where we can go over the digital and maybe compare notes?"

It was a stupid question Lavin had asked—neither Cramer nor Johnson bothered to answer—just turned and walked toward *Puckshaw's* alarmingly busy police station. A young female officer met them at the door.

"Mel Abrams? You've got a telephone call; you can take it right here at the desk."

"Thanks. I'll meet you guys in a minute; where are you going to be?"

Johnson was pissed and he showed it. "Upstairs."

Puckshaw was abuzz with gossip and crazed with excitement. The press hounds were hanging around the police station and camped out at *Puckshaw's* signature twin-span bridge, prepared to follow the officers into Boston for the arraignment. Charlie's was packed to its advantage, doing a busy lunch trade. All the daily papers were sold out and strewn around the counter and booths. Businessmen in suits sat across from fishermen and old ladies while summer and year-round residents chatted, mingling easily as they waited for a booth.

Today, at Charlie's, everyone was equal.

Any observer would have immediately noticed the lack of youngsters out and about the island. Most of the teens who had been at the party were grounded, having been instructed by their parents and lawyers to stay out of the line of fire, lest they be caught off guard and say something stupid. The youngsters who had not been invited to the Macguires on that fateful night—the *B* and *C* listers—thanked the Almighty for their good fortune although they, too, knew enough to keep to themselves.

The kids were constantly reminded that Cassie Albright's murderer was still out there. Teenagers throughout the island who were usually on the beaches or the docks, were tucked away in their palatial homes, exercising their God-given right to universal communication. They were listening to music, watching television, and talking to one another through continuous and frantic e-mails, texts, Twitter, and *Flutter,* the latest rage.

A few brave souls had even remembered to e-mail the popular victim's parents to express their condolences.

Cassie's funeral was private and unannounced. Her parents had taken her bruised and bashed body—further defaced by the deep surgical cuts of an autopsy—back to the family seat in Vermont, to be laid to rest peacefully. The island's *rumor mill* was hard at work and already had it that Mrs. Albright might not even return to *Puckshaw*—ever. No one could blame her. Parents shouldn't have to bury their children—not on *Puckshaw—it just wasn't right.*

To the outside world, *Puckshaw* was growing up. It had become a melting pot of the rich and *almost* rich. Bridges, schools, a publishing house, and even a small emergency clinic, stood as proud witnesses to the island's growing maturity. All across the island—from the *Macguire* oceanfront mansion, where a family was huddled in shock and under virtual house arrest, to the *Jenkins'* inter-coastal villa, where a gin-soaked mother stared through a window, pondering her son's fate—the saddened residents of *Puckshaw* were still not ready to pay the price of the Island's budding status as the tiny *Metropole of the Cape.*

The over-populated island had reacted with shock over the death of Cassie Albright; sinking into deep mourning, young *Mollie Simon* was no exception.

She was holed up in her extravagantly furnished bedroom, red-eyed and jumpy. She hoped no one would find out that she was lying about sleeping over Cassie's house. She reasoned that she wasn't really lying; she just hadn't gotten a chance to ask Cassie if she *could* sleep over. Everyone knew you could crash at Cassie's—anytime—even if it was early in the morning when her parents were rising. They were *cool* parents; the kids loved them. The Albrights never questioned anything as long as Cassie came home at night. That's all that was important. They didn't care where she was or whom she was with as long as she was in her own bed by morning. As Mollie would later say, "They were *so* cool they were referred to as the *iciest.*"

Today, Mollie wished she had left with Timmy Jenkins. If only he hadn't been in such a hurry. She had asked him to wait just a few minutes until she could find Cassie and ask her to cover for her in case her parents questioned her whereabouts—he couldn't.

She recalled how thrilled she was about going to an *all-nighter* with Timmy Jenkins. She had had a crush on him since seventh grade and now she was finally sixteen and he was eighteen and had his own car. It would be the *first time* for her; after all, Cassie was going to *do it* with Eddie Macguire sometime during or after the party, too. She had been looking forward to comparing notes with her the next day.

Now, staring up at the ceiling, she knew Timmy was in a lot of trouble and she didn't have the slightest idea why. She wished she could talk to him. She couldn't stop thinking about the kiss he had planted on her when he came up from the beach. He claimed ignorance about what was going on down there and said couldn't wait to take her to the party later on.

She flipped over and buried her face in her pillow and faked sleep as her mother entered her room and softly called her name. She just couldn't take anymore. After all, she reasoned, she was only sixteen. She needed somebody to talk to and decided to call Jenny Holmes—as soon as her mother was safely out of earshot.

The cell phone rang out loudly in the empty bedroom of the opulent Holmes residence. Jennifer was sitting in Dr. Allen Godfrey's office. The surgery had been planned since the day before the party. Her mother had made a big fuss and didn't want her to attend the Macguire party in her condition, but Jenny had belligerently insisted on going. She had argued bitterly with her mother before leaving for the birthday bash on Saturday night.

"What do I have to worry about? It's not like I can get *pregnant!*"

Her father quietly drove her to the party and dropped her off with the usual warning about being careful.

She had responded with, "Yeh, right dad!"

The night of the party she had been picked up around midnight and was in bed by twelve-forty-five according to her father and mother. They had picked her up on their way home from a late dinner. She told them she had spent most of the night dancing with Harry Macguire and had a great time. Everyone had seen her with Harry and that was the reason she was on Lavin's list for questioning. She had been spending a lot of time with Harry in the last few months. More time than she should have; now she faced Dr. Godfrey's hostile needle and the termination of her unwelcome pregnancy.

It wasn't his first or last rescue of a young female islander. Dr. Godfrey was well known and had experienced a few close calls over the years that had *slightly* tarnished his image, but it never stopped him from having his morning coffee at Charlie's and cocktails at *the club*.

Ensconced in the back booth at Charlie's, Ed Sims was feeling the effects of the depression that had crept into the very soul of *Puckshaw*. He had been quietly reading page after yellow page of blurry notes and rested his eyes for a moment only to be enveloped by a deep reflection on the present situation he found himself in.

The number of crises that had occurred within *The Macguire clan* in the last twenty-five years amazed him. He recalled his dear friend, Henry Macguire, whom he had loved like a brother. Deeply distressed by his tragic suicide, he had moved forward to assist and eventually bond with Scott, Henry's only son. Then there was the unexpected appearance of *Lila* and her untimely death, along with the revelation of Scott's young and grief-stricken daughter, Lenora. And just when Scott seemed to settle into prosperity and family living, cancer had come to claim the life of Victoria Macguire, his beloved wife and the mother of his children—taking her before the year had passed.

Now, the very real pain that Sims felt in the center of his chest when he thought he might be called upon to defend one or both of the Macguire kids—*in a murder case*—made him physically sick. He worked and reworked his list of questions and scenarios to be discussed with the two young attorneys who had been called in from Boston to assist him. He hoped for the best as he prepared himself for the ugliest of possibilities. His two assistants were already taking care of any legal matters involving Thea Schults and Francesca Covel—the two women in Scott Macguire's life—but he would represent Scott, his twin boys, Eddie and Harry, and the youngest Macguire of all, *Amelia*.

Francesca Covel was going about her busy schedule with an imperceptible glow. Scott was the first man she had loved since an aborted romance she had bolted from in her early twenties. Now she knew he felt the same attraction and satisfaction she did and that made it easier to bear his absence from the publishing house. Maybe it was just as well, for she didn't know how they would be able to keep their hands off each other after their early morning tryst. In spite of her private joy, she was troubled by the horrible death of the young Albright girl.

She had never been so close to a crime in her whole life as she was at the moment. That it actually had happened while she was at Scott's house helping with the supervision gave her the shivers. She wondered how Harry, Eddie, and the rest of them were holding up under all the accusations that were being hurled about. Though she hardly knew them, she cared about their well-being. She still found it hard to believe she had been on the premises all evening, albeit distracted.

Today her job was to assure department heads that everything was fine and business was to be conducted as usual. As she went about phoning, e-mailing, and faxing documents to demanding clients; she wondered if this new romance was going to be the *real thing* for her.

She hoped that the hopelessly, grief-stricken widower hadn't fallen for the first woman who showed any interest in him; then she thought about Thea and she knew she wasn't really the *first* woman to show him affection. Thea had been doing the very same thing all along. All the signs were there—the utter devotion to him and his children, complete accessibility, and obvious infatuation. Had Scott missed all the signs or was he just not interested in or attracted to Thea? Whatever the reason, Frankie was grateful that he had responded so spontaneously and with such fierce passion to her obvious attraction to him. Maybe this was a bad time for Thea but it was a thrilling time for Francesca Covel and she wasn't going to waste another moment feeling sorry for the competition.

Thea was moving around the mansion's well-stocked kitchen and thinking about how soon she would be leaving. She admitted that she had become more than a little spoiled by the attendant privileges of wealth that had accompanied her tenure in the Macguire household.

It had been a little over a year since she had arrived with a small suitcase and a few possessions during the trying time for her sister and her family. During Vicky's subsequent illness and especially after her death, Thea had demonstrated such strength and support that Scott and the children couldn't imagine moving forward without her help. With little fanfare, Thea Schultz settled into the near-opulence that the Macguire family was nonchalantly accustomed to. She hadn't thought about paying a bill or even driving her own car since arriving at the ocean side mansion over a year ago.

Months of grief and sadness had engulfed the whole family, but she had emerged as the strong one—looking after everyone else's needs. She often thought she was as much *a Macguire* as the rest of the household was. She cried only at night when she was alone—and Amelia wasn't in her bed holding on to her.

The boys had counted on her to take them to Boston for clothes and the latest electronic educational devices that they would need for school. They went to Thea when they needed advice on asking a girl to a dance. In general, Thea took the responsibility for everything from dispensing lunch allowances to helping with homework to mothering Amelia on a full time basis. She had been particularly effective in talking Scott into allowing the boys to get a driver's permit as soon as their sixteenth birthday arrived.

Scott, too, had depended on her for many time-consuming tasks, such as school conferences and dental check-ups for the kids.

Early on, he had even asked her to accompany him to a social function or two, but once the newly promoted Francesca Covel entered the picture, Scott had the perfect partner at his side for all formal affairs connected with the new and thriving publishing house. Thea was rarely invited.

Everything had changed; for the first time, Thea felt used. She no longer came and went with her usual enthusiasm and joy, but rather with resentment. She loved the kids too much to let things go sour and she readily admitted to herself that she loved Scott; the stark reality was that he did not love her. She would leave soon—probably as soon as the *Albright mess* was cleared up. She was convinced that the boys had nothing to do with the whole thing but wondered why Cramer and Johnson never really assured her that everything was going to be fine. Only earlier in the day Johnson had said that he had to work out a lot of things and he *hoped* everything would be okay. His cautious wording had frightened her.

The house was quiet. The boys were upstairs in their room and Amelia was watching Thea as she sorted out some vegetables for *cook* to chop on the marble cutting board. The silence was eerie. It was very quiet throughout the house. Thea heard a sound and looked around. *Probably Amelia, she thought.*

It was Scott; he was pacing the family room floor. Sims had just left and he was put off by the serious mood his attorney and friend was in. Now, hell-bent on working himself up into a full lather, he paced.

He believed Amelia and he believed his boys. Why wouldn't he and why shouldn't he? True, he was pissed about the smoking and drinking and just the thought that one of his kids would *plan* to have sex in that damn little shed infuriated him. Still, they had given their word about everything that went on and he trusted them. Even though Eddie had failed to mention a few things in the beginning, Scott chalked that up to his jangled nerves and fear of being yelled at. Other than *that* little glitch, he felt that both of the boys had been more than cooperative and extremely truthful.

Of course, he hadn't heard the recording of Timmy Jenkins' account of the events. No one had, accept Detectives Mel Abrams and Tom Lavin; Cramer and Johnson were probably hearing it for the first time at the moment. Scott wished *he* could hear the damn thing, but there wasn't a ghost of a chance that he would.

The truth of the matter was that Scott Macguire really wanted to do *more* to help with the *Albright* case; he was just trying too hard to be all things to his kids, Thea, Frankie, the publishing company, and anyone else who might need him; it was getting to be too much for him.

He thought about Thea and felt as though he had let her down. He couldn't help that he wasn't attracted to her in any way. She had been a tremendous help to him—a savior—but he never had the urge to hold her in his arms or kiss her and never, ever, dreamed of making love to her. She was his wife's sister, his kids' aunt—fantasizing over her was out of the question.

Then he thought of Francesca and he felt weak-kneed for a moment. He wished she were here to give him some of her steely strength. Scott padded his pockets down for his cell phone and then stepped into the hall looking on the little table for the cordless. His private cell phone was probably on the front seat of his car. If he could just hear Francesca's voice, he would make it through the day. Out of the corner of his eye he caught a glimpse of Thea in the kitchen doorway again—looking at him, dog-eyed. He walked right by the telephone and went upstairs to his bedroom and closed the door. He was annoyed by her constant surveillance; something would have to be done about that—soon.

He thought about checking on the boys but a quick reconsideration told him he should leave them alone for a while. Besides that, he just didn't want make them say something he didn't want to hear.

Harry and Eddie had hardly spoken to each other all day. Tension had been mounting steadily and was close to erupting into open warfare.

Eddie lay on his bed with headphones clamped over his ears and the beautiful image of Cassie Albright emblazoned in his memory; he had never seen, felt, or smelled anything so beautiful in all his young life. He didn't know or care if it was love, lust or ignorance; he only knew he would never be able to forget her. Eddie Macguire was a very normal teenager given to normal adolescent sexual fantasies, but there seemed to be nothing normal about the situation he found himself in. Another thing he couldn't seem to figure out was what the hell was wrong with his brother, Harry. He was acting strange and it was the first time that he couldn't get him to open up, or even make him laugh with some stupid 'knock-knock' joke. He felt shut out.

Harry, moodily riveted to a flashy computer game, seemed distracted from the day's new tensions. Deftly launching rockets and missiles at an unseen enemy was helping him to avoid talking to Eddie. Today he played with little enthusiasm, not caring if he won or lost. He missed not laughing at Eddie's jokes; they usually broke him up—no matter how bad his mood or the jokes were. He had no desire to listen to music or read his e-mails—he felt utter despair.

The truth was that Harry Macguire could no longer look his brother in the eye and only *he* knew why. It was all about kissing Cassie down on the beach and kissing her *again* when he ran into her at the side of the house. He wished he hadn't done that. She had told him she was waiting for Eddie who was standing just a few feet away from the shed with a group of friends. He thought no one had seen him until Jenkins had come up behind him and jumped on his back and scared the hell out of him.

"*Shame on you Harry,*" Jenkins chided.

"Shut up, Jenkins. We were just talking. Come on, I'll buy you a beer."

Jenkins had refused Harry's offer, saying he was leaving soon and didn't want to drink too much. He was going to another party and he *was* driving his *new* car—the new preventative for drinking.

He spun around and did a little dance singing, "I got Mollie Simon tonight, ha ha!"

Harry congratulated him, while out of the corner of his eye he spotted *Cassie* moving the wide plank to one side and ducking into the little shed. He wasn't sure if Timmy Jenkins had seen the same thing so he tried to distract him away from the area. Timmy said he was leaving in a few minutes; he just had to get something out of his car and then he was going to find Mollie Simon.

Now, in the sanctity of his bedroom, Harry was thinking of Timmy and waiting for him to e-mail him or Eddie. They were not the best of friends but Timmy posted a lot of funny stuff and he was really anxious to hear from him. He wanted to ask his brother if he had heard from Timmy but he already knew the answer. So where the hell was he? Deep down he knew it was Timmy putting out those lies about him and Eddie. Who the hell *else* would dare say *anything* against the *Macguire Twins?* With little humility, he thought about their prestige and popularity and concluded that only Timmy was *that* stupid.

He considered the likes of Mollie Simon and Jennifer Holmes. Mollie was too scared to say anything about anybody and Jennifer Holmes was in the middle of some kind of crisis and everyone thought she was just playing sick to avoid being questioned. It *had* to be Timmy Jenkins who was spreading rumors. Harry finally flung his A-pad aside and clicked the television on. He waited a few minutes and the local news came on.

Some youngster was being held in Boston to be arraigned at five-thirty.

"What the hell? Damn!" Harry was shouting. He knew it was Timmy. He jumped on Eddie, who was lying on his bed with his eyes closed.

"Eddie, get up and watch this."

"What's going on?"

"I'll tell you what's going on. That goddamned Jenkins is telling lies about us. I'll bet he's the kid they're holding in Boston. Who the hell else could it be? "

"Harry, I think you're crazy and full of shit! Who said they're holding a kid in Boston? Did dad say anything about it? Jesus! You're making me sick; just knock it off. Anyway, Timmy Jenkins doesn't have anything to do with this whole thing. Get off his case. Just leave him alone, will ya?

Timmy Jenkins took a shower in the tiny curtained cubicle at the police headquarters holding center with an officer standing outside the stall, barely a foot away. He hadn't been supervised this closely during a bath or shower since he was six or seven years old and he didn't like it. He dried himself off and was careful about the scratches he had underneath one of his arms. He wondered where the hell they came from, but dismissed them when the officer handed him an electric shaver and a small mirror. He was surprised at the coat of yellow fuzz that had accumulated in only twenty-four hours. His hand was a little shaky and he attributed that to little sleep and not enough food. He hadn't eaten since early the day before and he was a skinny kid who was used to eating all day long—especially sweets. His mother was always saying something about 'low blood sugar' and he suddenly missed her and wondered how she was holding up under this crazed situation.

He shaved quickly and handed the shaver and mirror back to the young officer who had never taken his eyes of him.

They walked back to his cubicle where a tan suit, white shirt, and *quiet* tie, were carefully laid out on his cot with a pair of newly shined shoes glowing on the chair beside the cot. Timmy appreciated his father's taste; he probably would have chosen the same outfit for such a somber occasion. In a few hours he would go before Judge Carol Kenny and he *needed* to make a good impression.

He sat down on the edge of the bed to put the clean socks on and as he bent down, a sudden flash of light passed before his eyes. He shook his head for a second; this was the second time he had seen the flash of light and felt a pain under his arm at the same time. He looked up at the young officer with some alarm.

"What's the matter, kid? Gotta use the bathroom?"

"No. No, thanks, I'm just fine."

Timmy continued getting dressed and asked with feigned nonchalance, "Is my father here?"

"Yep, he's got about ten lawyers with him, too. You'll see him pretty soon."

"What time is it?" (They had taken all his jewelry, including his expensive *Rollandi* watch.)

"Almost noon; night shift said you had a pretty hard time getting to sleep last night; that's why I let you sleep all morning. It's understandable. I'll get you some food and a toothbrush then your father and his lawyers are going to talk to you and get you ready to go before the judge. How's that sound, kid?"

"Swell. Thanks." Timmy cocked his head and shrugged his shoulders. "I really don't have a choice, do I?"

"Not really, kid."

Timmy thought he looked pretty good—considering what he had been through in the last few days. He turned to his officer companion and asked him if he had a pair of scissors.

"Jesus! Are you crazy?"

"No, I just want to shorten my ponytail a little. Please. I'm not suicidal or anything like *that*. You can stand right next to me. Listen, you can even cut it for me."

The young man kept his eye on Timmy and stepped away to a desk in the hall and retrieved a pair of scissors from the bottom drawer. He knew he shouldn't do this, but he judged the kid to be harmless.

"Okay, turn around. How much do you want me to cut off?"

"You can cut right below my fingers," and he grabbed his ponytail and held it close to the back of his head.

"Wow! Are you sure?"

"Just do it before I change my mind."

The cop held up the mirror for Timmy to see himself. The rubber band fell out easily and Timmy shook the clump of bleached hair hanging on the back of his otherwise bald head and admired himself in the mirror.

"See? Just like Goldilocks, right? My father will love this."

A tray was delivered—cereal, milk, and an overripe banana. The boy picked up the carton of milk, pulled the top open, and slugged it down. He was thirsty. Then he opened the box of dry cereal and poured it into his hand and ate it like popcorn. It made him think of his mother and he actually wanted to cry; instead he picked up the banana and pointed it at the officer.

"Bang, bang, you're dead."

"Not funny, kid."

"I know—sorry."

Timmy was tired and wanted to lie down, but wouldn't think of wrinkling his clothes so he sat in the straight chair and let his head hang over the back of it. The flash of light and its accompanying pain struck without warning, yet, again. A shiny object was moving up and down and the pain under his arm frightened him. He kept his eyes closed for a long time, almost falling back to sleep. He wondered, as if in a dream, if he would get a chance to talk to Miss Melanie Abrams again. She had been nicer to him than anyone else had. Timmy thought she was the only one who really believed him.

Then the young officer was at his side speaking in a whisper. "Let's go *Goldilocks;* your father is here with a *posse* of lawyers. I'll be waiting for you when you get finished. By the way, you look great, kid. Good luck."

"Thanks."

Traffic was bumper to bumper as Mel and Lavin drove slowly, without saying much; Johnson and Cramer were right behind them. It was a somber moment for all of them. They were heading toward the downtown Boston courthouse to the much-ballyhooed arraignment. It probably wouldn't last more than two or three minutes, yet it was the first step on the way to a jury trial that would either convict or acquit Timmy Jenkins. He could sit in jail and rot while the case was prepared for trial or loll away the days at his villa or a hotel suite until the case was ready to go to trial. It was a distinct possibility that a conviction was on the horizon or…maybe not.

Several press cars followed them even after being forewarned by Boston Highway Patrol that the area around the courthouse had been closed off to regular traffic. Tommy swore under his breath and shook his head.

"Goddamn vultures."

"Be nice, Tommy; you never know when you might need their good will."

"Don't get *too* soft on them, *Cherry*; they can be almost as dangerous as the *bad* guys*".*

Lavin wanted to get there at least a couple of hours early not only to rub elbows with whomever he could—he called it swapping spit—but to get another close look at the kid as he arrived. Maybe he'd see something in the kid that had eluded him thus far. He wouldn't be talking to him anymore, now that the charges were prepared and he was all "lawyered up".

The district attorney would lay the charges before the Judge and Timmy Jenkins' lawyers would have already advised him how to plead. It was all up to Judge Carol Kenny after that; she could set bail and release him into his father's care or remand him to a holding center as a dangerous criminal or a serious flight-risk—pending trial. She was fanatical about human rights and privacy issues, but her ire knew no bounds when it came to the violent loss of a young life, such as *Cassie Albright.*

The basement of the courthouse was cold and damp. Boston had had a lot of rain in the last three months and it was a "smelly shell" of an old building. Mel shook her head and made a face at the odor as they got off the elevator. A guard pointed to where they could stand and wait. Timmy would arrive through this entrance and then be transported upstairs to Room 206—Kenny's courtroom. Everyone else would scramble up after them. Lavin and Mel both nodded to the DA, who waived a sheaf of papers and gave the thumbs up sign. Mel didn't like him, but she wouldn't think of expressing her sentiments openly. She might need him as a *friend* some day. She smiled congenially and turned to talk to Cramer and Johnson. Johnson walked away to answer his cell phone and left the three of them looking at each other.

Lavin snickered, "Christ, here we go again." He crunched his empty coffee cup and tossed it into a trashcan. "This place really stinks, doesn't it?"

No one bothered to answer; they were watching Johnson gesticulating wildly and shaking his head.

It was a few minutes before five o'clock when there was a flurry of activity and an officer came over and escorted Lavin and Mel to another area right near the elevator. They would get a good look at the kid now; he had been held for just about twenty-four hours and the wear and tear would have started to show.

The garage elevator was in descent, indicating that someone was coming from the lobby; the drama of the moment rendered the small group mute. When the doors opened, it was Mr. Jenkins and his small army of lawyers and a young officer sent to accompany them to the courtroom. The elevator was called up and everyone started talking again.

Mel felt sorry for the haggard-looking father. He and his lawyers had kept their eyes straight ahead, speaking to no one. Mel figured the six gray serge suits totaling about six grand an hour were going to do their level best to get the judge to set bail, though she doubted that would happen.

The second time the elevator came down heads turned in silent unison, yet again. Three officers and Timmy Jenkins stepped out. Each officer was assigned to a position to effectively protect the young suspect who was helplessly cuffed and chained.

427

Mel's heart sagged at the sight of the kid who had been so self-assured and free from fear barely thirty-six hours ago. He looked like a pathetic child playing a grown-up. Someone was holding the side-by-side elevators open and the officers led Timmy from one elevator to another and took him up to the courtroom.

The small group scattered in all directions; some to the freight elevator while others fled outside the building to take the stairs up to the third floor. The quiet foursome, Cramer, Johnson, Lavin and Mel waited for the elevator to become available again. They were secretly grateful for the time to be left alone with their thoughts.

The hearing was less than fifteen minutes—still longer than usual. After the charges were read, the plea was entered and the lawyers presented their case for bail. It was impressive enough for the Judge to excuse herself for five minutes. On her return, she rendered her decision: bail was set at $750,000.00. Lavin swore under his breath and Johnson and Cramer shook their heads. Only Mel showed no reaction. Lavin had a sneaky feeling she was happy.

"Goddamn it!"

"What's wrong, Tom, your numbers not adding up?" Mel chided him in a gentle way. "You know, you could think of it this way. If Timmy isn't our guy, another suspect just might be flushed out of his complacency."

Tommy Lavin hated it when she talked so high-classed; he didn't bother to respond.

There was a reminder for silence and everyone rose for Judge Carol Kenny's departure from the courtroom. The DA was furious and thought maybe the charges should have been more severe. They should have pushed for *premeditated* or *first degree* all the way. Of course, lack of motive, weapon, and eyewitnesses to the actual commission of the crime, were all missing.

And then there were the ramblings of an eleven-year-old.

Timmy Jenkins had no prior record besides a speeding ticket or two—definitely a low risk for bail. He would be remanded to the custody of his father and his lawyers with all the usual attendant conditions—except one. Timmy was to be taken to Boston General to give blood samples for DNA testing and a semen sample just in case there was a sexual assault involving more than one male. They wouldn't know that until the autopsy report was released and even then…it could be a crapshoot.

The Judge reminded everyone that things could change quickly once the autopsy report, DNA testing, and contents of the car in question, were confirmed. After all, it was barely a week since the murder and everything took time; could be weeks or months—or days—or hours.

The lawyers surrounded the father and son and led them out of court to a waiting limo. They never acknowledged the presence or the questions of the mob of media people.

Lavin, Mel, the Sheriff, and his Deputy, all left by a side entrance—they too ignoring the shouting media.

Mel picked up her car at headquarters and told Lavin she would meet him in the morning. She looked at her watch; she wanted to get to her parents' home as soon as possible. She was on her way to make some casseroles and finish the laundry, after which she wouldn't be on duty again for three weeks. Although she stopped in a couple of times a week to say hello, she always felt guilty about the relief she felt when she left on Sunday night.

Lavin sensed her urgency, but didn't want to meddle by asking questions. Mel being the type of person that she was, would never have even considered discussing her personal life with him, anyway. She did want to make one stop on her way home; she had a friend at the police garage where Timmy Jenkins' car was impounded, so she headed in that direction. It was uncharacteristic of Melanie Abrams not to have noticed that Lavin had remained about a half a block behind her all the way.

It was Sunday morning, exactly one week since the mangled body of Cassie Albright had been found bludgeoned and strangled under the family room of one of *Puckshaw's* proudest residents: Scott Macguire.

Most of the results of the testing were to be turned over to the district attorney and his staff as soon as they were completed. *Rapid Testing Inc.* made it all pretty simple these days.

Lavin had been awake almost all night and rightly assumed that Mel and the others had probably not slept a wink either. He predicted a testy morning meeting would start out the day in the far corner office that was usually occupied by his chief. He was right. The meeting turned out to be a hodge-podge of hindsight regrets with everyone blaming each other. They broke up at ten o'clock, agreeing to go to the basement cafeteria for some strong coffee and an attitude repair job. It usually worked. The little band of warriors was grateful that it had worked, yet again, for them this morning. They no longer felt the need to leap upon one another at the slightest provocation, as they had an hour ago.

The coffee had actually cast a magical spell over them as they huddled around the table like a football team, scripting every move in response to any and every test result, no matter how expected or surprising it might be. They wanted a grand jury and an indictment and they wanted it fast—before this case took on a life of its own and somebody slipped up and did something stupid. It wouldn't be the first time; each of them could rattle off a half dozen of high profile cases that had fallen flat on their asses because of sloppy police work or "slam-dunk" premature pomposity.

Lavin had regained some of his usual control and commanded the small group to tighten it up and be prepared for anything. The pep talk did them all some good. It was ten to twelve and they were expected to be in the DA's office—now. They hopped into two cars and sped down the two-block alley. Lavin secretly wished they could pick up the kid and throw the whole goddamn book at him, but that was a long shot.

Timmy's mother ran upstairs at eleven-thirty a.m. shouting to her son and husband to get out of bed.

"Something is wrong! They're here! Timmy, Timmy, hurry up!"

Mr. Jenkins sat up in the king-sized bed—he did not share with his wife—mumbling under his breath. He thought immediately that she had probably started drinking very early.

Timmy was lying in a double bed with his headphones still on—fast asleep. He wouldn't have heard anything anyway.

He had the volume on high and was sleeping through Metallica's rendition of *Stone Cold Crazy*—one of his favorite oldies. He had spent a good part of the night dreaming of that bright flashing light and the shiny object that moved around in circles. With each new dream the pain under his right arm flared up and woke him. He saw Cassie Albright's face over and over; first laughing then crying. Where was the blood coming from? He felt pain again and again until finally exhausted, he slept, but not without seeing Cassie's smiling face as she pulled him down on top of her.

Timothy Jenkins Sr. rose and ran to his son's room, but not before grabbing the cell phone next to his bed to call his lawyers and alert them to impending trouble.

"Wake up, son. Something is going on but don't worry, we'll handle it. The lawyers told me we should stay upstairs until they get here."

Mrs. Jenkins was back downstairs in the sun porch watching in amazement as car after car pulled up with police officers piling out with guns drawn to surround the huge villa.. Her hand shook violently as she poured herself a drink at the tiny bar set up in the corner of the sun-porch.

In her early-morning sobriety she knew this was going to be the worst day of her life.

Mr. Jenkins noted the time. It was eleven thirty-five a.m.; the preliminary testing results could be released at noon from the DA's office.

Rapid Testing Inc. was nothing short of a miracle, but there must have been a terrible leak.

Two of the kid's lawyers were posted outside the DA's office and were to call Jenkins if anything went awry.

For the first time in many years Mr. Timothy Jenkins felt fear. Fear of losing his only son. He put his arm around him and whispered in a hoarse, angry voice, "Son of a bitch! Son of a bitch! Son of a bitch! They leaked the results; they faked them, right son? I've known right along that you were telling the truth. Right Timmy; am I right or not, son?"

"You're right, Dad."

Timmy was a million miles away. He was sitting on top of Cassie Albright's stomach, groping her breasts in the dark. She was laughing and cooing and he couldn't believe he had gotten so lucky. Stealing a girl away from one of the *Macguire* twins! That was really something! He, Timmy Jenkins, had pulled off a terrific *coup* right in Eddie Macguire's own back yard—literally! Cassie was pulling him down on top of her, urging him on. He had his eyes open and was just getting accustomed to the darkness when a flash of light appeared above his head and then bounced around the little shed's walls erratically.

"Cassie? Cassie? Where the hell are you?"

Timmy tried to lie perfectly still on top of her. He could feel her heart beating hard against his bare chest and she was clutching him tightly around his waist. His uncontrollable physical inclination drove him to continue what he had started; he began to move slowly on top of her until the light was directly on the back of his neck and spilling over to Cassie's face. He was just slightly put off by the look of fear in her eyes.

"What the hell? Who is it? Come, on get the hell out of here; can't you see we're busy?"

"Is that you Jenkins? It's me Harry. How about sharing the pie?"

Cassie was making little distressful noises and trying to get up from under him. She was whimpering, "Let me up, Timmy. Harry, go away, go on."

Timmy was lost in a moment of the sheer, physical phenomena that was taking place in his lower body and could *not* let her up. Deep in the back of his mind he could hear Cassie crying louder, almost screaming. He had to stop her and there was only one way. He reached up and put his hand over her mouth. At the precise moment he exhausted his ecstasy he was startled by the pain under his right armpit. Cassie was clawing at it. He sat up, dripping with sweat, and found himself face to face with Harry Macguire—in a partial state of undress.

"Hold the flashlight, damn it," Harry whispered.

"Come on Harry, get out of here. Can't you see? She's really upset. Jesus, we were having so much fun before you came."

By now, Cassie was terrified. "Timmy, get me out of here, now. Please!"

Before she could say anything more, she felt a sharp blow to the side of her head and though dazed by distant pain and suffocating fear, she continued to struggle.

Timmy had seen the flashlight, raised in a half-arc, as it came crashing down on the side of Cassie Albright's head. He had watched the blood as it ran down her cheek and neck, slowing down to trickle between her breasts. She was still trying to get up when Harry pushed Timmy off of her and lowered his own shaking body on top of hers.

"Hold the flashlight, asshole; watch!"

Timmy Jenkins watched in wonderment; this was a sight he had only seen in porn magazines and videos. Was it wrong? He didn't care; he was lost in it. By the time it was over, Harry was sitting up, panting, with his hands wrapped tightly around Cassie's throat. She was quiet—finally.

"I think she's asleep or passed out," Harry noted dryly, pulling up his khakis and wiping his face with his bare arm. "Just leave her alone, she'll wake up on her own—they always do. They love it when you choke them!"

Timmy, fully alert and aware of his actions said, "Jesus! She said *stop*, and we did it anyway. I think we should have stopped. I hope she doesn't go the cops; we could get in real trouble if she does. We'll make it up to her, right dude? Don't tell anybody about this or she'll be really pissed."

Harry was still on his knees when he grasped the end of the beach towel she was lying on and wiped the side of her face and the blood around her ear and neck. It didn't look too bad, but Timmy was scared. They had done the *unthinkable*. He knew what it was called and it sounded *impossible* to him. After all the girls he had had sex with….how could this have happened?

"Harry, can you tell if she's still breathing?"

"I don't know. I think she is. We better get the hell out of here. Get going! Go—now! Here take the flashlight with you.

Throw it away on your way home. Okay, you go to your car and I'll sneak around the back lawn and go down to the water and wash up."

Timmy crawled out and wrapped the bloody flashlight up in his yellow scarf and threw it in his trunk; then he went to say good-bye to the rest of the kids. He told Mollie he couldn't wait for her but he'd see her later. He ran into the house, wanting to wash his hands and face, but saw the little kid on the love seat and changed his mind. He just wanted to get the hell out of there. No party. No Mollie. He just wanted to get home and into bed. He knew he would wake up in the morning and find it was all a bad dream.

Now he lay crosswise on his bed and admitted to himself that Cassie was dead from the moment he crawled out of the shed and right now he wished that he were dead, too. If he couldn't be dead, then he wanted to talk to Mel Abrams. He wanted to tell her that they should get blood samples from Harry Macguire and he would swear that he wasn't lying. He needed to get a hold of the sympathetic detective, but the noise and confusion coming from downstairs indicated that he might be too late. He wondered where his father had gone; he was alone, afraid, and disoriented. Where was everybody?

The corner office at headquarters in downtown Boston was overcrowded and Mel tried to snag a position near the window to catch an occasional whiff of fresh air. The county coroner, his staff, and a toxicologist from Buffalo Metro were all on hand to explain the autopsy report, as well as the results of hair, skin, and semen that had been found on Miss Albright. The results would explain how and *if* there was any relationship between the tests made on Cassie Albright and the blood, semen, and hair, taken from Timmy Jenkins.

Reports and graphic pictures were in large manila envelopes marked with FYEO and were passed out to Lavin, who was to share his packet with Mel, and Cramer, who was to share with Johnson. Of course, the DA had his own and the coroner and his staff of supporting technicians all had their own personal copies to work from.

Mel didn't like the way Johnson kept going out into the hall to talk on his phone. She conveyed her concern to Lavin who nodded his awareness of the situation. She wished she had a bionic ear when Johnson came in and spoke behind his hand to Cramer.

He had whispered, "All hell has broken loose at the Jenkins place. It's surrounded by Boston PD; there's been a terrible leak. These reports are going to confirm that Timmy Jenkins is our man and guess who he wants to talk to?"

Cramer was impatient, "Christ, who?"

"That little lady over there: Miss Melanie Abrams."

The coroner droned on and on upon deaf ears. Johnson and Cramer wanted to get out of there before Lavin and Mel began to draw their own conclusions.

Mel tried to concentrate on the pathologist who seemed to be a million miles away. There was only *one* big problem: *Bits of hair, skin, semen, and some random palm prints pointed to the presence of another person besides Timmy Jenkins.*

Mel wrote frantically in her notebook and held it before Lavin's eyes. "Timmy's presence undeniably accounted for but who the hell is the *other* one?"

A young female officer had come in to tell her she had a phone call. She thought it might be one of her sisters calling to chastise her for being gone for so much of the weekend that she was supposed to spend with her parents. She was surprised to hear the voice of her chief; he was calling from his home.

"What the hell is happening? You got trouble? I thought it was a clean sweep; the kid is guilty as hell, right?"

"Well, you're almost right, chief. The kid is a perfect match but it seems that there was a third person present. We need to figure that out. You want to talk to Tom?"

"No. The kid, Timmy; he wants to talk to *you*. He's been picked up at his home already and is on his way downtown and has asked Corky to contact you. He contacted me first to make sure it was okay. You understand, don't you? He's just a rookie and wants to make sure he does the right thing."

Mel was pissed that the rookie had checked with her chief on that; there would have been no question if Timmy

Jenkins had wanted to talk to *Lavin*. She was insulted, but she would keep that to herself, for now.

"So what do you want me to do, chief?"

"I want you to be downstairs in a half hour when they bring the kid in. You have priority clearance to speak to him. Get him on your recorder. He's going to tell you who the other person is. I think it was kind of a threesome sort of thing that got out of control. These goddamn kids! When are they ever going to learn? When does it stop? I'm so fucking glad that I'm going to retire next year; I don't understand a fucking thing about how these fucking kids think, today. Anyway, I expect to hear from you as soon as you finish with him. And *Cherry,* don't be a pussy; cut deep, otherwise you're going to miss the big dance."

Then the chief did something unusual; he apologized for his foul language. He mumbled something about still having respect for women.

Mel was shaken. She re-entered the conference room, which was decimated by at least twenty-five per cent. She walked over to Lavin and put her hand over her mouth. She knew Johnson was watching her so now she returned his courtesy. She gave Tommy Lavin the bullet and they both backed out of the office and headed downstairs to greet Timmy Jenkins. On the way down in the elevator, she decided to tell Lavin that it hadn't been made public yet, but a flashlight with traces of Cassie Albright's blood on it had been found in the trunk of Timmy's car. He didn't show much surprise until Mel had added with disgust that there were two sets of fingerprints: Timmy's and the person that better be found within the next twenty-four hours or this case was going to shit the bed.

Lavin grinned his approval. He liked the way Mel was behaving now. She seemed to be filled with his kind of excitement as she stepped off the elevator.

The Macguire household was glued to the television set—as was the whole Island of *Puckshaw*. Things were happening so fast that you had to stay tuned to stay informed.

Thea was talking to her mother non-stop; trying to make arrangements to leave in the next week or so; or at least as soon as Amelia settled down in school.

Scott was on his cell phone talking to Francesca who was coming to see him right from the office. She was just winding down a few last minute schedule changes for the coming week. She, too, was glued to the television and asked how the boys were doing. Scott assumed they were okay, holed up in their bedroom, laying low like everybody else was.

"What about Amelia, is she okay?"

"Yah, she's fine, I think she's out for a walk with Thea right now."

"Great. Well, I guess I should be out there in about an hour. Okay?"

"Sure. I'll tell Thea to tell *cook* we'll order in from Alfredo's. I can't wait to see you. Bye."

The next hour would prove to be one of excruciating pain and horror for Scott Macguire and his children; it would forever besmirch the good name of Henry Macguire and all his descendents.

Lavin and Mel arrived first—followed by Johnson and Cramer. All four of them stood before the front door while Mel, using the highly polished brass fixture, knocked on the door. Scott was on his way upstairs but instead, stopped and swung open the ornate door. What he saw frightened him. The drawn faces of his two old friends and the impassive presence of Mel Abrams and Tommy Lavin made him reel in dizziness. In a flash the driveway had become filled with police cars and officers with guns drawn. The house was under siege.

"What is it?" Scott was ashen.

Johnson and Cramer were stupefied into a frozen silence and Mel quickly covered for them.

"Mr. Macguire, please believe me when I say how sorry I am to be the one to tell you this, but your son, Harry, has been seriously implicated in the murder of Cassie Albright. Would you please step aside and allow a couple of our men to enter your home and apprehend him? They won't hurt him, but they will put restraints on him for everybody's safety. Now, may I ask you to please step aside? Please?"

Scott started to shout for Sims who was holed up in the little office off the family room, but Mel put her hand on his arm to calm him down.

"Please, Mr. Macguire, let me do my job. Your lawyer can follow us down to the station and wait while we question Harry. You can come too, if you wish. This is painful for everyone involved, but we have to do it."

Melanie looked up toward the top of the stairs and Scott followed her eyes. He let out a wrenching cry when he saw Harry being led down the stairs with his hands in nylon cuffs. Two uniformed officers had entered through the patio door and had gone up the backstairs to Harry's bedroom. Surprise was game, here. No one was hurt. Mel had covered all the bases.

The boy wasn't making a sound; just looked dazed—almost like the lamb of innocence being led to the slaughter.

Mel looked at one of the young officers. "Did you read him his rights?"

"Yes ma'am, I did."

"Good. Let's go."

E *pilogue*

The young man was startled as he walked along the private beach hidden in a tiny cove on the well-guarded *Island of Puckshaw*.

What appeared to be an elderly security officer blocked his path. "What is it you want around here, boy? Don't know that I've seen *you* before. This is all government property and you could get yourself in a bit of trouble."

"Sir! My name is Mac Simon. I'm a photojournalist doing some post graduate work at Boston International Institute. I'm researching this island for a series of articles and pictures for the *Boston Trumpet*. I don't mean to cause you any problem, sir. I'm just roaming around, trying to gather my thoughts. Actually, I already know quite a bit about the island; I know some people that knew some people that grew up here."

"Well, come on—walk along with me while I check out the rest of the cove. Once in a while someone roams onto the beach and I have to tell them to move on; that's my job."

They walked along for several minutes and then the young man spoke.

"I guess this island has quite an interesting history—a *checkered past, one might say.*"

"*Is th*at so? Well now, what *exactly* makes you say that?"

"Well, I guess just a lot of family history that has been passed down to me. You see sir, I should have told you the truth; I'm related to the *Macguires of Puckshaw*. Does that name ring a bell with you? I've been told that four generations lived on the island dating back to 1970. It's strange, but I can almost feel my ancestors' presence here."

The old man didn't answer and seemed to be trying to hide any expression from coming through his natural frown.

With several cameras hanging from his shoulder and around his neck, the young man walked beside the aging stranger for several minutes before finally speaking again. He didn't speak like the youngster that he really was; he sounded more like a man of experience and wisdom.

"You know, there's only a few of these little pearls left," he said waving his hand in a panoramic gesture. He let his eyes sweep around the cove and shook his head, "Just tiny, isolated communities which were lucky enough to have survived the population and technology boom in all their glory—not to mention the ruinous bloodletting. But just look at this spot; breathtaking isn't it?"

Suddenly, he was on his knees snapping from all angles at nature's display of beauty and power. Switching cameras and twisting lenses with speed and determination; he was very comfortable and confident in *his* world.

"Imagine, miles of sparkling sand, untamed waters, and endless skies; a modern utopia, isn't it?"

He shaded his eyes from the setting sun and turned his body a full 360 degrees, as if he was looking for something. Then he continued in a sweet voice.

"I heard there used to be a twin span bridge connecting this island to the mainland maybe seventy-five to a hundred years ago. I actually have some old photographs of it—electronic, you know?"

The old man squinted and faced the young man. "What's your real business here son?"

"Well, you might say I *came* from this island a long, long time ago. Of course, what I mean is my *relatives* did. I have pictures of some of the beautiful mansions that used to stand atop that cliff up there. God, I wish they were still here. They must have been something to see. Maybe I'm in the wrong spot; but I was just wondering if there are any of them left anyplace on the island. I've seen a few pictures of the oceanfront mansions and the inlet estates that would have been on the other side of the island. Do you know what I'm talking about, sir?"

"Well, young man, if you studied the history of this island, you probably read about how life—no—the island itself was *interrupted.* Years of storms and erosion took most of those ocean front mansions and the villas along the inter-coastal area, too. The bad weather started slowly, I believe. Yep, then winter storms raged against this island for almost six straight months out of the year. It was considered some kind of phenomena—*global warming* or something, they called it. Summer heat was so dangerous that those who stayed around stayed indoors. They said that it was caused by some big hole in the ozone—you probably know all about those things, but anyway, everything was ruined—the fishing, the docks, the beaches, and the cottages—all gone. It was said that the weather literally ran the year-round residents right out—they just couldn't make it through the winter—too dangerous, I guess. You might say that was the Almighty's way of thinning out the population on *Puckshaw*—sort of a cleansing. *It stopped the island in its tracks.*

My own grandfather had a small place inland and he was able to withstand the bad times. He owned what they called a coffee house. I think it was called *Charlie's*, though that wasn't *his* name.

I wasn't born until 2024 and I don't know too much of what went on after I left. You see, we left the island when I was about four years old; it was horribly overcrowded and everyone was in a panic. No money, property in ruins, and lots of crime. We headed toward the great mid-west. I guess you might say we were part of the *second* great Western movement.

I grew up there and raised my family and even saw my grandchildren before I decided to move back here. My wife and two of my sons were already gone and I wanted to come back to the ocean to live; or maybe I should say to die. I'll be seventy-seven pretty soon—not too bad for an old-timer, huh? Now I stay in a little apartment above what used to be an old publishing house. I do a little walking on the beach, just sort of report anything unusual, you know. It's all government property now but I heard they are going to start selling off parcels and populate the island again. Sort of restore it to its previous glory—without the crime."

"Wow! Well, I'm twenty-six and I thought I should come and see where my great, great, grandparents and great uncles and aunts once lived. My great, great, grandfather was a journalist who lived on the island for twenty-five years and left some journals that were published about life right here on *Puckshaw*. My mother has a copy of one of his books—it was really something. I guess there were two women who died right around here on one of the beaches and my great, great, grandfather *Henry Macguire*, wrote extensively about them. After the book was published, Henry's son, Scott who was my great grandfather, opened a small publishing house and named it after him.

My grandmother, Amelia, was one of the first female Macguires to be born on the island of *Puckshaw*. She lived in a huge mansion that might have been right up there, according to my calculations." The young man pointed high above the cliff to his left. "I think I'm pretty close to the original site of the old cottage, which was swept into the ocean during a storm. Henry Macguire bought the land and left it to his son, Scott—my great grandfather. He built the family mansion on the triangular parcel of land overlooking a beautiful cove—just like this one.

But please tell me more about the old publishing house that you live above—do you know if it was the *Macguire Publishing* house? Wow; that would be something wouldn't it?"

The old man smiled and then cocked his head to one side with a chuckle.

"Hmm, now that you mention it, I might have heard that *Macguire* name around here a time or two; could be the very building that I live in now. That *would* be something, wouldn't it? You know, there are boxes and shelves of newspapers, books, and old manuscripts down in the basement. It's sort of a walk-in vault. It survived the devastation and serves as an archive of sorts; the door swings wide open and I bet you might just be interested in seeing some of that stuff. What do you think about that?"

Young Mac smiled and shook his head, unbelieving of his good fortune. The strangers walked in silence for a while longer before the younger of the two began to speak again, this time in rather sad tones.

"My great grandfather, Scott Macguire, came to live on this island after he buried his father: the journalist and author, Henry Macguire. Scott had two sons and two daughters. The youngest of his daughters was named Amelia Macguire who eventually became Amelia Macguire Simon. Amelia had a daughter whom she called Thea. Thea Simon never married but gave birth to me in 2075 and to my sister in 2077. By the time we came along, the family had been living in West Virginia for some time.

I was named Macguire Simon to keep the *Macguire* name in the family. My sister and I have already made a pact to keep the name alive when and if we have children of our own. My sister's name is Victoria, after our great grandmother. People used to tell me I was a lot like my grandmother Amelia whom they loved to call 'Miss Mac'.

Today, there are only three dozen Macguire descendents left and up to about ten years ago, we used to have some great reunions. My mother, Thea, is the family archivist right now, but I imagine the job will pass on down to me in the future; naturally I want to learn as much as I can about the island. Believe it or not, we recently located an old great aunt up in New Hampshire; she is Scott Maguire's grand-daughter. She descended from his eldest daughter, Lenora Powers Macguire who was born from a relationship with a Miss Lila Powers."

The old man stopped and asked Mac if he minded resting for a few minutes. He had been walking slowly and limping a little which prompted the young man to help him lower his frail body onto the sand for a rest.

"You sure will make a fine family historian someday. So tell me, young squire, what else do you know about our island and it's *checkered* past?"

"Once, when I was small, I saw some old newspaper clippings about a great uncle of mine. He was twin. It seems he was involved in the brutal murder of young girl. Yes, it's true! As far as I know, it happened right around here—somewhere up on one of those cliffs where the mansion stood. He was only sixteen years old then. He was sent away to a private school shortly after the trial and had very little to do with the family after that. Well, except maybe with his younger sister Amelia, my grandmother.

She was only eleven years old at the time of the murder, but it was her clear and unshakeable testimony that saved her brother, Harry, from a life in prison. She was able to identify a young acquaintance as the murderer and tenaciously claimed that he, and he alone, was the only one to enter the little shed where the victim was found brutally bludgeoned and sexually assaulted. Amelia had watched the whole scenario from beginning to end. The twin boys provided alibis for each other which their sister corroborated. Then some girl by the name of Mollie Simon testified that she had seen Harry Macguire in, shall we say, *a compromising position* on the beach with the very girl who was murdered—a Miss Cassie Albright.

The family attorney defended him brilliantly, claiming that his earlier contact with the girl accounted for the presence of his DNA on her body. His blood was said to have been found on her beach towel because he had earlier stepped on a broken shell while they cavorted on the beach. The boy produced a small cut on the bottom of his foot that *could have* accounted for his bloody palm print.

The other poor kid, by the name of Jenkins, took his own life after one year in prison. I'm sad to say that there was a lot of talk about a cover-up because he was a "Macguire", but Harry Macguire claimed he was innocent until his dying day. The case was chronicled in *Puckshaw's Sunny Islander* for two straight years and my mother has all the original articles.

My apologies, sir; sorry that I've been doing all the talking, but I didn't think I'd meet anyone down here. I've been here since yesterday—even camped out on the beach about a half-mile away from here, last night—but you're the first person I've seen today. I guess it is good to be alone once in a while. Are you alone a lot? I'm sorry, sir. That was an insensitive question, wasn't it?"

The old man shook his head. "No, not at all—and yes, I'm alone most of the time, but I don't mind it too much. I guess I've talked enough in my lifetime, so it's kind of good to be quiet now. What do you think about that?"

Mac Simon was very pensive, resembling a young Henry Macguire. "Well, some good came from my being alone for the last couple of days. I've had plenty of time to think something through. I'm thinking that it would be a hell of an idea to have the next *Macguire Descendants Reunion* right here, on *Puckshaw*. I'd love the rest of my cousins and their children to actually see the places that our elders have talked about for so long. I think it would be a great thrill. You could even be our guest; what do you think about that, sir?"

"For such a young man, you sure have a lot of good ideas in that head of yours! I guess young people are a lot smarter these days. But then, you should be; you been through a lot. So young squire, how long are you staying around here?"

The old man didn't wait for an answer. "Why don't you come up to my little apartment and have some dinner with me; I'd love to hear more about the famous *Macguires*. Who knows, I might be able to tell you a thing or two about them myself." His grey eyes twinkled.

The young man shook his head incredulously, wondering what this old man *really* knew about the island or better still—*the Macguires*. His shy grin and twinkling eyes just might mean that he knew more than he was saying.

"Stay right there!"

Mac snapped several photos of the old man and hoped he was capturing those eyes that seemed to have seen so much and those large rubbery lips that said so little.

"Hmm."

The wrinkled face and the gray mass of curly wool might make a great magazine cover, thought Mac. He continued to snap photo after photo as they roamed the beach, idly talking about things only perfect strangers can talk about with such abandon. He wondered, wistfully, if the old man would still be here by the time he returned for the reunion.

"Did you say you'd join me tonight, *young Mac*?"

"Yes sir! I did."

"Good! Now give me a lift up these broken down steps. They can be pretty slippery at times. I've often wondered where the hell they led, but then, like you say, there was probably a *big old mansion* up here, somewhere. Some days, I actually wish I hadn't moved away from here when I was so young; I feel like I missed something. I feel like I've missed a lot!"

The silence was comfortable until the old man spoke in a hoarse whisper.

"I bet that someday, *Puckshaw* will once again be a great place to grow up on."

The young squire, known as *Mac Simon*, had a near-angelic look on his face as he murmured in a barely audible voice, "Yes, sir, I bet it will."

~ * ~ * ~ * ~ * ~ * ~ * ~ * ~

Made in the USA
Charleston, SC
25 March 2012